PRAISE FOR MARK TEPPO'S
THE CODEX OF SOULS

"*Lightbreaker* is the best book about magic that I have read since Peter Straub's *Shadowland*. This book is simply amazing. It is a richly layered journey into the occult; it is complex, dark and one hell of a ride."

— *Famous Monsters of Filmland*

"Dark and urban, this paranormal thriller is more cerebral than most as it explores the philosophy behind the nature of good and evil in an unusual blending of Tarot cards, Hermetic tradition and a myriad of spiritual beliefs."

— *Monsters and Critics*

"An urban fantasy novel that is a lot more *Hellblazer*, *Mage*, and *Highlander* than it is high heels, hot pants and horizontal vampire mambo."

— *NFSF Reader*

"I would most definitely recommend this author to my readers, and he's going on my short list of Authors Whose New Books Get Preordered."

— *Pagan Book Reviews*

"*Lightbreaker* is a damn good book. It throws some new curves into the Urban Fantasy ride. I think you've got a big, fat hit in your hands."

— Kat Richardson, author of *Vanished* and *Underground*

"...good story with a nice twist."

— *Post-Weird Thoughts*

"With *Lightbreaker*, Mark Teppo has built something out of shadow and starlight that grabs the reader and simply won't let go. The story is dark and dense and beautifully written. It is also eerie and morally complex and yet ultimately hopeful. Perhaps more to the point, it's simply a damn good read and I'm very much looking forward to seeing what Teppo does next."

— Kelly McCullough, author of *WebMage* and *Cybermancy*

"...awash in unpredictable emotions."

— *The Green Man Review*

EARTH THIRST

Other books by Mark Teppo

The Codex of Souls
Lightbreaker
Heartland
Angel Tongue (forthcoming)

The Mongoliad (with Neal Stephenson, Greg Bear, and friends)

EARTH

MARK TEPPO

THIRST

NIGHT SHADE BOOKS
SAN FRANCISCO

First Edition

ISBN: 978-1-59780-445-5

Night Shade Books
www.nightshadebooks.com

This one is for H. R. and Barth,
who have been waiting patiently for some time.

Here are cool springs, soft mead and grove,
Here might our lives with time have worn away.
But me mad love of the stern war-god holds
Armed amid weapons and opposing foes.

—Virgil, *Eclogue X*

BOOK ONE

THALASSA

ONE

"**I**t's her, isn't it?"

She tries very hard to look like the rest of the crew—bulky sweater, heavy pants, rubber boots, red hair pulled back into a pony tail beneath a worn Yankees baseball cap—but there is a tiny stutter in her step that gives her away. She hasn't quite figured out how to walk in sync with the motion of the boat.

Nigel leans forward, lowering his face so that he can be sure I see his expression. "Why is she here?"

I suspect I'm supposed to know the answer to his question, but I don't and so I shrug as I return my attention to my mug.

The woman has paused, blocking the people behind her. She's looking at our table. The mess on the *Cetacean Liberty* is already tiny, and with so many volunteers on board, the room feels even smaller. There are only four tables, and no one ever sits with us. We've done nothing to dissuade the rumor that we're here in case things go wrong, and most of them afford us the space you would any dangerous animal.

I can see the scar that wraps itself around the base of her throat. The one she got from the Chechen gangster. It's part of the reason the network never picked her up after the exposé. She hasn't let it stop her though—her reporting has only gotten better since. Probably due, in no small part, to the fact that she hasn't been trapped in the vicious cycle of appealing to a fickle television audience.

"Mind if I join you?"

Nigel stares straight at her, his gaze hard and empty of any emotion—as if she wasn't there. The woman doesn't flinch, and when the moment of silence stretches too long, Phoebe's leg bumps mine under the table.

"Sure," I say, nodding at the empty spot across from me.

She looks at Nigel for a second, and then slaps her tray down. The gravy pooling around her mashed potatoes is more gray than brown, and the carrots are a sickly orange color. For all the lip service to ecological principles, Prime Earth doesn't feed its volunteers well. Too many things come out of cans—corporate cans. "It's pretty bad, isn't it?" she says as she sits down. "The food." Picking up her silverware, she points at our mugs with her fork. "I should probably stick to the tea like you guys."

"Probably," I say. Phoebe wraps her fingers—long and delicate—around her mug. Right over left, trigger finger slightly curled and tapping against the middle knuckle of the opposite number on her left hand. It's an old tic of hers.

The woman ignores Phoebe's icy stare and digs in to her meal. We watch her eat, and she lets us watch her—this is the game we play. Patience. Indifference. Slow death by boredom. She plays the game well, but I can read a shiver of excitement in the way she eats too quickly. She gulps air between bites, as if she were drowning, and she fidgets, her right foot tapping against the deck.

"So," she says, once the island of mashed potatoes is decimated, sunk beneath the gray-brown sea of swill. "You came aboard at Adelaide, didn't you?"

The *Cetacean Liberty* had left Adelaide three days ago—the last port for supplies and volunteers.

"Did we?" I volunteer.

"The captain isn't very good at keeping track of volunteers, but by my count, we're at least four over this boat's listed occupancy."

"I'm sure the captain is keeping a close eye on the number of people onboard."

She snorts. Nigel shifts in his chair, not finding her reaction the least bit amusing.

"You seem to be very conversant with the ship's crew roster," I point out. "What's your role on this vessel?"

The game becomes more entertaining now, with a bit of daring mixed in. She meets my gaze and returns my smile. We both know more than we should, and the mystery of the game is how much to reveal? How much can you get the other to tell you without letting them know how little you truly know?

"Last time," she says, toying with her fork, "someone took a shot at

Captain Morse. The bullet hole is still in the railing; he likes to show it off."

"I've seen it."

"Is that why you're here?"

"To see the bullet hole?"

"No," she shakes her head. "To shoot back."

"What would we be shooting at?" I ask innocently.

She puts her fork down and leans forward. There's a gleam in her eye, and the twisted skin in the hollow of her throat flutters with her pulse. "Are you—" She glances at the table next to us, gauging whether its occupants are paying any attention to our conversation at all. "—*Arcadia?*"

I know who you are, her question says, leaping right to the end game.

"Yes, Mere," I reply, using the familiar form of her name. *I know who you are too.* "We are."

▼▼

"There's a woman here. An investigative reporter," Nigel tells Talus when we return from the mess. "Her name is Meredith Vanderhaven. She has a history with Silas."

"Why is she here?" Talus echoes Nigel's question. He stalks back and forth across the tiny room we've made our own, his restless energy making the room feel even smaller. His beard bristles and the top of his bald head gleams in the wan light.

"Why else would a prize-winning investigative journalist be on a Prime Earth boat in the middle of the Southern Ocean?" I go for the "playing dumb yet being helpful" answer.

"Why else?" Talus replies, not being taken in by my feigned innocence.

"I don't know," I say with a shrug.

"But you know her."

"I do."

"What does she know of you? Of us?"

"Little or nothing," I say.

"She knows Arcadia," Nigel points out.

I shake my head. "She knows the name, but she doesn't know anything else. She is, for lack of a better word, *fishing*. Nigel, frankly, knows more about her than she knows about us."

Talus doesn't like my answers; they don't fit his mission profile. I wish I could tell him otherwise, but I'm telling him the truth as far as the woman's presence goes. She's an aberration, an unexpected element that could cause all manner of trouble, and I don't like not having the answers as little as Talus does. Why *is* she here? Even that question has produced a palpable tension in our quartet. There is little trust among us, and we do not fit together as a cohesive team. There is something awry with this mission—we all know it—and we're jumping at the slightest provocation. There is a poison in our roots, and we fear that it will spread.

It's the water. None of the others have spent any time at sea; it unsettles them. I remember the back-breaking rhythm of rowing and the howl of enraged storms that could never quite capsize a ship, but the memory is very old and frayed.

"Where are the whalers?" Talus asks Nigel.

"A hundred nautical miles due south, but Morse isn't looking in that direction." Nigel might not have been a sailor, but he had an unerring sense of direction. He always knew where the prey was.

Talus growls in his throat, an ursine sound that belies his size. "Show him," he tells Nigel. "Let's get this job done and get back on land." He had never been on a boat during his previous life, and he didn't like the way the floor squirmed beneath his feet, or the way the horizon moved—when we could see it. The weather gnaws on his psyche too. He had fallen during Napoleon's march on Moscow, and the ground had been too hard and the weather too brutal for the dead to be buried. He had lain in the snow for five months before the ground could claim him, and his bones never quite forgot the touch of winter.

"How?" I ask. "This boat is scheduled to be out here for three weeks."

"That doesn't matter," Talus says. "Once we're done, we'll convince Morse to return."

There's a lot about his response that I don't like, and I'm sure my displeasure is clear on my face so I don't bother vocalizing what's on my mind.

"Who is this woman?" Talus ignores my annoyance, and gives me a hard stare that probably terrified Cossack cavalry, but which is wasted on me.

"A reporter," I tell him again.

"What story is she chasing?"

"I have no idea." I let some of my annoyance show in my voice. Our conversation is becoming circular.

"She wants Arcadia," Nigel says.

"We don't know that," I counter.

"Why do you care?" Talus snaps.

"She's useful to us," I say. "Do you remember the *E. coli* scandal around

Beering Foods two years ago? She broke the story for the *Boston Herald*. Nearly won the Pulitzer."

"What was our involvement?"

"The Grove wanted me to give her some data. We found a way to give her a trail to its location. We weren't exposed."

"So how does she know you then?"

I have to be careful now. "I was assigned to watch her. Until the data was understood. Until we were sure she would run with the story."

"And you weren't exposed?"

"No, of course not."

Talus isn't convinced.

"Look, she took a gamble when she approached our table. It's what she does. She makes people make mistakes—little tics in how they interact with her. That's how she knows she's on to something. Nigel and Phoebe blew our cover back in the mess by getting all worked up about her presence. I simply acknowledged we know who she is. It cut through a dance that could have gone on for days. She knows *Arcadia*, but has no sense what it means. There are a couple of places where she might have gotten the name."

"Are you sure?"

His stare is relentless, and I don't like how his guard is up. Nigel is giving me the Evil Eye as well. Phoebe's expression is one of feigned indifference, masking a not entirely concealed dislike; but she's been giving me that look for more than two hundred years now. I've given up trying to read anything in Phoebe's face. The other two, though? They're too edgy, too paranoid, and their decisions are based on bad data.

"I'm sure," I tell them, even though I know trying to dampen their curiosity is wasted effort.

Talus calls my bluff. "Find out what she knows," he says to Nigel.

"She doesn't know anything," I interrupt. "If you do anything—short of killing her outright—she'll know she's right. All that is going to do is make her dig harder."

"I'll just kill her then," Nigel says. "Simple solution. I like simple."

"Simple isn't better," I sigh. "Black and white; us versus them: it's not that simple." It never was. When are they going to figure it out? Even in the old days, so many conflicts rose out of such myopic awareness.

Phoebe stirs at my declaration and seems about to say something.

"Explain it to us then, Silas," Talus snaps, his patience running thin. "Use short words if you think that'll help."

"We don't know why she is here, but we do know it's not because of us," I say, ignoring the venom in his voice. "She was already on-board the ship at Adelaide, which means she's here for a story about Prime Earth and the whalers. How could she have known we were going to be here? The simplest answer is that she didn't know. We're a happy accident, and she's good enough at what she does that she knows how to take advantage of any opportunity that presents itself. Killing her accomplishes nothing, but if we consider the most likely reason for her to be here, she might actually be useful to us. We're short on intel for this mission as it is." I play to their paranoia, feeding the serpents of unease we all have twisting in our guts. *We shouldn't be here. This mission is wrong.*

Phoebe narrows her eyes, glancing back and forth between Talus and me. I don't like the hardness of her eyes. Before this mission, I hadn't seen Phoebe in more than two decades, and we didn't part on the best of terms—our long-standing antagonism had been tenser than normal. The Grove should know better than to pair us on an isolated mission like this, and neither of us is pleased to not know why. Talus is known for being a bullheaded commander, but he gets the job done in the worst of conditions. Phoebe's a wildcard, and watching her watch us, I'm unsettled, once again, by her enigmatic independence.

Talus clenches and unclenches his fist, watching the way his flesh tightens across his bones. "Stay close to her," he orders. His eyes flick up at me so that I know I am being given this responsibility. "Feed her enough to keep her interested. Find out what she knows."

"And then what?" I sense he's not finished.

He shows me his teeth. "Remember your priorities, Silas."

"Remember who is family," Phoebe adds, though she is looking at Talus and not me when she speaks.

TWO

The whaling fleet belongs to Kyodo Kujira Ltd, a Japanese fishing company, and is comprised of a processing ship, two harpoon boats, and a support boat. They are, ostensibly, hunting whales for research purposes—a gray area in international legislation and the Japanese haven't bothered to hide the fact they've been skirting the gray for many years. In the past, little more than lip service was ever paid to *scientific research*, but six months ago, Kyodo Kujira—who had been on the verge of bankruptcy—suddenly developed a change of heart.

It probably had something to do with a massive infusion of cash from the corporate giants who rule the biopharmaceutical and agrichemical industries.

There's an entire speculative industry in the medical and pharmaceutical literature, and more than one startup has bet its entire existence upon a bit of specious speculation in the literature. In this case, there was an article that caught fire in the community last year about the wide-ranging physiological properties of cetacean cartilage. Suddenly, the whaling market—which had been suffering recently due to a downturn in whale meat prices—is hot again.

Prime Earth is one of those militant environmental groups with more money than sense, and armed with a boat and a plan, they think they're going to be able to make some sort of difference for a few whale pods. It's all very reductionist and symbolic—save the whales, save the planet—and it is the sort of Neo New Age argument that gets a lot of play with the easily manipulated nouveau wealthy housewife that wants to do something to offset her carbon footprint. It's the sort of part-time environmentalist ethos that puts a boat overflowing with zealous volunteers out in the middle of the Southern Ocean, intent on getting between a pair of harpoon boats and their target, and will ultimately be about as effective a deterrent as chaining yourself to a tree has been on the logging industry. It's an ugly setup that has all sorts of opportunities for someone to do something stupid and, out here in the middle of the Southern Ocean, the repercussions of stupidity could be lethal.

We're several hundred miles from solid ground. I wasn't worried about drowning, but salt water is corrosive to Arcadian flesh. Too long in sea water and the flesh becomes tainted and doesn't absorb nutrients well. The four of us are much more resilient than the rest of the crew, but we aren't indestructible.

Remember who is family.

Sometimes it is hard to know who to trust. It is hard to know a person's true motivation. You trust your family with your life because that is the way it has always been. That is what keeps us strong. But those bonds can only take so much stress for so long before they start to fray. Before they weaken.

Keep her close.

I wanted to know why Meredith Vanderhaven was on this boat. Regardless of the story I had sold Talus, the coincidence bothered me. Given her contentious history with the food industry and Big Ag, it was possible that our paths would cross again, but I didn't like the way she had beat the odds. Was there something else going on? Had she known we were going to be here?

Behind all these questions lay others. Whispers I want to ignore, questions I want to dismiss as nothing more than distorted echoes. *What did she remember from that night? What have I forgotten?*

The disease of neglected memory is an eventual consequence of leaving Mother's embrace, but seeing Mere again has triggered that nagging uneasiness much sooner than I would like. It contributes to my own paranoia and confounds my ability to think clearly. I get easier to spook. We all do.

There is something rotten about this mission.

ᴠᴠ

"Do you know what Prime Earth is going to do when we find the whalers?" I ask Mere. We are standing on the starboard side of the upper deck, sheltered from the wind that is pushing us toward the heavy storm in the south. It's mid-afternoon, and even if the sun wasn't obscured by the clouds, it wouldn't be very high in the sky.

She is wearing a heavy coat, a thick stocking cap, and her throat is hidden by the voluminous folds of a wool scarf. The tip of her nose and her cheeks are red. She stamps her feet and I know she's thinking about going inside, but she won't go in. Not while I'm in a sharing mood. The air is clean enough that I could go without my coat and hat, but that would only draw attention to me. It's the second week of July—mid-winter in the Southern Ocean. The air is always cleaner in winter climates.

"I've seen the videos from last year," she says. "A lot of playing chicken and throwing—what is it?—that acid on deck."

"Butyric. Stink gas, essentially. When they take a whale on and carve it up, the acid gets into the flesh and ruins it. They can't sell it."

"So they just have to throw it away?"

"Yes, unless they can find another use for it. Some other buyer."

She glances at me shrewdly. "Is there?"

"A buyer? I wouldn't know."

Mere steps a little closer, letting my body act as a wind break. "Why are you here?" she asks.

"Why do you think we're here?" I throw the question back on her. "You're the one who took an extended vacation to come down and join the cruise. How many weeks have you been playing at sailor?"

"Two. And a half."

"And what have you seen during that time?"

She shakes her head. "Lots of open water. Some birds; I think they were terns. I've been propositioned nearly a dozen times—only two of them have been poor sports about being turned down—and I've won around a hundred dollars in that endless poker game they run in the mess after dinner." She lifts her shoulders and stares out at the sea. "Everyone is waiting for something to happen. Some of them are better at it than others. A few are... wound a little tight..." She trails off, and her words would have been lost in the bruising roar of the ocean against the hull of the boat if my hearing hadn't been so good.

"What are they waiting for?"

"Do you know what the whale market is like?" she asks, and when I don't immediately reply, she tells me. "Prime made an impact last year, but there's no sign any of their leadership actually bothered to notice. Japanese consumption of whale meat is down thirty percent from this time last year, and it's not from a lack of supply. Public perception has started to swing in an eco-friendly direction, and yet Kyodo Kujira sends out four boats for an extended whaling trip. In winter. They've been out for three weeks already, and I hear they're in no rush to return to port. Do you know how much it costs to keep these boats at sea for that long?"

"More than I make in a year," I reply, a tiny smile touching the corners of my mouth.

"Really? How much does a private consultant like you make?"

"Less than you think. My tax rate is insane."

"You should diversify your portfolio better."

"I would if I knew what those words meant."

She stands close to me, rising on her toes slightly to look closely at my eyes. I don't step back, though the smell of her breath and her blood is almost too much. "It's a matter of making good investments," she breathes. "The wholesale price of whale meat is down forty percent. Over half the whalers never put out to sea this year, and yet Kyodo Kujira doesn't seem to be worrying about their burn rate. The Japanese are notorious for keeping up appearances, but this is ridiculous. Two years ago, they were looking for someone to buy their boats, and I heard they weren't having much luck finding a buyer. Now? This is either suicidal desperation—not a trait commonly found in your typical Japanese businessman—or…"

"Someone else is paying for it," I say.

"Who?"

"Why do you think I know?"

"Why else would you be here?"

I smile at her. "Remember the bullet hole? Captain Morse, all bluster and bravery for the crew's sake aside, feels more secure with some… protection."

That sounds convenient," she says. "Is that the story he's supposed to tell?"

"You could ask him."

"I have. He pretends to not know what I'm talking about."

"It probably just slipped his mind."

She takes one more step, and even through the thick layers of her coat, I can feel the heat of her skin. "Maybe," she says. Her eyes are bright, and I can hear her lungs expanding and contracting. "But I suspect getting any real information out of him is a waste of time. Especially when I could ask someone else, someone who would actually know."

My hand is on her arm when Nigel makes a noise behind us. "The captain has spotted the whalers. They're on the edge of the storm front. About sixty nautical miles to the west," he says, ignoring the way we step back from one another, like teenagers caught by their parents, sitting too close to one another on the old couch in the basement.

THREE

We wait until the end of the day, even though there isn't much change in the available light in the sky. Winter near the Antarctic Circle is many days of near darkness, and for their own sanity, humans try to maintain a semblance of normalcy during these months. Sleep cycles and shift changes still occur in the last few hours of the nominal day, which makes this block of time optimal for our reconnaissance.

The whaling fleet is ten nautical miles south of us, holding position in a half-arc with the two harpoon boats positioned at either end. We take a single Zodiac and head west, our rubber boat rising and falling across the restless sea. We mean to approach them from the south. This route will take an extra half-hour—time we don't really have, but it is a calculated risk.

I'm not driving the boat, nor am I spotting, which means I get to bail. The rubber shield stretched across the front of the boat disperses the brunt of the spray from the ocean, but a lot of it still manages to get in the boat, and I spend most of my time hunched over in several inches of water, working the manual pump. The water is cold and tenacious, undeterred by the dry suits we are wearing; by the time we reach the research vessel, I've started to lose feeling in my toes. As Nigel cuts the engine of the Zodiac, and we glide the short distance remaining between us and the factory ship, I let myself think of the warm embrace of Mother for a moment. How good it would feel to be buried in her humus, surrounded by that warmth—that familiar security.

But then the Zodiac bumps against the ugly steel plates of the research boat, and I'm wrenched back to the present, to the cold semi-darkness of the short night on the Southern Ocean. The tight embrace of the dry suits and Gore-Tex balaclavas isn't the same thing. Nigel eschews the headgear entirely, wearing a black stocking cap instead, and I can't say I blame him. Being in the tight grip of synthetic fabrics can be too constricting. It makes you clumsy.

Phoebe goes first, the metal spikes in her gloves and boots giving her enough purchase to scale the side of the boat. The nylon line spools out in her wake, wiggling back and forth with the motion of her body as she climbs. With the sun below the horizon, we can keep our optic protection low; it is easy to follow her progress—a black glob of ink against the dull metal of the boat. She reaches the top, disappears, and then a few seconds later, the rope snaps tight.

All clear.

I go next, as Nigel secures the Zodiac to the hull with a pair of mag-clamps. He follows after and, just like that, we're on board the research ship.

We all have the same map memorized, and with Phoebe on point, we move quickly across the rain-slick deck. All our individual paranoia is set aside as soon as we climb aboard the boat. We've done this drill too many times over our lengthy lives. We know our jobs.

The meat-processing equipment is in place, and I give it a cursory glance at first, but then there is something that nags me about the general disarray and decrepitude of the hooks and blades. It hasn't been used. Even if they haven't been catching whales for the meat, they'd still need to process them for the research. And there are large barrels with hose-mounted assemblies bolted to the deck that look like recent additions. A cleansing system? It doesn't make sense. Why wouldn't they just use sea water pumps?

"*Silas—*" Nigel and Phoebe are already inside the central stack. She gestures at me to stop dawdling, and I tear myself away from the scattered equipment on deck. I join them, and we slip down two levels and then through a cluster of tight hatches.

The boat creaks around us, and the sound of the engines are a dull throb, but there is no other sound. It's as if we are ghosts on a ghost ship. I fall behind the other two, growing more and more suspicious of the emptiness of the boat. With modern equipment, you could pilot a boat this size with a crew of six, but that sort of skeleton crew was normally reserved for massive shipping boats, not whalers who were ostensibly on a fishing expedition. If you caught a whale, you'd need at least twenty able bodies to run the processors; you could do it with less, but the risk to the crew was exponentially more dangerous than the savings in labor. And if this was supposed to be a research boat, wouldn't there be a scientific crew?

So where is everyone?

I pause at the next hatch. The lining is thicker than I'd expect it to be on a boat like this, even if it had been retrofitted into a high-tech floating bio-pharmaceutical laboratory. It's more like the sort found on a submarine: thick enough to hold back water and atmosphere. I hiss at Phoebe and wave her over.

"Something's wrong," I say as she drifts back to my position. "Look at this seal."

She touches the heavy hatch door we're standing next to, and it moves sluggishly under her finger. "Hydraulics," she says.

The hatch can be opened and closed remotely. Remote control means remote viewing, and we both step back from the hatch, suddenly interested in the maze of conduits and cables running along the ceiling. Looking for security cameras, thermal scanners, motion triggers.

Someone could be watching us right now.

"Nigel." Phoebe leans through the hatch and hisses at Nigel.

He is standing beside a hatch with a security panel, and his hand is poised over the keypad. His expression is both annoyed and startled.

"It's all wrong," Phoebe whispers.

"Don't touch anything," I add.

His eyes flicker toward his hand and the keypad.

Too late.

In the wall, there is a sudden hiss of escaping air, and the hydraulics controlling the hatch start to swing it closed. Phoebe grabs at the hatch, slowing its motion as I turn and race back to the previous hatch. The hydraulics are retrofits, exposed machinery welded to the inside of the hatch. From this side, I can break things. I go to work, and dark oil squirts over my hands as I tear apart critical pieces of the hydraulic system.

A mist starts to descend from the ceiling, a pale yellow mist, and it burns where it touches my exposed skin. I inhale reflexively and try to stop myself from filling my lungs with the aerosol. What gets in though feels like I've just inhaled fire. An old memory stirs. Naphtha—oh, how it used to burn the wood decks and hulls of the old triremes. I fight my flight impulse, and throw my weight against the hatch, fighting the sluggish hydraulics.

Nigel is screaming behind me, a sound no one should make, much less hear.

Phoebe slams into the hatch beside me, combining my weight with hers, and we force the hatch back until it is wide enough for her to slip through. She moves like a shadow, and the metal hatch groans as she levers it from the other side. As soon as it is wide enough for me, I go through and then take over for her.

Nigel staggers through. His face is a wreck. The poison has melted his skin down to the bone in several places and his eyes are gone, weeping holes in his face.

The remaining hatch isn't as hermetically sealed as the others, and I hear it crash open as Phoebe clears our path. As I try to help Nigel without actually touching him, I hear shouts from the deck, followed by the faint rattle of Phoebe's silenced pistols. Clearing a path for us.

Nigel can't see, and he bangs his skull against the frame before I can shove his head down enough for him to clear the last portal. My skin crawls at the touch, even though I'm wearing gloves. Tendrils of acrid smoke are spiraling off Nigel's melted skin.

Phoebe is waiting for us by the railing, covering our retreat. There are six bodies on the deck, and the reek of their blood makes my throat constrict. The hoses have been unrolled from the mounted tanks, and they lie on the deck like dead serpents. The nozzle of one is open, and it is spewing a frothing fluid on the deck. My skin crawls at the sight of the pale, bubbling liquid and my eyes water as we skirt the flood that is threatening to cover the deck.

Our rope is still in place. Nigel is coherent enough to know what to do when I shove the rope into his hands. I mean to go first, but he leaps off, nearly in free-fall in his frantic need to get off the boat. I go after him, the water-slick rope twisting in my hands as I slide down the side of the boat. The fabric of my gloves burns away as I squeeze the rope and slow myself down. Nigel hadn't even bothered trying to stop. He is lying in the briny bilge in the bottom of the boat, whimpering and moaning. Phoebe lands lightly, the rope cascading down beside her.

Phoebe shoves us away from the hull of the processing ship as I start the engine of the Zodiac. I don't worry about making a silent retreat; I open the throttle all the way, and we flee as fast as the tiny rotor will go.

Nigel lies in the bottom of the Zodiac the whole way back, half-covered in a netting of loosely coiled rope. He makes a whistling noise through the ruin of his mouth. Phoebe and I don't talk, not for a lack of things to say, but because we are both gripped by the same fear.

They were waiting for us.

FOUR

I know the cream is working, because my skin is twitching and the urge to scratch is unbearable. I sit on my hands to keep from tearing at my flesh. Phoebe must be feeling the same thing, though I can only tell by the way her eyes are moving—back and forth, like she is watching a tennis match. My lungs still hurt, and when I take a deep breath, the webbing of new tissue threatens to tear. My throat is raw, and I sound like a three-pack-a-day cigarette junkie when I speak.

When he is finished with Nigel, Talus strips off the rubber gloves, turning them inside out, and discards them in the nearby waste bin. His skin is shiny with sweat, and when he raises his hand to wipe his forehead, he pauses. Even though he has been wearing the heavy rubber gloves, he's still not sure he wants to touch his face with his hand. He realizes I'm watching him and he finishes the motion, though he uses his sleeve to wipe his forehead. I don't blame him; Phoebe and I both know the same apprehension. We've just had more time with it, more time to bury the fear deep in our hearts.

"They were waiting for us," Phoebe says.

"Give me your report," Talus says. He hunches forward slightly, turning his back to the bed where Nigel is lying. It forces us to cluster around him, as if we are sharing a secret, and I dislike the subtle inference in his motion, but I let it go, focusing instead on telling him what happened. Our intel had been bad. Whoever was funding Kyodo Kujira had wanted Arcadia to send a team. Would we be so curious that we'd leave solid ground, that we'd expose ourselves, just to find out what they were doing? Out on the open water, we couldn't hide as readily—we couldn't run away. "They're conducting tests, all right," I say, "but it's got nothing to do with cetacean research. That boat hasn't processed a whale in over a year. They just wanted to test a new chemical agent, one that"—I wave a hand to indicate the three of us—"reacts strongly to our physiology."

"Aerosol dispersal," he mutters when I finish. He looks over his shoulder at Nigel's quivering form. "Idiot."

Nigel hadn't been wearing Gore-Tex on his head. The stocking cap soaked up the poisonous mist, and the cotton fabric turned into a concentrated glob of corrosive acid. Whatever that mist was—whatever was pumping out of that hose on the deck—reacted strongly to flesh. *Our flesh.* It had no effect on the slick surface of our dry suits, or any other surface.

Phoebe and I had gotten a light dose, and our burns would heal in time, but Nigel was much worse. Most of the flesh on his head was gone. His eyes were ruined, and his throat was badly burned. His lungs were in bad shape; each shallow breath caused his body to quake with pain. He had forgotten what it was like to die, and so he kept on breathing, kept on trying to heal. The process would take a long time and it would be filled with pain.

Sometimes it is only Mother who can stop the pain, but she is so far away. Solid ground is so very far away.

"He needs blood." Talus says out loud what we've been thinking.

"It won't be enough," Phoebe says.

Talus lifts his shoulders. "He's family." As if that is all the justification we need.

Phoebe looks at me since Talus won't meet her gaze. "It won't be enough," she repeats.

"I know," I reply. "But if we can get him stabilized, he might manage to hold the thirst off until we can get back to land."

My words are meaningless, and I can tell Phoebe is disappointed in my response. But to say anything else would be to contradict Talus, who has invoked the most primal justification.

Family.

We know what this means: everyone else dies, because that is the only way to ensure our survival.

Ⱦ Ⱦ

"Silas."

I should ignore her. I should pretend I didn't hear her over the omnipresent growl of the boat and the ocean. I should just keep walking. But I don't. "Mere."

The hallway is dim and the hood of my coat is up so she can't see my face, but she gets real close. Her hand falls on my arm. "What's going on?"

"Nothing," I say, though the ragged sound of my voice reveals the word as the lie that it is.

"I saw you leave. You and your friends. You took a boat and went out there."

I look down at her hand, and think how easily it would be to take her for Nigel. A simple rotation of my arm to break her grip; my other hand around her throat. The panic light in her eyes as I carry her back to the room. The smell of her fear. The hammering sound of her heart. The smell of all that blood.

It would be so easy.

"You didn't see anything," I say as I carefully remove her hand from my arm.

In the corridor behind her, Talus is watching. I lift my head fractionally and she looks—a quick glance over her shoulder—and it is enough of a distraction for me to walk away from her. This time I don't stop or turn around when she calls my name.

The hallway is too narrow. The ceiling is too low. My breath hurts my throat, and through a film of tears, I mistake the deck door for an airtight hatch, and I'm transported back to the factory ship again. My face, beneath all the topical cream, itches and burns. I start to run. All I want to do is get away; all I want is to get out of this metal prison. Away from all the toxins spewed by these mouth-breathers. Away from all the sterile death of this construct. Back to Mother's embrace. Back to the earth.

I hit the door at a run, and the metal bends beneath my hands. The wind strikes my face with a stinging slap, and I suck in a huge lungful of cold air, ignoring the fiery tearing in my chest. The railing is cold under my hands, slick with water, and I grip it tightly. The ocean isn't the ground, but it still teems with life, and I can feel it. I can feel all that vibrant energy.

Mere grabs my shoulder. I react, spinning out from beneath her grip, and my hands bury themselves in the fabric of her coat. She shrieks as I lift her over the railing, and her feet drum against the side of the boat.

The wind blows my hood back, and seeing my face frightens her even more. I tighten my grip. "Stop struggling," I say. "I might let go."

Her hands are on my arms, and even though the panic light is bright in her eyes, she stops thrashing.

"We survive," I tell her, "because we know who to trust. Everything else—*every other person on this planet*—does not matter. That is the first law of Arcadia. Do you understand?"

I wait, my arms strong and unburdened by her weight, until she nods. A tiny sob escapes from her as I bring her back to the deck. She backs away from me when I let go, though she runs into the railing before she can take more than a single step. Her hands clutch the front of her coat, and she won't look at me. "I'm sorry," she says, her voice so soft against the noise of the sea.

"For what?" I say, even though I know I shouldn't reply—that I shouldn't be drawn into this conversation.

The corner of her mouth moves, and I realize I've just given myself away. She raises her head and looks at me. She doesn't flinch at the sight of my face, and the weak light from the yellow line on the horizon highlights the scar on her throat. "It must be very lonely," she says and there is a different light in her eyes now.

She isn't afraid.

V V

"You should have brought the reporter." Talus is standing too close to me. I can smell the stale stink of his breath. We've been away from land too long; our bodies are retaining too many toxins. "She's too curious."

I swallow my rage. "What did you expect?" I snap.

Phoebe gives me her enigmatic glare, saying nothing. Talus doesn't notice her—he's unaware of the tension in her frame. How close she is to doing violence. The wet sounds coming from Nigel and the young Prime Earth volunteer aren't helping. We're all feeling the thirst. The boy's eyes are open; there's still life in that flesh, and though he can't speak, he's trying to get our attention. Trying to beg for his life.

His name is Francis, and his tragic flaw is his nicotine addiction. If he hadn't been heading out to the deck for a cigarette, I wouldn't have met him in the corridor. If he had stayed in his tiny bunk, he might have had a chance to become a helpful statistic in the media war against the tobacco companies. Forty-three percent chance of contracting lung cancer by his fortieth birthday. As it stands, he won't turn twenty-six.

His blood is polluted, of course, awash with a cocktail of carcinogens and nicotine, but there are still raw nutrients that Nigel can extract. It won't be enough, like Phoebe warned us, but Nigel will be able to repair some of the caustic damage from the aerosol spray. *The blood will help.*

"We have to be strategic," I say to Talus. "There might be a few assets we can leverage here. We need to be careful with our resources."

We're in the middle of the fucking ocean, I don't say, *we can't afford to let our fear rule us. That's what they want us to do.*

"They don't know how well it worked," Phoebe says.

"That's right," I echo. "We got off the boat. All they'll have is video footage, but it won't tell them much. They don't know how well it works. Until they can be sure, they'll be cautious. They'll want more data."

Talus chewed on the inside of his cheek for a moment, his attention straying toward the dying boy. "Nigel will need more blood," he says.

"No." I shut that conversation down.

He whirls on me, a blur of motion, and his hand moves even faster. I feel it coming, but I don't move out of the way. My head snaps to the side, and my mouth fills with the warm taste of blood. "Know your place, *liar,*" he hisses.

I don't cringe, nor do I reply right away. I take a moment or two to watch his eyes. "I *do* know my place," I respond. "And that is to respect and serve. But if you fail to uphold the first, then I am not bound to the second."

He starts to sneer at me, and then his gaze flickers to Phoebe behind me, and the expression vanishes like a shadow fleeing the rising moon. "The reporter is dangerous," he says, recovering and retreating to a safer position.

"Agreed," I reply, meeting him halfway. "But to whom?"

He growls in his throat, and I hear the accusation caught there. *Liar.*

Suddenly weary of this conversation, I turn away from Talus. "I will find out what she knows—because she will tell me—and then we will decide if she can still be useful to us," I say. "We will decide together. It will be a group decision."

I watch the light go out of the boy's eyes. His face goes slack, and Nigel lifts his mouth from the boy's neck. A shudder runs through his frame, and it isn't the same sort of spasm he had been exhibiting earlier.

Talus glares at me. I've challenged his authority. I will have to answer for my insubordination eventually, but he's smart enough—he's old enough—to know the truth of my words. We need better intel. We need to know who we are fighting and why. He doesn't like it, but we need Mere.

He doesn't like having to trust a human.

I don't blame him, but we don't have any choice.

We're cut off from Arcadia. On our own and in dangerous terrain. In such conditions, there are rarely good choices. Only the expedient ones that increase your chance of survival.

FIVE

Ostensibly, our mission was an intelligence-gathering assignment, but I had been party to enough cluster-fucks designed by an armchair committee to know the signs. We were being exiled, and the Grove wouldn't be terribly saddened if none of us returned. I suspected my previous incident with Meredith was the reason I had been chosen—and it was starting to occur to me that her presence on the boat simply made things easier if the Grove was attempting to purge *weeds* from the garden. It had been a couple of decades since I had seen Phoebe, and it had never been easy to tell what she was thinking. She was like that though—perpetually inscrutable. In many ways, it didn't matter if we were talking to one another. She and I were bound together. There may be more animosity than love between us, but there would always be respect.

I had heard stories about Talus—the man had a hair-trigger and a history of letting the bloodlust rule him. Nigel was the odd man out—nothing I had heard suggested he was anything other than a perfect soldier—and perhaps his secondary objective was to push the rest of the team overboard somewhere below the sixtieth parallel. By the time we managed to return to Arcadia, we'd crave Mother's embrace so much that we'd agree to anything. She'd strip the incendiary memories from our heads while we lay in her arms—the revolutionary zeal, the incessant need to question authority—and when we were born again, we'd be resplendent with the pure spirit of Arcadia.

It never worked quite right with me, and I suspected it had something to do with the auguries I had performed before coming to Arcadia. I had seen the world differently than the rest. I remembered more than I was supposed to—I knew there were holes in my history that weren't entirely the result of decades-long slumber. I could remember the way Arcadia used to be. We used to not fear the sun. We used to be able to breathe the air. We used to be able to sleep anywhere.

But so much has changed in the last two hundred years.

The seed of our panic had been laid by the Romantics and had been steadily nurtured by the Modernists and their hyphenated children. Stir in the nihilism of Nietzsche, Dostoyevsky, Lovecraft, and Camus—as well as the brutal reality of two World Wars—and the resulting harvest was rife with fear, despair, and a mad yearning to be coddled. Capitalism, Communism, and a few other -isms tried their best, but it took corporate greed to finally figure out how to yoke humanity, and once yoked, they were easy to lead.

We became the bogeymen, the terror that threatened everything they were told they needed. The message spread, always the same. At first it was just the Internet, magnified by the vitriolic half-percent that purports to be the reasonable voice of the popular consensus, and then talk radio, in all the big markets, began to treat it as something other than a bad Internet meme that wouldn't die. Eventually, the networks discovered there was money in fear-mongering and the modern monster was given a face and a mission statement: we were the children of anarchy, the sons and daughters of Free Love radicals who wanted to turn the world into a socialist prison camp; the world was a free market economy, and we were the barbarians who only wanted to pillage and plunder the marketplace.

All the while, their dark Satanic mills kept pumping poisons into the air, earth, and water. We didn't stop them because we were afraid to, and that fear has started to seep up from Mother's roots.

▼▼

There is whisky in Captain Morse's mug, and the alcohol blurs his eyes and taints his breath. It gives him strength too, a ruddy flush in his cheeks, and his gestures are big and exaggerated. As if he were playing for a television audience, the one he imagines due to him for his courageous stance against corporate malfeasance and ecological destruction. "They're going hunting," he tells me as I enter the bridge. He points out the curved window at the two narrow shapes on the water. "Both of them."

The harpooners are moving away from the factory ship, heading in an easterly direction. Hugging the edge of the persistent storm that never quite breaks. I don't see the patrol boat. "Any whale sign?" I ask.

Captain Morse's mouth flaps for a second and then he gestures off toward port, mumbling something about radar echoes. He strides across the deck and jabs the sailor standing in front of the navigation console in the shoulder. "Get in front of them," he commands. "We need to be beat them to the pod."

The man, one of three able-bodied sailors who came with the boat, glances at me briefly and then nods. "Aye aye, Cap'n," he replies as he complies. The growling sound beneath our feet grows louder, and the persistent tremor in the deck increases. In my gut, I can feel the slow twist of our changing aspect as the *Cetacean Liberty* responds to the sailor's commands. The factory ship begins to drift to starboard, and I finally spot the thin blade of the patrol boat peeking from around the bow of the bigger ship.

The pair of harpooners stay squarely in front of us.

"Tuna," Captain Morse says.

"Excuse me?" I inquire.

"It's not 'chicken' when we're on water. Right? So, what's the 'chicken of the sea'? Tuna." He laughs, a bray of open-mouthed laughter, punctuated by a long pull on his mug. "Let's go show these bitches how to play *tuna*."

I wonder how long he's been waiting to say that, and as I watch the factory ship and its armored shadow grow smaller and smaller, I also wonder if there's another game being played. A wild what? A wild *salmon* chase, to keep with the captain's nautical vernacular. Both harpoon boats make sense if they are actually trying to harvest a whale. Realistically, we can only engage one boat at a time, leaving the other to go about its bloody business. But if that were the case, they'd be splitting up, trying to put as much distance between themselves as they approached the pod. Making us choose one or the other. *Why the tag-team approach?*

I sense another presence behind me. Mere. Her scent is easy to pick up in the close quarters of the bridge.

"Is your girl going to be ready?" Captain Morse asks. "If any of those bastards even think about shooting at us, I want to know before they get the courage to try it. Okay?"

"Aye-aye, Cap'n," I echo. "She'll be ready."

ⅤⅤ

"Was that little show for my sake?" Mere asks me a few moments later as we navigate the narrow hallway outside the bridge.

"No."

"Is she actually going to shoot first?"

I stop, and turn on her, showing her my teeth. "We never shoot first," I snarl.

She holds her ground. "What if they don't miss?" Her cheeks are flushed, and her eyes are bright.

"Then—" I break off, looking away from her face. *Then, there will be one less whisky-tainted mouth-breather to leech off her resources. Then, there will be more for the rest of us.*

"Why are you here?" I shake off the other thoughts. *Remember your priorities.*

"This is where the action is," she says.

"There's action in Afghanistan, too."

"Not the same sort." She shakes her head. "Besides, I don't care for the heat. Nor, I suspect, do you."

"You don't know me." Still on edge from my conversation with Talus, from the threats and accusations rumbling beneath his words.

"I think I do."

A bark of laughter escapes me—a hyena-like bray of noise. "Do you now?"

"The Beering data. It wasn't an accident that my guy found it. He was supposed to give it to me."

The laugh dies. "Who?" I try.

"Not 'what?'"

"What?" It isn't hard to be confused.

"You asked me 'who,' not 'what.'"

"What are you talking about?"

"I'm talking about you're not as clever as you think; I'm talking about how much danger you're in, and how this little excursion had better be worth a great deal to your people because it is going to cost you."

"You have no idea what you're talking about. What do you know about *costs?*"

"You tell me." She lifts her chin, and the scar is like a serpent coiling down into the hollow of her throat. "You killed him, didn't you?" she asks. "You killed Kirkov."

I look away again, unwilling to let her question in. Talus's accusation echoes in my head. I have lied to him, as I've lied to everyone since that night.

Up the old fire escape outside the run-down apartment he's lured her to. The old Chechen gangster, Illytch Dmitri Kirkov, wanting revenge for the damage her story has done to his organization—not Beering Foods, but the other organization that was piggy-backing off Beering. Kirkov limps, an old wound from the First Chechen War, but his grip is strong and secure. He's got a knee in the small of her back, and he's pulling her head up. The knife is the only thing he's kept from his old life, back in Chechnya, and it's worn with age and use. He goes to cut her throat, and he almost makes it.

But not quite.

The first lie—the one that has set me on this path—is the one I tell myself that night: *She didn't see anything.*

I tried to forget. But we're not good at letting go of memory. It's so fragile. We can't help ourselves.

And so we lie instead.

V V

The captain plays *tuna* with the harpoon boats for the rest of the day, completely oblivious to the fact that we never spot a single whale. Whoever is in command aboard the factory ship knows we're hiding in plain sight onboard the *Cetacean Liberty*. They know we're somewhat at the mercy of the captain's whims. By catering to his blind desire to be the man who *saved the whales*, they've lured us away with the two harpoon boats.

Eight hours, spent watching three boats engage in a clumsy game of *Chase Me! Chase Me!* The captains of the harpoon boats clearly have orders to lead us on, and they participate in Morse's game just enough to feed his ego. Just enough to keep his adrenaline up. To keep his focus on them.

Phoebe is frustrated too. She stalks along the starboard railing, her hands clenching and unclenching as she strides back and forth. All the way, watching the nearest boat for any provocation, any sign that they're going to do anything other than tease us. But they won't, and everyone knows it.

Everyone except Captain Morse.

I know something is wrong when Talus appears on deck. He staggers slightly in the half-light, his optics darker than necessary against the wan sunlight. He walks slowly, like the deck is slick beneath his feet or like a man who has been shaken from a long slumber. I get Phoebe's attention and we meet Talus in the lee of the bridge.

"Nigel's gone," he says. He shakes his head when Phoebe starts to say something. "I've already looked. He's not there."

I look out at the nearest ship, trying to gauge the distance. "How long?"

"I don't know. An hour, perhaps. Maybe more. I thought he was meditating."

I cast my mind back over the last hour, trying to map the relative positions of all the boats during that time. There had been a near miss with the smaller of the two harpoon boats—the one known as the *White Egret*—close enough we could see the expression on the faces of the half-dozen crewmen who had gathered at the rail to stare, mouths open, at our fancy boat. Since then, the *White Egret* had fallen behind, and the captain had claimed a victory—"she's lost her nerve!"—but now I wasn't so sure.

I use my optics to zoom in on the trailing vessel. There isn't any activity on the upper deck. Not that that means anything. As there were no whales, there was no need to have any of the harpooning stations manned. Yet another sign that this was all a ruse. I scan the tiny rectangles of the bridge windows, but the sun is behind me and all I can see is glare, even with the light reduction lens on my optics.

White Egret's aspect begins to change, her nose drifting to port.

A door slams open on our ship, metal against metal, and we all hear the chatter from the bridge. From the upper deck, the first mate whistles, a piercing shriek of sound, and we flinch as one. Having gotten our attention, he waves frantically, and Phoebe—understanding more intuitively how badly the situation has deteriorated—moves faster than the human eye can track. Talus and I cling to our fraying illusion of normalcy, and by the time we reach the bridge, Phoebe has come and gone.

Captain Morse is slumped in his chair, shivering violently. He tries to make himself even smaller as Talus and I enter the bridge. The first mate's knuckles are white on the wheel, and he won't look at us. The young man manning the radar is trying to hide his fear by being helpful. He knows Japanese, and he's translating the radio signal as quickly as he can.

Talus speaks the language too, but he lets the boy translate. Something for his brain to focus on.

"Over and over, he's saying '*Kyuu*—'…'*Kyuuketsuki*.' And: 'they're all dead…'" He trails off. Talus doesn't bother translating the one word. The boy's imagination is doing a pretty good job already.

"Come about to port," Talus instructs the first mate. "Bring us close to *Cherry Blossom*, the other boat."

"The other boat?" The captain finds his voice and some of his courage. "What the fuck are you doing? We've got to—"

"Do what?" Talus interrupts.

"The *White Egret*. They're in trou—" The captain's gaze flickers back and forth between us. "We can't just…"

"You heard him. There's no one to rescue."

"There's one guy," Captain Morse tries. "Listen to him. He's screaming for help."

"*Cherry Blossom*," Talus repeats quietly, and the first mate spins the wheel. The engines groan and grumble with the sudden strain, and our boat begins to turn away from the drifting harpoon boat. The other boat has already begun to flee, and the gap is widening between us. In a flat-out race across the sea, we might not be fast enough to catch them.

Phoebe is in the forward observation blister on the boat. Her blonde hair is tied back in a pony tail so the wind can't play with it. She ignores the spray of water coming up from the sea as the boat churns across the ocean. Her rifle, a Sako TRG-42, is set up on a plinth, and she's completely focused on what she sees through the rifle's optics.

When the man on the radio begins shrieking incoherently, Talus tells the boy to turn it off.

Kyuuketsuki. Vampire.

Our cover is blown.

SIX

All it takes is several rounds from Phoebe's Sako TRG-42 and the *Cherry Blossom* begins to drift; no longer is it a question of whether we will catch her, but when. It's not clear how Nigel got to the other boat, but he didn't take our Zodiac, which is fine with me. I get the prop turning before it hits the water, and it skips across the ocean like a flat pebble. As soon as I am close enough to jump aboard the tender, I kill the small engine on the Zodiac. My leap carries me over the railing and I land on the deck just below the bridge house. I hear a distant pop—Phoebe providing me cover—and a small circle of glass falls out of the bridge's side window, like an extra star in Orion's belt.

There's no movement following this last shot, and so I dart up the stairs to the bridge. There are several bodies, all of whom have been hit by Phoebe's sniping. She's using .338 Lapau Magnum rounds, heavier and more devastating at distance than the standard .308 Winchester round— one of her few concessions to modern technology—and the bullet tends to make a mess of people. The one guy who is still alive took one in the shoulder (unlike the other two who took rounds to the head and are spattered rather dramatically across the small bridge), and he's rolling around on the floor, making a lot of noise about the exit wound that has demolished most of his right shoulder blade.

I resist the urge to drag my finger through the bloody mess.

A thirsty man, lost in a desert, will drink anything that is more fluid than sand and call it *water*.

There should be more men on this boat, and I'm a little concerned to find it so deserted. I don't like this setup; it smacks too much like the processing ship the other night. Like someone is expecting an Arcadian response.

The Japanese sailor is slipping into shock. I try to get some answers out of him, but he only shakes his head wildly, shrieking with pain, and then sprints into unconsciousness.

All of the men on the bridge are all carrying sidearms. SIG Sauer P226s. Two of them are so new I'm sure their users have never fired them. The P226 is a fine pistol, though unexpected on Japanese sailors; I take the new pair of pistols and the clip from the third.

The men below deck are better armed. It's only because I'm expecting trouble that I don't walk straight into their ambush. As it is, I empty one of the two pistols driving them back into the depth of the ship. The hallway is filled with smoke, and my ears are ringing from all the gunfire, but I creep forward. I've killed two men—neither is Japanese—and I pause long enough to check their bodies. The only thing they're carrying is extra magazines for guns that the others have taken. No wallets; no IDs; no receipts from a favorite lunch place back on the Continent. Professional mercenary behavior.

Who are these guys?

I check their teeth and dental work, both of which suggest American backgrounds with time spent on overseas military bases. I inspect the extra magazines again: .40 S&W rounds. Same as the pistols.

I don't know the layout of the boat, and playing hide and seek with these guys doesn't sound like much fun, and I'm wary that I'm *supposed* to follow them. I don't need another repeat of the aerosol incident from the factory ship. I go back to the upper deck and head for the engine room instead. There are two guys waiting down there, trying to be stealthy, but the cloying stench of the diesel engine doesn't hide the scent of their sweat. The first tries to gut me with his tactical knife like I'm a wild sturgeon. I catch his wrist, break it, and take the knife from his slack fingers. The knife blade is long, and it reminds me of my first *kopis*. I show him an old technique, one that works just as well now as it did back then. I like the way the blade feels in my hand, and cutting the second man's throat feels like a home-coming.

I lick the blade, feeling like a junkie as my body shivers at the taste. The blood is foul and I want to spit it out, but much like Nigel when he was drinking from the student, once it hits the back of my throat, there's no denying the shivering joy that sweeps through my body.

I hack through a number of critical pipes and tubes, mainly to coat the blade with enough oil-based products to take the edge off my desire, but also to reduce the boat's ability to do more than drift with the current until the oncoming storm can have its way with the derelict vessel.

The rest of the tactical team hasn't been waiting for me to find them, and as I return to the upper deck, they try to catch me in a furious hail of bullets. I'm not so easily caught unaware, and I don't stroll blithely into the gunfire. The pair in the engine room carried Heckler & Koch UMPs—the magazines I found on the other men match—and I return fire, catching one of the team. He staggers over the rail, and pitches off the boat. The remaining pair head for high ground, and I let them think they've got the advantage of high ground. They're just going to get picked off by Phoebe.

Nothing happens after a minute or so, and I finally crab-walk to a position where I can look to the rear of the boat. Why isn't Phoebe firing?

The answer is clear as soon as I look. The *Cetacean Liberty* isn't following the *Cherry Blossom* any longer. The Prime Earth vessel's aspect is all wrong. She's heading off on a different course entirely.

As I stare, wondering what is going on, one of the two mercenaries pops out of the bridge and empties a clip in my direction. Bullets chew up the deck and railing around me, and more than a few chew on me too. I drop out of sight, gasping from the pain. It's been a long time since I've been hit this badly. Not since… when? Verdun? The fall of 1914? I gape at the sight of my blood. So many holes. I am going to lose blood.

Mother will be so displeased. Such a waste.

The mercenary drops down to the deck, coming to look for me. We get in a stand-off, both firing at the same time. He panics; I get lucky. The .40 S&W round is heavy, and firing it causes the gun to jerk more than the old 9mm round. He doesn't control his weapon, and his bullets stitch a line in the wall over my head. My bullets run right up his hip and belly. He drops, screaming, and curls into a fetal position on the deck. I drag my leaking body across the deck.

He is close to passing out when I reach him, and he finds a reserve of strength when I latch on to his leg. He starts screaming again, and I shove my fist into his mouth to shut him up.

One more. I'll take care of him in a minute. As soon as I drain what blood is left in this one.

The last guy bolts from the other side of the bridge, and I waste a few seconds wondering where he's going to go. The harpoon boat isn't that big. He can't hide forever. Then I hear the sound of a motor running, and a gurgling noise. Like a hose filling.

I dart forward, racing toward the nose of the boat where I discover why there hadn't been anyone manning the harpoon guns. They've been replaced with something more akin to a mounted fire hose, except this hose is attached to a series of tanks lashed along the front rail of the boat. The last mercenary has turned the hose around, and as I come limping into his field of vision, he lets loose with a spray of a pale yellow liquid.

I back-pedal, slipping on the wet deck, and the chemical spray douses my legs. As it soaks through the fabric of my pants, the burning starts. My legs feel like they are being devoured by an infestation of fire ants. I'm firing my gun indiscriminately—trying to hit him, trying to get him to stop—anything to make the pain go away. Several of my rounds perforate the hose leading to the nozzle, and the pressure drops. The deck is awash with the chemical. My boots are splashing in it.

He's firing his gun at me now. Bullets are shredding the deck all around me. I'm hit again, in the upper arms and chest. My rifle clicks, the hammer falling on an empty chamber. I throw the weapon aside, and dig out one of the pistols. I snap off a trio of shots as he ducks around the fire hose assembly, and I hear him fall and splash on the deck.

My legs are shaking badly. Standing is hard. Doing so without touching the deck is even harder. But I manage. I creep forward, peering around the edge of the bridge housing.

The mercenary is lying on his back. The main hose is still spewing yellow chemicals on the deck. I raise my gun, squinting through the sights.

The mercenary's hands fall away from his chest, and the hand I can see opens, releasing a round object.

Grenade.

I get two steps away when the incendiary goes off, rocking the boat. A flume of water cascades over me. It's tainted by the chemicals, and while it is diluted, it still burns. My hair feels like it is on fire. The boat lurches to the right, starting to list, and the only good news inherent in this change is that the deck is now titled away from me. I'm climbing as I stagger toward the stern of the boat, which means I'm getting away from the chemical agent. It's going in the water, though, and unless I can get off this boat before it sinks, I'm going to end up in a toxic slick that is going to corrode my flesh.

The wind is picking up too. It's as if the storm that has been gathering strength to the south has finally decided to move. In another hour or so, the sea is going to be very unstable.

I reach the stern and look for my Zodiac. I hadn't attached it to the harpoon boat, thinking that, after I had taken over the *Cherry Blossom*, I would have simply piloted it back to the *Cetacean Liberty*. Or they would have come and gotten me.

A bad plan, that one. Easy to see now in hindsight. Also easy to get side-tracked in kicking myself for not thinking the plan through. Chalk it up to sea-spawned dread.

The *Cherry Blossom* has to have its own life boats. Its own inflatable rafts.

The boat is listing more now, tilting a few degrees to starboard.

I don't have much time.

In a locker beneath the rail along the stern, I find the large yellow shape of an inflatable raft. And long plastic oars.

On the open sea. With a storm coming.

It's an easy choice, really. Given how much my legs are shaking. How much my body is quivering with adrenaline and fear.

I have to get off this boat.

I yank the cord that starts inflating the raft, and shove the expanding lifeboat over the railing. I throw two sets of oars down into it as soon as it starts to take on an oblong shape. I shouldn't delay, but I take a few minutes and find the galley of the ship, retrieving as many bottles of drinkable water that I can carry. When I return to the deck, the raft has finished inflating, but it has floated a good twenty meters away.

I'm going to have to swim.

I find a mesh bag for the water bottles and tie the end around my belt. As I clamber up to the rail of the *Cherry Blossom*, I catch sight of my Zodiac. It's a faint black dot against the sea. Too far away for me to reach it now, but not so far that I don't spend a second lamenting that it isn't closer.

The *Cherry Blossom* lurches beneath me, and I spill off the railing and hit the water headfirst. My legs start burning all over again as sea water gets in my burns.

When I surface, I've forgotten all about the Zodiac. All I can think about is getting to my raft. Getting out of the ocean.

The storm is coming. The sea is beginning to churn.

I'm a long way from land.

SEVEN

don't even know how long I cling to the raft. The storm tries to have its way with me, but it is a mild spring bluster compared to the tempests I have survived. It tries to drown me with rain, but I welcome the fresh water. It blows me about the ocean for a day or so, and then relinquishes its hold, casting me adrift. I float for a long time, lost in a delirium of pain, until I realize the raft is caught on something.

I peer over the edge of the raft and spot tiny waves disturbing the water. I've floated into a coral reef, one that nearly breaches the surface. My body is dehydrated and wracked with painful tremors when I try to move, but I have to turn my head. I need to look around. Coral reefs are typically found in shallow water. I have to be close to land.

I am, but it's not as much land as I would like.

On my left is an atoll, a wedge of red stone rising out of the water like a crooked thumb. The end that would be the nail is encrusted with rock and it rises to a flat point that has been claimed by sea birds. A dry sob rattles its way out of my chest when I spot loose collections of long strands coyly peeking over the knuckle of the thumb. *Trees.*

You could almost call it paradise.

The coral tears a hole in the raft as I use the oars to swing the inflatable boat toward the shore. I paddle as quickly as I can in my debilitated state, but the raft takes on too much water to be viable as a seaworthy vessel a hundred meters or so from shore. I'm forced to swim again, and the pain starts in my legs again when I submerge myself in the ocean. I have an incentive to swim fast, and my feet soon touch the bottom of the narrow beach on the atoll. I drag myself into the dismal shade of the knuckle-like ridge. The ground is hard, more like petrified coral than stone, and there is very little loose dirt. Not enough to cover me. Still, there is shade. Enough to suggest that the thumb of the island points north. I am on the eastern side, and as I lie on the cool stone, the shadows get longer.

It's been a busy day, I think. *I'll start again tomorrow.*

I sleep, for the first time in many days. It does seem like I've found paradise.

▼▼

I'm woken by the sound of boots on wood and the buzz of voices. As I struggle out of a dreamless valley of sleep, I struggle to remember where I am. Am I still on the *Cetacean Liberty*? I twitch, moving my legs, and the twinges of pain bring everything back. My eyes are glued shut by both tears and dried salt spray.

I'm not alone on this rock. Moving sluggish—every muscle in my body aches—I slither up the slope of the knuckle until I can peek over the other side of the hill. Unlike the eastern side, the west is home to a slender collection of lancewood—tall trees with naked trunks and clusters of leaves shaped not unlike Grecian *kopides*. Beyond the tufted lancewoods is a white beach, pristine and clean. At the southern end of the island, at the base of the thumb, there is a gentle groove in the rocky atoll. At the top of the arc of the groove is a partially concealed shelter, and along the rim of the natural lagoon are a series of wooden poles sunk into the water. It's a cheap harbor, probably indiscernible from a kilometer out. You almost have to be on top of the atoll before you would notice the man-made modifications.

The harbor is easy for me to pick out now because there is a boat anchored there. It might have been a commercial fishing boat once, but that time is well past. A frenzy of antennae and satellite dishes festoon the roof of the narrow bridge like a cluster of mushrooms. The seamen I see are dark-skinned, and they're wearing an assortment of clothing. Nothing that looks like a uniform. Unless you considered the distinctive shape of the AK-47 each carries as an adequate stand-in for a squad patch.

It's hard to tell what they are doing from my vantage point, though it looks like they are offloading cargo and reconfiguring it. Repackaging and dividing. It's oddly familiar all of a sudden as I recall doing not-dissimilar work while transporting contraband for the French Resistance. You get the goods from the supplier, repackage them to meet the requirements of your buyer, and then make the delivery. Neither end knows how much you skimmed off during the transaction. Everyone goes home happy.

The captain of the ship, an angular man in a black pea coat and woolen hat, ambles up the beach. Taking a nature hike while his crew does their work. I crawl over the top of the hill and start sliding down the other side. This gentleman and I have a matter to discuss.

He spots me coming. I am a black shadow tumbling down the red rock hillside, a bird of bad omen coming to roost. He tugs a large revolver out of his waistband as I reach the base of the hill, and he waits out in the middle of the beach for me as I weave through the copse of lancewoods. I've been exposed to a lot of sun the last few days and my skin is red and peeling. I'm worn out, like a husk of dried fruit, and my mood is as foul as my skin.

I'm going to try to be nice, though. Just in case politeness will make a difference.

The captain's got a bulge in his cheek, and as I cross the pale beach, tiny shards of bleached coral, his jaw moves and he spits a squirt of black goo onto the beach.

I come to an abrupt halt, staring at the dark stain on the coral.

"Um, hey," he says, thumbing back the hammer on his revolver.

I raise my head and stare at him.

"Oh, shit," he says, his hand trembling. The barrel of the revolver wiggles off-target.

I really should be polite, but I'm thirsty.

He manages to pull the trigger once, the report of the firearm breaking the calm respite of the island. On the rocky nail, birds startle, flooding into the sky.

His blood is foul, tainted by years of chewing tobacco. I drink it anyway, because I don't want to stain the beach.

VV

The sailors are Maori, their dark skins covered with tribal tattoos, and they don't appear overly agitated. Apparently this isn't the first time their captain has fired his hand cannon on the island. I can only imagine what sort of target shooting he's been doing with the birds, which only makes me happier that I killed him. The sailors have finished whatever unloading and loading they needed to do, and a couple of them are still wandering around the beach as I walk up.

"Nice boat," I say. I'm wearing the captain's coat and hat, the handgun shoved in the front of my pants in much the same lackadaisical fashion as he carried it. I don't expect my disguise to fool the sailors; more that I hope to suggest a starting point for our conversation. Ship needs a captain. Captain needs a crew. Everything else is negotiable. To a point. I could probably manage the boat myself, but I'd prefer not to.

"It's a bucket of rust," one of the sailors replies. The others begin to wander back toward the boat, trying to look nonchalant, but I can tell from the tension in their shoulders that they are trying hard not to run.

I keep my gaze on the spokesperson. I'm not terribly concerned about the others. Yet. "What's your name, sailor?" I ask.

"Winston," he replies. "Where did you come from?"

I indicate the landscape behind me. "From the other side of that hill there."

He offers a polite laugh. "Where are you going?" he asks.

"That depends on a small matter, doesn't it?"

"Aye," he nods. "It does."

"You going to miss your late captain?"

"Captain Henry was an asshole," Winston says. "He never paid us shit."

"Well," I point out, "he was captain of a rusty old trawler. What did you expect?"

Winston laughs at that. He has a lot of strong-looking teeth. A good sign. Virility and self-confidence.

"I need a ride, Winston. You think that boat will remain seaworthy long enough to get back to Australia?"

He shakes his head lightly. "It is bad luck to give rides to stranded spirits. Especially *kiri mate*."

"I'd be happy to give you what is in my wallet, except..." I shrug, suggesting that the story of how I lost my wallet isn't that interesting. I don't know what a *kiri mate* is, but it isn't too hard to guess. "Well, here's the thing," I continue, taking the late captain's hat off and tossing it to Winston, "I need a ride more than I need a ship."

Winston catches the hat and turns it over in his hands for a moment. His gaze strays to the gun stuck in my belt. "Where?" he asks eventually.

"Somewhere near Adelaide."

He puts the hat on, adjusts it to his liking, and smiles at me again. "I might know how to get to somewhere near Kangaroo Island," he says.

It is my turn to laugh. It's a small island off the Australian coast, at the mouth of the Gulf of St. Vincent. The Aboriginals call it the island of the dead. "That'll work," I say.

"And?" he asks.

"And you can keep the boat, and as far as I am concerned, there is no cargo below deck.

"Nothing but empty boxes," he says, touching the brim of the cap.

Several of the crew are now standing on the deck of the boat, their AK-47s hanging loosely in their hands. Not in a threatening way. They're just letting me see them.

I doubt any of them could actually hit me at this range, but I don't need to make them try. "I hope the crew is as lazy as they look and not prone to sudden spurts of curiosity," I say.

"The previous captain's quarters are very small, and they smell bad," Winston says. "But the door locks."

"Finally," I sigh, "something on that rust bucket that works."

Winston smiles as he turns his head and shouts at the crew in Maori. The guns disappear and the crew starts to make preparations for departure.

"Welcome aboard the *Black Starling*," Winston says, indicating the boat. "We'll be departing shortly."

BOOK TWO

APORIA

EIGHT

Kangaroo Island was the site of one of the first European settlements in Southern Australia; it's still an island and the lure of millions of hectares of unclaimed land just a short boat ride away won out. Now, the island is split between national parks and wineries, which keeps the population density down and the natural vegetation up.

The *Black Starling* comes within sight of Kangaroo Island during the endless dusk, and for a parting gift, Captain Winston gives me a rubber raft and a pair of plastic oars. I don't complain as the weather is pleasant and the mild current pushes me toward shore. I float/row for about an hour, and in that time, the *Black Starling* slips around the curve of the island. I doubt I'll see Captain Winston and his crew again, which, I'm sure, suits them fine.

I never did find out what *kiri mate* means.

My destination is a thin stretch of rugged beach, more rocky spurs than smooth sand. I run the raft aground, and splash through the last few meters of tidewater. As soon as I feel firm ground beneath my feet, I start to run.

I used to be able to run from sunset to sunrise without stop, and now I barely get five kilometers before I'm winded. Another kilometer and my legs begin to cramp.

Fortunately, I'm deep in uncontrolled woodlands now, where the ground is soft underneath broad-limbed trees. Even though all I want to do is lie down and breathe all the rich oxygen the trees are exhaling, I drop to my knees and dig. The ground accepts me, but it doesn't want to hold me tight. It doesn't remember me like it should. Mother is too far away, and I've been gone too long.

I'm tainted.

V V

I rest for a few days, and when the itching in my legs becomes too distracting, I claw my way out of the ground. Low in the northern sky, a pale half-closed eye of a moon winks at me, and the forest is quiet but for the scattered calls of silvereyes and grey warblers. I lean against the trunk of a black cypress and listen to the birds singing to each other. My fingers trace the patterns of the tree's bark, reading its history. It stands tall and straight, and there is very little warp in its bark. The birds sing openly, without concern of who might be listening to them.

It would be so easy to sit here all night. And the night after that. And the one after that. But I can't, because I don't have that kind of time anymore. My body is decaying.

My bullet wounds—a good half-dozen of them scattered across my chest and two more on my upper right arm—are still there, sullen and weeping holes in my flesh. They're infected, slick with a sickly yellow pus. My legs are trembling beneath the tattered remnants of my pants, and the skin is a tangled map of knotted flesh—half-melted, half-healed. The chemicals are in my bloodstream too and until I can flush it out, my immune system is compromised. The airborne toxins of the twenty-first century are going to gang up on me, and it's a battle I'm already losing. I'm rotting, slowly and surely.

If I could get back to Arcadia, Mother could heal me, but I'd have to convince the Grove to let me return to her embrace. I have no idea what has happened to the others. Did any of them survive? I've had more than a few nights to reflect on what happened during the last hours of the mission, and I'm not sure who fucked who. I can't be sure that Talus and Nigel haven't poisoned the Grove against me.

Even then, Mother might still reject me, even after I make the journey back home.

I get wearily to my feet, dust off the worst of the dirt stains, and go looking for something to eat.

One problem at a time. Start small; work your way up. An old soldier's rule.

V V

The first house I break into doesn't have a landline. The second has an old rotary phone, and the resident is on an equally antique phone service plan. I can't even get an international operator. I settle for stealing a change of clothes from the master bedroom closet and a half-gallon jug of unfiltered organic apple juice that I find in a small refrigerator.

The next house I stumble across is a tiny cabin nestled in the vee-shaped clearing. The land to the north has been cleared and converted to a vineyard; on the east and west, the forest comes in close to the house. It's fairly isolated, and I know better, but it is too tempting. The apple juice has taken the edge off my hunger, but my skin still itches. I can almost feel the poisons swirling in my blood.

There's only one person in the house, an elderly caretaker, and he wakes up when I bite him, but it is easy to hold him still. Afterward, I close his eyes and pull the heavy covers up over his face.

I should burn the house down, but that is liable to draw unwanted attention more than cover my tracks. I'll just leave all the doors open when I leave. Maybe there are enough four-legged predators on the island that they'll find the dead body.

The phone works. I dial a memorized number and a computerized voice tells me the call is subject to international charges, and I quietly tell it to proceed. The line clicks, a surprisingly analog sound for a digital connection, and then I hear the ghostly echo of a harpsichord—just a few notes. One of Callis's original compositions. Just enough to let me know that I'm being recorded. I speak quickly, outlining my situation, and I end my request with the ritual words used by Arcadians. When I am done, I hear a series of clicks and then the line goes dead. No confirmation necessary; I know my message will be heard.

I hang up the phone and raid the refrigerator.

Ten minutes later, as I'm polishing off my third piece of honey-slathered sourdough toast, the phone rings. As it is the middle of the night and since I'm expecting the call, I answer the phone.

"Hello?" I say around the last bite of toast.

"Hello, Silas."

I swallow, clearing my mouth. "Hello, Callis."

"It's been a long time since you've needed rescuing," he says.

"It was the other way around last time," I remind him.

"Was it?" he muses. "I don't remember."

He says it offhandedly, but the fact that it might actually be true strikes a sour note in our conversation, and neither of us say anything for a moment.

"We haven't heard from your team," he says after clearing his throat. "There's been a lot of attention."

"I'm out of touch," I say. "I fell overboard..." I realize I don't even know the date. "What happened?" I ask instead, figuring I'll get the news straight from him.

"Where are you?" he asks, and I know he's asking about the security of our conversation.

"I'm in a two-room house in the middle of Kangaroo Island," I point out with a laugh. "I'm the only one for a couple of kilometers in any direction. It's pretty fucking secure."

"Nothing is secure," he says. "Your mission was compromised. Maybe from the beginning. Maybe from this end. I do not know how deep the infection goes.

"What infection? I thought this was an isolated mission."

"As did I, but there is something amiss, something that goes back into our roots. Why was the reporter there?"

My hand tightens on the phone. "Which reporter?" I ask.

"Vanderhaven. She was on the boat..."

It's almost a question from him, but not quite, and I hesitate on the cusp of replying.

Callis and I have known each other for a long time. We've schemed our way into and out of a number of tight situations over the centuries. Typically, he plays the scoundrel role—the charming and devious one—while I play the silent and invisible heavy, and I've seen him extract information with an insouciant ease simply by leaving a sentence hanging, neglecting a final piece of punctuation that his listeners instinctively leap to supply. In doing so, they also tumble along a path he has arranged for them to take.

"Vanderhaven," I reply. "The one who did the Beering story?"

"That was your job."

"It was."

"The Grove has been expressing some concern."

"Now? That was two years ago. I've been in Mother's care since then. Up until about a month before we went to Adelaide and got on the boat."

"Why was she on the boat, Silas?"

I glance around. The phone is on the wall outside the kitchen, and I'm standing at the mouth of a narrow hall that runs from the living room of the small cabin to the other rooms. There's a single entrance to this cabin, and I can see it from where I'm standing, but there are also windows in the rooms. The doors to the rooms are shut. If there's a good place to be standing in this cabin, I'm in it.

I am in an isolated location, and I am the only one in the house, but his questions have set off a survival check in my brain. I'm doing a tactical assessment of my location. Figuring out my exit strategy. Wondering about my security.

"I didn't say she was," I reply carefully.

"There's a poison at work here," he says. "I fear it may touch members of the Grove. I don't know who you can trust."

"Suggestions?"

"Stay away from Arcadia. Be rootless."

Rootless. My breath catches in my throat. It's a hard word to hear. On my own, unable to return to Arcadia and to Mother's embrace. I have only the foul soil of the world to sustain me.

"Why?" I croak.

"The Grove is protecting its interests," he says. "They started as soon as the story broke. It's been three weeks, Silas. We haven't heard from any of the team. We had to assume you were all lost, or compromised. The Grove doesn't want to lose the mission data, but they have to protect Arcadia."

"Of course," I say. I know the drill. We all do—the priority is always family. Arcadia must be protected. Nothing else matters. That is the price we pay. Rooted, we live forever. The rootless—those who can't return to Arcadia and Mother's embrace—they simply... die.

"Your assets have been reclaimed," he says, a touch embarrassed, and I suspect the task of seizing my assets fell to him. Arcadia has managed to survive as long as it has by maintaining deep relationships with long-standing banking houses. It makes it easier for us to survive the ebb and flow of global finance, but it also means we are centrally managed. That much easier to excise the rootless from their allowances.

"Spend it on some tree farms, would you?" I ask.

"Gladly," he laughs. "Silas," he says, his voice becoming serious. "I'm not telling you to give up. Don't crawl off into the woods and let the humus have you. Stay hidden. Do you understand? It'll be the only way you can find out what is going on."

"What is going on?" I ask.

He ignores my question. "Do you remember Victoria's Diamond Jubilee?" he asks.

"Vaguely," I reply. We had been in London for the celebration, and he had dragged me into some scam involving gold from Witwatersrand. He had claimed it was an opportunity investment for Arcadia, but I hadn't entirely bought that line of bullshit. I had been right too; the other party had tried to cheat us, and a rather straight-forward enterprise had become complicated. And bloody.

"There was a party we attended. A masked ball."

"There was?" I have the same memory problems as Callis—all Arcadians did—and the older memories suffered the most. But Queen Victoria's Diamond Jubilee had only been a little over a hundred years ago.

"I met a woman there, a banker's daughter. She introduced me to her father. I made a small investment with him before we left London."

"Ah," I say, suddenly understanding why he was telling me this. "And this investment has been quietly maturing ever since, hasn't it?"

"The bank has a branch in Adelaide," he says. He tells me the name of the bank. "They'll be expecting you."

"And then what?" I ask.

"Find out what happened," he says. "Find the reporter."

Mere.

A strange emotion tugs at me. "And then what?" I repeat, at a loss of what else to say.

"Help me find the root of this poison before it infects all of Arcadia," he says.

What other choice do I have, really? The rootless die after a while. They can't find soil that will nourish them, and the other method of staying alive is bloody.

It never ends well.

He gives me a different number to reach him at—a private line I can call directly. After I hang up, I scour the house, looking for a source of useful news. Fortunately, the caretaker is one of those who prefers to thumb through a paper over breakfast rather than scan a newsfeed on a computer. I find a stack of newspapers in a recycling bin in the spare bedroom, but there's only a week's worth. If there was a story to be found in the Southern Ocean, the world has moved on already.

Australian elections are coming up and the front-runner has just been caught in the sort of scandal that would derail a US candidate, but as Down Under isn't as tightly wound as North America, the media has to work pretty hard to make the story seem worthy of the attention they're giving it. Piracy is up along the Somalian coast. People are still killing each other in Central Africa. Countries in the Middle East are changing governments. Again. Though it has been a long time since much dramatic change swept across Outremer. It used to take centuries for these lands to change hands, and now it is a matter of decades. A pipeline rupture near the Black Sea has caught the media's fancy as well as a story about infidelity between a Hollywood power couple. Based on the amount of column inches devoted to each story, it's hard to gauge which is the worse disaster, though I suspect the Hollywood couple's agents are milking the story a bit as neither has had a decent hit in the last five years.

The ecological and environmental impact of the pipeline rupture makes me want to run back to the woods and hide underground, but that's been the reaction for decades now and what has it gotten us? Arcadia weeps as the world dies a little bit more, and we're all incrementally closer to death. All of us.

Some more quickly than others.

There are scabs on the knuckles of my right hand and, compulsively, I pick one off. There is no blood, but the flesh underneath is pale.

"Careful," I whisper to myself, "you could scar."

Wouldn't that be a novelty?

I could bury myself beneath the roots of any of the cypress out there and wait for the world to change again. Would I wake up or would the chemical poison in my blood kill me while I slept? Would my decaying corpse end up poisoning the tree that was wrapped around me?

That's what Callis had warned me about. Poison, getting at the roots. Killing Mother, the Grove, Arcadia—everything.

Crawling into the ground and waiting for the end wasn't a soldier's death, anyway. I have fought on Mother's behalf for a very long time. My head is filled with half-remembered dreams of a thousand wars. I've been a good soldier. I deserve something more.

Who backed Kyodo Kujira? What does Prime Earth know? What happened to the *Cetacean Liberty*?

Mere will know how to find the answers.

NINE

Everything but the forward prow of the *Cetacean Liberty* is wrapped up tight in white plastic wrap, and it lolls in the water like a burn victim soaking in a saline bath. A harbor patrol car is parked on the dock nearby, and only one of its two occupants is awake. The other has his seat levered halfway back, his cap pulled down low on his face to block out the half-dozen mercury vapor lights permanently trained on the shrink-wrapped boat. The light reflects harshly off the white wrap, and there isn't a shadow anywhere within thirty yards of the *Cetacean Liberty*.

Either Prime Earth or the South Australian government has turned the boat into a floating art installation—a minimalist *tabula rasa* that waits for meaning to be imprinted upon its slick nakedness. What do we see when we look upon this abstract symbol? This bleached blot, waiting for its Rorschach stain.

I don't loiter, but I do make a second pass, walking in the opposite direction. The guy in the car doesn't even look up from his phone. The other one continues to sleep.

Reefie's is a noisy pub three blocks away, and after I enter and gauge my choices, I head for the bar and find an open spot next to a guy drinking alone. A half-dozen plasma screen TVs are competing for the patrons' attention with three different football games (two of the three are broadcasting Australian games), a pair of soccer games, and a US basketball game. Lakers versus someone else—no one seems to care, including the network that is broadcasting the game.

The bartender, a well-groomed man with precision-razored stubble, flips a coaster on the bar in front of me and I order a beer. "A lager.

Whatever you've got on tap that isn't the tourist beer." He squints at me for a second, trying to gauge if I'm trying to be a smart-ass, and when I put a bill on the bar, he stops wondering.

"Not a fan of the local?" The man sitting next to me stinks of fish, and his blond hair has been permanently stiffened by sea and sky.

"It's like that American coffee company," I reply. "You can get it anywhere, but that doesn't make it good."

He chuckles and raises his pint glass in my direction. I clink my glass off his, notice how empty his is compared to mine, and catch the bartender's eye. "Thanks, mate," he says when another full pint is deposited in front of him. "So, journalist or investigator?" he asks.

"Excuse me?"

"If you're looking to chat me up, you're bad at picking out men who might be your type."

"Was I trying to pick you up?" I ask.

My answer confuses him for a second, though it isn't hard to confuse him in his state. "I ain't got much else to offer," he says, "and I don't believe in random charity."

"And the world is a poorer place for it," I say.

"Which are you?" He squints at me. "Angling for a payout or writing a story?"

"Journalist," I say, figuring that's the answer he's looking for.

He nods and sticks out a hand. "I'm Ted."

"Silas." His hand is calloused, rough from the nets and a fishing knife. "You want to tell me something about that boat out there?"

He grins. We both know which boat I'm referring to. "Aye," he says, "I can tell you a story or two." He takes a long pull from his glass, moistening his tongue and making me wait a few seconds. Ted is a garrulous local, pre-greased by the media, and a bit of a drunk; he knows the routine and is happy to play along. I'm a good listener, and I have a pocket full of money taken from the caretaker's wallet.

We're going to be good friends.

V V

Ted takes me back about two and a half weeks when stories began circulating among the fishing boats out of Adelaide that something had happened out on the water. A few days later the *Cetacean Liberty* was found, adrift, in the Great Australian Bight. She had suffered a fire, and all of her life boats were gone. The Royal Australian Navy flooded the Bight with ships and found a few drifting life boats. What survivors were in them were suffering from burns in addition to exposure and dehydration.

Ted doesn't know how many survived, but it doesn't sound like many.

The *Cetacean Liberty* was towed back to Adelaide and wrapped up tight. Prime Earth's management—back in San Diego and quick to point out that they are miles and miles from any sort of altercation in the Southern Ocean—stuffed their fingers in their ears and pretended nothing had happened other than an unfortunate galley fire.

Ted tries to milk me for a few drinks, but once I establish that he knows nothing about the whaling fleet, it's clear he isn't quite the fount of knowledge that he thinks he is, which makes sense, given the lack of ongoing speculation I hadn't seen in the local papers. The media did their routine of scrounging for scraps, looking for some morsel that they can worry long enough to show an upward trend in their readership metrics at their next quarterly shareholder meeting. But without some immediate scandal to keep their audiences' attention, their corporate overlords will simply can the stories. The story is lacking a champion, someone like Meredith Vanderhaven, to keep it alive. It dies with a whimper, a final update buried on the back page of the local news section, and the conspiracy community wanders off, looking for something with a bit more meat on it.

No one cares.

Much like this crowd's attitude toward the Lakers' game.

The world is a big place. It's easy to get lost.

▼▼

I go to ground at a cheap hotel, spending half of what remains from the money I took from the caretaker's wallet. I had gotten to Adelaide too late to visit Callis's bank, and after spending most of a day and part of the previous night in wait mode, I had gone down to the docks. I had to do something; the night was too precious a time to waste.

Wasting time. It's an odd thing to worry about. To be concerned that I might not have enough.

I get a room on the north-facing side of the hotel, put out the *Do Not Disturb* sign, and hang the comforter over the curtain rod for the windows. I am restless, but I force myself to lie down. Hurry up and wait: all soldiers know how to do it. Sleep when you can. Eat when you can. Keep your weapons ready. The violence will come later.

After a thirst-inducing nightmare of knocking over a blood bank, I get up, shower, and try to find some enthusiasm for going out. Adelaide's smog index isn't as high as many cities in the United States, but it is high enough that I can't be in the sun too long—my skin will have even worse reactions than it did during my idle days on the life boat. I find a coffee shop with computer rentals in the back, where I can spend a few hours. On the Internet and as far away as possible from the sun-warmed air that lies over Adelaide like a heavy blanket.

After a cursory search for mention of my fellow Arcadians, I scan the original stories written about the *Cetacean Liberty* accident. There is mention of another boat, but no names are given, and certainly no mention of the harpoon boat I wrecked or the one that Nigel attacked.

A search on Kyodo Kujira turns up a number of recent stories. The company's senior management is all dead, lost in a freak fire that ripped through a private facility outside of Ehime, where they were all gathered for a corporate retreat. The timing is awfully coincidental too: three days after Nigel and I went after the harpoon boats. Other than stating the barest of facts, Japanese investigators aren't speculating about the cause of the blaze. *A need for further investigation*, they say. *The blaze was too hot*, they explain in a press conference, *we can't be sure what really happened.*

I go back to the local news, noting the names of the writers who covered the incident for the major news outlets in Adelaide. I even find the name of the hospital where the survivors were airlifted. I find it curious there are no eyewitness reports of what happened. Eventually, I find a single, illuminating sentence tucked on the back page of one of the last stories written. All attempts to interview the survivors were referred to Prime Earth's lawyers—a firm with a long, comma-filled name. It isn't hard to guess the firm's basic response to anyone asking.

Captain Morse's name does come up, and it's only because it is common knowledge that he was the captain of the ship. I learn his first name is Thaddeus. There is no crew or passenger roster, and we're as much guilty of that lack of data as anyone else on the boat. Our own need for anonymity working against me.

I do a web search for Meredith Vanderhaven and find nothing but her byline on articles that are four months old. No hits on what she might have been doing in Australia. No hits on what story she is working on.

Which isn't surprising either. After Beering, she knew to keep her stories under wraps until they were ready for publication. Less time for her targets to prepare. Less time for people to shred documents, disappear sources, and hide the dump sites.

ⱽ ⱽ

When the sun starts to get lost behind the taller buildings, I get a cab and go visit Callis's bank. It's more centrally located than I want to be in the city, but there's enough of a brisk wind that everyone on the street is more interested in getting to their destinations than eyeballing a haggard tourist like myself. The cab drops me off in front of a worn four-story building that is the lone holdout for modernization on the corner of King Williams Street and Waymouth Street. I keep my back turned to the high-rise going up across the wide boulevard of King Williams; the windows are in, and they're reflecting the sunlight directly across the street.

The bank's windows, on the other hand, are heavily tinted and the climate is tightly controlled at a reasonable temperature. The décor goes for ostentatious in its effort at replicating someone's vision of an aristocratic drawing room from a century ago. The ubiquitous security guard near the entrance straightens slightly when I enter. He's wearing a dark blue wool suit and an expensive silk tie.

It's that sort of bank.

I ignore the security guard who is eyeing me because I'm dressed down for bank's normal clientele, and I adopt the sort of laconic swagger that suggests more money than fashion sense as I head for the client services desks in the back. The ones with the comfortable leather chairs next to them. I throw myself down into one of the chairs, kick my legs out, and stare at the finely attired young man behind the desk.

The nameplate on the desk reads *Rupert Gillam*, and his sandy brown hair is cut very precisely across the back of his head, a scant millimeter above the finely tailored line of his collar. His suit is perfectly muted for a conservative banker, and his tie is a shade of purple somewhere between aubergine and plum.

"How may I help you?" he asks, setting aside whatever he had been pretending to be working on as I had approached.

"I need some money," I say with just enough bluntness that he hesitates for a second, his eyes flicking across my attire and general scruffy condition. I smile, and it is my pristine dentition that convinces him that I'm not some homeless person who has come in to rob the bank.

"Certainly, Mister…"

I tell him the family name Callis and I had been using during our jaunt through late-nineteenth-century London. "Call me Silas though," I say.

He pulls out a keyboard tray and clacks on the keys. "Do you know your account number?" he asks.

I stare at him and he fidgets for a moment, his eyes flickering back and forth from me to his computer screen. "Oh," he says as he spots something on his monitor. "Oh," he says again as he starts to read. "Yes," he continues, licking his lips nervously, and I imagine he's gotten to the part where the account history goes back a hundred plus years. "Certainly, sir," he finishes. "There's… ah… there's a password."

"Of course there is," I say, briefly wondering what it could be. Genevieve," I settle on. Callis hadn't warned me, which meant it had to be something obvious to both of us. The name of the banker's daughter who Callis had a thing for, for instance.

Rupert nods. "Well," he says, placing his hands on his desk. He smiles. His dental work isn't as good as mine, though it looks to have cost his family a great deal. "What can I do for you today?"

Finally, some good news. "I'll need some cash. About this much." I hold two fingers several centimeters apart. "And a debit card of some kind. Something I can use to get more. Oh, and the name of the place where you get your suits."

TEN

Where Rupert gets his suits turns out to be a place a few blocks away. The stack of cash is easy enough—that only requires a looping scrawl that passes for a signature—but the card will take an hour or two and so I spend it being fitted for a suit I'll never pick up. I buy other clothes too, an outfit that makes me indistinguishable from any other fashion-aware man in Adelaide. Afterward, I stop at a juice shop on the way back to the bank. A mega dose of chia and wheatgrass powder. Processing kills a lot of the green but in large enough quantities, it'll help keep the thirst at bay.

I'm heading to the hospital next, and I can't afford to lose control there. Regardless of what it smells like, most of the blood in the building is going to be compromised. My immune system is already under enough stress.

The Royal Adelaide Hospital is located in North Adelaide, on the south side of the River Torrens, and I cross the gently flowing water on a pedestrian foot bridge near the zoo. I'm tempted by the plethora of aromas wafting out of the Botanical Gardens and I promise myself that I'll scale the fence and admire the sleeping flowers later. The hospital is a brightly lit contrast to the dark embrace of the Botanical Gardens, and I find my way into P wing where the burn wards are located.

The scent of the chemicals makes my skin crawl. Western medicine relies on its science too much. If it comes out of a laboratory and cost more than a billion dollars to create, then it must do something. And these products do, but it's not what these patients need. They need to know their skin will heal, that they'll be able to wear clothing without having to worry about how the synthetic fabric is going to irritate their flesh. They need to know their families won't look away when they enter the room; that someone will look past their melted skin and see the person inside. The creams and salves with the trademark names won't do any of those things. The pharmaceuticals will only make the pain go away. For a little while. But it's okay; there's a solution for the pain that persists after the creams have done their work. It has a trademarked name too, and the insurance companies will cover most of it. Maybe in a few years, the patient can talk about weaning themselves off the drugs. Maybe.

There's a handful of people in the lobby, draped across the uncomfortable furniture. They don't know how to keep a vigil for their loved ones, and the fluorescent lights have sucked all the hope out of their jaundiced faces. The staff move efficiently—some of them make eye contact, but most don't. The only reason they look up is to check the hands on the large clock over the nurses' station.

Patient rooms are on the first two floors, and no one shows any interest in me on the ground floor. As soon as the elevator doors open on the second, I lean forward and press the button for four, trying to appear annoyed that the elevator has decided to slow my ascent down.

There are two men in the waiting area, right in front of the elevator. They look like they bought their suits off the same rack, and they both glance up as the elevator doors open. They're good, but they stare a little too long.

I get off on four, and discover there is no place for me to go but back down. There is no waiting area; instead, there's a nursing station right in front of the door, and the single nurse sitting at it has already spotted me. "Can I help you?" she asks.

"Hi," I say, spontaneously deciding to be the sort of guy who asks for directions. "I'm trying to find a client of mine," I say. "His name is Morse. I'm with—" I rattle off the long name of Prime Earth's legal team, adding an extra partner for good measure. "They told me he's on the third floor. 'Get off the elevator and turn right. You can't miss them.' That's what they said."

"This is the fourth floor," she says.

"It is?" I glance around, as if I don't quite understand how I managed to arrive where I'm at. "So confusing—kind of like casinos in the US. They want you to come in, but they don't want you to leave."

The nurse's nametag reads Kelly, and her long brown hair has been clipped back into a loose bun. It hasn't started to escape her efforts at restraining it, which suggests she hasn't been on shift too long. "There are no patient rooms up here," she says.

I try for charming, recollecting that Callis had always been the ladies' man between the two of us. I've done my fair share of playing the rake over the centuries, but I've fallen out of practice since World War II. "I was just down on the ground floor," I say, leaning on the counter, "and my client—Morse—wasn't there."

"He wouldn't be on the third either," she says. "He's probably on the second floor." She slides her chair over in front of the computer monitor. "Morse," she says, tapping the keys. "What was the first name?"

"Thaddeus," I reply reflexively, recalling the news article I read earlier.

Her eyebrows pull together slightly as she reads the results of her database search. "Who did you say you were with again?" she asks.

I repeat the law firm's name, reducing it to just the first two partners' names. Like someone who says it over and over again would. They probably even reduce it to a three-letter acronym, but that might be selling the lie a bit hard.

She looks at me again, and I can tell she's actually looking at me this time instead of the cursory boredom elicited from staff by the sight of the lost and aimless. "I'm sorry," she says. "You've been given some wrong information somewhere. There aren't any patients by that name in the ward."

"Well, goddamn it," I say. "Those sons of bitches!"

She pushes her chair back from the desk, startled by my invective. "Excuse me?"

"Listen," I say, leaning forward. "Can you do me a favor?" When she doesn't immediately flee, I take that as a *yes*. "Look, I'm not really with that firm. I'm an independent. I do personal injury. You know, fighting the insurance companies—those bastards who turn everything into a shit show of red tape, you know?" She nods slightly. "Here's the thing. I got a call from Sally Morse—Thaddeus's wife, back in San Diego, California. She told me her husband—Thaddeus, though everyone calls him *Capt'n* actually—was going to get screwed by these other guys. She asked me to come down and straighten things out for Thaddeus—for Captain Morse. I get here, and these two dickheads downstairs try to tell me that Captain Morse isn't here—that none of them are here—and I can't believe it. Where the hell did they go? And why the hell doesn't his wife know?"

She's trying to follow all of this, and I can tell from her expression that she's following the important part—that Morse isn't here anymore. "Which guys?" she asks.

"Downstairs," I reiterate. "Look, call down and see if they're still there. I just saw them not five minutes ago. They got off on the second floor as I was coming up."

Somewhat automatically, she reaches for the phone. I pretend to fume, but I'm keeping an eye on her fingers as they move across the keypad. She dials an extension and it's picked up almost immediately on the other end. "Hi," she says. "It's Kelly up on four. Listen, can you do me a favor?" Her eyes flick up at me and I smile. "Are there two guys just... I don't know..." Her back stiffens slightly. "In the waiting area?" she says. "Are they—?" She looks at me.

"Dickheads," I say. "One and two. You can't tell them apart."

A tiny smile catches the edge of her mouth, and she relaxes slightly. "Yeah," she says, listening. "Yeah, that sounds like them." She looks up at me again, the smile still there. "Secutores," she says, repeating what she has just been told.

It's been a long time since I've heard that word, but I smack the counter as if it is confirmation of what I had been telling her.

"Okay. Thanks, Shelli." She hangs up the phone. "I don't know what's going on, Mr...."

"Mickelli," I say, falling back on an alias I haven't used in decades. "David Mickelli." From Florence, of course. The thing with creating aliases that stick over time is to make them easy to remember.

"Mr. Mickelli," she repeats. "I can't reveal anything about patient data, and I don't want to get involved in whatever is going on with the insurance companies and any law firm that might be representing patients. It's probably best if you just called—"

"No," I say, nodding. "I get it. I'll totally forget I was up here, okay?" I take a step back from the counter, far enough that I can't see her name tag any more. "What was your name? See? I've forgotten already." I keep backing up until I reach the elevator, and I reach over and push the button. "I'll call Sally. I guess I'll have to call those bastards at the firm too, even though they're just going to give me the runaround. And these guys—Hippocampus, Hoplomachus—"

"Secutores," she corrects me.

I wave a hand. "Secutores," I say. "They're just being dickheads, right? There's no reason for that." The elevator arrives, and I stomp into it theatrically. "I'm not going to cause a scene," I tell her. "I'm just going to talk to them. Tell them I don't appreciate them fucking with me like that. There's no reason at all for it." I press the button for the second floor.

"Good luck," she offers as the door starts to close. I smile and nod.

My smile disappears as soon as the doors close. I press the ground floor button too, and then position myself against the back of the elevator. It trundles down two floors and then opens. I stare at the pair in the lobby, assessing them.

They stare back, and none of us blink until the elevator doors close.

The *secutores* were Roman gladiators, back in the day. They fought in the

Grecian style—sword or spear and shield. I knew the techniques as readily as I knew how to breathe.

Those two aren't lawyers.

▼▼

One of the things I had Rupert at the bank procure for me was a pay-as-you-go phone. It's as cheap and disposable as they get, but it has a working phone number. I leave the hospital and find a judiciously situated internet café within line of sight of the P wing. I do a quick search for Secutores with a couple other key words and am not surprised at what I find. I do a bit of reading, which only serves to amuse me.

They have no idea who the *secutores* really were. Still, the name serves its purpose.

I open another tab and click through the website of *The Independent* until I find an email address for the journalist—Ralph Abernathy—who wrote the articles about the *Cetacean Liberty*. I have to sign up for a free webmail service and that takes longer than I'd like, but I finally get a screen where I can send an email. I title it "Secutores," and keep the note brief. "Why does the Royal Adelaide Hospital not have any patients from the *Cetacean Liberty*? And why are there men from Secutores Security hanging around the burn ward if there are no patients?"

I sign it with my new cell phone number, hit send, and wander over to the counter and order a cup of herb tea.

Fifteen minutes later my phone rings. "It's the wrong time of year to be fishing," says a male voice when I answer.

"Same could be said for whaling," I reply.

He's quiet for a minute. "There's no story here," he says.

"No? Then why did you call me?" I ask.

"I'm recording this call," he says. "I'll be sending a copy to my editor immediately after we're done."

"Okay," I say.

He's a little put off when I don't offer anything else, and after another long silence, he clears his throat. "So, ah, why did you send me that email?"

"Where are they?" I ask.

"Who?"

"The survivors."

"What survivors?"

I hang up the phone. This game is silly, and I don't really have time for it, but I don't have any other leads.

I have never been very good at investigative work; I have always had a different role in field work. It's always been that way, even before I became an Arcadian. I was the one who read the signs in the wind and the waves, who listened to bird song, and who saw the patterns in viscera. After lying with Mother, she showed me I no longer needed those skills; she wanted me for other reasons. I was happy to oblige her and my new family. I became tooth and claw—a sword for Arcadia. Being polite and knowing how to ask questions were not part of my requisite skill set.

Mere, though, is good at this sort of thing. During the time I had been watching her, I'd seen her play a version of this with a number of contacts. Her trick was always to play hard to get, to suggest she knew more than she did, and to get them to come to her.

As I wait for Ralph to get with the game, I recall the first time we had seen Mere on the *Cetacean Liberty*. The rest of the team had played her game so readily.

My phone rings again. "Give me something," he says.

"Kyodo Kujira," I reply. "Your turn."

"Not yet," Ralph says. "What's your connection?"

"One of Kyodo Kujira's vessels was a harpoon boat with a name that translates to *Cherry Blossom*."

"Was," he says, picking up on my verb tense.

"I know what happened to it."

He breathes heavily into the phone, and I hear the distant sound of his fingers hitting keys on a laptop. "Okay," he says after a minute. "Not on the phone, though."

"Of course not," I reply. I glance over at the café's counter and read him the name that runs across the top of the reader board behind the counter. "I look like any other hipster in here, but older. And I'm drinking tea."

"Very Colonial of you."

"Old habits," I reply. "I know what you look like. The paper very conveniently posts a picture next to your articles."

"It's… that picture was taken a few years ago."

"I'll extrapolate."

"I'll… uh, I'll be there in a half-hour."

That's a lot of tea to drink, I think as we end the call.

Patience. Time enough.

I kind of hope one of the Secutores guys shows up while I'm waiting. That would be more fun than sitting here.

ELEVEN

Ralph Abernathy takes closer to forty-five to find the café. He wasn't kidding when he said his press picture was several years old. The last few turns around the sun haven't been kind to him. He stands near the entrance of the café, fussing with his cell phone while trying to be surreptitious in his examination of the room. I'm the only one paying him any sort of attention, and after a few minutes of pretending to be coy, he shoves his phone into his pocket and marches up to the counter.

Mid-forties. Divorced or never married. Certainly single. Obsessive about all the wrong things. Good shoes, though. The man knows the importance of decent footwear. His coat is an old leather bombardier jacket, nicely distressed and worn in. It's a little snug across the back, and I doubt he can zip it up anymore, but it's clearly the one aspect of his old life—his wistfully remembered twenties—that he can't quite let go of.

He sits down heavily across from me—a complicated espresso drink in a wide ceramic cup, a half-eaten cookie in his hand. He needs a haircut more than he needs a shave; more than both, he looks like he could use a break from the relentless of his life.

I wonder if this is what I'll look like in a few months, or if it'll happen more quickly.

"Fishing," he says by way of greeting. "Shall I call you *Fisherman*?" He's given this some thought on the drive over.

"David is fine."

He takes a big bite of the cookie. "You don't look like a David," he says, trying to hide his disappointment that I'm not keen on his code name.

I don't have the heart to tell him about the statue in Florence that I modeled for once upon a time.

"You wrote the stories about the *Cetacean Liberty*," I say, getting to the point. "I read all the press. You were the one who kept asking questions."

He nods, sitting up in his chair—pleased that I know his work. "It never made sense, and then, yeah, I did some digging and found about the tragedy in Japan, with Kyodo Kujira." He shoved the rest of the cookie in his mouth and leaned forward. "I paid a translator for some port reports. Out of my own pocket. I knew Kyodo had put a fleet in the water. In June. They'd been out for nearly a month when the accident on the *Liberty* happened."

"A long time when you're not actually catching whales," I say.

"Exactly." His head bobs up and down again. "The reports are gone now. Kyodo's fleet is now listed as having been moved from Ishinomaki to Shimonoseki, which is bullshit. They've never had boats in Shimonoseki."

"New management," I suggest.

He chokes on a laugh, and covers it up by taking a drink from his beverage. "That's not funny," he protests when he has recovered. He glances around. "Do you know who these Secutores guys are?"

"They're independent contractors," I say, using the phrase that is *de rigueur* in this decade for *mercenaries*. "I suppose they can work in Japan as readily as they can here in Adelaide, yes?"

"Jesus," he swears, putting his hands on the table and stiffening his fingers to gesture at me to keep my voice down.

I lean forward. "Why do they have two guys sitting in the second floor waiting area of the P wing at the hospital?" I ask.

"They're still there?" When I nod, he shakes his head. "Why? There's no one there any more."

"Who isn't there?"

"The people from the *Liberty*."

"How many?"

"I don't know. I could never find out. That's where they went, though. I talked to a couple of the pilots who airlifted people out of the rafts. Some of them in pretty bad shape. Burns and exposure. Somewhere around twenty is my guess."

"And?"

"And nothing. Prime Earth's lawyers showed up." He tries to rattle off the firm's name but gets it wrong. He nods when I correct him. "Yeah, bunch of tight-assed corporate hacks from the US. Flown in. Didn't give a shit that they had no clue about Australian law. Buried the hospital in a ton of paperwork, and threatened litigation on everyone—down to the fucking interns who were emptying bedpans. A couple of days later, these other guys show up—Secutores—and everyone's asshole puckers even more."

"Why does Prime Earth send in independent security consultants if they've already gotten everyone running scared with lawyers?"

"Oh, these guys aren't with Prime Earth." He shakes his head. "No, no. Prime Earth takes off as soon as these guys arrive. They're still dumping paperwork on the hospital, but it's all hands-off now. Secutores is in charge."

"And then?"

"A week ago, I manage to get one of the nurses to talk to me. She won't tell me anything useful, but she tells me the ward has gotten really quiet. Like 'no one there' sort of quiet."

"They released them?"

"How? And where did they go?"

"They moved them, then."

"Again: How? And where?"

"I don't know, Ralph. That's why I'm asking you."

He fidgets in his chair, one of his legs bouncing up and down. Arguing with himself. "Ah, fuck," he whispers, shaking his head. "Look—" he starts.

I pick up my mug and take a swallow of tea. "I'm almost done with my tea," I say. "When I finish, I'm leaving." He needs a push.

"Okay, okay," he says. "There's this guy. I don't know what happened, but somehow he got lost in the shuffle when everyone was being brought in. He says he just got up and walked out of the ER. Came back the next day with some story about an accident in his garage." He shakes his head. "I don't know how he got away with it, but they didn't make the connection. Old dude. Veteran of some kind. Vietnam, I think."

I know who he's referring to, but I let him continue. Gus had been one of the engineers on the boat, a retired Navy enlisted man. As a young man, he had been a Riverine in Vietnam, running the engines on one of the converted monitors that harried the Viet Cong in the Mekong Delta. His boat had been overrun one night, and he and three other Navy men disappeared into the jungle for five years as POWs. A lot of the crew thought Gus was the craggiest bad-ass that had ever lived, and he certainly leaned into the part, but I knew from the tremor in his hands and the way he pressed himself against the bulkhead, eyes downcast, the few times I had passed him in the ship that his bad-ass days were far behind him.

"I was looking for anything, any sort of lead that I could use to convince my editor this story was worth following up. That there was more going on than some bullshit US company getting all squirrelly about getting sued. I got in and found this guy. Talked to him one night. He was going to be my source to blow the whole thing wide open…"

"They figure it out and disappear him too?"

Ralph shakes his head. "He died. In his sleep, I guess. His room was just empty one morning."

Death. It comes quickly to some. I suppress a shudder. "What was he going to tell you?" I ask. "He give you any hint?"

"You read my last story," Ralph snorts. "What do you think?"

I had, and knowing about Gus's death, I understood the underlying bitterness that ran through the story. No reporter likes losing a source, especially when the story they know is there suddenly slips away from them. However, I know how to reel him back in.

"I was there too," I tell him. "On the *Cetacean Liberty*."

"Bullshit," he says, but his disbelief doesn't reach his eyes.

"That man's name was Gus," I tell him, and I go on to describe the scars on Gus's hands and the tattoo he had on his right shoulder. Ralph eats it up, that hardened nugget of hope that he hadn't been able to let go of suddenly softening in his hands, threatening to become malleable again. Something that he could shape into that story he dreamed about.

"Holy shit," he whispers when I finish.

"Now," I say, putting my hands on the table. "let's talk about those two guys at the hospital right now. How many more of them are there? What's their routine?"

"Why? What are you going to do?"

"I'm going to ask them some questions."

"I… I don't think that's a very good idea," he blanches.

"Why, Ralph? Don't you want some answers? I know I do."

I can tell he is not a fan of the direct approach, and I concede there's some prudence there. He's not entirely sure why they are there at all if everyone has been moved somewhere else. I suspect it is because they're waiting for someone like me to show up. And I did, which means I have a short window of time before word gets back to wherever the Secutores command center is. The two guys I saw tonight didn't recognize me, but they had noticed me. Judging from the lack of any excitement around the hospital during the time I'd been in the café, I don't think they've called in their suspicions, which meant it will go in their nightly report. A line item to establish a baseline pattern. If they spot me again, Secutores will upgrade me to active threat status.

I have to either not be seen again or be long gone by the time they find out that I'm still around. I can't take them in the hospital itself, even the parking garage is going to be tricky, but taking them after they leave the hospital opens me up to an entirely different set of risks though. Pros and cons. Every mission has them. The deciding factor, as always, comes down to which "things have gone to shit" scenario is the most recoverable. When things go awry—and they will—where do I have the best chance of survival.

And Ralph too. Short of banging him over the head and dumping him in the trunk of his car, I'm not going to be able to get rid of him. That's the cost sometimes of hooking a source. They can be hard to get rid of.

Visiting hours are going to be over in an hour or so, and I doubt the Secutores men are going to remain in the waiting area after that. Their job is to keep watch for strays like me who might come wandering in; they're not protecting any assets at the hospital. Not anymore. They're just watchers. Once there's nothing to watch, they'll call it and head back to wherever they spend the night.

"Ralph, here's the deal," I lay it out for him. "You can wait for me, and either I'll come back in a while or there will be a sudden surge in police activity around the hospital, which will be your one and only clue that I'm not coming back."

"Maybe I should come with you..." he tries.

See? Hooked. Can't shake him off the line. I try to push him off a bit with a simple question. "Do you want to be a material witness?"

He sits there, looking like he is actually thinking about my question.

"Mull it over from your car," I tell him as I stand up.

"That... yes, that makes better sense," he says.

I leave Ralph and the café, and walk back to the hospital to scout the route the mercenaries will probably take. There's a new parking structure and it's got a floor plan for maximizing parking, which leaves little in the way of places to hide and blind spots, but there are enough.

The pair exit P wing shortly after nine o'clock, heading for the parking garage. They're walking assuredly. Not excited. Not bored. They've got something on their minds, and they're looking forward to reporting in. In the last few hours, they've decided I'm worth making some noise about to their superiors.

All the more reason to act now.

I slip around the exterior of the garage and enter by one of the pedestrian access points near the back. There's a man sitting in a silver Mercedes along the back wall of the ground floor, his car pointing the opposite direction of every other vehicle. He's reading a newspaper, his window cracked slightly, and he glances up as I walk by. There's something about him that seems familiar, but I can't place it, and the setup looks like a bored town car driver waiting for his ride to finish whatever they're doing in the hospital. The guy doesn't seem interested in me, and I push him out of my mind as I stroll toward the low railing that separates the floors of the garage.

General parking starts the floor above. I check to make sure no one is watching and leap up through the narrow gap between the floors. Cars are packed along every up and down ramp—these half-floors are separated by a combination of steel wire and heavy concrete blocks. There's just enough room between them for a body to slip through. It's the sort of architectural layout that parkour aficionados love.

The mercenaries take the elevator, and I move up quickly enough to stay ahead of their ride. When the elevator opens on the third floor, I'm already there, crouched behind a hulking SUV.

The two cross to a dark sedan parked close to the half-wall, and in that moment of time when all four doors are unlocked and they're getting in, I dash over and slip into the back seat on the passenger side.

The driver has buckled his seat belt and is reaching for the ignition when I crack him in the side of the neck with my fist. The passenger goes for a weapon in the glove box. He gets it out, and I let him thumb off the safety before I take it from him and break his nose with the butt. The driver is still reeling from my punch, but he quiets down when he feels the barrel of the pistol press against his head. It's a familiar looking model. SIG Sauer P226 with a short magazine. In the car, the .40 S&W round will do quite well. I don't need a lot of bullets.

"Hello, gentlemen," I say. "I think it's time we had a chat." The smell of Passenger's blood is making me tense, making the thirst knot my stomach, and I bleed off a lot of that tension in my voice.

They both go still, waiting for me to make the next move. It's always nice to do business with professionals.

"Hands on your heads," I tell them, "interlace your fingers." Driver seems to be the one who is going to test me, and so I thumb back the hammer on the gun. It's a double action pistol, and pulling back the hammer lets them know I mean business.

Passenger starts breathing out of his mouth, and tiny strands of blood fly from his lips.

"You don't want to do this," Driver says.

"Do what? I just want to ask a couple of questions. This doesn't have to get complicated."

I sit back, taking the pressure off Driver's head. This way I can keep the gun on both of them. Driver looks at me in the rearview mirror, and if I had a silencer on this pistol, I'd put a bullet through the mirror, but I settle for making sure he can see the pistol.

"Who's paying for your services?" I ask.

"Fuck and You," Driver says.

"They pay well?"

The question isn't what he was expecting and he blinks heavily at me. Passenger starts to turn his head, and I kick the back of his seat to let him know that I don't think that is a good idea.

"Where are the people from the boat?" I ask. I tap the barrel of the pistol against Driver's shoulder. "And Fuck and You's house isn't the right answer."

"You're not going to shoot us," Driver sneers.

"No?" I lower the pistol and press it against the back of his seat. The trigger action is good and clean, and I fire the gun twice. The leather seat is a decent noise-suppressor, and Driver jerks and coughs very dramatically, spitting blood on the dash and windshield. With a rattling groan that I know well, he slumps forward against the inside of his door.

The barrel of the gun is hot and I press it against the back of Passenger's neck, shushing him because he's starting to make a bit of a high-pitched whining noise.

"Where are they?" I ask when he calms down enough to hear me.

"E… Eden Park," he stutters.

"See? Not very complicated at all." I hit him hard enough to put him out, and toss the gun into the driver's side footwell. I get out and walk away.

It would have been easy to kill the other one too, but that turns the car into a crime scene that Adelaide Police are going to be all over. With Passenger still alive, he's going to call it in to Secutores. They're going to scramble to do clean up, and I did Driver discretely enough that they'll probably get away with it. The job will tap their resources though, leaving less guys to be waiting for me at Eden Park.

That's the first thing Passenger will do when he wakes up. Let his command know what he told me. If he lied, it means nothing; if he told me the truth—and I suspect he did—I've got a very small window of opportunity.

Ralph is startled when I appear next to his Volvo. I tap on the glass and he unlocks the passenger side. "Eden Park," I say as I climb in. "Drive and talk. We don't have a lot of time."

TWELVE

His phone is more modern than my crap pay-as-you-go phone, and it offers us a route to a place far enough from the city center that the buildings get replaced by trees. His phone also has access to the Internet, and I can run a search on *Eden Park* while he drives. His phone's screen is small, and the search results are tiny, but I find enough to jog his memory.

"Yeah," he says. "I've heard of the place. I thought it was shut down though. It used to be a lunatic asylum when it was first opened, like, forty years ago. And that's why it closed, I think. The term fell out of favor, and other places that were more politically correct started springing up." He laughs nervously. "A cottage industry, you know? The pharmaceutical companies want us taking more pills, right? They don't want us to get over our depression or our phobias. They want us to be taking some sort of medication for them. We can't make you normal, but we can make you *look* normal."

"Appearances are important," I say, staring out the window.

"What happened on the boat?" he asks suddenly, trying to catch me out.

"Someone panicked," I reply. "And then they tried to hide their mistakes."

"Why do you care?"

"It's good to care about something, Ralph," I say, turning my head toward him. "Don't you think?"

He gets flustered and the car wiggles on the road a bit as he fusses with the steeling wheel.

"What happened at the hospital?" he asks.

"Nothing you want to put in any story you write," I tell him.

"If you did anything illegal for this information—"

I cut him off with a laugh. "Do you think the people at Eden Park—if this is where they're all locked up—are there *legally*? Do you think Secutores is doing anything other than helping to establish a *legal* precedence for curtailing people's rights?"

"That's not the point," he sputters. "Where does it end if I don't—I mean, how does the system work if no one adheres to it?"

"How old are you, Ralph?"

"Forty—forty-six."

"Keep holding on to that childlike idealism as long as you can," I say.

V V

From the outside, Eden Park looks like a respectable private estate. Set back from the road and hidden by a wide screen of oak trees, the main grounds are nicely manicured and the three buildings try hard to pass for Nouveau Colonial. The only sign it is something other than it appears is the lack of shadows. Mounted floodlights keep the darkness at bay, and the grass shines unnaturally in the harsh light. There's no sign of external patrols, but I'm sure the persistent light is to ensure a clear picture on the many closed-circuit cameras.

It's quiet in the trees around Eden Park. I haven't heard a single car pass since Ralph slowed down enough along the main road for me to hop out. No sound comes from the buildings either. This iteration of Eden Park is one of those kinder and gentler psychiatric facilities than its original incarnation, and the lack of B-movie shrieks certainly suggest the *unfortunates* are resting quietly.

It's certainly not the same as Bedlam in its heyday.

I skulk around the perimeter, a ghost among the trees. If there are motion detectors, no one is paying any attention to them, and the only activity I see is a pair of gray rabbits who I flush out of a squat bush as I pass along the northern verge of the property.

The staff parking lot is in the back, and it's where shadows are allowed to gather. I slither across the damp grass and hug the tailgate of a pickup truck. I count cars, and making a guess purely based on the make and model of the cars in the lot, I surmise most of the staff on-hand tonight are only a notch or two above hourly wage.

The trio of identical black sedans parked in a row gets my attention.

Same make and model as the car the mercenaries were driving in the garage. *Rentals*, I realize.

I'm considering the brazen approach when a door opens on the rear of the closest building. A pair of suits exits. One is fumbling in her purse for keys and the other has his ear glued to his cell phone. Their outfits match, though the man's jacket is ill-fitted in comparison to the woman's tailored top. Her haircut is more precise than his as well, and I'm a bit surprised when she finds her keys, clicks off the alarm to one of the three sedans, and holds open the back door for the guy. He ducks into the car without missing a word in his conversation, and she shuts the door. She opens the driver-side door, climbs in, starts the car, and then gets back out. Leaning against the car, she lights a cigarette, and stares at the building which they had just vacated. She's waiting for him to finish his call, and judging from her expression, this isn't the first time he's made her wait.

I wonder who he is talking to.

She finishes her cigarette—a Gauloises Blonde from the smell—and crushes it out beneath the smart heel of her black oxford pump. She looks around, as if she senses me watching, and I can tell from the slackness of her face that it's been a long day. She's not really looking, even though the lizard part of her brain just reached up and yanked on her consciousness.

I consider taking both of them. Certainly easier than any sort of assault I had considered in the parking garage. Drop her first; yank open the back door of the car; lean in and pop the guy on the phone. It would take me ten seconds, max; but then I would have to decide what to do with them later. And the first few suggestions that float to mind aren't really options, as much as I'd like to fantasize otherwise.

Invisibility is better, and so I stay put as she gets back into the car. It backs out of its space, pivots, and drives around toward the front of the facility and the long driveway to the main road. After it is gone, the silence returns.

Two rentals left. Somewhere between four and eight passengers. It's after ten o'clock. If there is a shift change coming anytime soon, it'll be midnight. I have two hours.

The scent of the Gauloises hangs in the air, a tantalizing hint of an idea.

The smoker's corner is under the overhanging eaves on the northern back corner of the main building. There are two plastic chairs and a tall cylindrical ashtray. A single video camera points directly down on the spot, the baleful eye of Eden Park's administration offering not-so-subtle distain for the lung-burners.

Having seen the unedited toxicological reports from the 1960s, I can't say I blame them.

Fortunately for me, any serious smoker is going to need a couple smoke breaks during an eight-hour shift. I shouldn't have to wait too long.

ᵥᵥ

He's a three-pack-a-day man and although he washes his hands obsessively, there's still a nicotine stain on the inside of his right middle finger. He breathes heavily from the mouth when he's afraid, and I gag at the rot coming out of his lungs. His circulation is bad enough that it doesn't take much pressure on his neck to make his pass out. I lay him out on the ground, swipe his ID badge and his wallet, and after a moment's hesitation, I dig through his pockets for his pack of cigarettes and shred them.

The video camera hangs crookedly on its post, its eye no longer watchful.

I swipe the ID card on the nearby door and slip into the main building.

Inside, it's all puce walls and off-white trim. Prints of very restful landscapes are arranged neatly along the walls. Someone left the mood music on—Chopin, from the sounds of it—though it's so quiet most wouldn't know they were actually humming along with it. Got to keep the natives placid.

I'm behind the scenes at the psychiatric hospital, and there aren't any cameras watching the watchers. The first floor is most likely administration, with the upper floors and basement given over to the rooms for the residents and rooms filled with therapeutic opportunities, respectively. A pair of orderlies is hanging out in a break room not far from the staff kitchen, and as they're staring tiredly at a video feed from a sports channel, it's not too hard to slip past them. I ponder putting the pair of slightly less bored guards in the security cage to sleep, but I suspect the current administration at Eden Park isn't keen on putting real names on the room roster.

I'm going to have to do this the old-fashioned way.

THIRTEEN

Mere is in a corner room on the second floor. She's asleep when I peek in, but she's thrown her sheet off and even though she's curled up and her head is turned away from the observation peephole in the door, I recognize her shape.

There are a lot of things I can't forget. Sometimes I wish I could. Though, times like this, I relish having the memories I do. Too many are gone—good and bad.

The lock on the door is solid, and I could probably rip the door off its hinges, but that'll be noisy. I go looking for someone with keys instead—like the two guards in the security cage on the first floor.

When I get back downstairs, one is not there. When he returns a few minutes later, he gawks at his unconscious buddy for a second before joining him. While I've been waiting, I've had time to collect the set of master keys and read over the resident roster. It's all first names and last initial only, and I find "Mere V" as well as "Thaddeus M."

Sally will be pleased.

The master key makes it easy to open room 216 quietly, and I consider slinging Mere over my shoulder and making a run for it. But I don't know what the drugs have done to her; if she wakes up and freaks out, then I'm carrying the equivalent of a sack full of cats. I opt for stealth, though it is going to take more time. I sit and bounce on the edge of her uncomfortable bed until she stirs. Her breathing changes around the third bounce and her eyelids start to flutter. She turns, notices my presence, and opens one eye enough to look up àt me. She burrows into her pillow, pulling it over her already messy and limp hair. She mumbles something unintelligible.

"I'm not a dream," I say.

"You have to be," she slurs. "Otherwise the rest is true too." I stroke her hair. Other than when I held her out over the railing on the boat, it's the first time I've touched her when she's been aware of my presence. She whimpers slightly, and when she speaks, her voice is muffled by the pillow. "I can't feel anything," she whispers.

"It's the drugs," I tell her.

"That's what my last boyfriend said." She giggles and I'm not happy to hear the sound. It's unhinged, disconnected, and we're back to a sack of cats. She's got quite a cocktail screwing with her head. My hands tighten on the edge of her bed, my nails tearing through the sheet and slick cover of the mattress.

"Let's go somewhere else," I try. "How about a trip to the spa? We'll have native children rub your feet."

"Don't," she says. She flips over, keeping the pillow over her face. "You're making it worse."

I glance toward the door, mentally considering how long I've been sitting here. "I need you to come back," I say. "I need you to walk out of here."

With a sob, she bolts upright and throws her arms around me, burying her face in the crock of my neck. She squeezes me tight and I embrace her awkwardly. "I hate you," she says and then, without taking a breath, "I've been dreaming about you."

"It's just the drugs," I tell her gently.

"Before the drugs," she says with a short laugh.

I don't know what to say to that, and there's an awkward moment of silence between us. "We should go," I finally say, feeling like I should be saying something else instead, but my ready supply of snappy one-liners has run out.

"To the spa?" she asks, a dreamy smile on her lips.

"Sure," I reply, grabbing on to anything that'll keep her attention. That'll get her upright, compliant, and heading for the door.

"What about the others?"

I hesitate, and even in her addled state, she's aware enough to read my answer in my silence.

"That's not okay, Silas."

This, of all things, is what brings her back to reality.

"What do you want me to do? Release everyone?"

"Yes," she hisses.

I regret my honesty and am about to reconsider how much I'm going to tell Mere when the light through the observation peephole flickers. I'm off the bed and at the door in a second, but I'm too late. I hear the lock click and the heavy sound of the key being removed. I have a set of keys too, though there is no keyhole on this side, and when someone puts their face up to the observation peephole, I slip one of the keys on my keyring between my fingers and jab it forcefully through the glass port.

Someone is screaming outside the room as I return to the bed and grab Mere's arm roughly. "So much for stealth," I say. "Come on. Spa time. Let's go."

I kick the door hard, and it comes off its hinges. The guy on the floor with his hand over his bloody eye looks up, other eye wide, and I punch him hard enough to snap several bones in his hand. The other security guard has a Taser, but it's cheaply made and breaks easily. A headbutt lays him out, and then I'm dragging Mere down the hall toward the stairs. The drugs make her clumsy and she stumbles twice before I pick her up and run with her in my arms.

Half a sack of sleepy cats. It could be worse.

The staircase is big and open, and it is easier to simply leap down to the landing of the first turn and then again to the lower floor. Mere is heavy in my arms, and she hangs on tight, her face pressed tight against my shoulder, as if she doesn't want to see what happens next.

The two orderlies who had been watching TV earlier are alert now, and shortly before they spill out into the hall, I hear the distant drone of the alarm and the lights in the hall immediately shift to red. The tone and the color are meant to confuse and disorient any escaping residents, but those parts of my brain aren't in charge right now.

The first orderly has a black nightstick, and he swings it sharply as he rushes me. I raise a shoulder and let the wooden stick bounce off harmlessly. I drop my shoulder and drive it into his chest, throwing him against the hallway wall. A picture frame cracks beneath him and glass tinkles to the floor. The second guy gets it into his head that if he targets Mere, I'll surrender.

He's wrong. Very, very wrong.

I hear a soft pop behind me, and fire explodes across my back. I stagger, nearly dropping Mere, and the hall is filled with a sickly crackling noise as my flesh burns and sizzles. I duck into the break room, depositing Mere on the nearby couch. The chairs scattered around the two small tables are plastic with metal struts, not terribly suitable for what I need. Ignoring the pain crawling up my back, I stagger over toward the counter where several modern appliances are sitting patiently, waiting for someone to put them to work.

Yanking the pot off the coffee maker, I whirl toward the door and throw the glass container toward the man in the dark suit who is entering the break room, a long-snouted pistol held out in front of him. He sees the coffee pot coming and dodges, but in the seconds it takes him to get out of the way, I get my hands on the microwave and throw it too. It's bigger and heavier, but it flies just as readily. It hits him in the face, and something snaps. He drops like all of his strings have been cut.

Another gunman is right behind him though. Same goofy looking pistol. When he pulls the trigger, his gun makes a staccato popping noise, hurling tiny round projectiles. They're like paintball pellets, but their contents are much worse. I dodge, moving slowly but more than fast enough to avoid compressed-air-propelled pellets. There's a design flaw someone hadn't considered.

Realizing the limitation of his weapon, the gunman drops back into the hallway. It's a smart move, forcing me to come through the narrow frame of the door if I'm going to attack him.

I'm not planning on it, though. There's a tall window on the far side of the room. That's where Mere and I will be going.

I cross the room and slam the door shut. There's a deadbolt on the inside frame, and I slot it into place. The guy on the floor is still conscious, bleeding heavily from a gash on the side of his head. Grabbing his pistol and shoving it down the front of my pants, I collect Mere from the couch and dash for the window. She shrieks, clawing at my face, as she sees where I'm going, but I hold her tight and jump.

ⅤⅤ

I hit the parking lot, the gravel chattering under my feet. The back door bangs open, and a handful of mercenaries run out. They've got more conventional weapons, and the night fills with the muttering noise of angry bees. Bullets spang off the cars around me, making more of a racket than the suppressed semiautomatic weapons being fired at me. I can't keep running with Mere; not with this much lead in the air. I dump her behind a van, and dart to my right, letting the night swallow me.

I feel my body loosen as I let the restraints go. We train constantly to keep ourselves in check, to keep ourselves moving in such a way that humans don't freak out when they see us, and it's glorious to let these self-managed shackles fall off. I'm not anywhere near my full ability, not with my veins still fucked up with the chemical agent. Whatever is in the pellet

I got spattered with is from the same batch. I can feel it soaking through the fabric of my jacket and shirt, and my skin burns like a thousand ants are all trying to slice pieces of my flesh off.

There are four of them and they move like a trained team—two focused on what's in front of them, one on either side, each sweeping their back trail as they move. It's a good tactic and they move well together, but they're too tightly packed. A single grenade could take out all four of them.

Or a single Arcadian.

I get a running start and launch myself off the front of a sedan, leaving a big dent in the hood. The closest of the quartet spots me as I sail through the air, but he can't get his gun up in time. My knees shatter every rib in his chest, driving shards of bone through most of his vital organs. Before he even hits the ground, I spring off him and take out the one on my left with a hard strike to his neck that shatters vertebrae. The one standing in front of me is still turning around as I kick him mid-spine, doing more damage than any chiropractic care will ever fix. The last one thinks he knows where I am, but I keep moving, dropping my right arm around his head as I pass. I spin, pulling his upper body in tight to my chest. He stumbles, losing his footing, and I tense my arm and bend at the waist. His neck snaps.

I don't bother checking them; none of them are coming after Mere and me. I run back to where I dropped her, scoop her up, and head off into the woods.

It's only as I reach the tree line that I realize there was a silver Mercedes in the parking lot that wasn't there earlier. There's no time to go back and check, and it might be a coincidence. I got what I came for; time to go. I run until my sides ache.

Mere clings fiercely to me as I run through the woods. I try to dodge low-hanging branches and the trunks of narrow saplings, but I know her dangling feet collide with at least one tree as I speed through the woods. I cross a narrow creek and angle upriver, looking for a suitable place to rest.

I could have gone back to the road, but that choice would have assumed Ralph was stupid enough to hang around and wait for me. On the one hand, it would have made for an easy getaway; on the other, the silver Mercedes was nagging at me. In the end, I didn't want to be in a car on the roads. Too structured. Too few exits and escapes.

Plus I'd have to trust Ralph's driving.

Mere winces as I set her down, favoring her right ankle.

"Sit." I indicate a grass-covered mound next to a row of red beech. "Let me look at it." She complies quietly, and as I crouch to look at her, the pistol shoved in my waistband digs into my hip. I pull it out and set it aside.

Mere pushes some of her lank hair back from her face, staring at the long muzzle of the gun. I notice that the sleeve of her shirt is ripped in several places. There are similar tears in her pants, closer to her bare feet, and a thin gash along the bottom of her left foot is stained with blood, a few smeared drops like tears.

My tongue is thick in my mouth, and my hand shakes as I carefully bend her leg so that the bottom of her foot rests against the ground. Out of sight, out of mind. Her right foot is the injured one. That's where I need to be focusing my attention.

Her ankle is tender and swelling already. I touch the skin, probing gently, and she hisses at me when I prod her too much. "It's not broken," I announce, wiggling her foot. "We can soak it in the water; that'll help bring the swelling down." I turn toward the creek, meaning to look for a good place for her to perch for a few minutes, but her gasp brings me around.

"Your back," she says.

"It's fine," I lie. I have no idea what she sees, but I can guess. There is no pain, which means I've already blocked out the nerve endings, leaving them to die in isolation. The flesh is necrotic, certainly, and given the way my shirt *clings* to me, I'm sure the melted slurry of skin and fabric isn't pleasant to look at.

"No, it's not fine," she argues. Her hands flutter as she talks. "I may be as high as a kite, but I know no one can run that fast—for that long. I saw you throw the microwave at that man like it was a… an empty milk carton. And—" Her hands start to flutter in the direction of my back.

"There's nothing to do about it now," I tell her. "Try not to think about it. *I'm* trying not to."

Her gaze returns to the pistol, and I know she's looking at the elongated barrel, and the bulbous shape attached to the back. It's a CO_2 pistol—elegant in a way, but cumbersome in many others. The grip of the gun contains the CO_2 cartridge, and there's a bulbous clump on the back of the gun where the hammer normally would be. I find the seal on the top and pop the blister open with my thumb. I shake out several of the pellets on the ground, unwilling to even touch them, and Mere leans over to pick one up. "What is it?" she asks, rolling the yellow-green pellet between her fingers.

I reseal the hopper, and point the pistol at a clump of weeds growing around a small rock. When I pull the trigger, compressed air forces one of the pellets out of the barrel with a hollow pop. The pellet hits the rock, breaks, and its contents spatter on the weeds, which all but burst into flame for as quickly as they shrivel and blacken.

"Defoliant," I say.

"Weed killer?" She stares at the blackened weeds. "But it never works that fast."

"You're thinking of herbicides which are a poison. Plants don't come back with herbicides. Defoliants are, like the name, meant to clear cover as quickly as possible. Agent Orange, for example."

She focuses on the tiny pellet between her fingers, her face moving through an exaggerated series of expressions. "This is Agent Orange?"

I offer her a bitter laugh. "No, this is much, much stronger."

She shudders and drops the pellet. "And it works on human flesh too."

"I doubt it," I say. Her head swivels around to look at me, and her pupils are still too large. I crawl over to the damp rock, and being careful to not touch any of the chemical stain, I pull it out of the ground. "Touch it," I say when I return with the chemical-stained rock.

"What?" She tries to bat my arm away. "Are you out of your fucking mind?"

"Unfortunately, I don't think I am," I say. "Please. Touch it."

"I'm not going to touch it."

I grab her hand and force it against the rock. She shrieks and pulls away, freeing herself from my now-loose grip. She tries to slap me with her other hand and I take the blow on my shoulder as I throw the rock away. It bounces into the underbrush where its taint can only hurt other plants.

"What the fuck are you doing?" she yells.

"Do you feel anything?"

She slaps at me again as I repeat my question. The words finally penetrate her outrage and she blinks several times before she looks down at her hand. "No," she says. With a shudder, she wipes her hand on a nearby patch of grass and, as we watch, the stalks brown and wither. "Oh my God," she whispers. "What is it?"

"The perfect weapon," I say.

It all makes sense now. The lure of the whaling fleet, the aerosol dispersion trap on the processing boat, Secutores and their obvious watchers, the pellet guns: this has all been a test environment set up by whoever is funding Kyodo Kujira.

They've finally figured out a way to kill us.

FOURTEEN

The trees are alight with the fire of dawn by the time we get back to my hotel, and Mere is asleep before I can cover her with a blanket. I lie down next to her—on my side since my back still hurts—and as soon as I close my eyes, most of the day vanishes. When I open them again, the light in the room has changed—the sun is on the other side of the sky now—and Mere isn't in the bed anymore.

I sit up slowly, feeling an unnatural stiffness in my back. Mere is sitting in the overstuffed wingback chair, dressed only in the white cotton robe that comes with the room. She's reading the morning paper. Some of her hair is damp and her face is clean and pink. I can smell the lavender scent of the hotel's complimentary soap on her skin.

"You don't breathe when you sleep," she says.

My mouth is dry—it's an unpleasant sensation—and when I move, I feel a layer of skin on my back cracking and shifting like loose shards of shale. "I'm a shallow breather," I say.

She lowers the paper and regards me. Her eyes are clear. Whatever they were doping her with at Eden Park doesn't linger long. "Just because I was drugged doesn't mean I wasn't paying attention. And that's not the only incident either. You picked me up like I weighed nothing and held me over the railing on the *Cetacean Liberty*. Do you remember that? And I saw Phoebe—"

"You saw Phoebe do what?"

"Gus—you remember Gus?—knows some Japanese. I asked him what '*kyuuketsuki*' means."

I was more curious about what Phoebe had done, but Mere has a point she wants to make. "What does it mean?" I prompt.

She folds the paper and puts it on the table. Without a word, she gets up and walks to the heavy curtains that are keeping most of the light out. She yanks them open and the room floods with sunlight. I put up a hand to keep the worst of the glare out. My optics are sitting on the dresser next to the TV. I wish they were a little closer, but I don't move to get them. The light hurts my eyes, but I won't suffer any permanent damage. Not right away, at least.

"This is stupid," Mere says with a snort. She walks back to the chair and sits down. "I mean, there you are. Sitting in full sunlight. You came out during the day on the boat too." She makes a noise in her throat and flaps her hand at my face. "Open your mouth. Show me."

"Show you what?" I ask, squinting at her.

"Let me see your teeth."

I stand, my back complaining again, and close the curtains before I grant her request.

My teeth are much like hers, except—

"No dental work," she notices.

"Why would there be?" I point out.

A laugh escapes her throat before she can stop it, and she puts a hand over her mouth as if she is embarrassed by the sound. "I'm sorry," she says, shaking her head. "I don't—this isn't… I'm having a hard time…"

"You wanted to know about Arcadia, Mere," I say as I wander over to the narrow desk and search for something to write on. "This is your chance."

"Huh. True enough, I guess." She rubs her hands across her arms as if she is catching a chill. "Okay, out with it, Mere," she sighs, talking herself into something. "Ah, shit. This is too weird, but what other explanation is there? I mean, I'm sure there's a *rational* explanation, but what does rational even mean, really? And then there's Clarke's Law, right? The whole *magic is just science we don't understand* argument."

Having found a piece of paper and a pen, I return to the bed and start making a list.

She interrupts her stream of consciousness thinking. "What are you doing?"

"I'm making a shopping list."

"Why?"

"We need a few things." I point at her robe. "Unless you want to go around wearing that."

"No." She is flustered for a moment, her hands touching the robe. "No, I don't. Silas, you're not answering my question."

I raise my eyes to her face. "You haven't asked one yet."

"What are you?"

"I was born a *Dardanoi,* in a place that was once called Troas, which later became Anatolia and is now part of Turkey. Later, I became an Arcadian."

"What's an Arcadian?" she asks.

I offer her a smile. "What do you think?"

"I think '*kyuuketsuki*' means '*vampire*,' and I also think you're not answering my question."

"I'm not using the words you want me to use, but I am answering your questions." I say. "You have to ask better questions."

She makes a face and fidgets. I know what she wants to know, and I'm not making it easy for her. Why? Because what she thinks she knows isn't true, anyway.

"Look," I say, "a vampire is a creature out of folklore. Stoker made his career out of sensationalizing what is a bit of propaganda that had its roots several hundred years earlier. The old stories were just a way to scare children and keep the locals malleable. It's all true inasmuch as it functions as an effective deterrent."

"But that doesn't explain what I saw."

I shrug. "Can you explain everything you see, Mere?"

"No," she says, "but you're just side-stepping my question. You and I both know what I saw, and you know damn well that's not normal." She levers a finger at me. "And don't give me that *But what is normal?* bullshit."

"Look, you know this as well as I: every story has a kernel of truth to it, doesn't it? All our folklore is based around an effort to explain something, right? You start with a key truth—something you are willing to believe is absolutely swear-to-God true—and then layers and layers of embellishments and other nonsense get piled on top, until no one can really remember what the original kernel was. Or whether it was really true, in an objective sense."

"If I come over there and punch you in the face, I think we can both agree there's some objective truth to the fact that it'll hurt."

I smile. "Do you want me to say that I'm a vampire, Mere?" I spread my arms. "I'm a vampire. Do you feel better? Safer?"

"No," she snaps, "because you're just saying it to placate me."

"It could also be true."

"But what if I don't believe in vampires?"

"That makes me a liar, then." I remember something Talus said to me on the boat. "You wouldn't be the first to think so of me." I write one more item down before I offer her the piece of paper.

"What is this?"

"A shopping list," I tell her again.

When it becomes clear that I'm not going to get up and bring it to her, Mere gets out of the chair and takes the list from me. She stands—legs slightly apart, body square to me—as she reads the list. "A loofa?" She looks up and notices my expression. "What?"

I shake my head and look away. She's made her decision already, even if she hasn't mentally accepted it. Her body language has given her away. "A loofa is one of nature's best exfoliators," I say.

"Why? Oh—" She wrinkles her nose. "Never mind. What am I going to do for clothes? And cash?"

When I stand up, we're close to one another, and we both pause for a second, gauging each other. "I have money," I say, spoiling the moment. I cast about for my coat and spot it on the floor of the shallow closet. I was going to offer it to her, but the back is a gnarled mess of melted fibers and bits of my skin. "Stick with the robe," I say. "Be eccentric until you can find some tourist crap."

"Spoken like a man who has done this before," she says.

A fragment of memory floats through my head. Yellow lights along a river. A two-spired cathedral with a rounded hump of flying buttresses. Gargoyle skyline. I'm wearing less than the robe Mere's wearing now. "Once or twice," I admit.

"What if I don't come back?" she asks. "What is stopping me from running to the police?"

"What are you going to tell them?"

She nods. "It's Kyodo Kujira, isn't it? Those pellets. Whoever is behind this is gunning for Arcadia, aren't they?"

"We can talk about it when you get back."

She laughs. "Of course. What better incentive could there be for me to not run screaming to the police?"

"I can't think of one," I reply.

The truth is: I need her help, and it'll be easier if she's already decided to stay for her own reasons. I need someone I can trust, even if it is only inasmuch as sharing convergent short-term goals.

Arcadia has been dying slowly for centuries now. As the planet becomes more and more toxic, we inch ever closer to extinction. Whoever is manufacturing this chemical is trying to accelerate the process, and with Arcadia gone, there will be no stewards left.

That sounds like the sort of story Mere might be interested in.

VV

I follow her, of course, even though I know she'll come back. I want to know if anyone notices her, eccentric style of clothing aside. Have we lost Secutores? Is there anyone else?

In the old days, we held to the Rule of Rome—kill everyone; leave nothing behind—but in the last few hundred years, as a general policy "salting the earth" has become less viable. It was easier to be invisible; to hide in the shadows and prey upon their fear of the dark. They welcomed any excuse to look away.

But we got lazy; we forgot our mission. We convinced ourselves that we didn't need to know, and like a field untended and unwatched, weeds grew. After several generations, they became strong and entrenched. Like clover with thousands of runners beneath the surface, binding everything together. Choking the life out of the native grasses.

It is easy to remain unseen when I follow Mere. I know her mannerisms: the way she tucks her hair behind her left ear when she stops at a street corner and looks both ways; how she makes tiny popping motions with her lips when she is reading and thinking; her quick, distance-devouring stride; she plays chicken with anyone walking in the opposite direction, unconsciously—oblivious, even—waiting for them to side-step first. Without her knowing, we fall into the same routine we had two years ago.

She was an up-and-coming investigative reporter for one of the network affiliates in Boston. Too brash for an anchor job, she preferred the deep research, investigative exposé—building a story, chasing down witnesses, and packaging it all together in five-minute segments that would be doled out over successive nights in the heart of the prime time news slot. The New York and Los Angeles markets were already sniffing around, and she was on the shit-list of more than one lobbyist group in D.C. Meredith Vanderhaven was going places; it was just a matter of time. Organized crime and double-speaking politicos in the Boston area could not wait for her to move on.

It didn't matter if she was chasing the money trail of city-wide construction contracts gone horribly over-budget, or the social media scandals of city government candidates who didn't understand the first rule of texting sexually explicit pictures, or the byzantine backroom dealings of the fulsomely corrupt city government, she dug into it all with the same tenacity. But Big Ag could turn her head quicker than anything else, and it had been her story about the cattle conditions at Hachette Falls that had caught Arcadia's attention.

A family-owned cattle ranch, Hachette Falls was two generations past its sell-date. The current operator was half again as unconcerned about the quality of the meat coming out of the Hachette slaughterhouse as his father had been, and as a result, the stockyards were beyond inhumane. Downer cows and electric prods were the order of the day, and the workers were masters at spotting the signs of brain damage and virulent distress in the herd. They knew how to shock the sluggish cows right into the chute.

Mere got a video camera on site and her clandestine video footage was story enough, but what made her story pop was the arrogant indifference of Hachette senior management, especially in light of government subsidies the company was receiving for being a test farm for a new GMO-based additive in the feed. The product was made by a miniscule biotech that was getting inordinate handouts from the same government program—collusion of the most scandalous sort. The biotech company disappeared within days of Mere's footage finding its way onto the Internet. No mere trick there.

It was as if, having seen the presence of the Devil, Mere was now a true believer, a crusading convert, who would face any hardship in her relentless quest to hunt Old Scratch down, to purge his influence off the surface of the planet. Hachette's BSE haven was almost forgotten in her zeal to track the influence. The money was easy—right out of D.C.—what was harder was finding out who pulled strings to get the cash flowing the way it had been. And who had the power to make a company of twelve suddenly disappear.

Her search led her to Beering Foods, a subsidiary of a subsidiary who made patties from the ground chuck that came out of Hachette Falls. They were part of a resurgence on a community level to buy and eat local, though the community was clearly oblivious to the corporate chain behind Beering. They were equally oblivious—for different reasons—to Beering's black market channel of organ trafficking. This channel was run by a bunch of Chechens who had been schooled in modern international business by "retired" officers of the pre-Glasnost Russian secret police.

A fun bunch and Mere, having reported from the floor of a recent Republican National Convention, was a little too fearless for her own good. Arcadia was watching Mere's progress, and it was my job to steer her toward a data cache that would crack Beering open and force the FDA—who had been trying their best to look away as they counted their payoff—to step in and shut the company down. A shutdown that would have included the backroom organ-legging. The Chechens would have rolled up their shop and gone somewhere else—which was victory enough for the time being— but Mere wanted more—she wanted to expose the whole operation.

Illytch Dmitri Kirkov had a different idea. One that involved a private conversation about some of the more exotic interrogation techniques he had learned during the First Chechen War.

I shouldn't have gotten involved. We had risked exposure in retrieving the corporate data and leading her to it. My surveillance of Mere had been ongoing. Twenty-four seven. We had an interest in her. We couldn't walk away. We had made an investment. She was a valuable asset. She could be useful, properly pointed at our enemies. If she died, we would have no voice in the media. This is how I justified taking the Chechen's knife from him, how I convinced myself that dragging him away and leaving Mere—unconscious and bleeding from the cut in her throat—was an acceptable risk for myself—for Arcadia.

I did what I did for Mother's sake. What son wouldn't have done the same?

VV

"You gave me a lot of money," she explains when she returns, laden with bags. "I bought some clothes for both of us. I… I guessed your size."

"I'm sure they'll be fine." I'm sitting by the window, a cup of tea on the table next to me. "There's more water," I point out, "if you want tea. I could make coffee too." Pretending I don't know that her first stop was a coffee shop where she ordered an enormous beverage that was more sugar and milk than espresso.

"I'm good," she says. She sorts through the clothes, laying them into several piles. She points to a white bag adorned with the logo of a local chain. "Toiletries and the like are in there," she says, "including your loofa."

"Thank you." I stand and walk over to the bag, inspecting its contents. "I guess I'll go clean up."

She makes a face. "I'll go first." She snatches the bag out of my hand and flees to the bathroom. The door shuts firmly behind her.

I can't say I blame her. I need to scrub off a lot of dead skin.

For me, she's picked out a few nondescript t-shirts, a pair of dark jeans, and a thin wool sweater. The color of the last isn't one I would have chosen for myself. Magenta, perhaps, maybe vermillion—it all depends on how upscale the brand marketing is meant to be. I run my fingers across the wool as I try to recall the last time a woman bought me clothes. Before World War II? Paris? No, somewhere else.

It's been a while.

In her rush, she didn't take her own new wardrobe into the bathroom. I carefully strip off all the tags and pile them neatly on a chair I set before the door. I return to my seat by the window and listen to the world rush by while she showers.

My hearing is getting better. I can hear her humming as she stands beneath the steaming water.

Memory gets slippery after a few centuries. There's too much to remember, and no good way to retain it all. After a millennium, you learn to not worry about what you've forgotten, but that doesn't mean the sense of loss is any less frustrating.

What was her name? I can see the café where we met, down the street from the theater. On Posthumalaan, yes, in Rotterdam. She had loved the movies. What had we seen at that theater? I remember her face. She had cut her hair short, a flagrant dismissal of her family's authority, and she was wildly ecstatic about her emancipation. *Valentien.* Yes, that was it. She let me call her Val.

She had bought me a suit.

I had been wearing it the night the German Blitz had started.

ᴠᴠ

"What are you thinking about?" Mere is wearing a gray t-shirt and loose shorts— the sort of casual wear that would look like undergarments on men, but women manage to turn them into *accidentally* alluring lounge wear. Her hair is still wet, and she's worrying sections of it with a towel as she wanders across the room.

"Someone I knew once," I say. The sun has gone down, and I've opened the curtains again. The sky is nearly black, and the clouds are outlined with a faint roseate glow.

"A woman?"

"Yes."

"Where is she now?"

Dust. Crushed beneath a ton of rubble when her apartment building collapsed.

"I don't know," I answer honestly.

"Are they going to find us?" She changes the topic, sensing there is nothing more of the previous subject that I wish to share.

"Eventually."

She winds her hair up into the towel and wanders over to look out the window. "What are we going to do?" she asks.

I let my gaze flick up to the towering white cone perched atop her head.

"After my hair dries," she amends.

"I suppose I can take my turn now."

She rolls her eyes. "You're going to make me wait, aren't you?"

"Not unless you want to scrub my back."

"Silas," she sighs, "*eeeew*. Not a turn-on. Really."

"I'm out of practice."

"Stick with being enigmatic and confounding. It works better for you." She jerks her head toward the bathroom. "Go. *Exfoliate*. And then you had better start talking when you come out."

V V

She is curled up on the bed when I finish with my shower. Her towel had slipped off her head, and her red hair curls around her face. I brush some of it back, my fingers lightly caressing her cheek.

I suddenly remember the way the morning sun used to stream in through the porthole-shaped windows in Val's bedroom. She would accuse me of purposefully leaving the curtains open. I was always apologetic, but continued to forget.

I liked watching the sun creep across her face.

Mere's breathing is slow and restful. Whatever dreams she had fallen through on the way to the deep trough of sleep were not troubling her.

When did I start caring for her? Was it when I entered the warehouse and took Kirkov's knife from him? Has Mother known since then? Had I become expendable? Was that why I had been chosen for Talus's mission? Mother doesn't love me anymore, and maybe that means it is time for me to finally die, after all these years. This is how it ends, like Eliot says. 'Not with a bang, but with a whimper.' I am one of his Hollow Men. Who will miss me when I'm gone?

"No one," I whisper.

They're all dead. Everyone I ever cared about. Mother took care of the pain. She always did. I would fall into her embrace, and she would take away the memories that hurt the most. That was why we went back to her; that was why we loved her as we did. She gave us life, and she helped us forget.

After Val, I had sworn that I was done with consorting with mortals.

I lie down next to Mere, as close as I can without actually touching her. When I inhale through my nose, I can smell her scent. Mere's right; I don't breathe when I sleep. None of us do. I close my eyes, but I don't let myself rest. *I'm not going to fade. Not yet.*

Maybe this is just a reaction to my exile from Arcadia, a sudden panic that my life—my three millennia plus, quasi-immortal existence—is coming to an end. Maybe I'm not ready to let this world consume me. Not having died, I don't quite know how to do it.

Or maybe I'm just an old soldier and it's been too long since I've had something worth dying for.

FIFTEEN

It finally dawns on me where the tiny buzzing noise is coming from. It started shortly after I lay down next to Mere, and I had been trying to sort through the pieces of this puzzle I had scattered in my head, but the tiny beelike buzz kept intruding. I get up from the bed, and find the noise-maker in the inner pocket of my wrecked coat. My cheap cell phone has been trying to tell me that I've missed a few calls. All from the same number.

There's only one person who has this number. I put on the clothes that Mere bought and slip out of the room, all without waking her. I take the back stairs down to the ground floor, and duck out into the open parking lot. The moon is peeking around the edge of the office building on my left, and the sky is clear. I stare up, wishing it were darker so that I could see the stars.

I call Ralph back and he answers on the second ring, out of breath and somewhat guarded. "Ah... hello?"

"It's me," I reply.

"Oh, you," he says. "Yes. You got my message?"

I glance at my phone and see the tiny blinking symbol that indicates that, yes, I do have voice mail. "No," I say. "Why don't you tell me again so I don't have to figure out how to access my voice mail."

"You haven't seen the papers?"

"No."

"There was a fire at Eden Park."

"When?"

He doesn't say anything, and I realize why he's being cagey. "You think I started it?"

"I… I don't know," he says. "Why don't you tell me your version of what happened."

"My version?" I stop myself before my anger takes over control of my tongue. "Are you covering the story for *The Independent*?"

He makes a noise in his throat that I take to be a *yes*.

"What about Secutores?" I ask. "You know they're involved. You know they had people at that location, that they want to keep things covered up. You know about Kyodo Kujira."

"Yes," he agrees. "But I don't know who *you* are."

I stop looking for the stars. "I'll have to call you back, Ralph," I say.

"No! Wait—"

I end the call before he can say anything else. He's got a valid point. He doesn't know me. He doesn't know what my motivation is or who I might be working for. I don't blame him. Until he knows enough to trust me, he's going to be worried that he's getting involved in a personal spat between me and Secutores. The type of disagreement that involves people with guns. Ralph strikes me as the type who steers clear of those sorts of disagreements.

I glance back at the hotel. Should I let him talk to Mere? He'll trust her; she trusts me. Can I keep things contained? Can I keep my secrets safe?

I dial another number. It rings a long time before it is answered; even then, the line clicks and hums for a bit before I hear his voice. "It's me," I say.

"Where are you?" Callis asks.

"Same place, more or less."

"Progress?"

"There's a private security company called Secutores that is running interference. They came in shortly after the boat was found and scared off Prime Earth's legal team. Spirited the survivors away to a place called Eden Park—old asylum outside of the city."

"This wouldn't be the same Eden Park that burned down less than twenty-four hours ago?"

"The same."

He waits for me to provide more information. I had been hoping that he'd be the one offering up news, and I exhale noisily before I continue. "I was there. They were waiting for me. Not just there. At the hospital too. They've been waiting for an Arcadian to show up." I tell him what has been bugging me about my mental puzzle. "They want one of us. They want to capture an Arcadian."

"Why?"

"I'm not sure." I'm starting to see the shape of the puzzle. The weed killer is lethal, but the CO_2 pistols are a clumsy delivery system, as evidenced by how readily I was able to avoid the pellets. They should be dipping ordinance into the chemical. Since they haven't been—so far—it means they're using it as a deterrent, like using dogs to flush quail toward a blind where the hunters are hiding. Like shocking cows to get them to move in the direction you want.

"How do they hope to manage this?" Callis asks. "Did you see anything that suggests they have a weapon of some kind? Something that could incapacitate us or…?"

"Oh, they have something all right," I laugh. "It's pretty nasty."

"What is it?"

"Something that makes Agent Orange look like Tang."

He's quiet for a moment. While he's thinking, I wander farther away from the hotel, heading for the darkness beyond the parking lot. Heading for someplace with more trees.

"Where did they get it?" he asks, following the same line of thinking that I've been chewing on. A security company like Secutores might have an R & D budget, but not for the sort of high-tech science that it would take to develop something like the weed killer. Someone gave it to them, which means they're following orders.

"Unknown," I tell him. "But it involves Kyodo Kujira." I give him a brief rundown of what happened on the *Cetacean Liberty*. My version. He doesn't ask about Mere, and I don't volunteer any tidbit that involves her.

"The whole mission was a trap," I finish. "It was all a setup to grab an Arcadian. We were supposed to lose someone on the processing boat, but we didn't. Then Nigel went out of his head and things got messy. They've been waiting ever since, hoping that one of us—or another Arcadian— would come and investigate what happened to the crew of the *Liberty*."

"What about the others?" he asks. "Talus and Phoebe? They were on the *Cetacean Liberty*, weren't they? It was just you and Nigel who were on the harpoon boats."

"We were," I say. "I don't know what happened to the other two. I'm assuming they didn't get snatched because why else would Secutores be hanging around?"

"Unless it's you they wanted."

I shake my head, rejecting that idea. I'm not that important. "That's too complicated," I say. "Keep it simple. They're ex-military. They know any mission gets astronomically more likely to be fucked up the more moving parts."

"So, any Arcadian then," he says.

"Probably, but where would the others go? We were out in the middle of the Southern Ocean. Australia is the closest land mass."

"It's not the best destination," he says. "Especially if you're damaged."

"Who?" I ask. "You think Nigel took his boat somewhere?"

"If you were him—body burned, poison in your system, half out of your mind with shock and pain—where would you go?"

"Back to Mother."

"And if you couldn't make it that far?"

I exhale slowly. "Some place safe," I say. "Some place where the soil was good." I shake my head, knowing the place he's thinking about. "The temple isn't there anymore. It's been gone for more than a hundred years."

"It's still there," Callis says. "The soil is still good, even if all the trees are gone. Even if there is no steward."

"You think he's gone to Rapa Nui," I say.

"Wouldn't you?"

"I don't know," I say, which is only partially true. My legs are still a mess, and my back is a solid slab of scarred flesh. If I had received as big a dose as Nigel, I'd want good soil too. The temple on Rapa Nui—Easter Island—has been abandoned for a long time, but he's right. The soil is better there than almost anywhere else. "Yeah, okay," I relent. "I'd consider it."

"Get out of Australia," Callis says. "Follow the money. Find the others."

"What about the reporter?" I ask.

"What about her?"

"The last time we talked, you said I should find her. And now you're telling me that I should find the others."

The line is quiet for a moment. "Well," he says, "you found her, didn't you?"

My hand tightens on the phone and I don't say anything.

Callis chuckles lightly. "I know you, Silas. I would have done the same. Don't let her get under your skin. Find the others. Let her follow the money. She's good at that."

▼▼

Mere is still asleep when I return, though she has rolled onto her back and tangled herself in the sheet. One of her legs sticks out, and I pull her toes gently until she starts to wake. She stretches languidly, unaware that

I can see perfectly well in the dim light spilling into the room from the partially open curtains.

I click on the lamp sitting on the side table, and the light chases away the thoughts starting to form in my head.

"What is it?" she asks as she sits up, pushing her hair back from her face. "I fell asleep."

"You did."

She glances around the room, still waking up. Still wondering what she's missed in the last few hours. "What time is it?"

"There's been a fire at Eden Park," I say.

Mere stares at me. "No, that's not—" she starts.

I toss my phone onto the bed. "Call the number in the log. The man who will answer the phone is Ralph Abernathy. He's a reporter for *The Independent*. He's on the story. He also covered the *Cetacean Liberty* fire."

Her face hardens, a mask meant to hide the torrent of emotions threatening to overwhelm her. "But. Why?"

"I don't know," I tell her. "Talk to Ralph." I stand up and walk toward the door.

"Where are you going?"

She hadn't picked up the phone. It lies there on the tousled sheets like a black blot, a stain that no amount of bleach could get out.

"I need to find... transportation," I tell her.

And, if my suspicions are correct, I will be the last person she wants around when Ralph tells her who died in the fire.

She asked me to save them, and I refused. It won't matter that Secutores kidnapped the survivors from the *Liberty* or that they started the fire. I didn't save them when she asked me to. That's what will gnaw at her.

I can't blame her. She's human, after all.

BOOK
THREE

HUMUS

SIXTEEN

hear voices coming from the hotel room as I exit the stairwell. I pick out Mere's voice easily enough, and after listening for a moment, I recognize the other voice. I fumble with the door handle, pretending that I'm having trouble with the electronic key, and by the time I figure it out, all sound from inside the room has stopped. I enter the room, casually looking around as I shut the door behind me. She is sitting in one of the chairs and the bathroom door is nearly closed.

"Don't slip in the dark," I call out to Ralph as I walk by the bathroom.

Mere's wearing comfortable jeans and a gray turtleneck sweater, made from the same grade of wool as the sweater she bought me. She's already started stretching the arms over her hands. Her hair is pulled back into a loose pony tail, and her eyes are bright—she's been crying, but not recently, and there are other emotions that have taken precedence.

"I have very good hearing," I remind her as Ralph catches his foot on the edge of the bathtub and nearly pulls the shower curtain off its rings.

"I know," she sighs. "He… I don't know what he was thinking."

Ralph comes out of the bathroom, and when he nervously steps past me, I can smell bourbon on his breath.

"I only made travel arrangements for two," I say.

"Where are we going?" Mere asks.

I glance at Ralph. "Why don't we start with why he's here."

"You told me to call him."

"Call, yes. Invite him over for a drink, no."

"We're not drinking," Ralph says. "Not… not now," he amends when I look at him again.

"What sort of travel arrangements?" Mere wants to know.

"Mere," I say patiently. "There's a Need to Know conversation we need to have. Is Ralph an asset or a liability?"

"Jesus Christ." Ralph backs away from me, and when the bed hits him on the back of the legs, he sits down heavily. "You did do it."

"Do what?" Mere demands.

"He set the fire. Oh, shit. The guys at the hospital. What did you do there?"

Ralph's had too much time to speculate and he's letting his ideas get the better of him. This meeting is going sideways, and it needs to get back on track. I move, slapping Ralph down on the bed and putting my hand over his mouth. He squirms for a second and I apply pressure. He quiets down, his eyes bulging with fear. Mere is half-out of her chair and I stop her with a word. "Don't."

She glares at me, not entirely cowed but smart enough to not make any sudden movement that I might interpret as threatening.

"Do you remember the boat?" I say. "Do you remember what I said when I held you?" She nods and I don't have to say anything more. "All of that still applies. More so, perhaps, because I am under a bit of stress right now. Do you understand?"

She nods again.

"Everything is either an asset or a liability," I explain, partially for Ralph's sake. "You want to be an asset."

"I know," she says quietly.

"Eden Park was not my doing, nor was it my responsibility. Why?" She doesn't answer at first and I repeat the last word. Firmly.

"Because you had retrieved your asset," she snaps, "and no one there was a liability."

"Correct."

Ralph starts to squirm under my hand, and judging from the amount of white I'm seeing of his eyes, his panic is getting the better of him.

"That's… You're a cold-hearted bastard," she interjects.

I bare my teeth at her. "I'm a soldier of Arcadia," I remind her.

She stares at me for a long time, still furious with me, but when I do nothing but wait for her to say something, she finally sets aside her outrage and thinks about what I just said. And why I am waiting. "He's an asset," she says, nodding toward Ralph.

I take my hand away; gasping and coughing, Ralph scuttles back on the bed until he runs into the headboard; even then, he tries to press himself as far away from me as possible. "Fuck, fuck, fuck," he says when he can breathe more readily. "What the fuck is going on?"

Mere sits down again and her shoulders slump as she leans back against the seat. "You heard him," she says. "He's a soldier. He follows orders." The last word comes out dripping with venom.

"Whose?"

Mere lets loose with a brittle laugh, and Ralph flinches at the sound.

"I don't understand," he whines. "I really don't. This... this is weird, and I don't know what is going on between you two, but it isn't going to be ..."

"Safe?" She shakes her head. "No, it probably isn't going to be. For any of us. So, the question becomes: What do you want, Ralph?"

"What... what do you mean?"

"You want in on this story or not?"

"What story?"

She smiles at him, a predatory curl of her lips. "How much do you know right now? Maybe you can slip some speculation past your boss, but you don't have much and Secutores is going to disappear. Unless you start making wild accusations and then, well, they've set two fires already, right? I don't think they'll have any problem starting a third."

"What about him?" His eyes dart toward me. "What did he say he was? A soldier of what?"

"He's mine," she says flatly. "But you can have the *Liberty* and Eden Park."

He licks his lips carefully, his eyes darting back and forth between us. "And...?" His fear is gone, replaced by an expression not unlike the one I had seen on Mere's face not a few minutes ago. Animal cunning. Looking for an angle.

"Anything more will make you a target," she says. When that doesn't make him blink, she continues. "I'll need someone I can trust for research—quiet research, without attracting attention."

"I'm a staff journalist with the largest independent Australian newspaper," he argues. He sits up straighter as his spine starts to come back. "I'm not an intern."

"Write whatever you want based on any research you do," she says. "But I don't have to tell you why I want things or what my conclusions are."

"Fair enough," he agrees.

"You play games with me, and I cut you off," she says. "You tell anyone *anything* that puts us in danger and—"

"Who would I tell?" he interjects. "I mean, willingly. Right? I know how this works. I'll keep my mouth shut."

"What if Secutores comes looking for you?" I ask.

He takes the question well. "I don't know," he says.

"Tell them everything," I say. "If it comes to torture, don't be a martyr. They'll probably know more than you anyway."

"Oh, that's reassuring. So they'll just be ripping out my fingernails and tasing my testicles because they're *that* sort of psycho perverts?"

"Well, they certainly won't be doing it because they think it'll make me come running to your rescue."

"Yeah." He glances down at his hands, which are balled up into fists in his lap. "I kind of figured that out already."

"What's it going to be, Ralph?" Mere asks again.

He exhales heavily and his fists tighten again. "Nnnnn," he starts, strangling a single letter. "Fuck it. I'm in."

"Okay," she says. "Then it's time for you to go."

"What?" He stares at her, looking as if she had just ripped his heart out and stomped on it.

"Silas says we're leaving," she says. "Do you really want to know where we're going?"

"Oh, right. Right." He nods, caught between elation and disappointment. "Right. I don't even want to know." He pushes away from the headboard and gets off the bed. "Okay, I'm gone. Yeah, I can be gone." He gives me a wide birth, but stops before he reaches the bathroom. "I can work with Secutores setting the fire. I can stir the pot a bit on that. I might even be able to get some speculation going about Kyodo Kujira, but I need something else. Something from the big picture."

Mere nods, and I step over to the dresser/armoire unit and pull out the bottom drawer. I grab the CO_2 pistol and offer it, butt first, to Ralph.

"What is it?" he asks, reaching for it as if it might bite him.

"One of the Secutores agents was carrying it."

"Which one?"

"Does it matter?"

He offers me a wry grin as he plucks the gun from my hand. "No," he says.

"Be careful," Mere says. "Whoever supplied that to Secutores isn't going to be very happy if they find out you have it."

"Yeah," Ralph nods. "I know. He hefts the gun and looks at both of us in turn. "Thanks," he says. "Thanks for the chance, and, uh, thanks for not killing me." The last is directed at me.

"No problem," I say.

"Shit," he says, more to himself than to us, and with that, he darts for the exit, his sense of self-preservation finally getting through to the motion control centers of his brain.

"So," Mere says after the door has shut behind Ralph. "Where are we going?"

"Easter Island," I tell her.

"And how are we getting there? I don't have any identification. I can't get on a plane."

I reach into the back pocket of my pants and produce the fruit of my recent labors. Two passports. "You get to be Madame Moreau, from France."

"I do?"

"I'm your other half, but I'm local—from one of the Marquesas Islands, not far from Tahiti. We met there four years ago. You were part of our archeological tour group. I was your local guide. We feel in love, and we're finally taking our honeymoon. Easter Island for a week and then on to South America. Maybe we'll see the Nazca Lines."

"Seriously?"

"Well, I had to book a flight that would match our story."

"No, the passports. You got them in what? Three hours?"

"I had to use what the guy had in stock."

"*In stock?* You make it sound like you went to a local head shop or something." She slides off the bed and pads over to investigate the folio I offer her. "Where did you get this picture?"

"Off the Internet. I think it's from some Christmas party you attended a few years ago. In Boston. At the mayor's estate. You wore a green—" I bite my tongue. *A green dress.* It had matched her eyes.

She looks at the picture for a moment, one hand idly straying to the scar on her throat. "I looked good that night, didn't I?" she says softly.

"Our flight leaves in two hours," I say gruffly, changing the topic. But it's too late; she's already caught me.

She already knows I was watching her. That's how I knew to step in when Kirkov went crazy, but what she's never known is how long I'd been watching her.

The incident with Kirkov happened in March. Three months after the Christmas party where she wore the green dress.

"I get that it's a romantic destination for a pair of newlywed archeology nuts, but why are *we* going there?" she asks, letting the topic drift happen. "You and I." She shakes her passport at me. "Not these two."

"There's a spa on the island. The soil of Rapa Nui has particular qualities not found anywhere else."

"A spa?" Her eyebrows pull together. "My god, I thought I dreamed you saying that. *A spa.* With native children who will massage my feet? Are you serious?" She gestures toward the door through which Ralph had just left. "You broke me out of an insane asylum, which was burned down hours after we left." She hits me on the chest with her passport. "And we're not done talking about that, by the way."

"I know," I acknowledge.

"You've just scared the shit out of a local contact—and me too, by the way. And if you're halfway not kidding with what you said, then we've got a private security company after us who seem to think they're not beholden to local laws. Or international ones, for that matter. Not to mention whoever hired them. All this, and you want to take me to a fucking spa?"

"An *Arcadian* spa."

"Oh," she blinks.

I tap her passport. "Freshen up, Madame Moreau. We're leaving in twenty minutes."

SEVENTEEN

The passports are functional, and getting on the flight is the least exciting hour we've had in the last day and a half.

Mere was more right than she knew about where I got the forged passports. I had started my search in the local head shops, looking for someone who could provide me with forged passports. I could have asked Callis to make some calls, but I wasn't ready to go there. His comments about knowing me too well stung, as did the impression that he knew more about my activities than he was letting on. For the moment, I wanted to be off everyone's radar.

Cash helped, and I only had to threaten two people before I found someone who could do the work I needed. He wasn't too keen on my deadline, but I was even less keen on waiting, and he became much more accommodating when I took both the knife and gun he was threatening me with and used the sharp one to dismantle the noisy one.

Functional is best. Functional works. Keep things simple.

The soil is good on Rapa Nui, and while looking for Nigel is key, dirt time wouldn't hurt. My equilibrium is off, my reflexes are slow, and my thirst has returned. If I can't go back to Mother, then a trip to the garden and temple—the *spa*—on Easter Island is going to have to do.

Provided it hasn't been completely filled in. Easter Island has changed dramatically over the last few hundred years, and I have some nagging memories of having been there—really nagging memories that I can't get a grip on—but Callis was right. Dirt is dirt. Sometimes we can't be too picky.

The first leg of the flight from Adelaide is a tiny prop-job that gets us to Tahiti's Faa'a International Airport; from there, we get on a slightly larger plane and take a longer flight, one that devours most of the day. And we lose even more time, flying east against the rotation of the planet.

"You're not a fan," she notes, eyeing how tightly I'm holding on to the armrests of my seat.

I manage a weak smile. "I know the science and I've watched birds fly for many, many years, but that doesn't mean I relish pretending to be one."

"Statistically speaking, you're more likely to die in a car accident or from lung cancer than in a plane flight."

Her statistics don't apply to me, and a fall from thirty thousand feet will pancake my body well enough that I might not have enough presence of mind to reconstitute. It's much like being on a boat in the middle of open sea: you tend to be hyper-aware of the ways that can really do you in and to avoid them.

"What's your favorite bird?" she asks, diverting my attention from the window.

"The sparrow."

"Really? I would have thought something more exotic like a kestrel or something."

"Sparrows remind me of home."

"Arcadia?"

I shake my head. "There aren't many birds in Arcadia."

"That's surprising. Isn't it supposed to be like paradise?"

"Blame the Romantic painters."

"I try to as often as possible." Her hand falls on mine, and she gives my fingers a light squeeze. "Especially Bosch."

"He wasn't a Romantic," I point out.

"That's what his wife thought too."

I laugh and turn my hand over so that our palms are touching. A light shiver runs up her arm but she doesn't move her hand. "Arcadia is as much a state of mind as it is a place," I tell her. "And it has changed too, over time. It might have been paradise once, and some will argue that it was the model for the Garden of Eden, but nothing lasts."

"But those who live in Arcadia"—she smiles—"those who, in their minds, dwell in Arcadia, they live longer than the rest of us, don't they?" When I nod, she continues. "How much longer?"

"That, too, is a state of mind," I tell her.

"How long for you?" she persists.

"You remember when you asked me who I was thinking about earlier?

Her name was Valentien. She died on the fourteenth of May, 1940, when Germany tried to wipe Rotterdam off the map. I was... I looked not much older than I do now. Well, the last few days haven't been terribly good. I'm sure I'm showing my age now."

"Hardly," she snorts. "But you do age, don't you? Or is that part... that part of those half-kernel folklore stories you were talking about earlier true?"

"I have good genes, and I heal well. That's a lot of it. 'Aging' is a process wherein cells die and aren't replaced. Where organs fail and the body decays. If you can stop all that, you essentially stop aging."

"And how do you stop it?"

"Ancient family secret."

"So someone knows?"

"Once upon a time, I suppose. We have to"—I cast about for the right words—"we have to trust our intuition when it comes to new members. They have to be of the right genetic proclivity."

"A mutation?"

"Somewhat. More of a throwback."

She smiles. "You're a knuckle-dragger? Somewhere between *Homo erectus* and *Homo sapien*?"

I close my hand and she wraps her fingers around my fist. "Somewhere," I say.

"How long?" she persists.

"A long time, Mere. A very long time."

V V

"Why were you on the *Cetacean Liberty*?" she asks a little while later. The flight is only half full, and the people seated near us are all catching up on the sleep they missed getting out of bed for this flight. Mere isn't interested in sleeping. Too much on her mind. "All four of you were—are—Arcadians?"

"Yes. Our mission was to investigate the whaling fleet. We had been led to believe they were doing illegal research. They weren't catching whales for food; they were doing studies on whale tissue for use in protein therapeutics."

"I heard the same thing," she says. "I was chasing a story on nootropics. A company out of Denver, Colorado. There's a complicated money structure behind them, a bunch of shells formed in the mid-'90s when the big agriculture and chemical companies started to diversify their holdings in an effort to lessen their visibility. Mitratech, Subloftco, AFH Venture

Group, Petriluminent, Hyacinth Holdings, Ionophaze: there's a long list. Most of them don't even know where their money is coming from. They, in turn, fund little biotech and biochem startups that focus on one product. The product does well, though its main buyers are part of the vast web of subsidiaries who rely on that product for their own efforts, and so on and so on. It keeps on going, and I keep thinking there's one master product that all of these little pieces are contributing to, but I can't figure out what it is.

"Anyway, this company out of Denver—Mnemosysia—is doing something with memory retention, and they've done some early Phase II tests in animals that have gotten some people at Stanford excited. There was a paper in one of the journals last year about some enzyme found in whale brains—blue whale brains—and this company thinks they've managed to replicate it in the laboratory. Groups like Prime Earth were all up in arms, of course, because the foundation of the research stems from having to, you know, dissect a blue whale brain."

"They're not very good at volunteering," I point out.

"No, they're not. So, I hear—via a circuitous chain of sources—that Mnemosysia's research is bogus. The enzyme is real enough, but their synthetic version has nasty side-effects and about a third of the efficacy of the naturally occurring enzyme. Mnemosysia is feeling pressure from someone else, someone who needs their product to work."

She leans toward me, her hand tightening on my arm. "This is the problem of sourcing your own product chain, right? It's like a pyramid. You need everything in each of the layers so that you can build up and reach that top point. But what happens when some part of the base doesn't work? Does the whole pyramid collapse?"

"So Mnemosysia started looking for a shortcut."

"Yes. The complicating part is that Kyodo Kujira wasn't talking about who was funding them. Mnemosysia would have benefited from the research, and there's a paper trail linking both Kyodo Kujira and Mnemosysia— they'd had a few exploratory conversations—but Mnemosysia is on life support. They don't have the ready cash to fund the whaling expedition."

"So the money is coming from somewhere else," I say. "And you think that company is the one who set up the tests."

She nods. "They used Mnemosysia as a lure, to get you to commit a team to the *Cetacean Liberty.*"

"Do you think Mnemosysia knows they were set up?"

She laughs. "When I'm really paranoid, I think Mnemosysia never had a product. I think they're a complete shell, and their only purpose was to look real enough to get your attention. But that means whoever is running things has been working on this for a long time."

"A long memory," I muse.

"There are only a couple of multi-national corporations that have that sort of corporate intelligence. Most of them go back nearly a hundred years. They got started in completely different markets—industrial chemicals, rubber, plastics. They've only drifted toward Big Ag and GMOs and biotech because their older markets have become completely poisoned with lawsuits and the market margins have all shrunk to nothing."

"You knew," I realize, "you said something else on the boat. Something about a cost associated with what we were doing out there. A danger we didn't know about."

It is her turn to hesitate, and I find myself unconsciously leaning toward her, my curiosity aroused.

"Upper Management at Prime Earth knew," she admits. "They knew Kyodo Kujira's fleet wasn't whaling, but they didn't tell Captain Morse. I didn't know why, and at first, I thought my source had been wrong, but then the four of you showed up in Adelaide and I knew. Mnemosysia was a lure. The whole setup was about Arcadia."

I swallow heavily and look away. Confirmation of what I told Callis. Arcadia is at risk. He's right. There is some poison in our roots.

"Something happened to one of your team—Nigel—when you went out to the whaler. Was it the weed killer?" she asks.

"Yes," I say. "Different dispersal method, but it was the same agent."

"And it's fatal to you, to your kind?"

"Eventually," I force the word out of my tight throat.

"Why do they want to kill you?"

"For the same reason any homeowner wants to get rid of any pernicious weed that is marring their otherwise pristine lawn."

She nods. "You said 'steward' earlier. You mean it, don't you? In, like, a *global* sense."

"Yes. But it's more than just us versus whoever wants us gone." I nod around at the other passengers. "Everyone is contributing to the disease that is slowly wiping us out. These companies think they can fix things with GMO seeds and new pesticides, but they don't have the long view. They're denying what the rest of humanity is doing every day."

"Doing what?"

"You're killing the planet, Mere. All of you. It's ecocide."

EIGHTEEN

Once we reach Rapa Nui, we pass through customs at Mataveri International Airport without much trouble. The agent inspecting our single suitcase raises an eyebrow at our minimalist packing until I say the word "honeymoon" and glance suggestively at Mere, who has the good grace to blush appropriately. The agent smirks, his eyes lingering on Mere's breasts, and stamps our passports, a quaint custom that hasn't gone out of style on Rapa Nui. It's the first real mark of approval these papers have seen.

Outside the airport, the air is warm and turgid. I have a headache from all the sun, and I collapse on the hard seats in the back of a cab, leaning to the side so that my head is out of the direct sunlight. I'm wearing my optics and they're dialed all the way down. I hear Mere ask the cabbie to take us to the best hotel on the island. "Yes," she says in response to his reply. "The Hanga Roa Royal Resort is fine."

The car lurches off, and we ride in silence for a few minutes. The windows of the cab are rolled down, and there is little breeze. The scent of Mere's skin wafts through the cab.

"Are they all like that?" she asks suddenly. "Looking inland."

I don't have to open my eyes to know what she's talking about. The *moai,* one of the impassive stone heads the island is known for.

I grunt enough of a response for her to know I'm listening.

"I've seen pictures," she says, "but it's a matter of context, I guess. You see the heads, and you know they're on an island and that they're remnants of some strange Cargo Cult religion. You just assume, I guess, that they're all facing outward."

"They were tribute, built by the natives in recognition of the clan leaders," I tell her. "Kind of like the pyramids in Egypt. Most of the *moai* were knocked over and broken shortly after the European discovery of the island. Inter-clan conflicts. You tend to break the other team's stuff, you know?"

She slaps my leg playfully and her touch is almost enough to get me to open my eyes. "Men," she says. "It never changes, does it?"

I think of the reasons why the Achaeans came east, their army covering the Plain of Skamandros like black ants. "No, it doesn't."

VV

The day clerk at the hotel finds us a mid-sized suite on the inland side of the hotel, and I hang back as Mere crosses to the heavy curtains and pulls them open. There's a sliding door behind them, and a narrow balcony. Mere opens the door and lets the warm air in as she steps out onto the balcony. The sun is a hand's-width over the horizon—the ragged edge of the dome of Rano Kau, one of the three volcanoes that make up the island. Lightening my optics a few clicks, I step up to the sliding glass door, bracing myself for what I'm going to see, what I've been avoiding.

But I have to.

"You look like someone ran over your dog," she says when she notices my expression.

"This island used to be covered with trees," I sigh. "I knew there had been a collapse, but I hadn't been…" I hadn't been paying attention.

"What are you, the Lorax?" She means the question as a joke, but it comes off too brittle, too close to the truth, and I can tell she regrets the jab as soon as she says it.

I've been trying to remember when I was here last, and my memory has holes. Has it been that long? When did the Dutch discover the island? Seventeenth century? Eighteenth?

"This used to be covered with a forest of broadleaf trees." I sweep my arm to indicate the nearby hills, covered with green grasses. "Toromiro and palm trees." I lean heavily against the frame of the door. "It takes more than a hundred years for the palms to grow to their full height. Why didn't they replant? Why was this place abandoned?"

"By who?" she asks quietly. "Arcadia or the natives? We're hundreds of miles from anywhere. If the ecosystem of the island gave out, how could the residents survive?"

What happened? My legs are weak, and I'm oddly short of breath. The skin on my back starts to prickle, a thousand needles jabbing at my burned skin. The thirst is building and, deep in my blood, something bubbles. An alien presence trying to change me. "I need to lie down," is what I say, but what I need is to sleep in the ground. I need to be covered in humus, the rich loam of the earth. My hands ache. The desire to dig is overwhelming.

As is the desire to hurt someone.

There were trees here the last time I was on Rapa Nui. Why can't I remember what happened? What has Mother taken from me?

❦❦

When I open my eyes again, the sun has slipped from the sky. A tiny breeze is flowing through the open glass door, and it toys with the bottom edge of the curtain. I smell cooked food and spices—lots of spices—and the potpourri of scents drags me upright.

Mere is sitting at the table, on which are several trays from room service. "I ordered a couple of things," she says, "figuring maybe some food would do you some good. It's mostly vegetarian with some fish. Is that okay? I didn't know if you needed raw meat or something…"

"It's fine," I manage. I take off my optics and blink heavily for a moment or two as my eyes water. "I don't eat a lot of meat."

"Really? But, don't you—?"

"I'm not a meat sucker, Mere. I don't need to cut up cubes of sirloin and stick them in my cheek for an hour."

"Thank God for that. You'd have the nastiest breath."

I sit down at the table with her, and my stomach makes a noisy rumble as I reach for a plate. I am hungry, and the hotel has a surprisingly good menu. There is baked shrimp with fennel and feta. Pan-seared cauliflower with wild rice and a rich tomato pesto colored like the heart of the sun. A plate of marinated eggplant, chilis, and—I have to taste the sauce to be sure—burrata over brown rice pasta. A slab of seared salmon with a black and shiny tapenade of anchovies and olive, complete with a sprig of freshly harvested rosemary lying idly across the top.

The food will help me not think about the fluttering pulse in her neck. She's pulled back her hair, showing a lot of the pale skin there.

"You were angry," she says after I've loaded my plate and started to shovel the food into my mouth. "While you were … *resting*, I guess you could call it. I tried to talk to you once or twice, but you snarled at me." She shows me her teeth like she's an angry dog. "I figured it was best to leave you alone. I was going to go out, but I didn't want to leave you here on the off-chance that…" She shrugs. "So I ordered food. It's always a good idea when you don't know what to do next, right? Get a meal in because you can't be sure when the next one is going to happen."

"It's a good plan," I say around a mouthful of broccoli.

She smiles, and her hand drifts up to the scar at the base of her throat. It's not very deep, but it will always be there, a curling reminder of how close she came to dying. Kirkov had been an old soldier; his brain didn't even need to tell his muscles what to do anymore. He operated on instinct, and part of him had sensed me coming. He had already started cutting when I put my hand through his chest.

"When you and the others came onboard the *Liberty*, you brought your best *don't fuck with us* vibe. It worked well, didn't it? They left you alone, but then, most of the kids on the boat had never been at sea before, much less taking part of in an environmental protest. I could make any number of them cry just by raising my voice. I've been around meth heads who've totally lost it, some bad-ass mercenaries who could probably kill me as easily as they picked their teeth with a toothpick, and a couple of political lobbyists who would sell a busload of their own children if it meant ramming a bill through Congress. It was going to take a little more to scare me off."

She shakes her head slightly, gathering a bit of courage, and continues. "You know what frightened me the most about being held over the railing? It's wasn't being held out like that. That was terrifying, sure, but what really scared me was the look on your face."

I pause, half a wide rice noodle hanging out of my mouth. "Like this?" I squint at her.

She smiles politely, but her fingers are still toying with the flesh of her throat. "No," she says. "I saw it on the others too. That day, on the *Cetacean Liberty*, when the harpoon boats got into trouble…"

She's reticent to talk about it and I haven't pressed her so far, knowing she'd tell me when the time came.

"I tried to get onto the bridge after you came storming out, but the other one—Talus?—he ordered the crewmen to take me below deck. I nailed one of the pair in the groin, but the other one got his arms around me. They were more frightened of Talus than me—and I can't blame them—and they were only going to get rougher with me if I kept fighting them. So I let them take me, and just as we were going down the stairs, I heard the first of the gun shots. That was Phoebe, right? With some sort of sniper rifle?"

I nod, still eating, but listening intently to her story.

"I thought I had seen her, up in the prow," Mere continues. "I didn't find out until later that she was clearing a path for you. You went out to one of the harpoon boats, didn't you? You and Nigel, both. You each took a boat."

"Nigel went rogue," I correct her. "He went off on his own and attacked the first boat. By the time Phoebe and I had gotten involved, it was already well underway."

"Nigel? Rogue? Is that what you think happened?" She shook her head. "An hour before, I had run into him coming out of the cabin you all shared. He had *that look* on his face. He stopped when he saw me, and when I squeezed past him, I saw Talus standing in the room, watching me too. I'm pretty good at reading people, Silas. They had made a decision. I was terrified when I realized what it was, and I didn't know what to do. Who could I tell? You? I had no idea if you weren't part of it. Captain Morse would have shit himself with fear if I had gone to him, and then he would have jumped overboard and been happily eaten by a shark. I went down to the mess and sat with as many people as I could find. It wasn't a good solution, but all I could hope was that all those innocent kids would be enough of a deterrent to keep Nigel away from me. But I knew they wouldn't. If he had wanted to kill me, it wouldn't have mattered how many there were. He would have killed them all to get to me."

She's not family. Remember your priorities.

I can't argue with anything she's said and so I don't try, keeping my attention on the food. There's a few slices of thin bread made from cassava flour on the tray, and I mop up the remaining bites on my plate. The tension in my muscles is easing and my skin is softening. I'm hydrating, but not quickly enough. I pour myself a glass of water from the pitcher and drain it quickly. The water is good too, untainted by too many cycles of filtering and chemical softening.

"But Nigel wasn't coming after you," I say, prompting her to continue her story. Nigel was going over the railing to assault the first harpoon boat. And Talus knew. His orders on the bridge made an ugly sense in light of Mere's story. He knew I wouldn't have agreed with his decision to fight back, and so he had had to create a situation where I would be inclined to do what he wanted. Where I would *volunteer*. With me gone, there would only be Phoebe to protect the crew of the *Cetacean Liberty*.

"When the shooting started, I was locked in my cabin," she continues, her frustration at being kept away from the action clear in her voice. "I made a racket for a while, more angry than anything else, and then I started to hear other people shouting and… screaming. And then it got real quite. I hid, or tried to, actually. There's not a lot of places to hide in those cabins. After a few hours, I started to wonder what was going to happen if no one ever came looking for me. How was I going to get out of this cabin? Was there anyone piloting the boat?

"I was starting to get hungry and having my second or third panic attack about being trapped, when I heard someone tapping at my door. It was the old guy, Gus—the engineer who'd been in Vietnam. He had been hiding down in the engine room. Once things quieted down, he started to sneak around the boat to see who was still alive. He found me and a couple of others. Gus had the clever idea of hiding in your cabin—the room where you four all stayed. At first, I thought it was a terrible idea, but he explained that none of you were on the boat anymore."

"What happened?"

She shakes her head. "I don't know. I asked everyone we rescued, but no one knew anything. They had all been below deck when things had gone sideways. By the time Gus let me out, the Japanese were running things."

"The Japanese? From the whaling fleet?"

"Captain Morse—or whoever was in charge on the bridge—sailed the *Cetacean Liberty* right up to the processing ship and handed it over. The Japanese put a crew on board and turned the boat around for Adelaide."

"Why?"

She shrugs. "I don't know. We stayed out of sight. They didn't come looking for us. But they had to know we were there. And they didn't care."

"What happened?"

"There was some British guy with them. Hard-looking guy. At the time I thought he was military of some sort, but now, I realize he was probably Secutores. Short gray hair, well-groomed stubble like he'd just come from a fashion shoot. I only caught sight of him a couple of times before Gus insisted I stay in the cabin. Anyway, as soon as we hit the Bight, there was another boat. The enforcer and his crew took off; Gus said it sounded like they were using a go-fast boat. 'Two engines, maybe a thousand horses,' is what he said. Ten minutes later, the bomb went off and the fire started.

"That's when we found out who was still on the boat; we could hear them screaming and shouting. Me and Tawni—she was the one who had the orca tattoo on the back of her neck—well, anyway, she and I tried to get all the rooms open, get people out and on deck where the life boats were. Gus and some of the other guys tried to fight the fire, but it spread too fast. It all happened so quickly. We didn't have any time. We barely got the life boats in the water in time. And then there was nothing we could do except wait for someone to spot the smoke."

"How many made it into the lifeboats?"

"I don't know. There were three boats. There were six—seven?—in the one I ended up in. At least that many in the others. I… don't really know. And once we got picked up and taken to the hospital, it was chaotic. There were lawyers from Prime Earth there. The police showed up. Hospital security was trying to get everyone out of the way. It was a mess. I don't even remember a lot of it. The next morning, the guys in dark suits show up, and I know they're friends of the guy from the boat."

"Secutores."

She nods. "And that's when I knew we were going to disappear. Those of us who were coherent enough to talk about what had happened. I had to get out of there or get a message out to someone, but before I could do anything, the nurses came in and put me out. When I woke up… well, I didn't really wake up again. Not until you came." She flushes slightly, and turns her attention to her food, which she has barely touched. "Your turn," she says. "What happened to you?"

I give her the short version—glossing over the parts where people died. She pretends not to notice the judicious editing.

NINETEEN

She wanders out onto the balcony again when we're done eating, and I stack dishes and clean up—giving her some space—before I join her. The sky is wide above us, and a bat flies by, a dark rag fluttering across a panoply of glittering stars.

"What's next?" she asks.

"Out there, past the airport, is Rano Kau," I say, pointing off into the darkness. "The island was formed by three volcanoes, which extruded over a relative short span of time—geologically speaking. Rano Kau was one of the last ones to form, and the rim of the crater makes for a good wind break. It makes for a good micro-climate: warmed by geothermals, a couple of rain basins that are large enough to call lakes, and a rich soil."

"Sort of like Ka-Zar's Savage Land."

"Whose?"

"Ka-Zar. He's a—never mind. Yes, I read comics as a kid. I was *that* girl."

"And look at you now. All grown up."

"Mostly." She looks at me over her shoulder, and I can see her face quite well in the ambient light. There is an impish curl on her lips. She leans back slightly, bumping her shoulder against me.

I don't know how I'm supposed to react. She's been sending me a variety of signals, and I've been wrestling with my own... what? To call it a *long-standing fascination* is to dissemble. To downplay what I've been feeling.

"There's a break in the rim of the crater," I say, ignoring the signals I may or may not be getting. "You can look out over the ocean there; it became a place where the natives performed religious ceremonies. Over time, they built a village."

"So there was a cult here," she says.

"Not a Cargo Cult. This was earlier, and it wasn't reliant upon manna dropping from Heaven as part of the ritual celebrations. It was called *tangata manu*. A bird cult."

"Didn't the Cargo Cults worship birds too—as in the giant planes that dropped supplies?"

"This was a different sort of bird cult."

"Did they worship chickens or something?"

"Terns, actually."

"Isn't that the local equivalent?" I can tell she's playing with me, and I find it both intriguing and distracting.

"The *tangata manu* rite was a manhood ritual," I say, keeping on topic. "Every year, hardy warriors from the tribes would gather at Orongo and they would race to see who could get to a tiny atoll that lies offshore. They would dive and swim to this rock and try to be the first one to collect an egg from one of the terns that nested there. They're not chickens, but they might as well be, as ubiquitous as they are. Though, by some quirk, they only nest on Motu Nui—the atoll—and not on the main island."

"A quirk, eh?"

"Well, if I were to hazard a guess, I'd say the island shamans banded together and wiped them out on the island. After a generation or two, the terns probably got the hint and stayed away."

"Smart birds."

"The guy who finds an egg first gets to stay on the rock as long as he likes—meditating, praying, whatever it is they think they're supposed to do—and then he comes back to the Orongo and gives the egg to his patron, who becomes the *tangata manu* for the next season."

"The bird man," she nods. "Does he get to wear a funny hat?"

"Of course. It's not a cult if it doesn't involve a funny hat."

"Okay," she laughs. "So what does this have to do with why we're here?"

"The *tangata manu* got to help tend the trees that grew in the crater. For that year, they were apprenticed to the steward of the garden. What they learned about tending the trees and the soil was knowledge they got to take back to their tribe. Remember how I said that the dirt here is different? Cultivating it was an ancient secret that was critical to any tribes' success in the growing season. The *tangata manu*'s tribe would be assured of having a good harvest the year after their champion won."

"They grew the trees everywhere else," Mere says.

I nod. "But they're all gone now, which means—" I pause as bits of memory fall into place in my head. White wings. Waves. Torchlight. An arc of carved stone. Figures of birdmen.

"The steward left," Mere finishes for me. "Is that why the island died?"

"I don't remember," I say.

VV

I should go alone, but Mere pretends not to hear me when I suggest the idea. It's not far to the crater—a couple of kilometers—but we have to go around the airport. It'd be easy enough to rent a bicycle from the hotel, but doing so at this time of night is just going to draw attention to us. We keep it simple instead, and as soon as we walk a block from the hotel, I pick her up and start jogging.

She feels good, nestled against my chest, her head tucked against my shoulder.

An airplane howls overhead as I follow the road around the end of Mataveri's main runway, and instead of sticking with the road as it doubles back on itself toward the main terminal, I head overland. It takes me about an hour to jog up the hill, and I'm out of breath when we reach the top and I put her down. I don't want to look, afraid I'm going to see as desolate a landscape as the sere terrain surrounding the city, but to my surprise, the valley of the crater is carpeted with a lush forest.

"Are there any trees?" she asks, unable to see as clearly as I can.

"Yes," I say, my voice breaking. "There are a lot of them."

"Silas." She fumbles for my arm, and I try to suppress the shiver that runs through my flesh as her fingers get hold of me. "When was the last time you were here? There haven't been trees on Easter Island for more than a hundred years."

"I know."

"When we were on the plane you said something about remembering World War II, and you said you were older than that. When I asked you how old, you dodged my question." Her hand tightens on my arm. "I know we laughed about the *vampire* thing, and what you said about being a *Dardanoi*…"

Her brain is starting to insist on some answers. Things are becoming too real. I understand her confusion—I have my own. She can't make the pieces work without accepting some things as being truth that are difficult to swallow.

"I was here," I admit. My memories are still fragmented, like the leftover pottery shards that get folded into raw soil. The growing loam.

"Are you familiar with Sirolimus?" I ask, changing the subject. "It's an immunosuppressant, used primarily to treat patients who've received organ transplants. It is sourced from a bacterium only found here in the island."

I close my eyes and try to remember the way Rano Kau used to be. "We cultivated a number of fragile species in the garden down there. Species of tree and bush that had gone extinct elsewhere in the world. It was its own ecosystem, and we had saved it. The soil here—the humus—is incredibly rich, almost the perfect proportions. In fact, we tried to grow a sapling from"—I pause, catching myself—"from an old, old tree that we had been tending for centuries. Our cutting lasted longer than a lot of people thought it would, but it didn't survive."

It was too far from Mother. Or too close, perhaps.

"Why is the soil important?" she asks. "Is it for you? Do you need to... you know, sleep in the ground?"

"We can. We do. But most of the ground has been tainted by all the chemicals leaching in from landfills or what seeps into the ground after being dumped in streams. We need clean dirt, and that's what this ground is. This garden and our steward were always here, even after the island was *discovered* by European explorers."

The image of a headdress of white feathers floats through my head. As does the sensation of jumping off a cliff. And black streaks on skin, like ash mixed with tears. I'm starting to build context. Remembering why I should know this place.

"I need to rest," I say, pushing the images aside. They're still a distracting mess. "My immune system is compromised. I need to flush my system clean. Any of the others would have the same need. They'd come here for the same reasons."

"And here we are," she says, "and there are trees, so what is the problem?"

"Why are there only trees here?" I ask. "If there is a steward here still, why did they let the rest of the island die?"

"We should go ask," she points out. "I wish I could see something," she sighs.

"This is why I didn't want you to come with me," I remind her. "I should take you back to the hotel."

"Yeah, well, that's not going to happen," she replies. "I should have brought a flashlight."

I offer her my optics. "Try these."

They're too big for her face, but she stuffs the ends of them into her hair and they look like they'll stay in place well enough. I show her how to work them, and as I do, her hand naturally rests on my hip. "Wow," she grins as she looks around. "These are cool. I knew being obstinate would totally work in my favor."

She fiddles with the settings, and I take advantage of her hand moving away to step out of her line of sight.

"Oh," she says, grabbing my arm without missing. "I see something. There's a blob out there. Sort of red and yellow."

"It's a heat bloom," I say, realizing she's got the thermal filter on. "Ambient heat. Usually from a building."

"Maybe it's Orongo," she suggests, "though…" She cocks her head to one side as if the change in perspective will help her decipher what she is seeing.

"It can't be," I tell her. "Orongo is on the western rim of the crater." She's looking off to our left, and since we're facing nearly south, she's looking in the wrong direction. My night vision is good, but whatever heat signature she has spotted is too subtle for me to pick out.

"It's almost like a cross."

"There shouldn't be anything like that out there. The natives weren't Christian. Nor would they build something like that if they were."

"Well, there's something out there now." She offers me the optics. "Here. Look for yourself."

I do, and I can tune the settings more delicately than she can. The shape wavers, solidifies.

"It's a building," I announce. "Four wings off a central hub."

"Well, I guess I know where we're going, then."

I hand back the optics. "I guess so."

Why would Arcadia build something like that?

V V

We work our way down the sloping rim of the crater and enter the rows of trees, and I'm struck almost immediately by the methodical organization of the trees.

There are toromiro, of course, a leafy tree almost fernlike in its appearance; it used to cover the hills of Rapa Nui. Ranks of miro stand in stately lines, while clumps of carambola—star fruit trees—huddle together like displaced children. I think I smell the tang of citrus trees, though I haven't seen any yet. There are several different species of palm trees, as well as two varieties of the plant whose fruit is known as the miracle berry. Both of these last two species are native to Africa, and their presence crystallizes a suspicion that has been building in the back of my brain.

"It's amazing," Mere says. The moon has risen, and she's taken off the optics as there's enough light to follow the track between the rows of trees. "It's a tree farm."

"Yes," I say, "but it's not right."

"What's wrong with this? There are species here that live nowhere else, right? I thought you'd be more excited about it."

"I am. Don't get me wrong. I thought the toromiro were extinct." I wave a hand up and down the row we're walking along. "But this isn't, well, *organic*. Notice how the toromiro are all exactly the same distance from one another." I point at the next row. "See those over there? Those are tualang. They're not much taller than the toromiro now, but give them time and they can grow to heights of more than seventy-five meters. Bees like them. The sorts of bees that build nests a meter across. They're not terribly aggressive, which makes it easy to harvest their honey and beeswax."

"So there are bees here too?"

"Perhaps. The use of honey as an antiseptic goes back thousands of years."

"You said this was a spa. That's exactly the sort of thing I'd expect to find here. The bacteria you were talking about earlier. The honey from bees. It all sounds like the sort of things you'd find at a private Beverly Hills spa for the stupidly rich."

"It's the organization," I say. "The building, too." It's obvious to me, and I know why she doesn't see it as I do. She's never been underground; she's never experienced the fulsome chaos of the systemic nervous system of plant life. The way roots of different species—weeds, flowers, shrubs, trees—all share the same space, the same water and nutrients. It only looks chaotic from the outside. If you are in it—if you can sense every other root and tendril around you—then it becomes part of you. Order out of chaos.

"This is too much like an orchard or a vineyard—the sort of layout that makes it easy to harvest fruit. This is order for order's sake," I explain. "This is the way corporations think."

That stops her. "Big Ag?"

I shake my head. "Does the thought of a multinational agricultural conglomerate investing in a tree farm in the middle of the Pacific Ocean make sense to you?"

"Only if there is a functional profit model. But why couldn't this be an Arcadian project?"

"We don't do things this way," I point out. "We know better."

"Silas," she says, tapping her lower lip as she walks along the row. "I don't like this. It doesn't track well."

I'm having similar thoughts. "I know." Secutores is the security arm of some corporate entity, one that has the wherewithal to make the chemical weed killer. There's no reason they couldn't also have an arm that does pharmaceutical or biotech research. I start to replay my conversation with Callis, wondering if there was something I missed.

"Silas," she says again.

"What?"

"There's a road."

I hurry over to where she is standing. I had thought the gap between the rows of trees was a grid border—how the planners were separating the distinct plots of specific tree species. But it is definitely a road of packed dirt, wide enough that two cars could squeeze past each other. I kneel and scrape up a handful of the dirt, sniffing it carefully. I don't smell anything terribly pungent and I taste the dirt cautiously.

"Okay," Mere says. "What are you doing?"

It's faint, but there's a bitterness to the soil that shouldn't be there. "They cleared this path," I say after spitting the dirt out.

"Cleared it? How?"

"I don't know, but it's not as toxic as I thought it might be."

"And yet I have just watched you eat dirt because you wanted to check toxicity?"

"TCDD," I say. "It's a persistent contaminant found in dioxins, which are the basis for a lot of herbicides."

"So you were tasting for poison. In the dirt."

"Yes. There was growth here that needed to be cleared away. Look, the Amazon rain forest takes up how much of Brazil?"

"Most of it?"

"And yet it started as a tree farm."

"It did?"

"Yes, but the natives didn't farm all of it. They only farmed the areas that were convenient for them. The rest they let grow wild. Over several thousand years. It didn't happen overnight. There is a mix of order and chaos in the arrangement of the trees." I gesture at the rows of trees around us. "This is order." I point at the road. "This is order, too, but it came *after* the trees. Do you see?"

"I get it," she says, nodding and looking at the trees again. "Not all of these trees are farmed. Some of them were here originally. Someone came later and, well, *farmed* it, I guess."

"And at that time, they needed a road."

"And someplace to hang out, like the cross-shaped building I saw." She nods and claps her hands together. "Well, mystery solved then. Is there more dirt eating to do or can we go find this place?"

"After you," I say, gesturing along the road.

We keep it on our left, walking between the rows of trees, and it doesn't take us long to reach the building site. It's not far from the wall of the crater, about a half kilometer from the gap which looks out over the ocean. There's nothing graceful about the building. It's made from pre-fab Chinese materials, and it looks like it was spit out of a first year architecture student's design program. Everything is framed by right angles. Calling it *utilitarian* would be to upsell the intent of the builders.

There are no external lights, though I can hear the distant rumble of a generator running. Motion-sensitive lamps run along the roofline, and we stay beneath the trees so as to not inadvertently announce ourselves. A field of antennae and a pair of satellite dishes huddle together on the roof of the northern wing. The only doors are an unmarked set in the front. There are no windows and no second floor, though over the central hub, there is a square concrete block—the sort of shape that would house the machinery for an elevator.

"What is it?" Mere asks when I lean against a nearby tree and massage my temples.

The memories are coming back again. The open sky. White feathers. Old stone carvings. A cistern of cold water. None of it is connected to anything, though. It's all out of reach. I've had this happen before, when I've gone someplace familiar. It kicks things loose. I know Mother helps us carry the burden of our years when we go into her embrace, and it rarely is a problem. Not like this.

"It's nothing," I say. I stare at Mere's moonlit face, her features knotted with concern, and I realize I can't remember what happened after I took Kirkov's knife.

Nothing is both a lie and the truth. There are chemicals in my blood. TCDDs, even. While I may have staved off the worst of the poisonous effects, there are some lingering malignances that are causing decay.

Remember your priorities. The voice in my head isn't mine, and it isn't Talus's either. Who said that to me first, or was it something beaten into the meat of my brain by years of soldering? *Know your mission. Make it to the next checkpoint. Don't think about the big picture, son. You're not trained to think. You're trained to kill. Kill one of the enemy. Find another one. Repeat. Keep it simple.* So many variations over the centuries. Don't think. Mind the plan.

Memory is insidious. It can become a burden too heavy to carry. That is why we let Mother leach it away when we rest in her embrace. *There. There. Let me take care of everything. Let Mother take away the pain.*

Remember your priorities. Survive. Kill everyone else.

No, that's not true.

I remember the boat and the storm. Aeneas holding on to the tiller. His eyes forward, not looking back. "Remember our families," he shouts at me.

Remember those we left behind.

I slump against the trunk. It's a Surian cedar. Australian Red Gold. Our boat was made from cedar planks, though the cedars of the ancient Mediterranean were much different from their Australian counterparts—not even the same family. But the wood, the wood was the same: strong, resilient. So much of history was built from trees like this. So much history was... burned.

I jerk upright, startling Mere who was reaching out to shake me.

"Smoke," I say. "I smell smoke."

It's faint, the sort of distant aroma of a wood fire a thousand yards away, and it's not from wood. There are chemicals in the smoke too. Plastics. Synthetic fibers. Paper. "You saw a heat bloom," I remind Mere.

She fumbles for my optics, puts them on, and stares at the building. "It's the whole building," she says, "but it's more yellow than red now."

"Because it is cooling off."

I walk out into the open area that has been cleared around the building. Mere squeaks behind me, but when nothing happens—when the motion-sensitive lights don't flash on—she follows. I walk up to the front doors of the lab and touch the panels gingerly. They're warmer than the outside air, but not by much. "There's been a fire," I tell Mere as she comes up behind me. "The building is a hermetic environment. Nothing gets in or out."

"Wait," Mere says as I grab the handle of the door. "If the fire has burned everything inside, then it's an oxygen starved environment. What happens when you open that door?"

"Nothing." I tap my ear. "Do you hear it? There's a generator running somewhere. And I can smell the burn. It's faint, but it's there. An environmental system is still running. There's a tiny leak somewhere."

There's a keycard reader next to the door, but the activity lights on it are dark. I brute force the door, and for a half-second, I fear Mere is right. The fire is waiting for us, and I've just given it a big dose of fresh air. But all that comes out of the lab is a foul commingling of everything that has been burned.

TWENTY

We prop the door open and wait a little while, just to be sure. When nothing seems to change, we venture inside.

The lab is dark, both from a lack of light and from the layer of ash that covers everything. The fire burned while it could, and the more combustible materials went up quickly. If there was a fire suppression system, it never went off. The walls are scorched black, the paint and wallpaper gone. Metal struts for movable walls and desk units are still there, but the synthetic and plastic overlays are all melted or gone. There's a large planter—several meters in diameter—in the center of the lobby that held a few flowering shrubs, but they're nothing but blackened sticks poking out of char-covered dirt.

There are a few bodies too, twisted in unnatural positions. Mere gags when we find the first one, though she doesn't vomit. "Were they dead before the fire reached...?" she mumbles through her hand.

"From smoke inhalation?" I shrug. "Let's hope so."

There are four wings off the central hub: the entrance, where the few rooms off the central hallway seem to have been administrative; two research wings, though it is difficult to tell exactly what sort of research was done—the lab equipment (what hasn't been melted and charred by the fire) is used for chemical analysis, protein therapy studies, and biological tissue analysis; and the last wing, opposite the entrance, that looks to be more administrative services—executive offices, a kitchen, a quartet of conferences rooms, and a break room. The elevator in the central hub has a large set of doors—freight-sized doors. There is only one button on the pad next to the doors, and it isn't marked.

"Only one way to go," Mere says. "Down." She pushes the button, and nothing happens.

She's sweating. The ambient temperature inside the lab is higher than outside, and not just because the central air handling system has failed.

It hasn't been that long since the fire snuffed itself out.

"There has to be another access," I point out. "Where's all the heat exchanges, the air control infrastructure? It's not up on the roof, which means it's all below ground. That has to vent somewhere."

She nods. "And the server room. I see computer workstations, but where does the network collapse back to?"

It's odd there's only one door into the building. No windows. No emergency exits. A good design criteria if you are building something that can be hermetically sealed, but, well, Mere and I are looking at what happens when good designs become deathtraps.

There's an unmarked door near the end of the right-hand lab wing that is thicker than the others. The seal hisses when I pull it open, and colder air wafts out. Stairs, going down. We prop this door open too, and descend, feeling our way in the dark.

We reach a landing and find—by feel—another heavy door. I force it open, and weak light streams out into the stairwell. Emergency lighting, a track of tiny lights that runs along the ceiling of the hallway beyond. The hallway is nondescript and I spot a few generalized signs. Maintenance and HVAC systems. Separate from the lab upstairs, and unaffected by the fire. They're in low power mode, but they're still functional.

"We should find flashlights," Mere says, squeezing past me.

I hesitate, looking back at the stairs that continue going down. The walls of the stairwell aren't the same prefab material of the lab. They're actually stone. We're in the bedrock of the island.

"This stairwell predates the lab," I point out. "I know what's down there." The old temple.

"Silas," Mere says, "wait a second, will you?" She's found a panel in the wall, a recessed locker of some kind. She rummages through its contents and produces a heavy flashlight. Shining its beam around, she does a quick visual check of the hall and then comes back to me. "Okay," she says, "let's go."

I let her lead and we descend one more floor. She shines the light down the next flight, and the stairs go down a few more metals and then end. A heavy metal grate lies across the floor. She moves the flashlight around too quickly for me to make out any details of what lies beneath the grate. I almost reach out and grab the light from her, but she steps out of reach.

Trying to get my attention, she raps the handle against another security door. "One more door," she says.

I drag myself away from the grate and pull open the door. The same dull glow of emergency lighting greets us, as well as the distinct odor of blood.

The short hall beyond the door leads to three rooms: two tiny observation lounges and an operating theater. The last has been recently used—dramatically so—and the last person out hadn't bothered to clean up. There's a dried crust of blood on the tile floor, some of it built up around the drain not far from the metal table. Several trays of used equipment sit nearby, and there are tracks in the blood as if a large cart was parked nearby for a while and then moved once the patient had been... emptied.

There's power too. Mere spots a workstation nearby with a laptop still attached to the network. She investigates it, and I hear her make a noise somewhere between surprise and alarm. "What is it?" I ask, still looking at the blood stains on the table.

I used to read the future this way, in the spatter of blood from an animal sacrifice.

Something's not right. I recognize the scent, though I can't place it. There's panic rising in my chest, a flight response brought on by the scent of the blood. I should know what is causing it. I should—

"Silas." Mere gets my attention. A second later, she's got her hand to her mouth and she's backing away from the laptop. As soon as the sound starts, she puts her hands over her ears.

The video is jerky, shot with a hand-held camera, but I recognize the room. And the chair. And the man in the chair.

He is being dissected while still alive, and judging by the noise he is making, they aren't using anesthetic.

I'm dimly aware of Mere running out of the room, but I can't move to stop her.

I can only watch as Nigel is taken apart.

Piece by piece.

⋎⋎

"They knew we were coming."

She's huddled in the stairwell, her back pressed against the stone wall. She doesn't want to look at me, her eyes dart up once—fixating on the oblong shape of the laptop in my right hand—and then return to staring at the floor directly in front of her feet.

"Yes," I agree.

"They burned this place less than a day ago. Maybe even after you sprung me from Eden Park."

I agree with that statement too. I put the laptop on the ground and Mere flinches from it.

"I've removed the video," I say. "At least, it doesn't auto-run anymore. I'm not sure I've wiped it off the drive."

"And you want me to do it?" Mere stares at me.

"No," I shake my head, "I want you to see if there's anything else on it."

"I'm not touching that thing."

I shrug and hold out my hand. "Give me the flashlight."

"Why?"

"I'm going to go look for something."

"I'm coming with you."

I shake my head. My hand stays outstretched.

"You're going to leave me here?" Her voice rises in pitch. "With that? With God knows what other sadistic shit is lying around for us to find."

"So don't go looking," I say. "Stay put." I nudge the laptop with my toe. "Look. Please."

"Where are you going?" she asks with a sigh, handing over the flashlight.

"Down," I say. "I want to know why there is a grate. Why isn't it a solid floor? What's on the other side?"

She looks at me again. "You know, don't you?"

"It's the old temple. The spa, remember?"

"They blocked it off," she says. "There's nothing down there anymore."

"I want to see it for myself," I argue.

"Why?" she asks again.

"I saw something," I tell her as truthfully as I can, "back there. Before the video started. I saw a… pattern."

"A what?"

"I'll explain later." I flap my hand at her. "Flashlight, please. Don't sit in the dark waiting for me to return. Do something to keep busy. Look at this computer. You know more about them than I do. Are you going to let a stupid trick like auto-running a video file keep you from digging for data?"

She nodded. "Yeah. Yeah, I can do that." She slowly offers me the flashlight. She doesn't move toward the laptop, though. I click on the flashlight and head downstairs. I give her a minute or so before she opens the laptop.

At the very least, it'll be a source of light.

As I descend to the grate that lies across the floor at the base of the stairs,

I try to remember the temple the way it used to be. Above ground, it had been a simple ring of raised stones—modeled on the old celestial calendars of Central America. In the center, there had been a triangular divot in the ground, a sloped incline that had led down into the first of several natural caves. Sunlight filtered down to the first cave, which was as deep as the native peoples were allowed to go. This was the offering chamber. Below had been a honeycomb of smaller niches, where the steward catalogued and kept the samples: tiny shoots growing in clay urns, long troughs filled with quiescent ferns, and a vast assortment of sealed jars that held seeds and nuts of lost and extinct species. It was a seed bank, and it would be incredibly valuable if it still existed.

So why had they blocked it off, but not sealed it?

The grate is securely wedged between the bottom of the stairwell and a lip of stone directly beneath it. There are a few large iron spikes pounded into the wall ensuring that the grate doesn't shift. I kneel on the metal floor and peer through the narrow gaps. The flashlight beam bounces off worn stone steps and vanishes into the darkness below. On the wall, winding down, is a painted line of narrow-petaled flowers and tiny birds. White sea birds and hyacinths.

I lean my forehead against the cool metal of the grate. The darkness of the stairwell seems more oppressive suddenly, and my palms are slick with sweat. I'm having all the symptoms of claustrophobia, which I know isn't the case. Arcadians don't get claustrophobic. But it's a feeling of being hemmed in, of being constricted and bound.

I remember white feathers. I remember the rush of wind on my face. The rocky ground rushing past. The spray of water as waves leap up, trying to catch me.

I hate falling.

What's down there? What am I afraid of finding?

Also, lying there, I realize there's something else too. What am I not supposed to remember? If I'm not hiding it from myself, then it was taken from me. Why would Mother do that?

TWENTY-ONE

Mere finds me lying on the grate, staring up at the stairs above my head. "There's nothing on the laptop," she says. "Just an unlocked guest account that was set to load when I brought it out of sleep mode. There's no sign it's ever been on a network or the Internet. The hardware isn't that new, so it looks like it was wiped and reformatted a couple of days ago, the video was loaded—probably from a CD or USB device—and then it was configured to surprise us. That's it."

Her words stir something in my head, and I try to grab it, but it remains elusive.

"What is it?" she asks, sensing my aggravation.

"I've been down there—" I indicate the open space beneath the grate. "But I can't remember when or why. We forget things after a while. It's too much to hang on to, all that history, and the brain starts to jettison bits and pieces of it after... Anyway, there are some practices we've adopted that ease the discomfort of memory loss, but it doesn't clean up everything. There are little shards that remain, tiny chips of history that lodge themselves in the brain. They're disassociated from the core memory that binds them together, and the brain struggles to keep itself ordered. These little pieces end up in strange spots and, as the brain folds them in, they become disconcerting breaks in your mental history."

"That sounds confusing."

"You get used to it. After a while."

I don't tell her how Mother helps us when we go into her embrace. She won't understand. She hasn't lived as long as I have.

"Is there any reason to stay here then?" she asks. "Is it going to get better?"

"No," I sigh. "Probably not." I look wistfully at the spikes in the wall once more. Would getting the grate removed help? Would I actually understand what I found down below? Our would it be something that I felt like I should remember, but couldn't?

Would that be worse?

"Come on," she says, offering me her hand. "I want to find the server room. Let's see if it is in that first subbasement. Maybe there's something left there."

Using her hand, I pull myself up. She doesn't let go and I end up standing close to her. She leans toward me for a second, squeezing my hand. "I'm sorry," she says.

"For what?"

"For what happened to Nigel."

Why? is the first word that had popped into my head. *He was a bastard.* I shudder slightly and, feeling the tremor in my body, she squeezes harder.

"Thanks," I say, even though she's misreading my reaction.

I don't feel any sadness at Nigel's death. I should, but I don't. He wasn't family. Not in the truest sense. Not even in the slightest sense.

I miss Mere's hand touching mine more than I miss Nigel.

ᴠᴠ

The lab server room is more of a closet, and the narrow space contains two racks of computer gear. It's a bunch of black boxes with a tangled mess of wires coming in and out of everything in an incomprehensible maze, but Mere looks at it like she understands what she's seeing. "Patch panel," she says to herself as she starts inventorying the boxes, "Router. One—no, two—switches. Four servers, and… shit."

"What?"

"See these lights?" She pops off a plastic panel and shows me a row of red lights next to empty slots. "The drives have all been pulled. Each of these slots should be filled with a hard drive, but they're all empty." She checks each one of the boxes that she counted as a server, and they're all the same.

"They really wanted to make sure we couldn't get any data off these. Probably put them all in a bag and tossed it into the ocean. That'd be the quickest way to ruin the data. Damnit. There's nothing here. Nothing at all." She leans tiredly against the rack. "This was just a waste of time," she says quietly. "Such a fucking waste of time."

"We're still alive," I say. "We're not in immediate danger. We have freedom to move about. It's—"

She whirls on me. "'It's not that bad.' Is that what you're going to say? This entire facility was burned because you took me out of that hospital. They burned Eden Park too! How many have died now? Secutores is covering their tracks, and they don't seem to care about collateral damage along the way. What are we going to do? Where are we going to go? Do you think they'll just let us wander off? We're loose ends. They're going to come after us. Shit, Silas, for all we know they're waiting upstairs for us, laughing at us as we stumble around down here in the dark." She taps me on the chest, punctuating her remarks. "We don't know *why*. We don't know *what* or even *where*. We don't know *anything*."

I grab her finger. "We're alive," I repeat. "It's a start."

"A start of what?"

"I don't know. That's why I found you. Intelligence gathering isn't my forte."

"Me? That's your whole plan? *Find Mere; she'll figure it out.* That's it?"

"Sort of."

"Oh, shit. That's not a plan, Silas. That's barely"—she searches for a nice way to say it—"that's like something on a grocery list. *Get eggs. Meat. Maybe some cheese.*"

"Short lists work well," I say.

"*Find Mere. Kill all the bad guys.* Like that?"

"Sure. It's easy to remember."

She stares at me. "You're a grunt," she says. She pulls her finger out of my grip. "That's what you are—what you *were*. How long have you been following orders, Silas? Jesus Christ. Who put you up to this? Is this your idea? Have you ever thought for yourself?"

"Yes," I say. "The night I saved your life, for one."

She looks away. "That's not fair," she says quietly.

"It's true."

"Goddamnit, Silas, I don't need that on me. You saved my life once. You do it again, and this time how many people have died?"

"You can't connect those events like that. It doesn't work."

"Why not?"

"Because it's not about you. It's—"

"What? It's about you?"

"No," I say, struggling to grab on to that elusive thought that has been darting out of reach every time I try to reach for it. "Yes," I change my mind. "It's about *us*. Arcadians." And then the thought stops hiding from me.

"Secutores didn't do this," I say.

"What? How do you know?"

"It was all a trap," I say. "Right? Everything was set up to capture an Arcadian. Even after the *Liberty*. Those pop guns couldn't stop me; they were meant to drive me in a specific direction. They wanted me alive."

"Secutores?"

I nod. "Yes. So if that video was made by Secutores, then they have Nigel. They already have an Arcadian. So why burn the lab? Why leave the laptop for us to find? There's no reason to leave that video other than to taunt us. To tell us we're too late. There's nothing we can do for Nigel. He's gone."

"Which means this lab belongs to someone else."

I nod. "And they didn't want Secutores finding anything useful here. Other than their message: *We have him; you don't.*"

"Wait. Were they expecting Secutores to show up?" she asks. "Or us? And if they weren't expecting us, then… oh shit, there was a plane coming in to the airport when we were coming here. Secutores might be coming here right now."

TWENTY-TWO

We see lights among the trees when we leave the burned facility—three pairs of headlights—and we dash for the security of the tree line. The cars stick to the road, and it's easy to stay hidden among the trees as the trio drive up to the facility and fan out into the open ground around the building. As the engine noises stop, we hear voices—men shouting at one another—and a flurry of smaller lights bounce toward the building. They find the open door, and a number of men go inside, while teams of two start to sweep the perimeter.

I tug Mere away from the tree trunk we're hiding behind. "They'll find the laptop," I whisper. "We don't need to be here." Mere had wanted to keep it, but I had argued that it was better for us to be invisible than to hang on to the video file of Nigel's dismemberment. Especially if the video file was meant for Secutores.

She doesn't want to go, but she lets me pull her away, and we follow the road back to the edge of the crater. Mere is tired and not used to running in the dark, and after a while, I pick her up again and carry her. The access road turns south once it reaches the crater wall, and I follow it even though it is going the wrong way for Hanga Roa. I could climb the crater wall, but doing so with Mere in my arms would be tough. She's still enough that I suspect she's fallen asleep.

The road bends back on itself fairly quickly, turning into a series of tight switchbacks that lead up to the rim. It ends in an old dirt road that runs north to south. I turn left, north, and start jogging toward the distant glow of the airport and Hanga Roa.

V V

It's nearly dawn by the time we get back to the hotel. I wake Mere up so that she can climb the stairs under her own power, and she does so listlessly. Once we reach our room, she kicks off her shoes and falls down on the bed, letting her exhaustion pull her back into dreamland.

The recent exercise and inhaling Mere's scent over the past few hours have made me restless, and if the sun weren't coming up, I would go back out again and prowl around the tiny town of Hanga Roa. But nothing good would come of that. The thirst is there, at the back of my throat. My body is still fighting the toxins. I had been hoping to get some dirt time at the spa, but with that option no longer available, I'm starting to consider Plan B.

It's not a long-term solution. Blood brings other complications.

Mere is sprawled on the bed, and I adjust her position slightly so that I can lie down too. I fold my hands across my stomach and stare at the ceiling, trying to ignore the steady beat of her heart. She turns onto her side, a mumbled sigh slipping from her parted lips...

I close my eyes so that I don't see here anymore, and when I hear her exhale again, it doesn't sound the same. It sounds like wind on water...

And I'm not lying next to Mere anymore. I'm on the boat again, fleeing the ruin of the fairest city ever built. Fleeing everything I ever knew and loved.

"We are no longer who we were," Aeneas says. "We were men who stood our ground, who swore to fight to the last for our king and country. Now, we are nameless scoundrels, running across the dark sea that will surely swallow us before the sun rises again."

The men are scattered on the deck—exhausted, wounded, close to death. No one is rowing, and it is up to the captain and me to hold the tiller straight, to keep us on course—the only course available we can take. The wind is behind us, and our sails are full. The timbers of our boat are our most valuable possession. Everything else is broken and worn.

"We will become something else," I tell him. "We will find new names."

"Have you seen this?" he asks me. "Have you heard such a prophecy from the birds?"

I shake my head. "That is all behind me now. Like everything else."

He laughs, a cold laugh of a man who feels he has no future. "So be it. Let us never look back again. We are *Dardanoi* no more, you and I. We are men of the west, and we will go as far as these timbers will carry us."

The wind blows us away from the war, and we try to forgot how to be soldiers, but our bodies know nothing else. The short list. Kill everyone else.

I sigh, and the boat vanishes. I am standing on a cliff now, and the sun is a blazing fire in the west, its flames licking across the surface of the ocean. The people of the clans are behind me, chanting and beating their drums. I am naked but for a headdress of white feathers and a pair of wings made from palm fronds strapped to my arms. The ocean is far away, but I leap anyway, spreading my wings. I dive gracefully, and the cliff rushes past me. The updraft is warm and strong, and when I spread my arms, my palm-frond wings fill with air. I don't hit the water—not yet—the air carries me across the waves. Away from the volcanic cliff behind me. Toward the tiny spur of rock, jutting from the sea.

I am flying.

I am not afraid of the waves beneath me. They will grab me soon and try to drown me, but I'm not afraid of them anymore. It has been a long time since I fled Troy; crossing the Mediterranean seems so easy compared to the distance I have traveled to reach this rock, to stand before these people and show them how to fly. To show them their gods are real.

I pull my arms in, and dive into the water. When I surface, I am not at sea anymore. I am in a bed with a woman. She is on top of me, her lips against mine. Her skin is warm and her mouth is wet. Her hands knead my arms and chest, and I wrap my arms around her. Her legs part, and she gasps lightly, her teeth pressing against my lower lip. My hands sink to her hips and I hold her close. We move back and forth, like waves against the beach, and she crushes her mouth to mine, our teeth clicking together. I want to bite her, but she won't let me go and so I bite her lip instead. She bites me back, and I moan as our blood mixes.

I am hard inside her, and her fingers are raking across my skin now. I want to bleed for her...

I sit up.

When I look in the bathroom mirror, I see a face covered in sweat. There is blood on my lips. I taste it, and it isn't mine.

Arcadians don't dream, and what I told Aeneas was the truth. I gave up being a seer when we left Troy.

There are too many holes in my head. And they're growing.

You're just a grunt. You follow orders.

What have I done?

ᐯᐯ

I find my optics and head out to get some air before the sun gets too high in the sky. Outside, the scrub grass glistens with dew and the gulls are calling out to one another across the bay. I walk through town, not really paying attention to where I'm going. I'm letting other factors guide me. The air, the light, the distant sound of surf and seabirds. This is how I used to do it when Aeneas asked me to seek guidance. If the birds and the wind were not forthcoming with insight, there were other, bloodier, methods that were, as a result, prone to violence and darkness. After our flight from Troy, I no longer wanted to use the old methods.

I watch terns flit across the sky, trying to discern the patterns in the flight paths. A fat gull with gray pinfeathers squawks noisily at me from a wooden post as I pass. I walk on, and eventually I realize my destination is one of the *moai*. It sits on a low bluff near the edge of town, looking over the shallow depression of the bay and valley. There's a tiny café at the bottom of the hill, and a well-worn trail meanders up the slope behind the tiny building. I make the climb and stand next to the giant head. Seeing what it sees. How many are left? I wonder. They were the guardians of the island; they watched over the trees and the clans. And the outsiders came. The cult of the Bird Man came to the island—the *tangata manu*—and the clans found something to fight over.

The Bird Man brought them jealousy, greed, and avarice—the age-old sins that could never be completely forgotten. How quickly they had fallen into savagery. And the *moai* were toppled; the clans did not want them to see what was the clans were becoming. They did not want the old gods to look upon the shining white feathers of their new god. *Pull them down*, the Bird Man had said to them, *they may not look upon me. I am for your eyes only.*

A large airplane shatters the quiet morning as it comes in for a landing at the airport behind me. It is a different airline than the one we came on from Adelaide and Tahiti. This is the connecting flight that goes east, all the way to Chile.

"Which way should we go?" I ask the sullen *moai*, which does not respond. Mere's words last night stun, more so because there was great truth to them. I'm not a planner. That was never my role. I would read bird sign once in a while, and the rest of the time, I simply followed orders. I did not question. I did not deviate. I was the one who could be counted on to complete the mission and come home.

I did it for hundreds of years. Across many continents. Under countless banners and generals. I served Mother, wherever she needed me. I did what she asked; in return, she healed my wounds and took the pain away.

The plane taxies down the runway and slows to a stop before the tiny terminal. There are only two gates, servicing the two directions the planes fly. East or west.

When Troy burned, we fled west. We had no choice. West was where the open water lay, where undiscovered regions awaited us. We fled the burning wreckage of our past, and became something new. The sun set in the west, and we followed it until we found a new home.

And where is my home now? Arcadia is closed to me. Troy has been lost for millennia. Home is where the hearth is. Where the family is. I have neither. "What does that make me?" I ask the giant head.

I rest my hand on the cool stone of the *moai*, feeling the texture of the weathered surface. It is a reminder of a different age. One that has atrophied and become fossilized over the last hundred years. The old gods are gone; the new ones did not dwell long among the people either. The island has been abandoned. The soul is gone. All that remains is an empty husk.

We become strangers, in the end. The world changes and we slip out of place. Nothing more than solitary wanderers who don't know where to go. Or who they are anymore.

TWENTY-THREE

I enter the hotel through the front, a lazy mistake, and as soon as I clear the door, I catch the lingering aroma of tobacco. Gauloises Blonde. I make a right-hand turn into the tiny gift shop and busy myself with examining the dizzying array of plastic and foam *moai* trinkets. Through the wire mesh of the display rack, I scan the lobby and spot the woman from the parking lot of Eden Park—the one who had waited outside the rental for her companion to make a call. She's sitting in one of the comfortable chairs opposite the main desk, pretending to read a magazine. Her eyes betray her, flicking up and scanning the room every time she turns the page.

The only reason she didn't make me immediately is because her attention was focused on the elevator and the stairs. There's no one else around in the lobby and, even though she didn't see my face, she saw me go into the gift shop. I can't leave without her getting a good look at me.

She never saw me at Eden Park, and I consider if it is possible that she knows my face. The guy in the passenger seat of the car at the hospital parking lot has seen me. He might be able to ID me from airport security footage, if they've got it. But it'll be a shitty picture at best, meaning the woman in the lobby will second-guess what she sees.

That'll be enough.

I walk out of the gift shop and stroll slowly across the lobby, giving her time to get a good look at my profile, and as I approach the elevator, I divert to the stairs instead. Once through the ground floor door, I dart up the steps to the second-floor landing. I open the door and wait, listening; in a few seconds, I hear the door open down below. I leave the stairwell, letting the second-floor door shut noisily behind me. Just so there's no confusion where I've gone. There's a narrow alcove across the hall that contains an ice and a vending machine as well as a door marked "Employees Only."

When the brunette comes through the stairwell door, I grab her roughly. One hand on her throat; the other on her wrist. She's got a gun in her hand, and my grip keeps her weapon low. I drag her across the hall and ram my shoulder against the marked door, splintering the lock. Beyond is a narrow closet, lined with racks of cleaning supplies and linens. I spin her against one of the racks, stunning her. She gets her act together fairly quickly, and starts to raise her gun. I intercept her motion, snapping her wrist and peeling the gun out of her hand. She starts to cry out, but I grab a pillow off a nearby shelf and press it firmly over her face. Using her own gun, I put a round through the fluffy layer between us.

After she falls down, I go through her pockets and take what I find.

The closet door doesn't latch, but it closes enough that no one will notice the broken jamb unless they are actually trying to open the door.

As I take the stairs up to the fourth floor, where our room is, I examine her phone. In the photo log, there's a grainy picture, pulled from some security feed somewhere. My face.

Secutores knows who they're looking for.

V V

Mere is standing in the bathroom of the hotel room, wrapped in one of the complementary robes. She is bent over the sink, her hair still wet from a shower, and she looks up as I come in, her eyes cataloguing the objects in my hands.

"Where did you get that?" she says, eyeing the pistol. Her fingers are probing behind her left ear, and she winces as she finds something tender.

"We're being watched," I say, as I enter the bathroom and dump my collection on the counter.

"It's Secutores, isn't it?" she says. "Shit, I knew it." She drops her head, pulling her hair to the side. "When I was showering, I felt a weird bump," she says, showing me what she's been trying to feel. Behind her ear, near her hairline, there is a tiny scabbed ridge. The surrounding skin is red and irritated since she's been worrying it.

"They chipped me, didn't they?" she says.

I run my thumb across the bump, nodding. "That would explain a few things, wouldn't it?"

"Yeah, it definitely would."

One of the items I took from the Secutores agent had been a folding tactical knife. Rifling through the pile, I retrieve it and flip it open. "This is going to hurt a bit," I say.

She grips the edge of the counter. "I know."

Blood wells out as I make a tiny incision. I catch the rivulet with my thumb, and my teeth snap together, grinding against one another as I hold myself in check. Her breath hisses, and I grab a washcloth to apply pressure against the cut. "Sorry," I mumble. Her blood is all over my thumb.

"It's—Silas," she says sharply. She stands up, snatching the washcloth out of my slack hand. She presses it against her neck with one hand, while grabbing my wrist with her other. "Silas!"

"What?" I say dumbly, still staring at my thumb. My tongue has forced its way through my clenched teeth, and I'm breathing heavily.

"Look at me, you knuckle-dragger!"

"That's—" I snarl, and as I tear my attention away from the glistening crimson coating my thumb, I snap out of my hyper-focus.

She is still holding on to my wrist. "Lower your arm, Silas," she says. "Look at my face."

I do, though my gaze flickers toward her neck when she lowers the washcloth. There's a smear of blood across the side of her neck, and it is almost too much.

"Eyes on me," she snaps. "Focus."

A growl rises in my chest as I comply, forcing myself to look away from her neck. My shoulders are twitching.

"As long as I have this thing in me, Secutores knows where we are," she says. "We have to get it out. Now. You have to focus."

I move my arm and her fingers tighten. "Okay," I say, effortlessly pulling free of her grip. "I hear you. Let me do it." Taking a deep breath and marshalling my restraint, I indicate she should turn so that I can do what needs to be done. She nods and holds her hair out of the way again. I place my thumbs on either side of the cut and massage her skin, feeling the shape of a foreign body. When I squeeze my thumbs together, more blood flows but a tiny cylinder floats up and protrudes from the slit in her skin. I tug it free and step back. It's a small transmitter, slippery with blood, and I drop it on the counter.

Grabbing a larger towel from the nearby rack, I move away until my back is against the bathroom wall. Focusing on her reflection in the mirror, I keep my attention away from what my hands are doing. They're turning and twisting over each other, trying to get the blood off before I lose control.

Mere glances at the blood-stained counter and the tiny transmitter as she presses the bloody washcloth against her neck. "What sort of range does this thing have?"

"Hard to say without opening it up," I say. "But it's definitely some sort of tracking chip."

She checks on the bleeding and satisfied that it seems to have slowed, she nods toward the pile of personal effects on the counter. "A watcher?" When I nod, she puts down the washcloth and starts rifling through the pile. "Did you...?" She shakes her head. "Where were they?" she asks instead.

"Lobby. Standard stake-out. Waiting for us to come downstairs."

"So they don't know which room we're in?"

"Or they don't want to corner us here," I point out. I try to remember if I had seen anyone loitering around when I had gone out for my walk. Were they covering the side exits too? I point at the tracking chip. "If they're keying in on that, we have a slight advantage now. They know where the chip is, but they don't know that it isn't in you anymore. If we leave it here, they'll think we're still in the room."

"How long will that illusion last, do you think?"

"Long enough for us to get to the airport."

"And then what? There are two flights out of here per day. One heading for Tahiti, and the other one goes east. To Santiago, Chile. It won't be hard to figure out which way we've gone. If they don't grab us as soon as we walk out of here." She shakes her head. "It'd be easier if we could just fly out of here ourselves." Her mouth quirks into a tiny smile. "Too bad we can't turn into sparrows. And fly home."

Sparrows.

I recall the painting on the wall of the crypt beneath the laboratory. Tiny birds wreathed in flowers.

"Hyacinths," I say. "That's it."

"What's it?" she says, but she's talking to my back as I leave the bathroom. "What are you doing?" she asks as she follows me.

"I'm looking for the folder that comes with the room," I tell her. "The one that has the room service menu and the listing of all the other services the hotel offers."

"Why?"

I find the leather-bound folio, and start flipping through it. "Because there's always a page filled with market speak about the hotel, and it always contains some reference—"

A buzzing noise interrupts me, the sound of an angry bee caught in the bathroom. "The phone," Mere says. "I'll get it."

I nod and stand there, holding the folder, staring at the page. The words are bending out of whack, and I struggle to bring them back into line, just as I'm struggling to bring my memory back.

What I need is in my head. I just can't get it ordered correctly. I can almost see the shape of the puzzle. I almost know where the pieces go.

Mere returns from the bathroom, holding the Secutores agent's cell phone. "Text message," she says, showing me the display.

It's a message from someone named *Albatross*, and it reads: "Sr loc?"

"Situation report," I translate. "And asking about her location."

"Sent a few minutes after nine. Do you think it's routine?"

"Top of the hour check-in?" I shrug. "Probably."

Mere's fingers fly over the phone's quartet of control buttons, easily navigating the maze of submenus. "Yeah," she says. "On the hour. One word responses. *Zero. Zero. Zero. Down.* And then nothing before that for something like twelve hours."

I nod, following the sequence. *Down* was the note that she had arrived on Easter Island. "Text *zero* back. Keep it simple."

Mere does so, and then starts looking at other screens. "These are cheap phones," she says. "Ah"—she finds something of interest—"here's her contact list. *Albatross. Bear. Caribou. Dingo. Falcon. Gopher.*" She ponders the list. "No 'E'?"

"She's 'E,'" I intuit. "*Albatross* is her commanding officer."

She giggles slightly. "Do you think it was assigned?"

"What was assigned?"

"That code name."

I think about it for a second, recalling albatrosses of legend and those that found their way into literature. "Probably not."

The phone buzzes in Mere's hands and she nearly drops it. "Shit," she reads the message. "It just says 'Loc' again."

"You didn't answer all of the question the first time," I say.

"What am I supposed to do?"

"Tell him something."

"Like what?"

In the maid closet. Second floor. I shake my head, putting that suggestion away. "Type 'pissing,'" I suggest.

Mere smiles. "'Pissing,'" she says as she works the phone's keypad. "And I'm adding 'K?'" She hits send.

"Good idea. That'll explain the delay."

She checks another menu. "That's the only one who has been texting. *Albatross*. God, what a goofy code name. A big white bird, hanging around your neck." She shakes her head.

Big white bird…

"That's it," I whisper as the pieces start falling into place.

"What? An albatross?"

I tap the page I've got open in the hotel folder, and she leans over to see what I'm trying to show her. "'The Hanga Roa Royal Resort is part of Hyacinth Worldwide, a network of family-owned hotels and resorts,'" she reads. "Okay, and…"

"On the plane flight out here, you were telling me about your research. One of the companies you mentioned was…"

"Hyacinth Holdings," she finishes.

"On the wall of the temple, there is an old mural. Most of it is gone, but the trim along the top is still there. An ornamental row of white-winged birds and hyacinths."

The pieces start clicking into place.

Hyacinths on the wall.

The Bird Man ceremony.

Hyacinth owns the hotel.

Big white bird, falling into the ocean.

Hyacinth is in the agriculture industry.

The albatross. The harbinger of ill luck.

"I remember," I tell Mere. "I remember why I came here before. Arcadia sent me. We were abandoning the island."

Mother sent me because I do what she asks. I follow orders.

I had been sent to kill the steward.

BOOK FOUR

HYACINTH

TWENTY-FOUR

We put together a plan to get off the island. We've got an hour or two before a sitrep of *zero* becomes odd, and we make the best of it. Mere calls the front desk to check into the next flight going east. We're booked on the midday flight to Santiago, Chile, in four days, but if we show up at the counter at the airport and make enough noise and wave enough cash around, we can probably get our flight changed.

Especially if we play up the disgruntled newlywed angle. No one likes to see relationships go sour that quickly.

Mere leaves first, heading out the front door since *E* was probably the only one watching from the lobby. I linger, mainly to get the body out of the maid's closet and up to our room. I slip the tracking chip into the pocket of E's pants, along with everything else I had taken from her.

I keep the phone. I send one more progress report on the way to the airport and then I shove the phone down behind the seat in the back of the cab.

Mere is waiting for me next to the security check-point. She's wearing a large hat and dark sunglasses, and she's got a handful of wadded tissue. Her glasses are big enough to hide the fact that she's been crying, pretty heavily.

"What happened?"

"I had to put on a real show," she says, offering me a boarding pass. The flight leaves in forty-five minutes.

V V

Once the doors of the plane shut, I stop staring up the aisle; once the plane is in the air, I start to relax. I've been anticipating the arrival of any number of people: airport security, Secutores, the captain of the plane. None of those people show. It's just a tiny trickle of tourists, and then it is time to go.

The six-hour flight is uneventful. Mere sleeps for most of it. When we land in Chile, we slip into the flow of passengers leaving the airport. Twenty minutes later, we're outside the main building, standing on Chilean soil, and no one appears to be the wiser. The flight wound back a number of time-zones, and I had been worried that during our actual flight time, our ruse would have been discovered and someone would have called ahead.

For the moment, though, we appear to be ahead of Secutores, and now that we are on a larger landmass, it'll be easier to disappear.

The airport is in Pudahuel, a short subway ride outside of the city. I change some of my dwindling cash into local currency while Mere examines a subway map, trying to figure out which line will take us into Santiago proper.

She's been full of questions since we landed, and I've managed to put her off to this point, but once we get on the subway, she starts up again. This time, I get the sense that she's not going to stop until I give her some answers.

"Let's just find a hotel," I try. "There will be time enough for all of this."

"Do we have enough cash? I need some things. What about our passports? Are they still good?"

"I can get more money, and we don't need to worry about the passports."

"What are we going to do for ID? Should I go to the US Consulate then?"

"Why?"

"I'm an American citizen. I've been kidnapped by an international security company. I was aboard the *Liberty* when—"

We're sitting next to each other in a pair of narrow seats, our thighs touching. I reach over and silence her with a touch on her leg. "Let's not worry about all that quite yet."

"I'm going to worry about something."

"I know."

"It's what I do."

"I know."

"These are the things I'm going to wonder about."

"Yeah, I see that."

"You need to give me something else to gnaw on."

"Like…"

"Hyacinth."

"Later," I tell her. "When I'm sure."

She sighs heavily, and flops her hand down on top of mine. As the subway pulls into an underground station, she looks out the window. "I typically project three to six months for research before I even start laying out my story. I tell no one what I'm working on. Maybe one or two people at the network," she says quietly, forcing me to lean toward her to hear the story. "But after Hachette Farms"—she swallows heavily, and her fingers tighten on mine—"after the incident with Kirkov, things changed. It all broke too big, and everyone knew my face. I couldn't do anything without someone—somewhere—trying to figure what my angle was. They didn't know the details, but they could guess as to the general shape of the piece. I wasn't a friend to Big Ag—they knew that—and research got harder. Sources were less inclined to go on the record. I had to dig deeper. I had to take more risks. I filed a couple of stories where my facts weren't quite solid, but I was close enough that public opinion did the rest for me. I couldn't stop them, but I could make them change how they did business. I could make them be more cautious about breaking the law."

She turns her head and looks at me. It would be easy to get lost in her gaze, but there's tension in her face that keeps me at bay. "I was never more than an annoyance. A line item on a budget: damage control, media spin, that sort of thing. And I had a network of people I could rely on; people who I knew would ask pointed questions if I disappeared. It was a game we played. I wrote a story, and they did a cost analysis internally. Was it cheaper to let me have my day and go do business some other way, or was it time to shut me down? You see? It's not personal. It's barely political. It's all about money. That's all they care about."

I recall Callis's command to follow the money. "Is that what is going on here?"

She shakes her head. "I don't know. Personal vendettas don't make any sense in the corporate world. Resolving a grudge isn't boardroom thinking, and if we're talking about an enormous corporate entity, we have to assume there's a lot of boardroom thinking that is driving decisions. Unless you pissed off an entire corporate board."

"Isn't that what you do with your stories?"

"Yes, but not like this. They don't come to my apartment and do awful things to my cat."

"You don't have a cat," I point out.

"Well, yeah—" She gives me a look that says such details are somewhat beside the point.

"Look, it all boils down to controlling the market. Whatever I do with my stories or whatever direction they're heading is all about locking down market share. Destroying the competition or beating up on your personal enemies is meaningless if you don't control the market."

"So where does the video fit into this?"

"They want us to react. They want us to be horrified and outraged. They want us to get all wound up and go off on a tear in one direction, while they do something sneaky in the other direction. It's a distraction. They're trying to keep us from thinking about the big picture."

"Hell of a distraction," I point out.

She nods absently, returning her attention to the window. We're still underground and the tunnel walls are a blur rushing by. "And expensive," she says pensively. "Which means what's at stake is worth significantly more." I can see her reflection in the window and I can tell she's looking at me.

What's at stake is Arcadia, and she knows it too.

ⅤⅤ

We get off the subway at the Baquedando stop, near the Bellavista district. The wooded slope of San Cristobal rises to the north of us, and I'm immediately set at ease to be close to trees again. We wander the streets awhile, getting our bearings, and stumble upon a two-level, open-air mall. Mere drags me into a restaurant that isn't subtle in its mood lighting—orange and red lamps pointed at the walls and ceiling give off the impression of dining in a cavernous lava dome. The dark booths rise like stones out of a lake of shadows that covers the floor.

"I thought you might like the ambience," Mere says after the host seats us. She has to raise her voice to be heard over the music, and as soon as she finishes speaking, she shakes her head and slides out of her side of the booth and comes over to mine, bumping me with her hip to make room. "Not very ambient," she says when she's settled next to me.

"It's a privacy screen," I say, trying to adjust myself in the seat so that I have a little more space between us.

"Yes," she nods. "That's a good word. *Privacy.* This is hardly the soundtrack to an intimate dinner." The music was banal, heavy with electronic beats, and I vaguely recognize it as something that had been popular in the US a few years ago.

"When was the last time you took someone to dinner?" she asks, trying to make the question seem casual as she looks over the menu. Making small talk. But I feel a tiny tremor running through her body. Her heart rate seems elevated, though I can't be sure I'm not hearing echoes of the music.

"Several years," I say. "You?"

She shakes her head. "We're not talking about me."

"We're not?"

A waiter glides up to our table, seemingly legless in black trousers and a red shirt that glows in the indirect light of the restaurant. He starts in Spanish, switches smoothly to English when Mere offers him a rustic "Hiya," runs us through the specials, and then glides away in response to her request for a couple of caipirinhas.

Mere puts the menu down on the table and rests her head on her hand so that she can give me her undivided attention. "Yes," she says, "we're talking about you. Because I'm in Chile—illegally—where I'm probably being targeted by a bunch of ex-military heavies, while chasing the biggest story of my life. Oh, and there's this whole semantic game we're playing about the word 'vampire,' which, yes, is another story *entirely*. And probably even bigger than the first one."

"Is this an interview then. Like that book?"

"No, not like *that* book."

"Off the record then?"

"Are you out of your mind?"

The waiter returns with our drinks and hovers, waiting for us to order food. Mere glances at him, frowns, and reaches for the menu. "*Tapas*," I tell him. "*Exquisitas combinaciones.*" I pick up my drink. "*Más bebidas, por favor,*" I add.

"*Gracias,*" he says, collecting our menus and disappearing again.

"What was that about?" Mere asks.

"I ordered."

"I figured that much out. What did you order?"

"Tapas. Chef's choice." I give her a guileless smile. "And more drinks. It sounds like we're going to be here awhile."

TWENTY-FIVE

It's not hard to get her drunk. She's tired, jetlagged, emotionally wrung out, still recovering from being doped by Secutores, and hasn't had a decent meal in more than twelve hours. What surprises me is that it takes as many drinks as it does.

After we've cleared a dozen plates and half as many drinks (of which I had one and a half), I have our waiter get us a cab. Mere's already half asleep by the time I coax her out of the booth. Once in the cab, I tell the driver to drive around for twenty minutes or so, and it only takes Mere five to fall asleep, her head resting against my shoulder. Fifteen minutes later, confident that we're not being followed, I tell the driver to take us to the hotel I had spotted near the open air mall.

I leave her in the car until I have a room, and then I carry her in. The concierge gets the elevator for me. "Thank you." I nod toward Mere's limp form. "Too much to drink."

"It happens," he replies with that nonjudgmental air that good hotel staff learn. I smile, trying to make it seem like I'm the long-suffering one in the relationship, as the elevator doors close.

We're on the eighth floor, in a corner room. I key in, arrange Mere on the bed, and cover her with the sheets. I prowl around the room for a few minutes, pausing to peek out at the parade of lights that are strung along the side of San Cristobel, and then I acknowledge that I'm too restless to sit and wait. I leave Mere a note and go back downstairs.

The mall is still open and I find a telecom shop where I buy a few international phone cards and a new pay-as-you-go phone. I get a small laptop too, using the debit card that I got from the bank in Adelaide. It creates a money trail, but I don't have any choice right now. I don't have enough pesos to pay for it, and changing the rest of my Australian money is going to require a bank.

If we're going to keep moving, changing money is going to be a problem. I'm going to have to trust that the bank channel is secure for the time being. If it isn't, it's better to find out now rather than later when I really need it.

Afterward, I find a quiet bench off the main thoroughfare of the mall and sit down to figure out how to make the phone cards work. Australia is on the other side of the International Date line, and with the time difference, it is tomorrow morning there. I follow the directions on the card and then punch in Ralph's cell phone number.

He answers on the third ring. "Hello?"

"Did I wake you?"

"What? No, no. No, I was just… is this—?"

"It is."

"Are you…? Is…?"

It's hard to ask questions when you're worried about who might be listening in.

"We're fine. Enjoying our honeymoon," I tell him. "How are the neighbors?"

"Restless. Some of the natives are getting curious too."

"Sounds like a party."

"I think the neighbors are leaving soon, though. If they haven't gone already."

"Any forwarding address?"

"Just the one on file."

"Well, sounds like that party is almost over. Should be nice and quiet after that."

"So, ah, look, the neighbors." I can almost hear him thinking through the code phrasing we've adopted, trying to fit it to what he wants to tell me. "The landlords—the ones who own the place the neighbors have been staying at—I think they pulled the lease."

I parse what he's telling me. "Interesting. Any idea on who the landlords are? Is someone else moving in?"

"Nada," he says dejectedly. "I got zilch."

"I was thinking about buying my new bride some hyacinths," I tell him. "But it's the wrong time of year. Could you look into it for me? Where I could find someone who could grow them out of season? Get them to hold them for me? Until we get back."

He's quiet for a minute. "Yeah, sure," he says eventually. "Holding on to some hyacinths. I can do that." From the stress he places on certain syllables, I think he's got my request figured out. *Hyacinth Holdings.*

"Great, thanks. I'll call later." I hang up.

I call Callis next. Rather, I try to, but he doesn't answer. I let the call ring for a long time, wondering why it doesn't go to voice mail. All I can imagine is an old rotary phone in a dusty room somewhere, in a house that no one lives in anymore.

I end the call and shove the phone in my pocket. I don't need to talk to Callis, and maybe this is his way of reminding me that I need to stay away from making contact. If I'm isolated, then not only am I safe from whatever is poisoning Arcadia, Arcadia is also safe from me.

Mere says this isn't personal, but I can't help but think of Talus's warning on the boat. *She's not family. Remember your priorities.*

The matter *is* personal, though. It has been for a long time.

I need to remember who the steward was on Rapa Nui.

I start walking toward San Cristobal. There will be trails, walking paths through the trees. If not, I'll just find my own way through the woods. I've done it before. All that really matters is that I get under the trees for a while.

They don't judge me. They still accept me as family. They'll let me rest, and maybe they'll even help me put my mind back together.

ⱽⱽ

Mere is still sleeping when I return to the room. Her hair is mussed around her head and her shirt is twisted around her body. The only part of her that moves is her chest and her throat. Watching both becomes hypnotic, and I can feel the thirst tickling at the back of my throat.

How many times have I been in a room like this, watching someone like this? There were others before Val, a long list of faces that are all out of focus. But it was different with the others. None of them knew about Arcadia. None of them knew *how* I was different. I was a man with an exotic past, loath to talk about family and where I had been before I met them. I lied to them all. I was good at dodging questions, at coming up with false emergencies and interruptions to derail persistent questions. After a while, most of them gave up trying. Some of the relationships failed for that reason. Some of them flourished because the exotic and unknown were perpetually exciting.

Mere knows too much already, and I fear that learning more is only going to make her want to stay.

I peel the plastic wrap and dozen stickers that constitute packaging on the laptop and switch it on. As it boots up, I figure out how to work the in-room coffee maker. The sound of the computer churning and the smell of brewing coffee work to bring Mere out of her stupor. She sits up slowly, trying to push her hair into a semblance of order. A lazy smile spreads across her face when I offer her a cup of hot coffee. She takes a large sip and then lies back in bed, the cup resting between her breasts. "Ah, you know how to greet a girl in the morning, don't you?"

"I bought you a laptop. It's got a Spanish operating system preinstalled, but there's an English version on the DVD that comes with it."

"Now you're just trying to get into my pants," she says.

"I don't think you're wearing any," I say, recalling a crumpled heap lying on the bathroom floor.

She lifts her head and peeks under the sheet. "Well, then," she says, taking another sip of coffee. "I guess we must have gotten along pretty well last night."

I ignore her comment and put the cell phone and the extra calling cards on the table, next to the laptop. "New phone and calling cards," I say.

"In case I want to call my girlfriends and talk about the awesome night I can't remember?"

"It couldn't have been that awesome if you can't remember it," I point out.

"Spoken like an experienced amnesiac," she says. She winces as soon as the words come out of her mouth. "Sorry."

"It's okay," I say. "I'll take acerbic as a sign that you're going to survive."

"It's the caffeine kicking in." She takes another large sip from the cup, her attention drifting toward the table with the phone and laptop. "By the way, when this headache goes away, I'm going to get out of bed and kick your ass."

"Why? Because I took your shoes off before I put you into bed last night?"

"*And* my pants."

I shake my head as I point to where her shoes are neatly arranged next to the dresser. "There are your shoes. Do you see your pants?"

"Well, they're not *on* me," she says.

"They're on the bathroom floor, where you must have left them when you got up to pee in the middle of the night."

Some expression flashes across her face, and I'm not sure if it is disappointment or outrage, but it is gone before I can really decide which it is. "Regardless of the location of my pants," she snaps, "that's not why I'm going to put my foot up your ass."

"I shouldn't have plied you with drinks while I was dodging your questions?"

She makes a gun with two of her fingers and slowly shoots me with it. "Bingo."

"Call Ralph," I say. "Maybe he'll play nicer."

"At least he'll play," she says. "You owe me some answers."

I shrug. "I'm going to get some breakfast," I say, heading for the door.

"Silas. Don't you run away from me."

I stop and look back at her. "I'm not. I'll be back in a bit."

"Why don't you stay and call room service," she says, "instead of running away?"

"Why don't I go get some food while you solve your lack of pants problem?"

"Why don't you throw me them since you're standing right there?"

I glance over at the pair under discussion. "I could take them with me," I suggest.

A wicked smile curls her lips. She leans over and sets the coffee cup on the nightstand. With a sweep of her arm, she throws the sheets back and hops off the bed. She wobbles slightly as she stands up, but she manages to not lose her balance. Wearing nothing but her sleep-wrinkled shirt and a pair of pale green bikini briefs, she walks over. Standing very close, she leans toward me so that her face is almost touching mine. "Go ahead," she says. She grabs the top button on her shirt. "You want this too?"

"I'm going to get breakfast," I growl. "More coffee?"

"Please," she whispers, locking eyes with me. Daring me to look down to see what her hands are doing with her shirt.

"And a tart," I say. "A very fresh fruit tart."

Her laughter follows me out of the room and all the way down the hall to the elevator. Only when I'm securely behind the closed doors of the elevator, do I look down at the marks my nails have made in my palm.

There is still alcohol in her blood. That, I tell myself, is the only reason I held back. Otherwise, I would have done something foolish.

I want her to stay too.

ᐯᐯ

She's wearing pants when I return, and appears to have been upright for most of the time that I've been gone. On the wall beside the dresser and TV unit, she's attached a white sheet and has been covering it with circles, lines, and scribbled writing.

"I asked the staff for tape and a marker," she says, stepping back from her work as I put my bags on the table. "In case you didn't get my psychic messages."

"I did," I reply glibly. "But I also knew you couldn't wait for me to come back with them and would badger the concierge instead." I open a small box filled with round, sugar-coated objects and hold it out to her. "*Berliner*? Or as the Germans call them: *pfannkuchen*."

"A what?"

"Jelly donut."

"Why didn't you say so in the first place?"

"When in Rome…"

"Is that an Arcadian saying?" She takes one and bites into it, discovering the jelly center. "Like, the First Rule of Arcadia is: pretend you're in Rome."

"It's the other way around," I say. "The First Rule of Rome is to pretend you're in Arcadia." I pause thoughtfully as I pluck a *berliner* from the box. "Though that may have been Nero."

She wrinkles her nose as she finishes the first *berliner* and reaches for another. "Before my time," she says.

Chewing my donut slowly, I look over what she's done on the sheet. "This seems a bit more recent," I say. "Corporate connections."

She nods. "Ralph gave me a bunch of it, and while I'm waiting for him to call me back, I started making notes."

Near the center are three circles: Secutores Security, Hyacinth Holdings, and Arcadia. From the first two, she's drawn a number of lines to smaller bubbles, and each line has tiny notes running above and below. Hyacinth is connected to Hyacinth Worldwide as well as Hyacinth Pharmaceuticals— easy connections to make—and she's drawn a line between Secutores and Kyodo Kujira, but the line has a lot of conjecture scribbled along it.

There are clusters of notes orbiting each of the three central circles, but no lines connecting them.

"There's a Hyacinth Pharmaceuticals?" I ask.

She picks up her laptop, selects one of the browser tabs she's got open, and hands me the small computer. It's a page from Hyacinth Pharmaceuticals' website—a lot of market speak extolling the natural medicinal virtues of star fruit. At the bottom of the page is a back button that takes me to a summary page that gushes about the majestic mystery of the natural world and how much humanity could benefit from a more holistic approach to naturopathic medicine.

"Pretty over-the-top marketing copy," she notes. "Notice anything about that list of trees and plants?"

I pay attention to the two columns at the bottom of the page. "Some of them are Polynesian. Some are African. These four are Chinese. That one is extinct—"

"I bet they're all growing in the crater at Rano Kau," she says, interrupting my recital. Her voice grows more animated; it is clear from my expression that she knows something I don't, and she's delighted to be the smart one in the room. "Those trees we saw were big and healthy. A farm like that doesn't spring up overnight. How many years would it take to grow a farm that size?"

"A couple decades," is my guess. "More, probably," I amend, thinking of the stately toromiro.

"Hyacinth Pharmaceuticals was incorporated three years ago. It's hard to tell without going back, but I'd be willing to bet that building out there in the crater isn't more than two years old. The Hanga Roa Royal Resort goes back thirty years, but four years ago, it went through major renovations—including that five-story building we were staying in. The resort increased its number of rooms from sixteen to a hundred and eighty. For an island that's a marginal tourist attraction and pretty much out of any cruise line routes, what would create such a boom in housing needs?"

"A workforce. One that needs temporary housing."

"Exactly."

She wanders over to the chart and taps Hyacinth Pharmaceuticals. "Figure Hyacinth Worldwide is managing the land, since they're already on the island. Maybe the hotel is originally built to facilitate the team that plants all the trees. They spend three decades growing that farm, and when the trees start to mature, they build the lab."

"That's some long-term thinking."

"Who thinks like that?"

"The Japanese."

"Big Ag," she says, rolling her eyes at me. Then, more seriously: "And Arcadians."

"We left the island," I tell her.

"Are you sure?" she asks. She still has that glint in her eye—that journalist delight at having uncovered some unexpected secret.

"No, I'm not sure," I say as my stomach starts to tighten.

"Okay, let's look at the list of what you'd get from a farm on Easter Island." She takes the laptop from me and switches over to a document that she was working on. "Sirolimus," she starts. "Sourced from a bacterium found only on the island. If we buy the marketing hype, star fruit is useful to combat infections and it also acts—and I quote—'as an inhibitor of certain isoforms.' What does that mean?"

I suspect she already knows, but I play along. "It increases the efficacy of other drugs."

She makes the popping noise with her lips as she points a finger at me. "There's *agbayun*," she continues, working down the list. "Also known as miracle berry—a source of miraculin. Handy when you're making native medicines. And African serendipity berry too, which has thaumatin in it, much like miraculin. They're also working with Amyruca, a natural source of DMT; *Oldenlandia affinis*, widely used in Africa to assist in childbirth; *Polygala tenuifolia*, a memory aid found in a number of Chinese herbal remedies; a couple others which I haven't figured out what they're useful for yet; and the jujube, which I thought was something that Lewis Carroll made up, but is apparently useful for a whole host of things."

"*Ziziphus*," I say. "*Ziziphus zizyphus*."

"Excuse me?"

"I know of it. We used to eat the fruit. We'd dry it and eat it." I shake my head at her raised eyebrow. "Never mind. Yes, I can see why it's on the list."

"A small pharmaceutical company could make its nut—if you will—off any one of these if they could figure out how to harvest and/or synthesize them in large enough quantities. Yet, if we believe the marketing copy isn't just for show, Hyacinth Pharmaceuticals is doing *all* of them. Doesn't that seem a tad...?"

"Ambitious?" I try. "Delusional?"

"Either. Both," she says. "Remember when I talked about the corporate pyramid? Every company is working on a piece of something else, and none of them know anything other than the part they're responsible for. Someone much higher up the chain knows the real score. They're the architects of the capital 'P' plan. This is like a compressed version of that sort of vision. It's all in one place. In one company. We've got psychedelics, antipsychotics, immunosuppressants, antibacterial, anti-inflammatory, antifibrinolytics, God knows how many other *anti-* agents there are. If you put them all together what have you got?"

"I got lost somewhere around the third *anti-*."

"Complete systemic disassociation."

"What does that mean?"

"You won't feel a thing, and your body won't reject anything you put in it. Or attach to it."

It clicks for me. "Nigel."

"They weren't just torturing Nigel," she says. "They were cutting him up for *parts*."

"Parts they could use for something—or *someone*—else." I struggle to wrap my head around the idea of *parts*. Not just organ transplants, but entire pieces of a body. Or even building an entirely new body out of disparate sections. How would this work? "Lemon trees," I breathe.

"What about lemon trees?" Mere asks.

"Do you know how a lemon tree is cultivated?" She shakes her head. "You grow lemons and oranges on the same trunk. It's done all the time. They're from the same family. You can graft a branch on, and the trunk will accept it. With this pharmacopeia, you could do the same with any genetically similar species."

"Like *Homo erectus*?"

I nod, knowing it's more than that. It'd be even easier with a species that is more refined, genetically-speaking. Something singularly sourced.

Hyacinth wants to grow their own Arcadians.

TWENTY-SIX

"**W**ho owns Hyacinth?" I ask, suppressing the serpentine twist of fear rising up my back. Focusing on what we know. Setting aside this line of speculation. Knowing who you are fighting is often times more important than why.

"That's turning out to be harder than I thought," she sighs. She runs her hand over the sheet. "The part where they all have 'Hyacinth' in their names is pretty easy, but beyond that it turns into a fucking rabbit hole of shell companies, subsidiaries, and corporate nepotism so off-the-record that I'm going to have to dig up the Twitter accounts of bored socialite CEO wives to figure out who's playing golf with whom—or fishing for marlin or whatever they do for male bonding these days. I can figure it out—I did something similar when I followed the money out of Hachette Falls—but it's going to take a few weeks."

"I don't think that is a luxury we have."

"I've got Ralph digging too, and that'll help, but it's just the two of us against a hundred or so lawyers who bill a lot of very expensive hours dirtying up the paper trail."

"We need a shortcut."

"And if there is one, I bet it is figuring out what is going on here." She points to the empty space between Secutores and Hyacinth Holdings. "What's the connection?"

"You don't think they work for Hyacinth?"

She shakes her head. "I know that divisions of a corporation can be working on projects that seem to cancel each other out, and it's typically for a market dominance reason, but it doesn't make sense for Hyacinth

Pharmaceuticals to be working on a weed killer with the efficacy of what we saw. These guys have got to be working for someone else."

She switches to another tab on the laptop's browser. "Secutores has a very dull website. They keep a pretty low profile. They have a page listing their previous 'employment opportunities.' What a phrase. Okay, here they are. Protection and security for more than two dozen government ambassadors. Intelligence gathering for a bunch of three-letter acronym agencies, a couple of investment firms, one Hollywood studio—I have no idea what the hell that's all about—and some technology companies. Operative training for four governments, a dozen agencies, and twice as many 'sanctioned' military organizations. And then it turns into a bullet list of services that mean something to some people, I guess: 'Unconventional Operational Planning,' 'Counter-drug Services,' 'Restricted Site Access,' 'Asset Acquisition,' and 'Ground Truth Validation.'"

"They sound competent," I say.

She gives me a raised eyebrow. "This is the sanitized bullshit list, of course. You know what I found on the Internet? Lots of people railing about black ops missions. Unverifiable and vigorously denied by corporate leadership, of course, but there's rumors of everything from espionage—both corporate and political—to aiding rebel insurgents to outright assassination. These guys aren't Boy Scouts."

"Neither am I," I point out. "And if you were trying to capture someone like me, these might be the sort of people you'd contract the job to, right?"

She doesn't like the direction I'm taking the conversation, but she nods. "Yeah. Yeah, I would."

"What about the corporate management? Are they bean counters or do they have field experience?"

"Their CEO is a guy named Tony Belfast. English." She fusses with the trackpad. "Hang on. Let's see if I can find a picture of this guy. There's nothing on the website." She types a name, hits return, and pops her lips twice while waiting for search results to come back. "Oh shit..." she whispers when the screen loads. She spins the computer around to show me. "That's him."

"Who?" I ask, my voice hard. The search result has returned a screen full of pictures, most of which are of men who are probably named "Tony" and are wandering around Belfast getting their pictures taken. But the first few are of the same man. Well-dressed, cropped gray hair, looking like an older model.

"The guy from the boat," Mere says.

And the guy who was in the silver Mercedes in the parking garage at the Adelaide hospital, and who showed up as we were leaving Eden Park.

"That's *Albatross*," I realize.

"How do you know?"

"He's a hands-on type. You and I have both seen him, in the field. He'll want to be in the loop on any operation. The others report directly to him. Simplest chain of command."

Mere shakes her head at my words. "Don't do it," she says.

"Do what?"

"I know what you're thinking," she says. "I can read it right there. On your face. 'I'm going to call him.' That's what your face is saying."

"I should call him. It's the easiest solution."

"And the dumbest. Not to mention awkward and more than a little dangerous."

"It's direct."

"So let's call it *Plan D* then, and how about we come up with a few other plans before we settle on this one?"

"D for *dumb,* is it?"

"*D* for *Desperate* is more like it."

"I suppose we try to rise above that for *Plan A* then. For *Amateur*, perhaps?"

"Yes," she says. "Or *Asinine*. And *B* for *Backwards*."

"And C would be?"

"Catastrophic. At best."

"I'm glad you're not pulling any punches with your assessment of my ideas, Mere."

"Just trying to be useful. You're the one who said you weren't much of a planner."

"Any other options?"

"Is there anyone else you could call? Who is your contact at Arcadia who is looking out for you?"

"I tried. There wasn't any answer."

"Really? That seems a little odd."

"I've never been exiled before either, so I'm going to pretend for a bit longer that this is a temporary technical glitch."

She sighs and flops down in the chair. "I've got a lot of reading to do." For a moment, her face sags and I see through her mask, and then she tightens up again and locks everything down with a brave smile. "Can you stay out of trouble for a few hours?"

"I could go get some more cash. You need anything?"

"A fabulous dress, some shoes, and someone to take me dancing."

"When in Rome...?"

"You know it, mister."

▼ ▼

My short-term memory is very good, especially with sequences like phone numbers. I buy another disposable phone and more calling cards on the way to the park land of San Cristobel. Sitting among the trees on the southern slope of the hill—where cell service is surprisingly good—I punch the number into my new phone and give Mr. Tony Belfast, CEO of Secutores Security, a call.

D for *dumb*. *Dumb* is also a synonym for *simple*. Like plans that work.

He answers with a crisp, British "go."

"You've been looking for me," I say.

There's a muffled pause and then his voice comes back again. "I may be. Where are you?"

"In the next room. Where else would I be?"

He laughs at that. "That's a good trick," he says, "because I'm in my car. You want to try that again?"

"I'm in my office," I respond, looking up at the sun-limned leaves overhead.

"Ah, a business call, then. To what do I owe the pleasure?"

"Your people find the laptop? Have you seen the video?"

He's silent for a moment. "I have."

"Not quite what was supposed to happen, was it?"

"Yes, well. There have been a number of things that haven't gone quite the way they were supposed to."

"Are you getting hazard pay for this?"

He laughs. "Of course. You think I'd take this job if there wasn't hazard pay?"

"What about bonuses? You get extra if one of us comes in untouched?"

"I'm not really interested in discussing the terms of my compensation package, thank you."

"How about Hyacinth Holdings?"

"I'm sorry. Hyacinth what?"

I sigh and shake my head. "You've got nothing," I say, making an informed guess. "You've had a lot of collateral damage—some of it involving American citizens. Too many people know your company is involved. And you haven't delivered what you were supposed to. Whoever is paying you isn't going to keep throwing money at this problem. I'm betting they're already reconsidering how much this is costing them."

Belfast doesn't say anything.

"You tell your people what you're hunting?" I ask.

"They're professionals," he replies.

"Sure. But they're getting taken out, and quickly too. I've left survivors. What are they saying?"

"You've gotten lucky," he snaps.

"Is that what you're telling them? 'Chins up, gang. His luck will run out.'"

"It already has."

"What? You think calling you is a mistake? You're not going to track this phone. I'm going to destroy it as soon as we finish talking."

"Yes, but it has a cell number attached to it, you bloody idiot," he sputters. "I already know where you're calling from."

"You're on the wrong continent, aren't you, Tony? It's a pretty big place over here. By the time you get boots on the ground, who knows where I'll be?"

He makes a noise in his throat that is almost a growl. "What do you want?"

"Operational freedom."

"And you think I'm going to give it to you?" He laughs.

"Who runs Hyacinth?" I say. "If it is someone in your command chain, then they're shitting where they sleep. If it isn't, you've got a competitor."

"What does it matter to you?"

"We might have a common enemy," I spell it out for him.

"What sort of operational freedom?" he asks after a moment of silence.

"Steer clear. Let me deal with them. When I'm done, you can have what's left over."

"Why? What's in it for me?"

"Which is the better payout? A chunk of wet flesh in a freezer bag or a living, breathing Arcadian? Which one is going to save your ass?"

"How can I trust you? You're talking about selling out some of your own."

"You can't. No more than I can you. But, look at your alternative."

"Which is?"

"I kill every single one of you."

"And?" he asks, acting tough and calling my bluff.

It is my turn to laugh. "Every death from here on is going to be slow and painful."

TWENTY-SEVEN

After breaking the phone and scattering the pieces in various trash bins, I go back to the mall and wander through the clothing stores. Most of them carry natural fabrics, locally sourced materials, indigenous designs, hand-woven textiles—the very sort of commercial products that give me hope for humanity—and most of it is too casual for evening wear.

I don't buy Mere a dress because I feel guilt for what I just did, but because she asked me to. This is what I tell myself as I look through racks of long dresses. I'm not the type to taunt my opponent—that was more Aeneas's style—but I wanted to hear his voice. I wanted to get an idea of what sort of man he was.

He's not an idiot. He was waiting in the parking garage for me to show up. When his men spotted me in the elevator, they didn't wait until the end of their shift to check in. They called immediately and Belfast left them in position. He set them up as bait, to see what I would do.

And I showed him.

He could have had a dozen men at Eden Park. The pair who had left when I arrived at the asylum had been pulled off their detail by him. To make it easier for me to get Mere out. She had the chip in her. He wanted me to break her out. He wanted me to take her wherever we were going to go next, which was why we didn't have any trouble getting out of Australia.

We led him to Hyacinth, but Hyacinth had already anticipated our arrival. I don't know who the laptop had been left for, but it didn't really matter. The real message was that both Secutores and I were fumbling around in the dark. We had no real idea the scope of the game, and I was starting to wonder if Callis was equally in the dark.

The more I tried to put the pieces together, the more it seemed like I was working on a tiny corner of a much larger puzzle. Mere was right about distractions too. As long as we kept butting heads with Secutores, we weren't going to have a chance to focus on the bigger picture.

So why am I buying a dress for Mere and thinking about taking her out for dinner?

Because I want to.

I watched her for six months and she never knew I was out there. If I hadn't stopped Kirkov, she would be dead; all I would have of her would be memories of my surveillance. How long would I keep those? Would Mother take them from me when I went into her embrace next? *You don't need these; let me ease your burden.*

For the first time in centuries, I'm making decisions that aren't based on mission parameters. My priorities are my own, and I'm starting to wonder what we gave up when we accepted Mother's gift.

▼▼

"What do you think?" she asks, executing a slow turn. Her hair is up, wound around a mother of pearl hair stick topped with a lacquered pink flower, though mussed enough to make it appear as if she's just come from either a rollercoaster ride or a serious romp in the sack. The dress clings to her body and shows off her neck, shoulders, and arms. It is covered with black and dark blue and white streaks, patterns that look like a cross between Jackson Pollack art and a jumble of bird feathers. I found a simple necklace of citrine stones—tiny stones dangling from silver studs—that highlights the hollow of her throat. Matching earrings that shine like chips of ice.

It's her shoes, though, that make my throat tighten and my tongue tap against my teeth.

They are sleek pumps that looked good in the store, but when she puts them on, the clever design of the cutaway sides becomes apparent. White satin finish, overlaid with a myriad of monarch butterflies, the colors of which are not found in nature, but that doesn't matter. Not in the slightest.

"So?" she prompts me.

"You look fantastic," I say, looking away.

"Good," she says as she steps close and rests a finger on my chest. "Now, let's go some place where I can show you what happens when you put a woman like me in a dress like this." She curls her finger as she walks toward the door of the room, beckoning me to follow her.

I do, watching her as we walk the length of the hall. There is none of the clumsiness in her gait that I saw on the boat, even though she's wearing much less sensible shoes. I've walked in heels before—Louis XIV insisted courtiers wear red-heeled shoes—but it was never a fashion statement I cared much for. Possibly because I kept snapping heels off my shoes.

The elevator arrives and Mere walks in, pivoting smoothly and placing her back against the wall of the elevator car. In the warm light reflecting off the gold paneling, she appears to float, suspended off the floor by a host of butterflies swarming around her toes.

I push the button for the ground floor, and spend the ride down staring at the yellow shards of fire that lie around the base of her neck. She watches the numbers descend on the elevator readout, her lips curving into a tiny smile.

V V

The cab drops us off at the edge of a sculpted square, complete with a fancy fountain and decorative hedges that glisten from water saturation. Our destination is a tall building that starts with a rose-colored marble facade at the street level and transforms into a spire of glittering glass and steel as it goes up several dozen floors. Intricate patterns are engraved in the marble—Pre-Columbian, probably Incan or Aztec in origin.

A well-proportioned bouncer gets the door for us, his eyes lingering on Mere as she passes, and she gets the same treatment from the pair in the spacious lobby. The reliance on marble continues inside, huge blocks that create a veritable maze. The stone is sculpted with more of the same symbols as the exterior, though figures start breaking up the endless mosaics. *Incan*, I decide, idly wondering about the design choice. Santiago seems a little south of the heart of the Incan empire.

We follow a wide, winding staircase that takes us to a mezzanine that looks down on the marble display. Mere leaves me to look at the sculpture while she talks to the hostess who is standing behind a podium beside a marble archway.

Distantly, I hear the thump-thump of an electronic beat, dance music drifting down through layers of sound-proofing. How convenient. Dinner and dancing at the same location.

One of the two security guards in the lobby is looking up at me. His hand is pulling at his lapel and his lips are moving.

Who's he talking to?

I hear my name being called and I look away from the security guard. Mere gestures for me to join her. I'm less smitten than I was five minutes ago, and I appraise her more coldly as I walk across the mezzanine. *What is she up to?*

The hostess takes us through the arch and into the restaurant. The ambient thunder of the dance club upstairs fades to a distant echo beneath the melodic etude coming from the white grand piano set up in the center of the room. A dozen stage lights are trained on the piano, and the reflected light provides most of the illumination in the room. The rest comes from small mushroom-shaped lamps that sit in the center of each table, shedding just enough illumination for the diners to see their plates and each other, if they lean close. On my left, lines of blue light illuminate the bottles on the shelves behind the bar.

The hostess takes us to a small booth that is neither in the center nor near the walls. Each booth is separate from its neighbors, a rounded three-quarter shell of plush leather around a lacquered table. Mere slides halfway around the booth and I slip in next to her. She leans over after the hostess leaves, her shoulder bumping mine. "It's rated as the most romantic restaurant in all of Santiago," she says.

"I can't imagine why," I say, looking at her. I nod toward the ceiling. "Let me guess: the hottest dance club is upstairs?"

She smiles, showing me her teeth. "I have no idea what you're talking about."

"How did you know I was going to bring back a dress?"

"Not only am I psychic, but I have mad powers of autosuggestion," she says. Her eyes dart toward my mouth. "If you hadn't, I would have been forced to take you shopping."

"I'm sure I would have survived."

"It's better this way."

"Why is that?"

"Now I know what you like to see me wearing."

"You can't give me a heart attack," I tell her.

"Says you." She bumps my shoulder with hers as she moves away a little. That smile is back, and she busies herself with the menu.

I do the same, knowing this is how the game is played. I'm out of practice, but she makes it easy.

VV

The food is startlingly good. At first, I write off the overly elegant descriptions on the menu as simply the efforts of a very experienced copy writer, as I start with a shaved radish and fennel salad, topped with Thai basil, thin slices of Asian pear, and a hint of coriander in the lemon-infused olive oil dressing. Mere has the carrot, leek, and rosemary soup, and the carrots are Imperators—Gold Pak, most likely, as they are well suited for soup.

"Good?" Mere asks when I don't give the spoon back right away.

"There's no chemical taste," I say.

"Hence the claim of being organic," she says.

"It's rare that there isn't some taint. You can't always control what gets into the soil and root vegetables—carrots, especially—suck up whatever they find. It's not just the vegetables themselves that are pure, though, it's the soil they were grown in too. I haven't tasted anything this clean since…"

And then it hits me: what's been bothering me about this place. It's too comfortable; it fits an Arcadian temperament too readily. And the food is so pure that it has to be drawn from an Arcadian garden.

"What?" she asks.

"Who owns this restaurant?"

She gets that look in her eye, the one that says she knows more than I do. "Alberto Montoya," she says. "He owns the building. Probably the whole block. He's quite the celebrity in Santiago. Devilishly handsome, educated in Spain, very single, and a constant topic of gossip tweeting. He's next in line to run the family business."

"Which is?" I don't like where this is heading.

"It's a private investment company. Supposedly. The trail gets murky. It's old money. Goes back a long time."

"What are you doing, Mere? Why did you bring us here?"

"I don't know, Silas. Why don't you tell me?" She's watching me carefully. "I spent all day doing research, and the whole time I'm wondering why it is that I'm wasting my time on the Internet when I should just be asking you. You claim to have been there, on Easter Island, but you can't remember anything useful. That seems awfully convenient. And then I start wondering what this convenient forgetfulness might be masking. What are you hiding?"

"I told you. There are holes in my memory."

"Yeah, there's a name for it. *Lacunar amnesia*. An hour's worth of research into the causes of amnesia makes me little more than an informed idiot, but I learned enough to know that whatever is going on in your brain is probably due to either some sort of psychological conditioning or chemical imbalance—a lack of chemicals, even. Sure, you have holes, but you never want to talk about *why* you have holes."

She gestures around the restaurant. "The other thing I learned? Amnesiacs *know*. They may not be able to remember everything consciously, but the data is there. They've just forgotten how to access it, and I've seen how you remember things when confronted with familiar things—places, people, objects."

"You brought me here hoping it would jar something loose out of my head?"

"Yes, I did," she says, "because whoever is running Hyacinth remembers you, and until you get your shit squared away, you're not going to see them coming."

I want to be furious with her, but she's right. I haven't told her the truth, mainly because I haven't been able to face it. I'm already uprooted from all that I know; I can't deal with the idea that what I knew might be a lie.

I close my eyes and sink back against the booth, trying to calm my thoughts. The memory shards are moving too quickly; they're trying to force themselves into patterns, some of which don't work. But it doesn't matter. My brain wants order. It wants clarity.

A laugh slowly works its way up my chest and I let it tumble out of my mouth. "I called Belfast this afternoon," I chuckle. "Even though you said it was a dumb idea. I did it anyway."

Mere colors slightly and looks down at the table.

"But you went one better, didn't you? Montoya's firm runs Hyacinth, doesn't it? Beneath all the corporate confusion, that's the simple truth. Montoya is Hyacinth, and you brought us to their favorite restaurant."

"So now you know who they are," she says.

"Mere, they're Arcadians."

TWENTY-EIGHT

Mere swallows, her fingers moving to touch the scar on her throat, but she catches herself, and fumbles with her necklace instead. "They're Arcadians," she repeats, buying time. I wait her out, watching to see how she deals with this piece of news.

I'm working through it myself. It makes sense, but in doing so, it opens up an entirely different line of inquiry in our suppositions. I had made noises during my conversation with Belfast about getting him an Arcadian, and I hadn't thought through that promise. It had been something to dangle in front of him, but now, sitting in the Montoya family restaurant, I see that my brain was putting words in my mouth that it knew were true.

Amnesiacs know.

"We knew this," she says finally. "Not in as many words, but we knew it had to be Arcadians." I nod. "But that means you've got an internal problem. You've got one faction slicing up another."

Callis's comments seem all too prescient now. How much of this did he know? Did he send me to Easter Island to stir up trouble? To flush out whoever was behind the incident out in the Southern Ocean?

"So who—?"

Our waiter arrives, bearing plates, and Mere shuts up, smiling at the young man. If he saw any body language that suggested anything was amiss, he does a fine job of appearing oblivious. He presents our plates, offers some praise for the food and a promise that we won't be disappointed, and then makes to disappear again.

"Actually," Mere calls after him. "I could use a cocktail. We both could. Two Jack Roses, please." She seems almost embarrassed when he nods and departs.

"A what?"

"Jack Rose. Two parts Calvados, one part lime juice, one part grenadine, I think." She tugs an errant strand of hair behind an ear. "I was going to surprise you. I thought it would be the kind of thing you'd like to drink. Calvados is apple brandy."

"I know what Calvados is," I say gently. She seems to be on the verge of tears, and I reach over and rest my hand on hers. "Mere, thank you."

She catches herself, holding back the emotional flood building inside her and manages a laugh instead. "I fucked up," she says. "I really did it this time." She pulls her hand out from under mine and touches the corner of her right eye, daubing at some tear that hadn't started. "I'm sitting on the biggest story of the decade—fuck! of the century—and part of me this afternoon was like, 'Mere, get out of there. Run for the Consulate. Forget all of this. Just forget it and get out.' But I didn't. I stayed, and I... I... walked us right into the shit, didn't I? But what else was I supposed to do? This is all too incredible for me to write some fluff piece about 'how vampires were real and they're not as bad as you think they are.' I mean, I'm not some washed up hack who sells creative fiction to the tabloids in order to keep paying my bar tab. I need to break this story, and break it big. And it's worked for me in the past. The brazen US reporter who is too tenacious, too dumb, to stay home. You either have to kill her or hide your shit because she won't stop coming after you. But the corporate bean counters always won; they always ran away. I thought I was doing good. I was making a difference.

"And then Kirkov came along, and he didn't blink. He didn't want to run away. It wasn't in his nature. He had staked out his piece of turf and it was his. No one was going to take it away from him. He would have killed me..."

"I know."

Her face softens. "But he didn't, right? I got this"—her fingers touch her throat—"and he was dead, so I had won again. My... *souvenir* was proof that I was invincible. It was a symbol to Big Ag to watch out. I wasn't going to stop coming..."

"It's like that the first few years after... after we become Arcadians," I say, filling the void that follows her last sentence. "We think we're invincible. We *are* invincible. But eventually, that feeling wears off and it gets replaced by an awareness of how fragile everything is. We have to be careful; we have to keep ourselves hidden because the human appetite is too ferocious." I don't mean to let all these words out, but now that I've started, they keep coming. "We waited too long, and humanity's hunger is out of control now.

They're like childish Arcadians, inured to their mortality. They want to feel something—anything—to give them hope that death is not the end. They're too frightened otherwise. Too frightened to sit in stillness and hear how inconsequential they are to the world, and yet how marvelous their entire existence is."

"We want to feel something in order to stop thinking about nothing," she whispers.

"And here we are," I say, glancing around. I spot our waiter returning with two drinks. We silently watch him put each on the table, perfectly aligned with our untouched food. He hesitates for a second, seeing that we've not taken a bite, and then takes his cue from the way Mere reaches for her drink. Intuiting the minefield he is standing beside, he bows slightly and vanishes again.

Mere holds her drink out. "To us," she says. "Stupidly blundering through life."

"Lying to ourselves," I say, picking up my glass and clinking it against hers.

"Making a wreck of things," she adds after taking a sip.

I tap glasses again. "Pretending we're not alone," I say. The drink is smooth and marvelous, and I try to remember if I was ever in Calvados during the apple harvest.

She takes a big swallow of hers. "Pretending we don't want each other," she says, offering her glass again. When I don't immediate tap my glass against hers, her eyebrows pull together. "Oh, da—" she starts, her words barely slipping out of her throat.

I tap her glass hard enough to make them ring. "To living long enough to laugh about our mistakes," I say, and then I down the rest of the cocktail. It's not that sort of drink, but I don't think I can handle any more sharing right now.

"Silas," she says. She's not looking at me, though; her gaze is on something over my shoulder. I look, and spot a familiar bald head near the archway into the restaurant. Talus and I make eye contact for a moment, and then he turns and leaves the restaurant.

"Eat up." I raise my hand, trying to catch our waiter's eye. When he comes to the table, I smile and indicate my empty glass. "Another round please," I say, "Oh, and I'll need a large bowl of raw spinach, the largest piece of raw beef you have, and an equal amount of raw tuna."

He nods, completely unfazed, and vanishes to do my bidding.

"Eat up," I tell Mere. "This may be our last meal."

Talus wanted to be seen. He'll be waiting outside. I don't see any reason to rush things. The food is good; the company is better. I might as well enjoy the respite we've been offered.

▼▼

He stands on the mezzanine with his back to the restaurant as if he is intently studying the sculptures below. He's wearing a dark gray suit made from polished virgin wool, and his skin is ruddy without being sun-burned. His head has been recently shaved and moisturized. He turns as we exit the restaurant; he's not wearing a tie and his beard has been groomed to a dignified shape. He looks well-rested and well-fed. When he smiles, I don't believe him, and the fact that he tries to be genial alarms me even more than seeing him here.

"How was dinner?" he asks. His nostrils tighten. "You had the beef?"

"I did," I reply.

"Bloody?"

"Very."

He nods as if that was to be expected and turns his gaze upon Mere. "It is good to see you again, Ms. Vanderhaven."

"Fuck you," Mere says. She had my second drink after bolting hers. I didn't mind.

For a split second, Talus struggles to maintain his veneer and I see the angry man who stared me down on the boat, but he manages to plaster another smile on his face and shrug off her comment.

"Any chance the lady gets to go home?" I ask.

He shakes his head. "Not yet."

Mere takes my arm. "Well," she says, "at least he didn't say 'no.'" She's shivering lightly, and I tamp my anger down.

Talus grins again, and this time I really see the man I remember. He wants me to do something stupid. He wants an excuse.

"So," I say instead. "What's the plan?"

"We're going upstairs," he says. "Señor Montoya wants to have a chat with you."

"Alberto?"

He laughs, and that's all I need to know about his feelings toward the dashingly handsome Alberto. "Señor *Escobar* Montoya," he corrects me.

I feel Mere stiffen slightly beside me, and as Talus indicates that we should join him at the private elevator on the other side of the mezzanine from the restaurant, she leans over and whispers in my ear: "The clan patriarch," she says. "I read about him. When the construction boom hit Santiago in the '30s, he was at the heart of it. He's got to be at least ninety. I thought he was dead."

"Not dead," Talus said, reminding Mere of his superior hearing. "He prefers a less public profile."

The elevator opens as Talus approaches it, triggered by an unseen hand, and he stands beside the doors, indicating that we should enter. I eye the narrow box, considering the risk of taking him once the doors close, but Talus shakes his head as I dawdle.

"You two first," he says. "I'll come up later."

I look at him, and my thoughts must be plain on my face, because he shoves me. "Get in," he snarls, all pretense of civility gone. He stands in the doorway, getting himself under control, until the doors close.

"Well," Mere says as we begin to ascend. "I guess this is the part where we find out just how stupid this whole evening was."

I stand in front of her, taking her hands in mine, and I look at her face. "It was a lovely dinner," I tell her, "and you look fantastic. Nothing else matters. Okay?"

She looks at me and a brave smile struggles to find its way across her lips. "Okay."

"If things go off the rails up here, take care of yourself. Okay? No heroics. No bullshit efforts to stick with the story. Keep your head down. Get out. Go to the Consulate. Call Ralph. Do whatev—"

"I get it, Silas," she says, cutting me off. "Fuck. I get it."

"Okay." I release her hands and start to move to stand beside her. She doesn't let me, surging off the wall to press herself against me, her arms around my neck. Her lips find mine, her teeth nipping at my mouth. I grab her and return the kiss. Her tongue flicks against my mouth, and I open my lips, letting her in. She presses herself even harder against me, her hands winding in my hair. My hands drop, and I step forward, crushing her between me and the wall. She makes a tiny noise, gasping, and then her mouth seeks mine again.

The elevator dings, announcing our arrival, and the doors open. She breaks contact first, and I step back, giving her room. Mere rests against the wall for a moment, catching her breath, and then raises a hand and wipes at the lipstick on my mouth. "Live to laugh," she says quietly, looking me in the eye.

"Absolutely," I reply, and she nods tightly before adjusting her dress and walking off the elevator, head held high.

TWENTY-NINE

I step out of the elevator and I'm in the center of the penthouse. There's nothing between Mere and me and the floor-to-ceiling windows but hardwood floors, a couple pieces of furniture, and an impressive art collection. Off to my left is an equally ostentatious kitchen; to my right are several mobile partitions filled with books and an assortment of smaller trinkets; beyond I spot the edge of a billiards table and an array of large-screen televisions. Somewhere back there is a real wall. The display is meant to be daunting in its dizzying display of wealth, and it succeeds in its efforts.

"What do you think of the view?" someone asks.

The voice comes from a burgundy-colored leather chair near the windows, facing away from the elevator. A narrow glass of wine sits on a nearby side table.

I touch Mere on the elbow, guiding her toward the windows, and we walk over to admire the view. The glass is tempered and there's a pattern to it that shifts when I look at it. Controlled tinting, the sort of atmospheric control that an Arcadian would have installed. "It's impressive," I say, looking out at the glittering skyline of Santiago. There is only one building that is as tall as the one we're in, and I suspect Montoya owns it too. Off in the distance, I can see the dark hump of Sero San Cristobal, the glowing figure of the Virgin Mary at the peak.

The man sitting in the chair on my left appears to be in his late sixties, but he sits too readily, too upright, to be bound by the physicality of that age. He's older, his physical appearance simply a disguise. Much like my own.

"Alberto's tastes are a bit grandiose," the older man says, "but it makes him feel more... at home. More like a *prince*."

Mere fidgets next to me, her hands twisting over themselves, and she finally turns to the older man and puts out her hand. "Hi, I'm Meredith Vanderhaven. I don't think we've met."

He takes her hand—gracefully, elegantly—and raises it slowly to his lips. "Escobar," he says. "Escobar Montoya."

"You were born in 1896," she says, not letting go of his hand. "Which means you've got to be an Arcadian, like Silas. Alberto is twenty-seven. So my first question is: great-grandson or grandson?"

"Neither," Escobar says. "Both." He laughs, glancing past her at me. "She knows." It isn't a question.

"Probably more than I do," I say dryly.

Escobar laughs again. "Oh, that I know."

I look at him fully, examining his face. Trying to recognize it. All I can see is a resemblance from the sculpture downstairs. "I don't know you," I tell him.

His nostrils flare for a second and his face clouds. "You're a liar, Silas Dardanidi," he says.

"So I've been told," I reply, and as if on cue, the elevator sounds.

I expect it contains Talus, but when I hear the echo of more than one pair of feet, I glance over my shoulder. Talus is there, but so is a younger version of Escobar. He wears his suit like he knows how to. Unlike Talus, who is putting on a good show, but looks like the half-thawed French peasant he is next to Alberto Montoya.

"Well," I hear Mere say, "look here. It's the prodigal grandson and your old pal. This is turning into quite the party."

Grandson.

Pieces click together. "He's not your grandson," I say to Escobar. "He's you."

Escobar chuckles. "I was never that young," he says.

One of the side effects of Mother's care: we may live forever, but we're never less aged than the day we first enter her embrace.

"How long has it been since you were truly *young*, Silas?" he asks.

My head is spinning. "Thirty-three centuries," I say, "give or take a few."

Mere stares at me, her mouth open.

"One of the first," he concedes. "But then, you always were one of her favorites."

I shrug. "I wasn't aware that she has favorites. And even if she does, I'm certainly not on the list anymore."

Mere is still staring at me, and Escobar carefully picks up his glass and takes a tiny sip. "Yes, being *aware* is sometimes difficult when you return to her so frequently, isn't it?"

"What do you mean?"

"How much do you remember of all those years?" he asks.

"Most of it," I counter, somewhat defensively, not meeting Mere's gaze.

He laughs. "Most? Silas, do you know how complex the pathways in your brain would have to be to sustain all that history? Haven't you ever wondered why, of all the things that are perfect about us, it is our memories that are the most fragile?"

"The world is fragile," I counter. "It's not like it used to be. It's become so toxic. Brain tissue degrades easily."

"Toxicity has nothing to do with it," he snorts. "Memory is just as easily *not restored.*"

"What do you mean?"

"Come now, Silas. You know she takes memories from you. But do you know how? When you go into Mother's embrace and she heals you, how do you think that works?"

"I—she—she restores us."

"*Restores you?* How? You've been part of her for thirty-three hundred years, and you've never wondered how she heals you? Is it just a matter of growing you new tissue? If you come back to her without legs, she grows you new ones. No arm? No problem. Missing a kidney, or a lung, or an eye? Just as easy. Is that how you think it is done? She buries you beneath her roots and you lie there like a blind worm, letting her knit you whole again."

"Wait a minute," Mere interjects. "This is all true? This is what happens?"

"More or less," I say, somewhat stung by Escobar's words.

"More or less?" Mere echoes.

"He knows so little about how it truly works, dear," Escobar says. "He's not just a passive recipient of her affection. Ask him what happens when he buries himself? Ask him if he can grow a new arm? You hide in the ground, Silas, don't you? You hide so that you can make new marrow from the humus. You can eat flesh to replace your own. You drink blood to flush toxins out of your own bloodstream. If you can do all this without her, then why do you need her at all?"

"I—" I suspect *"that's just the way it is done"* isn't the answer he's looking for.

"Mother says you need her, and you believe her. Like any good child does when its mother tells it the way the world works. But it's more insidious than that, Silas, because Mother has built you in a such a way that you *crave* her soil above all others, and the longer you are gone from her embrace, the more that craving builds. Don't you feel it?"

"No," I resist. "It's the air. It's this world. It's this... this poison that is in my blood. She would heal me. She would protect me."

"She would lie to you," Escobar says sadly. "It's what she's been doing for more than thirty-three centuries."

"No," I protest. "You're the one who is doing the lying." I look at Mere for help, but she's just standing there, listening. Taking it all in. Trying to grasp what she's hearing.

"He's trying to confuse me. Confuse us," I tell her. "We know that Hyacinth owns land on Rapa Nui. We know they built the lab. We know what they're doing. This has nothing to do with how Arcadia works. He knows that I'm rootless. He knows I can't call Arcadia."

"Why not?" she says softly.

"No, Mere. He's lying to us. You saw what he did to Nigel. He did that to one of his own."

"And you haven't?" Escobar snaps.

He wants me to deny it; he wants me to say the words that will seal my fate. He wants me to admit my ignorance of my own history. Because that will prove his point. He knows what I have done, what actions I have taken because Mother told me to.

Amnesiacs know.

"You don't know anything," he says coldly as if he can read my thoughts. "You know nothing about who we are. What we have done to become who we are. What we gave up." His voice rises in volume. "You don't *remember* anything."

I look at Mere again, and the expression on her face is too much to bear. It reminds me of...

I can't look at her all of a sudden, and I turn my gaze to the view, looking out at the darkening skyline of Santiago. A tiny sliver of light gets caught on the roofline of the building near us, a tiny flash of reflected sunlight that hasn't quite gone out yet.

I remember the sun setting in the west, letting the night loose across the sky; I remember how the torches colored all their faces, turning them red with blood. I remember the feathers, the white feathers stuck to my arms and shoulders and chest. The heavy headdress, covered with more feathers. I remember the one who was there before me. The steward.

I remember her face.

"This is a waste of time," Talus says, walking up behind me. "It's all buried too deep. He'll never remember. He prefers it this way. It makes him more efficient. Memory only clouds the mind. Silas doesn't want to know. He just wants to serve." He's standing right behind me. "He just wants to do what he's told."

Mere's eyes are bright, imploring me to say something.

Pieces, coming together. Grafting lemon trees. Tending gardens. Growing a sapling in pure soil.

"Mother sent me to the island to stop you," I say. "You were growing your own tree. You were trying to create a new Arcadia. Mother didn't want that, and so she sent me."

Behind Mere, Alberto is silent, but his mouth is twisted into a leer. I can see the old man in him now. I can see where he came from.

I look at Talus next, searching his face for any sense that he wasn't the bastard I thought he was. I see nothing that convinces me otherwise and so I turn away from him, letting my gaze swing across the view once more.

The sliver of sunlight has gone.

I gauge the distance between the two buildings, and wonder how much wind there is at this height.

Putting my hand on Mere's arm, I turn toward Escobar. "Jacinta Huaca Copihue." I say the name attached to the face I now remember. "Mother sent me to kill your wife. Mother sent me to kill *Hyacinth*."

Mere was right. I needed a trigger. I needed something to force my subconscious to remember what was buried.

And now, I remember too much.

Escobar starts to come out of his chair. Talus is reaching for me, and all I care about is Mere's reactions to my words. Her eyes are widening, and I can't tell if it is in shock or horror.

I hear the tiny plink of glass breaking, and then Talus's head explodes.

THIRTY

Talus is right about one thing, though. I know about efficiency. Escobar has been trying to confuse me, and I've been party to it enough times over the centuries that I should know better, but I let him get under my skin. Inside my head. This is the trouble with fractured memories—with all memory—you seek order. You seek structure. One of the most dangerous things an Arcadian can do is let himself be convinced something is true, because that's what will happen. We'll make it true. Our brains will fix these words—these images—into an unassailable truth.

Their mistake is to think that this confusion will be enough, but I've been a soldier too long. I don't *think* about fighting any more. It just happens.

Even before the jacketed rifle round makes a mess of Talus's head, I'm in motion. I kick at Escobar's chair, knocking it spinning. He's still half in it, and the sudden weight of the chair against his legs knocks him sprawling. I still have a hand on Mere, and I drag her with me as I back-pedal away from the mess that Talus's headless body is making on the hardwood floor.

Another tiny circle of glass falls out of the windows and Alberto spins around, roaring in pain.

I run parallel to the windows, toward the shelter afforded by the book-filled partitions. It's not Alberto I'm trying to hide from; if it were just him and me, I would stay and slug it out. No, I'm getting away from what I know is coming up in the elevator behind him.

He and Talus weren't going to kill me. They weren't going to risk getting hurt themselves. They were going to use Mere to hold me off until the strike team could arrive. And, as she and I reach the safety of the partitions, I hear the elevator ding and the sound of many boots on the floors. Alberto starts screaming at them to go after me.

The partitions are double-sided bookcases about three meters long with thick steel casters. Heavy, but mobile. Not a bad solution for breaking up large warehouse spaces. Useful if I was trying to build a fort.

The billiards table is equally impressive. Walnut frame with marble legs. The green wool cloth like a pristine glade of new grass. The balls are solid ivory, and I take several, stuffing extras into my pockets. The cues are nice too—solid pieces of lathed ash—but impractical against guns.

Mere, to her credit, is right behind me. I spot a hallway leading away from the billiards room and I jerk my chin toward it, telling her to lead the way.

The men are talking to each other as they approach the partitions, and I hear Alberto's voice in the background, maligning their inability to move quickly enough.

The trouble with rent-a-troops: it doesn't matter how well trained they are, Arcadians will always think they move too slowly. The strike teams come at us through two of the gaps in the partitions, and the first pair open fire as they spot me on the far side of the billiards table. Their bullets wreck a number of the television screens arranged along one of the few fixed walls in the penthouse as I run for the hallway.

The book-filled partitions form an L-shape, running from the windows for ten meters or so before making a right-angle and connecting with the wall. The narrow gap between the last partition and the wall allows access to an actual hallway, and I know it is a dead end, but it's a better space for Mere and me to be in than hiding under the billiards table, hoping no one will notice us.

Immediately on my left as I enter the hallway is a walk-in closet nearly the same size as the rec room, and a capacious master bath. The hallway turns to my right several meters ahead, and at the turn is the master bedroom. Around the corner are several other bedrooms, and Mere is standing in the middle of this hallway, looking at me as if I know which door will lead us to safety.

I wave at Mere to stay close to the wall while I peek in on the master bedroom. It's impressive, and worth a more measured look, but behind me is the long and straight hallway back to the rec room. Standing here, gawking, is going to be bad for my health. I sense motion behind me, and I throw one of the billiard balls as I dart out of the doorway. The ball hits one of the strike team members and he goes down heavily, and the way he sprawls on the floor suggests he's not getting back up.

We're behind the elevator shaft now, on the opposite side of the floor, and there are four doors off this hallway. Two that will undoubtedly lead to guest rooms with good views, the one on the opposite side will mostly be a windowless—joyless—utility room of some kind. The last one is at the somewhat abrupt end of the hallway.

"They're behind us," I hiss at Mere. "We can't go back. These rooms"—I gesture around me—"they're not going anywhere either. We have to go forward."

She nods, still in shock. But she's still thinking. "It goes around, doesn't it? There's got to be a way through—a way back to the kitchen. He wouldn't build a place like this without a way to walk around, would he?"

"Let's hope not," I say.

The doors are all closed, which doesn't surprise me terribly if they aren't in use, but the door at the end of the hall shouldn't be there. According to my mental map, I'm not even halfway across the floor. There should be another space—the same size as the master bedroom, these other rooms, and the rest—on the other side of that door. *So why is there a door at all?*

I step back to the turn in the hallway and risk a peek. The gunmen are alert, and all I get is a quick glimpse before someone starts shooting. A fusillade of bullets pepper the wall around the frame of the master bedroom door.

But I get a head count. Four. And I only have two billiard balls left. I'm going to run out of ammo before I run out of targets.

"There's no stairwell either," Mere says. "What happens when the power goes out? Does Montoya stay up here until someone turns the power back on?"

"He's not that stupid," I say, thinking about the number of men who are stalking us. Five doesn't seem like enough. "There's got to be another exit." And then I realize why the number seems off. "They're coming up the stairs," I say.

"Who is?"

"The other team." I point at the way we came. "These guys are driving us toward this door. They haven't rushed us yet, and they haven't thrown any gas or flashbangs. They want us to go through that door first. Into a kill box."

Mere nods that she understands what a kill box is.

"How many do you think are on the other side of that door?" I ask Mere, flashing her a quick smile.

"I don't know, Silas."

"Guess."

"Fifty," she says.

I nod back in the other direction. "There are five back there. Which seems like better odds?"

"That way," she says, pointing back the way we came.

"Then that's the way we'll go." I take her hand and we start sidling along the wall. The door at the end of the hall is inset in the wall, and there's about a meter on either side. If I have to trust one or the other to be thick enough to stop bullets, I'm going to bet on the wall. As we approach the turn in the hallway, I stop and put my mouth close to her ear. "When I tell you to, start screaming," I whisper. "Give it all you got, okay? Think of being skinned alive or something."

"Or *something*?" she hisses back.

"Something that takes a little while. And is truly awful, okay?"

She looks at me.

"What?"

"Can I think of something pleasant first?"

"Sure," I say, leaning over and brushing my lips across hers. They're warm and soft, and all I can think is that I'd rather keep doing this than kill five men. "But don't think about it too long, okay?" I say as I stop.

"Okay," she says. A second later, before I've even had a chance to position myself to peek around the corner, she lets loose with an unholy blood-curdling shriek.

▼▼

The penthouse is on the twelfth floor. The dance club is on the fourth. In between, it's nothing but luxury condos. The tenants are all sheep, and they start flooding for the exits when I pull the fire alarm.

After Mere's distraction and my subsequent judicious use of billiard balls, we found a distinct lack of Montoya family members in the main area of the penthouse. The elevator never arrives, and our jaunt down eleven flights of stairs is fraught with a number of frightened residents who are either surly or terrified by the fire alarm that Mere pulled on the eleventh floor. It's good cover, and we ride it out to the street and the plaza around the building. The first of many fire trucks arrives, as well as a number of police cars, and the whole area becomes a hotbed of sirens and lights and activity.

Mere and I slip away. We walk four blocks north and catch a cab. It's as simple as that.

Which makes it too easy.

She presses herself against the door of the cab, shivering—both from chills and trauma. I offer her my coat, and she doesn't seem to register its presence around her shoulders. I don't push it. I let her sit and shiver and think, clutching my coat around her shoulders.

I lean against the other window and watch the city go by. I've got some things to think about too.

Phoebe was on the other rooftop. She's the only person I know who could have made a shot like that. And she took it, blowing Talus's brains all over Montoya's fine hardwood floors.

I'm more than a little curious as to why.

THIRTY-ONE

The cab pulls into the roundabout in front of our hotel and Mere responds to the familiar sight of the hotel facade. I get out and open her door, letting her get herself out of the car while I pay the driver. She's still in shock, stumbling like a sleepwalker through the lobby toward the elevator. I follow, keeping my distance, but still letting her know I am beside her. I get the hotel room door open, and step aside to let her in before I realize what a fool I've been.

Someone grabs her, yanks her inside, and the door is slammed in my face. A hotel room door isn't going to stop me, and I shatter the lock assembly with my hand, smashing the door open. The gunman inside starts firing, the suppressed noise of his submachine gun nothing more than a shuddering whisper, and his bullets make a mess of the door across the hall.

They're going to fall back since I've breached the door, and I can't imagine they're dumb enough to not have a fallback position. After the guy waiting for me to be stupid enough to stand there and let him fill me with bullets runs out of ammo and reloads, I push off from the wall next to the door of our room, and perform the same entry trick on the next room over.

There's a flurry under the covers as I dash through the room and I don't blame the residents of the room for pretending to be nothing more than a profusion of pillows. I yank open the sliding door to the balcony, and get outside in time to watch Mere and three mercenaries leap off the balcony of our room, letting their rappel lines guide them on their fast descent to street level.

There are two gunmen remaining, and one of them sees me coming. He gets one burst off, and I feel a burn across my arm and side, but it doesn't slow me down. The second guy was too busy watching for me to come into the room through the front door, and he reacts too slowly to the sound of his partner dying.

There are three rappel lines. I figure out which one Mere and her captor are on, and I yank the other two free from their hooks, letting the men on them fall. Wrapping the strap of one of the dead merc's weapon around the remaining line, I go after Mere.

Our room looks down on the bean-shaped pool. The hotel keeps it heated, but there aren't many deck chairs out given the time of year. The two mercs whose lines I cut are sprawled on the pavement around the pool, and the third man has reached the bottom of his line and is trying to extricate himself and Mere from the rope without losing control of her. Four more men are coming from my left, all dressed in the same black BDUs.

They're not dressed the same as the team at the penthouse, and they've got different weapons. These guys are Secutores.

Mere gets free of her captor, sees the men coming from the left, turns to run the other way, and is grabbed again by the man who had brought her down. She yanks free, takes two steps back, and goes into the pool.

It's a good distraction. I'm coming down fast, and I tighten my grip on the strap to slow my descent marginally. Timing the rapid passage of balconies, I kick off of one and let go of the strap, falling free the last ten meters. The guy who had brought Mere down is the cushion I'm aiming for.

He breaks my fall, though the impact is deathly traumatic for him. I'm up and into the midst of the other four in a heartbeat. They're trying to figure out how not to shoot each other with their silenced submachine guns as I throat punch one, shatter the kneecap of another, grab the third and throw him into the fourth. Shattered kneecap is down, and I twist his neck until I feel it snap, and then I strip his weapon from him. It's an HK MP7 and not an UMP like I expected it to be. The gun is lightweight, has a laser sight and a noise suppressor, and it shoots a smaller cartridge than the .40 S&W that the UMP carries. A better weapon for urban environments. I point the gun at the pair who are trying to get off each other, and pull the trigger. This one is set to semiautomatic fire. I have to pull the trigger again before the pair stop moving.

Mere is splashing in the water, making a lot of noise. "Are you hurt?" I call out, sweeping my gaze around the perimeter of the pool. She keeps making noise, but I hear a "no!" among all the other sounds.

I wave my gun toward the stairs at the shallow end. "Get out of the water," I tell her.

"Come and get me," she sputters, which makes me smile as I pad in the direction the team of four had come from. When I reach the wall surrounding the pool and peek over, looking over the manicured landscaping to the hotel parking lot, I wonder how many men Belfast has. And their transportation plans.

Nine men down, I count. If it is a twelve-man team, that leaves one to command and two to drive. Two vehicles. Six men each. I look for larger vehicles. Hummers. Luxury SUVs. Short buses. Anything that fits the profile.

My side aches, and the cut along my inner arm still hurts too. The bullets grazed me, taking a bit of flesh, but I shouldn't still be feeling pain from these wounds. I slip the magazine out of the gun and raise it to my face, sniffing at the top bullet in the stack. The chemical stink makes goose flesh race down my neck and across my back.

They've dipped their bullets in the weed killer.

The tips are dark in the light reflecting from the pool, tiny triangles atop copper jackets. I don't like these bullets, and I shove the top of the magazine in my pants pocket and with my other hand, fumble one of the bullets out of the magazine so that it falls into my pocket. I tap the base of the magazine once against the butt of the pistol and slap it back into the gun.

Out in the parking lot, a dark shape flicks its lights on twice. Behind me, I hear Mere say my name. I hear the sound of a hammer clicking back as I turn, and I make sure my finger is clear of the trigger on the MP7.

Mere is out of the pool—her dress clinging to her body, her hair wet and tangled. Standing partially behind her, his right side exposed enough that I can see the pistol in his hand, is Tony Belfast. He's wearing a dark sweater and slacks, the pants missing the numerous pockets typical of assault gear, but I have no doubt he'd be equally comfortable in that get up at a gallery opening as he is right now.

"Put it down," he says.

I set the safety and grab the sling as I let go of the weapon. It drops and hangs a few centimeters above the ground, swaying back and forth.

Mere is shivering.

"Let her go," I say.

"I can't do that," Belfast says.

"Why not? She's not an Arcadian."

"I know," Belfast says. He doesn't say anything else, waiting for me to figure it out. Mere gets it first. "They want me too," she says, her teeth chattering.

"She's a smart woman," he says. "A pain in the ass too, from what I hear, But hey, not my decision. I just follow orders."

"Yeah," I say, "there's a lot of that going around."

"Can I offer you some advice?" he says, stepping behind Mere so I can't see him as well. He puts his free hand on her shoulder. "Get some perspective. I don't think your masters have your best interest in mind."

There's nearly twenty yards separating us. He'll be able to pull the trigger at least once before I can cover that ground. And if I try to shoot him, he'll just shield himself behind her. Any move I make has deadly consequences for Mere, and so I do nothing as he starts to back away.

A scuffling noise of leather sole against brick sounds to my left, and I turn my head a fraction, still trying to keep an eye on Belfast and Mere.

"He's all yours," Belfast calls out, pulling Mere with him as he starts to walk backward.

I turn my head more and catch a glimpse of Alberto Montoya as he launches himself off the wall. I whip the strap up, swinging the gun like a mace as he flies toward me. The gun hits him in the head, doing absolutely nothing to distract him, and he plows into me, forcing me back several steps. Far enough that I tumble into the pool.

At least I drag him with me.

Underwater, there are no shadows and everything is cool and blue. We're in the deep end, and I let myself sink down to the bottom where I can launch myself upward off the tiled floor. Alberto is swimming overhead, spread out like a frog, and I come up fast. He twists as I hit him in the stomach, bending around me as we both break the surface of the pool. He tries to headbutt me, but missing, cracking his skull against the tip of my shoulder. I don't try to hit him; I just hang on, and when we fall back into the pool, I'm on top. Kicking ferociously, I drive us down to the bottom, trying to drive him head-first into the tile.

His shoulder hits first, and a flood of air comes rushing out his mouth. He claws at me, trying to tear my clothes. Trying to get at what lies underneath. I punch him in the left arm—somewhere in the vicinity of the ragged hole left by Phoebe's sniper bullet—and I'm rewarded with more bubbles coming from his mouth. And a thin strand of blood, swirling like smoke as it leaks out of the hole in his jacket.

He twists away from me. Since he's got the bottom beneath him his leverage is better, and when he gets his feet up and against my thighs, I know I'm going to lose this contest. He shoves, and I let go, letting the power of his kick send me rocketing back toward the surface of the pool.

I don't go after him. Breaking the surface like a rising whale, I suck in a lungful of air and swim for the edge. Whoever gets out first will have a height advantage against the other. I haul myself out of the pool, swipe the water from my face, and look for Alberto.

As I'm tracking the dark shape under the water, out of the corner of my eye I notice movement along the edge of the pool. Throat punch isn't dead, and he has rolled onto his side and he's got his gun pointed in my direction.

I dart for the shallow end, a direction that he can't track very well from his position, as bullets chew up the pavement where I had been standing a moment before.

There's no sign of Mere or Belfast. With a growl, I launch myself across the width of the pool. Throat punch senses me landing behind him, and he tries to roll over, but he's awfully slow.

This time I make sure he stays down.

Grabbing one of the other guns lying nearby, I pepper the water with bullets, letting Alberto know it isn't safe to come out of the water yet. Grabbing an extra set of magazines, I run for the wall separating the pool from the parking lot.

Mere and Belfast went out the wrong side of the pool. They're going to have to go all the way around to get to the parking lot. By heading straight for the wall, I'll make up a lot of lost ground.

I leap over the wall, landing in the park lot. A half-dozen rows over, I spot two figures hurrying toward a dark SUV with its lights on.

Alberto body-checks me, and I sprawl against the pavement, losing the gun. I spin, trying to get back to my feet, and he clips me across the chin with a vicious kick. I keep spinning and slam against a sedan, setting off its alarm. He follows up the kick with several hard punches to my kidneys.

He's strong and well-fed. Even after the protein cram at dinner, I'm not well enough to go the distance with him.

He hits me again, and I fall to my knees. His next kick bounces me off the car I'm kneeling beside, and my head leaves a nice dent in the back of the trunk.

Alberto is on me before I can get my bearings, and he drags me to my feet, throwing me into the back window of the car. I go halfway through the frame, shards of glass raking across my chest. The inside of the car is dark and there's something wet filling my left eye socket. The car alarm is wailing, and the lights on the dashboard wink on and off in time with the siren. I scrabble for anything that might be useful as a weapon, my hand sliding across the leather seat, and then I'm dragged out of the car by my feet. Alberto grunts as he pivots, throwing me across the aisle. I slam into another car, creasing the trunk and fracturing the back window.

I start to slide off the car, and he's right there to help, bodily slamming me onto the pavement. The wind is knocked out of me, and before I can get my breath back, he plants himself on my chest so that he can pound my face with his fists.

Bones moves unnaturally in my cheek after the third punch, and I can't see anything out of my left eye now. I try to shift beneath him, but he's a ten ton rock sitting on my pelvis. He hits me again and I feel something snap near the back of my jaw.

I'm suddenly back on the ship, fleeing from Troy. The storm is trying to capsize our leaking boat, the wounded soldiers are cowering down on the benches, and the masts are moaning as the winds try to tear through our canvas sails. No one expects to survive the night. Troy is behind us—its towers burning, its street slick with blood. Only Aeneas is laughing, his hand firm on the tiller. *We are being reborn. We are no longer who we were.*

I was a soldier of Troy, and then I became a soldier of Arcadia. I fought, bled, *died* for others. Time and again, my dead flesh was buried beneath Mother's roots, where I was reborn. Cleansed. Purified. My hands clean of blood. My mind free to make the same mistakes again and again.

I used to hear the voice of the Goddess in bird song. I used to be able to read the stars. I used to be able to see the shape of what might be. I gave all of that up when I let them bury me. I did so willingly because I thought I was getting something better.

Alberto breaks my nose. He knocks teeth loose in my mouth. With my one good eye, I can see his face above me—his lips pulled back from his teeth in a feral grin. I can feel his hips grind against me with each blow; I can feel how much he's enjoying beating me to death.

I see the ceremonial circle at the edge of the cliff near Orongo. The ring of torches, guttering and smoking. The natives, their faces painted white and black. Their naked bodies shining with whale fat to keep them warm in the water. The feathered headdress. The white wings. The steward with her dark eyes and dark hair. Hating me. Hating Arcadia.

I killed the matriarch of his familial clan. I put a knife in her chest, tore out her heart, and tossed her body off the cliff.

I was following orders.

Alberto stops hitting me. He's breathing heavily and he raises his reddened knuckles to his mouth so that he can taste my blood. I want to tell him something, but my jaw doesn't work. My throat is filling with blood; all I can do is choke and sputter, spewing my life all over his jacket.

He shivers as he tastes me, the electric sensation of fresh blood lighting up the pleasure receptors in his brain. Making him want more. Making him thirsty. He licks his knuckles again, his hips pressing against me as he leans forward. The thirst is rising in him. My face is a bloody mess, and the smell is going right into his brain. When he reaches for me again, it's not with a fist, but with an open hand. He's done playing. He's going to drain me now. Drain every last ounce of my life from my tired body.

I wait until he lowers his head, opening his mouth and showing me his teeth. And then I hit him with the only part of my head that isn't wrecked—the crown of my skull. The hard part. It's a glancing blow, mashing his nose enough to draw blood but not enough to break it. More importantly, he jerks his head back and shifts his weight.

I buck him off and roll away. He gets a hand on my pant leg, and I twist around, getting both of my hands on his and snap two of his fingers back before he lets go.

The face is the least dangerous tool a fighter has. Alberto should have focused on making sure I couldn't fight back before knocking my bones around. I'm down an eye, but both of my hands still work. This fight isn't over.

I leap and scramble over a pair of cars, and I get as far as the hood of the second car when he catches up, slamming into me and knocking me off the car. I spin off the car, landing on my right knee which distracts me momentarily from the pain in my face. He lands nearby, and tries to stomp on my chest. I evade his descending foot, and as I roll across the parking lot pavement, I pass over a ridged metal shape—a manhole cover. Stamped steel, and heavy.

I roll back, slipping two fingers into the access slot of the manhole cover. Alberto steps in, meaning to break some ribs with his foot, and I wrench the cover up. The force of his kick knocks the cover into me, but I take far less of the impact than he does.

He howls, stumbling as he tries to keep the weight off his foot. I swing the manhole cover in an arc and catch him across the other ankle. He comes down to the ground and gets his arms up in time to deflect my first attack, but it rocks him up on his side. He tries to turn the motion into a roll, but I bang the edge of the manhole cover against the back of his hip and lower back. He flops onto his face, and I scramble across the pavement. He tries to get up and I hit him in the back of the skull, ricocheting his face off the pavement. Flipping the steel cover around in my hand, I bring the edge down on the curve of his back, and he flops down again and goes limp.

He'll live but he'll be paralyzed until he can get a lot of dirt time. I decide I don't want to give him another chance to come after me, and I swing the manhole cover down again, putting a lot of force in the blow. Right across the back of his neck. The pavement dents, and his head rolls to the side, no longer connected to his body.

There's a lot of blood spurting from the ragged stump of his neck, and I collapse to my knees, whimpering with pain as my tongue forces my jaw to move. I'm head down, trying to lap up blood like a wounded dog, when I hear the sound of tires screeching against pavement.

Mere. Belfast. The SUV.

Growling and gagging with rage and frustration, I tear myself away from the bloody mess of Alberto Montoya. His blood mixes with mine, and it's a glorious taste. The pain of my shattered face recedes, and as I run, I don't feel anything in my right kneecap. The manhole cover, its rim edged with gore, is as light as a Frisbee in my hands.

When I get to the road, I spot the receding lights of the SUV on my right. I chase after it, and when its brake lights flare, I change my step and hurl the manhole cover like a discus. It's larger and heavier than the ones we used to throw in our seasonal games, but it is aerodynamic enough. As the SUV slows, making a right turn, the manhole cover shears into its back end, cutting through the paneling and destroying one of the back tires. The SUV slews widely, a rooster tail of sparks trailing behind it, and it slams into an oncoming car in the other lane.

The passenger side doors open, spilling two dark shapes out into the street. They orient on me, tiny spurts of flame flickering from their guns as they start shooting. As I dodge behind a car parked along the street, a black sedan shoots past me.

As the car nears the intersection, the driver slams on the brake, twisting the wheel to the left. The car skids, putting its length between me and the gunmen. I hear two muffled reports, noise suppressor on a larger gun, and both gunmen are knocked off their feet. Another cough, and the back window of the SUV shatters.

The driver of the sedan looks back at me. I don't recognize her at first— her skin is too tan and her hair is black. But I know that face; I know those eyes. The long barrel of a sniper rifle is propped up on the open passenger side window.

"Phoebe," I croak.

One of the other doors of the SUV opens and a slender figure in a blue dress spills out.

"Get her," Phoebe says without the slightest inflection in her voice. As if she hasn't been missing for the last few weeks. As if it wasn't her an hour ago putting rounds through the window of Montoya's penthouse.

I stagger toward Mere, who is shakily moving toward the black sedan, trying her best not to look at the pair of dead men on the ground beside her. My legs start shaking as I near the car, and I lean against the trunk, trying to breathe. Mere is close enough that she can see my face, and she shakes her head in horror at what she sees. There are black lines running down her face, a combination of shadows and mascara.

White bird. Black lines. Red blood.

I close my eyes and see Jacinta's face one more time, and then I don't know anything else but darkness.

BOOK FIVE

DENDRA

THIRTY-TWO

As I wake, I start to dig.

My body knows what to do. I'm not even fully conscious yet, but already my hands are scrabbling at the dirt around me. It's dry and loose, and my skin tingles from having been buried for... more than a few days. My clawed hand breaks through, and I've shifted enough in my makeshift grave to get my feet under my body and shove my way to the surface.

I flop on the ground, spitting dirt out of my mouth. My jaw aches, but it moves like it should, and I spend a few moments exploring my face with my fingers. My skin is tender in places and my eyes water if I press too hard on the bridge of my nose, but my face has healed.

It's just as Escobar said. We can heal ourselves. It isn't a truly revolutionary idea—any time in the humus heals—and most of the minor scrapes and cuts I've sustained over the last few weeks are gone. But I needed serious work on my face, and my other wounds were still tainted by the weed killer. I can still feel the poisons in my blood, too, but their influence has been lessened. I am *stained* now, instead of being *foul*, and the act of making such a distinction is troubling.

I'm in the shade of several palm trees, behind a nondescript villa with a plain porch. The setting sun makes the sere hills glow, and the sky overhead is vast and blue and I can see the glint of a few stars already. Next to the villa is the tall trunk of an aged monkey-puzzle tree, its burred branches curling like simian tails. I smell the air, and it's clean and dry with just a hint of fermenting fruit. It's the wrong season to be growing grapes, but there are vineyards nearby.

There's a light on in the villa. I drag myself out of the grave and brush off the worst of the dirt and dust. I'm not wearing any shoes, and it feels good to walk across the tiny yard with bare feet.

There's a screen door in the back of the villa, and the interior door is open. Through the wire mesh, I spot Mere standing in the kitchen. She's standing at the counter, preparing a plate of fruit, and she's wearing tan cotton pants and a cerulean-colored top. Her hair is pulled back but left unrestrained. She glances up as I enter, and then goes back to finishing the task at hand. "Well," she says, "there you are." As calmly as if I was just returning from a walk.

"Here I am," I reply somewhat hoarsely. My throat is dry. "And where is here?"

A ghost of a smile crosses her lips. "About an hour outside of La Serena, up the Valle de Elqui."

I nod, though I'm not sure of where that is.

"About a day's travel north of Santiago," she says. "It's a bit of a tourist spot, what with the observatories and all the pisco distillers, but Phoebe said the soil was good."

"It is," I say. "How long have you been waiting for me?" I ask. There are several dozen other questions queuing up behind that one. Observatories? Pisco distilleries? La Serena? And, farther back: Montoya; Belfast and Secutores; Jacinta and the garden on Rapa Nui; my role in what happened on the island. And Phoebe. Where had she come from? How long had she been watching us?

"Five days," she says. She looks at me again out of the corner of her eye and she can't quite suppress the shudder that runs up her arms.

"My face is healed," I give voice to what she doesn't want to acknowledge.

"I can see that," she says, visibly tensing. "I couldn't handle it," she continues. "I had Phoebe pull over before we had even left the city. It was either you or I in the trunk. The back seat wasn't good enough. I could still hear you trying to breathe through…" She raises her hand toward her face. "And I let Phoebe dig the hole out back. I couldn't look at you. It was awful, Silas. It was really awful."

"I'm sorry, Mere. I didn't do it on purpose."

She chokes out a laugh. "Did you kill him?"

Him being Alberto Montoya. "Yes."

"And is the rest true too?"

"That I killed Escobar's wife? Yes."

She finishes preparing the fruit and brings the plate over to the table.

She sits down, and when she doesn't say otherwise, I join her, figuring that there will be time enough to talk about everything.

There are bananas of differing sizes and colors on the plate, along with slices of oranges, papayas, passion fruit, lemons, as well as a couple of other fruits I don't immediately recognize. I try to savor them, to not grab the plate and immediately shovel all of it in my mouth, but the fresh fruit is a cup of water to a man dying of thirst. We eat in silence for a few minutes, as if we can put off plunging back into a strange reality we both set aside for a few days.

The round fruit with the shadowed green skin is dark inside—it isn't a date or a plum or a persimmon, though it tastes like the mixture of all three. I scrape the skin with my teeth, getting every last bit, and then I chew on pieces of the rind. "What is this?"

"Sapote," Mere says. There's half of one left, which she shoves toward me as she goes for a long slice of papaya.

I don't give her a chance to change her mind, and my fingers are stained black when I'm done, like I've been dipping them in ink or as if I've been burned.

"If I close my eyes and wish really hard, I can imagine that it is just the two of us," Mere says, lightly sucking at the tips of her fingers. "Look at you. Sleeping in until nearly sunset. A plate of fresh fruit prepared for you by a beautiful woman. An entire valley filled with vineyards. The quintessential romantic vacation."

"That would be nice," I tell her.

She raises her head and takes a long, hard look at me. The corner of her mouth turns up, and there's a glimmer of something in her eyes that I can't quite capture, and then she looks down at her hands again. "I've had some time to think," she says. "Lots of time. And Phoebe… well, she's not the best conversationalist, but once I figured out how to interpret her silences, it got easier."

"She tell you what happened? How she got to Santiago?"

"A little. Talus drove her off the boat. Says she knew something was wrong as soon as you reached the tender, but that Talus was already coming at her. She had no choice but to go overboard."

I wince at the idea. "And?"

Mere shakes her head. "She won't say. I think she swam."

I shook my head. "That's not possible."

"Well, she's here, isn't she?" Mere rubs her arms. "Is that what did it to her?"

I think back about how different Phoebe had looked in the car. So dark, like a vengeful shadow. "She's been out in the sun," I say.

"But it's only been a few weeks since we were all aboard the boat. You can't get that good of a tan in that time. And her hair? It's purple. Almost black, but not quite."

"It's what happens," I say with a shrug.

"But I thought you didn't like sunlight."

"It's not sunlight that's bad for us. It's what's in the air that causes grief. It's like any viral infection. As long as you can keep the bad stuff out, you can shrug off a lot of things that could kill you. Once it gets in, things get a little dicier." I remember a summer—in Iceland, a long time ago—and smile. "Sunlight is good, Mere. It makes things grow." I hold up one of the small bananas. So green and sweet. "But then the Industrial Revolution came along and changed so much."

"Yeah," she says, dropping her gaze. "Things changed." She wrestles with something for a minute, arguing with herself. "Look," she starts, "I should probably apologize for—ah, maybe, I don't know…"

"It's okay. You don't need to. We survived. That's all that matters."

"Yes, but—" She breaks off, and I wait—patiently, anxiously—wondering why my heart is tripping in my chest. "How many died in Santiago? How many men did you kill?"

I shrug as if the number isn't that important, even though I realize such indifference isn't the right answer. But what can I tell her? I've killed a lot of men over the centuries. These last dozen or so don't change the total that much.

"And Alberto Montoya. You killed Escobar's wife and grandson. You've killed his family, Silas. You're just perpetuating a cycle. Don't you see?"

I think of Priam, wreathed in silence, collecting the mutilated body of his son from the Grecian camp. All the violence and destruction that had come prior to Hector's duel with Achilles, and how Hector's death—the brief peace surrounding the funeral notwithstanding—did nothing to quell the bloodlust that burned in the hearts of both armies.

This is what Mother does. She hides the past from us, so that we don't get caught up in regret. So that we don't overthink what it is that we are supposed to do.

She rubs her face with her hands. "I'm an accessory. Don't you get that? I'm responsible."

"No you aren't," I say softly. "What happened in Santiago is not your fault."

"I took us to the restaurant. I knew who owned the place. Come on, Silas. I knew what was going to happen."

"Did you want it to happen?"

"No," she sputters, "but that's beside the point."

I shake my head. "There's a difference between seeking to cause bloodshed and being capable of doing it. That's the difference between being an animal and being a warrior."

"It doesn't make it right."

"Whatever you have to do to survive is the right thing to do." I reach over and catch her hands. "It's okay, Mere. No one will fault you for wanting to live."

She shivers slightly, but doesn't pull her hands away. "But that is what frightens me," she whispers. "That I'm going to be *okay* with *wanting to live*. With doing whatever…"

She's fighting the loss of her innocence, and I wish I could undo what has been done. That I could keep her safe and untouched by the bloodshed that surrounds me. But it's too late. War changes everyone—not for the better, most of the time. Mere is going to have to find her own way to deal with the emotional and psychological trauma. In her own time.

Mere is staring at my mouth, her teeth worrying her own bottom lip. "Phoebe said if we couldn't find good soil that you would need blood."

"I don't," I tell her.

"But that's part of how it works, isn't it? It's part of being an Arcadian. You really do drink blood. Like a…"

"Like a vampire? Yes."

Her teeth nip harder at her lip. "Would you have…?"

"You're not my type," I tell her, but my gaze belies my words. I'm fascinated with her lower lip. I can see her pulse in her throat, a tiny butterfly moving beneath her skin.

She smiles, a curl of her mouth that is both shy and sensual. "I'm O negative," she says, trying for some levity. "I'm everyone's type."

I laugh, and the noise tears something in my chest. She laughs too, and yes, for a moment, I can imagine the same dream she did. It's just the two of us. A romantic vacation. Nothing else exists. Nothing else is true.

And then the distant buzz of a tiny motor outside breaks the illusion. I go completely still and hold her in place too. "Are you expecting anyone?"

Her shoulders sag and she sits back in her chair. "That's, ah, that's probably Pedro," she says.

"Pedro?"

"He's just a kid. My local scout. I recruited him a day or so after we arrived." Mere extricates her hands from mine, and the last glimmer of the illusion vanishes as soon as the connection between our flesh goes away. "He comes by around now. Brings us groceries and gossip."

She gets up and comes around the table, laying her hand on my shoulder in a signal for me to stay seated. "He doesn't know you. You'll spook him. Plus—" She brushes dust off my shoulder. "You're dirty."

VV

I settle for listening from around the corner. Pedro sounds like nothing more than an eager teenager taken with the flame-haired American woman hiding out in this villa. His Spanish is inflected by a syllable-swallowing accent, and it's a bit hard to follow the torrent of words that come out of his mouth, but at the very least, it is clear he takes his job of being Mere's eyes in the valley seriously. Either he doesn't know that she understands little of what he is saying or he doesn't care. He delivers his report earnestly and breathlessly. I pay attention when he starts talking about cars. Mercedes and Land Rovers. Or maybe it is the same car; it is hard to be sure.

Mere knows how to work a source, and she makes the appropriate noises during his rapid-fire monologue. When he finishes, she congratulates him on his diligence, and in my mind, I can see him standing taller upon receiving her warm encouragement.

"He's too eager to please."

I glance over my shoulder. Phoebe is sitting in the chair Mere was recently in. Phoebe's skin is a warm bronze color and her hair is a dark and vibrant purple. She doesn't have it pulled back into a pony tail, and it lies loosely about her shoulders like a bruised shadow. *How clean is the air here?* I wonder. My chest aches at the thought of being able to walk about so freely in the sun. She's calmly cutting a papaya into long wedges, completely oblivious to my scrutiny.

Distantly, I hear the tiny motor of Pedro's scooter start up, the fierce roar of a tiny lion, and then it quickly starts to fade away.

"Do you think he's drawing attention?" I ask.

Phoebe nods as she finishes sectioning the papaya. She picks up a wedge, strips off the skin with a single smooth motion of the knife, and then—delicately, showing very little teeth—starts biting off pieces from one end.

"Is it going to be a problem?"

She pauses, a tiny slice poised to disappear into her mouth, and shrugs. Not a problem for us, apparently.

I want to ask Phoebe about what happened on the *Cetacean Liberty*—where she's been for the last few weeks, how she managed to find us, *did she really swim all the way back?*—but Mere returns to the kitchen before I can start.

"So," Mere says as she enters the room, "what did he say?" She doesn't seem terribly surprised to see Phoebe.

"Mercedes," Phoebe says as she picks up a second piece, unconcerned about the strip of black seeds along the inner edge of the wedge. "G Class. They look like Land Rovers."

"I thought it might be something like that," Mere says. "I heard him say 'Mercedes' a couple of times. Expensive, right? Otherwise he wouldn't have noticed."

Phoebe nods.

"And not just passing through," I note.

"Right," Mere says. "What's our plan?"

Phoebe finishes her second slice. "Where are we going?" she asks.

We both look at Mere, who raises her hands helplessly. "I don't know. I'm still working on it."

"Work faster," Phoebe suggests, reaching for another piece with more calm than her words suggest.

Mere grabs my arm and hauls me from the kitchen. "Come on," she says. "Now that you're awake, let me show you what I've got."

THIRTY-THREE

S he leads me down a narrow, unadorned hallway into a room that looks out over the front of the villa. The room is spartan—wooden chair, desk, and tiny chaise lounge—and a full-sized laptop, not the tiny netbook I had bought back in Santiago, is the only indicator that we're still in the twenty-first century. Tacked up on the opposite wall from the desk are Mere's charts: another version of the sheet from the hotel, even more byzantine now with its lines and bubbles, and a narrow strip of brown paper upon which she has drawn a crude map of the western side of South America.

I wander over to the maps and start examining them, listening as Mere runs through the highlights of the news over the past week. The fire alarm at Montoya's penthouse turned out to be a fortuitous act on a resident's part as a bomb explosion not two hours later decimated the top floor of the building. The Chilean military wanted to call it a terrorist attack and the local Santiago police were claiming it was an assassination attempt by a industrial competitor of the Montoya family. Either way, most of the city got locked down and the news media was still scrambling to figure out which of the thousands of rumors flying around were true. The entire country was in an uproar over the event, even though no one knew anything specific.

It sounds like a pretty standard cluster-fuck and cover-up. Montoya blows the penthouse, covering the dead strike team up there, and the resultant confusion allows him to spirit away the mess at the hotel as well. The martial lockdown might have been meant to seal us inside the city limits, but Phoebe did the right thing by getting us out immediately after rescuing Mere. We've done it a thousand times. Go in, do the deed, get out. Don't be there when the local media and police swarm the area. Keep moving as far away as fast as possible. In twelve hours, there won't be enough useful data to track anyone.

Though only a day's drive was a little close to go to ground, and as I decipher Mere's notes on the geography map, I realize why they chose the spot they did. "You're charting Arcadian-friendly spots."

"Yes," she agrees. "Phoebe gave me the idea when she said you needed good dirt. During the drive up from Santiago, I realized that was the way I was going to find them."

"Them?"

"Hyacinth." She joins me at the map and elucidates some of her squiggles. "You remember Mnemosysia? They're the ones out of Denver, Colorado, who are trying to create memory retention therapies. I thought they were running out of money, and I don't have my notes on hand to be sure, but over the last few days, I haven't been able to find nearly as much data as I had thought I had. I know it's impossible to scrub the Internet, but it certainly feels like someone has been trying. But let's stick with that basic assumption, okay? Let's assume Mnemosysia is having money troubles. They need a miracle to get them to their next milestone, and someone comes up with a shortcut."

"Whale brains," I provide, indicating that I remember our previous conversation.

"Right. And so they need a supply of raw material." Her finger traces along a line on the sheet. "Now, Kyodo Kujira is in similar financial straits. They happen to have a whaling fleet that's ready to go if someone would actually cover the costs of putting them out to sea." There's a question mark in a triangle next to Mere's notation of Kyodo Kujira. "If Mnemosysia doesn't have the money, then who steps up? And what are they getting out of the deal? And why are they a silent partner?" Mere looks at me and raises her eyebrow.

"Memory drugs," I say.

"Memory drugs," she repeats. "I didn't make the connection earlier, but now, knowing you a little better—knowing what happens to Arcadians—it seems obvious. Arcadia would fund this research, wouldn't they?"

"Except for the bit about having to kill whales for the research," I point out.

"True, but that's the hook, isn't it? That's what gets Arcadia interested. It's not about whaling. Whaling has been going on for centuries. It's about the reason *why* they're whaling, and that reason is one that Arcadia would be interested in, yes?"

I nod. I wasn't privy to the Grove's decision to send the team—team members typically aren't informed of all the various intricacies of their missions—and, given what has happened since, it's easy to say that I was an idiot for going along without asking more questions. But there's never been a reason to ask questions before. We're good soldiers. Mother takes care of us.

"But it's a trap. It's a way for someone to get their hands on an Arcadian."

"How is Hyacinth involved?" I ask. "If it is owned by the Montoyas, they already have access to Arcadians."

"Would you volunteer one of your own for what they did to Nigel?"

I concede that point.

"But that's what has been bugging me these last few days. Aren't there less invasive ways to get tissue samples? If that was the point, then you should be able to find a volunteer. Companies turn to their employees all the time for this sort of thing. Some of them even offer a pretty good honorarium for volunteering. So why the medical drama? Was that all just for us?"

"No," I say. "That went well beyond acceptable limits."

Mere nods. "So they were harvesting Nigel, which leads me to the burning question: *Who are they?*"

I cock my head to the side. "Not why?"

She shakes her head as she runs her fingers over her chart. "The more I dig into Hyacinth Holdings, the more it seems like it has to be a front for Arcadian research, but it doesn't make sense that it would be completely covert from the rest of Arcadia, or that it would be involved in some scheme to trap one of their own."

"But they're not Arcadian any more, are they?" I realize.

She nods. "You killed Jacinta. You wrecked the garden they were building. The garden that was going to create a place that wasn't beholden to Arcadian rules. You were supposed to bring them home again, but they didn't come home, did they? They went underground and kept working on how to be free of Arcadia."

How to be free of Mother, I think, trying to process what she is telling me.

"Escobar was trying to convince you that Arcadia is poisoning you," she continues. "When you go back home and... do whatever it is that happens there... you get injected with some sort of time-release virus—a mimetic agent, I guess—that makes you crave returning to Arcadia. Right? Your brain gets infected with this idea that you're going to die if you stay away. You self-sabotage, don't you? The longer you stay away, the harder it gets for you to stay healthy."

I don't disagree with her, but agreeing with her puts a lot of what Escobar was saying in a different light. And I'm not ready to make that jump yet.

"But, here's the problem with this theory," Mere says. "There's no money trail from Hyacinth to Mnemosysia."

"I thought you said someone was footing the bill?"

"Someone is, but as near as I can tell, it isn't Hyacinth." She taps the chart. "And here's the thing, why would Hyacinth get involved with Kyodo Kujira and all this mess with Arcadia if they already had access to Mnemosysia's data."

"They made a deal," I say, following her line of thinking.

She nods. "This is where Secutores comes in. They're the front for someone else. Their job is to get an Arcadian. They built the framework of the trap—one that would hold up to scrutiny and would tantalize Arcadia to send a team."

"Hyacinth's job was to make sure a team got sent," I say.

"Yep," Mere says. "They may have walked away from the family, but they still have some influence back home."

"So in return for an Arcadian, they'd get the Mnemosysia data?"

"But that's not what happened, is it?" she continues. "Your team didn't play ball the way they were supposed to, and Secutores's trap failed to catch anyone."

I shake my head. "No, it failed to capture me."

Mere snorts. "I thought we covered this. It's not about you."

"But it is," I tell her. "Phoebe and I have worked together in the past, and we have a working relationship. I'm point. She's support. That's the way we've always done it. I should have been lead on the processing boat, but I got distracted by the whaling equipment. Phoebe would have waited for me if it had been the two of us, but we had Nigel. We weren't used to working as a trio, and when I fell back, he naturally stepped up. He got the chemical dose that was meant for me."

And then I understand Talus's role in all of it. "Talus was the plant," I say. "How did he survive all of this if it wasn't simply by turning the boat over to Secutores? He talked Nigel into attacking the harpoon boat, specifically to force Phoebe and me to do what we did. To separate us." I cast my mind back and dredge up details about the fight on the harpoon boat. Little things that had been odd, but not so much that I had stopped and looked more closely. But now, a different picture emerged. "They were supposed to catch me, but they hadn't counted on Phoebe and her rifle. That threw things off enough that I was able to engage them. And then..."

I recall the errant grenade and the explosion that had holed the boat. The sound of water, rushing into the breach. The ocean, eager to claim the tender. When the storm rolled in, any chance of reuniting with the Prime Earth boat vanished.

"Escobar wanted to hand you over," Mere says.

I nod. "Do you see how that fits? Talus came back to shore. Secutores built a new trap—knowing that I'd come find you—and we managed to get away from them again."

"But Hyacinth had Nigel. Why'd they cut up Nigel?"

"It's like you said: to get us angry. To keep us from looking at the big picture." I lean against the desk. "What if Talus and Escobar didn't know about the chemical agent? What if all they were told was that Secutores was going to capture an Arcadian. Escobar gave them enough data to create an effective trap. That's why it was out on the water. It makes it easier to keep one of us in one place if we can't flee. But they didn't know about the chemical agent. When Talus saw what Secutores had, he realized what was really going on. Whoever had come to Escobar was playing off his alienation from Arcadia. They hoped he wouldn't think too hard about why they wanted an Arcadian, and maybe he didn't care, but when Talus saw the weed killer, that changed things.

"That compound comes out of defoliation research, and there's no way any Arcadian would have anything to do with that research. And why would Hyacinth create something that is just as deadly to them as it is to Arcadians? It's not strategically useful. However, to an organization like Secutores?"

"They were delivering the means of their own deaths."

"Right. That's what Nigel's death is all about. It's a big *fuck you* to Secutores. *You get nothing.*"

Mere nods, following my line of thinking "Nigel was harvested for another reason, wasn't he?" she says. "It wasn't just cutting him up to give Secutores the middle finger. He was tainted, wasn't he? He had had a big dose of that chemical agent. Hyacinth was taking tissue samples, because if they can develop something that is resistant to it, they go back to having the advantage. It's an arms race."

"And Arcadia has no idea that the war has started."

"Unless you tell them," she says.

"Unless either of us tell them," I amend, understanding why Belfast wanted to snatch Mere. Mere nods, eyes downcast, as she accepts the idea of her value.

"So, who was in the Mercedes?" Phoebe asks suddenly.

She's leaning against the doorframe. "The Mercedes," she repeats. "They're still looking for you two. There's nothing stopping either of you reaching out to Arcadia or any news outlet. But you haven't yet. You don't know who you can trust, which means you're unclaimed assets. Both sides want you."

"That's why you killed Talus," I say. "He was the only one who knew both parties."

"I killed Talus because he betrayed us," Phoebe says.

"You're right, though," Mere says. "We're the only connection between Escobar and Secutores. Secutores is still trying to finish their job and deliver an Arcadian; Escobar—"

"Escobar just wants me dead," I interrupt. "Let's not make it grander than it is."

"He wants revenge on Arcadia," Phoebe says. "It really isn't about you."

Mere coughs, putting her hand to her mouth to hide her smile. "It doesn't seem like Escobar's style," she says.

"You want to go find out who is in those cars, don't you?" I ask Phoebe.

She nods, her eyes gleaming with excitement.

THIRTY-FOUR

Phoebe's all for going into La Serena and finding out immediately, but I talk her into waiting until the morning. During the night, if the squad is Arcadian, they'll outnumber us—even if we manage to surprise them; if they're Secutores, they're going to be extra vigilant against an Arcadian assault. We don't have enough intel to perform an effective raid.

Plus, Mere points out that we're going to have to leave immediately after the raid, and she wouldn't mind a decent night's sleep before we start running again.

After Mere turns in, Phoebe and I assess our arsenal. The villa is set back from the main road that winds through the Valle de Elqui, and so we don't worry about being conspicuous as Phoebe opens the trunk of the car to reveal three aluminum cases.

"When did you start following us?" I ask as I open the first case on the right. Foam padding with slots for four pistols and extra magazines. Only three of the four slots are filled. I can guess where the missing pistol is.

"Pudahuel," Phoebe says. "I didn't bother with Rapa Nui."

"Why?" I ask as I tug one of the pistols out of its foam slot. A CZ 75. The gun is in pristine condition, and it seems small in my hand.

"P-01," Phoebe says, reading my confusion. "The Czech Republic has been making guns again. Has been for more than a decade."

I remember the arms markets near the end of the twentieth century. The CZ was a Czech gun, created by a pair of brothers, but its design was a state secret. They couldn't sell it in Czechoslovakia, and so all of their production was focused on the international arms market. At some point, the Czech government started to have second thoughts about being labeled as arms dealers in the historical record, and gun exports stopped.

I couldn't help but think of Kirkov as I held the gun. He had carried a 75 as well, though his had been one of the older models. Forged barrel with steel slide and frame. Ring loop on the hammer. Much heavier in the hand. The weapon of an old soldier.

I put the pistol back in its slot. It's not the right weapon for me.

"You didn't get off the plane in Rapa Nui," I say as I open the next case, getting back to the question I had been asking. "Why?"

"It's an island," Phoebe says, "in the middle of the Pacific Ocean."

Her explanation brings a smile to my lips. "Had enough of islands?"

"You weren't going to stay long," Phoebe says, ignoring my jibe. "Santiago was the obvious next stop."

The second case contains the parts for a sniper rifle. Another Sako, judging from the skeletal frame of the stock. "There's a garden on Rapa Nui. Mere says you swam all the way back to Australia. Wouldn't the garden have been restorative?"

"There is no garden on Rapa Nui," Phoebe says. "There hasn't been for two hundred years since you killed the steward."

"You knew?"

"Of course," she says. She sighs, seeing my expression. "How could you have forgotten? It wasn't that long ago."

"It…" I stop. How could she know? Had she been there? If so, why had Mother let her keep the memory and take it from me? "Phoebe, do you know what happens when we go into Mother's embrace? She takes some of our memories away."

A strange expression crosses Phoebe's face, something almost like fear or revulsion. "Why would you let her do that?"

"I… I don't have a choice. At least, I didn't," I say. "Wait. Are you saying that you remember everything? How is that possible?"

"I've never let Mother embrace me, Silas," Phoebe says.

I sit down heavily on the edge of the trunk. "Never?"

She looks at me, and the revulsion flashes across her features again, though in its wake what is left on her face is a growing anger. "You were there when I died, Silas," she says. "You let them put me in the ground and let Mother embrace me."

"I was," I say, saddened that I can't recall all the details of how Phoebe had become an Arcadian.

"I never wanted to forget what happened," she says. She flips the car keys at me, and I catch them awkwardly. She turns and walks off without a word. Not toward the house, but toward the trees that line the road. She moves gracefully and efficiently. Not in a rush, but moving away from me in the most expedient manner possible.

I sit there and watch her go, trying to figure out what centuries of hate would do to a person. *How old was her body?* I wondered, doing the math. *How fractured was her mind?* But it wasn't. *Of all of us*, I realized with a start, *she might be the least damaged.*

▼▼

The third case contained grenades. A mixed dozen of flashbangs, concussive, and incendiary. More than enough to cause trouble. While I wander around the villa, waiting for dawn, I have more than a few hours to ponder how Phoebe managed to procure this arsenal. I stare at Mere's chart until I have it memorized, and I surf through the news cycles, filling my head with the banality of the human world. I make my own timeline, examining what we think has happened over the past few weeks and how that might look from both Secutores's perspective and from Hyacinth. I think about Arcadia and my various conversations with Callis, as well as the possible reasons why he hadn't answered the phone in Santiago. I examine Mere's map with her tiny marginalia about various sites, and I think about this data the way that a good commander would. The way that Secutores would.

Shortly after the sun rises, I start rummaging around the kitchen. There isn't much, but the smell of freshly brewed coffee is enough to rouse Mere from the bedroom. She wanders into the kitchen, still yawning, and she perks up noticeably at the sight of the full coffee pot. She's wearing a gray t-shirt, no bra, and a pair of loose cotton pants decorated with green and red and yellow triangles. Her hair is both matted and frenzied, a sure sign that her sleep wasn't all that restful.

"Morning, sunshine," I quip.

She growls at me as she pours a cup of coffee. Shuffling over to the table, she sits and wraps her hands around her cup. I can feel her glaring at the back of my head as I work at the stove. "What are you so chipper about?" she grouses.

I glance over my shoulder. "I thought you'd be more pleased to have breakfast waiting for you when you got up," I say.

She pastes a false smile on her face as she cocks her head to the side. "Oh, Silas, you shouldn't have," she says mockingly. "What a lucky girl I am. Are you going to take me shopping later?"

"Of course, my darling," I respond. "I thought maybe we could get some diamonds and a puppy."

She makes a noise like the strangled sound of air escaping from a balloon, and it takes me a moment to realize she's imitating a squeal of delight.

"No diamonds, then?"

She turns the escaping air sound into the flatulence of a raspberry, and then devotes all of her attention to the cup of coffee in front of her.

I fill up a plate with the hodge-podge ensemble I've managed to create from the various leftovers in the tiny refrigerator. Standing behind her chair, I lean over and arrange the plate and silverware in front of Mere. I catch myself before I touch her hair, and I return to the stove where I can busy my hands with cleaning up. Behind me, I hear the clink of the fork against the plate.

"No puppy," she says after a while. "Not right now."

I stop washing the pan. "Okay."

"You have a plan, don't you?" she says.

I nod. "I do."

"I can tell," she says. "You're being sweet about it, but I can tell you're ready to go. You don't like waiting."

I turn around. "No soldier does. Not when he knows his mission."

"And what is our mission?"

I smile.

She sighs. "Maybe what I should be shopping for is a bulletproof vest," she says.

▼▼

After breakfast, I clean up the rest of the villa while Mere takes a shower. I have no idea how long she rented the place, but there's no reason to leave any sign that we'd been there at all. I haul the sack of garbage out into the back yard and dump it into the hole I had been planted in. As we're loading the car, Phoebe emerges from the trees and calmly gets into the back of the car. Mere gives me a withering look, and I'm left wondering what exactly has been decided was my fault.

On the way to La Serena, I outline the plan to Phoebe. Her frosty demeanor thaws, as I suspected it would at the idea of doing violence. As we reach the outskirts of the city, Mere diverts into a shopping district where Phoebe and I get supplies: heavy tape, carabiners, horrifically touristy ponchos, disposable cell phones with preloaded blocks of minutes, Bluetooth headsets, sunblock, and hats.

It's going to be a warm day. Unlike Phoebe, I need a little skin protection.

Mere drives to the central market, letting us off a few blocks prior. By the time we get to the edge of the square, Mere's already deep in the teeming chaos of the farmer's market. She's wearing a light blue scarf in her hair, making her easy to spot. She's got a basket on her arm, and is strolling slowly along the aisles, shopping for fresh fruit and vegetables.

Mere has Pedro's cell phone number, and she was supposed to call him after she parked the car, asking him to meet her at the market. He shows, not long after Phoebe and I get into position, and I watch him circle the market until he's on the same side as Mere's car. He parks his scooter in the shade of a building, and with a nervous glance around him, starts walking toward the market.

I can't blame him. I can tell he's very proud of the scooter, which means it's well cared for. As soon as he walks past me and is swallowed by the market, I get up from the chair I've been sitting in outside a tiny café and wander toward the scooter.

It's not very big, and not made for two, but it'll do. The ignition key—on a tiny chain with a silver medallion—is hanging across the base of the handlebars, just as Mere asked. It's not obvious if you aren't looking for it. Without breaking stride, I snatch it up and keep walking.

We've had to make some assumptions in our planning. Phoebe has been watching the road near the villa all week, and she's confident that whoever is in town hasn't made Pedro as our contact. But they're looking for Mere and me; they know what we look like. The market is an obvious spot to buy fresh produce. It'll be one of several places they have eyes. We just need to make sure they're just watching and not lying in ambush.

I keep an eye out for a G-class Mercedes. *Like a Land Rover*, Phoebe said. Should be easy enough to spot.

As I turn the corner at the end of the block, I catch sight of a suitable candidate, coming from the west. I duck into a nearby shop—one selling women's clothing—and idle near the front windows. A few minutes later, a silver G-class Mercedes drifts by. Tinted windows, but I can see well enough to count four men inside. As I look over a rack of scarves, I pull my new cell phone out of my pocket. Under my coat, a pair of grenades shift against my side.

I speed dial the first number. "One and four," I say when Phoebe answers.

"Four," she confirms quietly, and through my earpiece I hear the background noise of the market as she leaves the line open. "Two in market," she tells me. "Locals."

Mere has been made by two people in the market, both locals. The strike teams had circulated pictures. *See these people? Call this number.*

The four guys in the Mercedes were the response team. Quick, too, which suggested they were based nearby. Where was the other car?

I buy one of the scarves, green with streaks of purple and red in it. *One Mere might like*, I find myself thinking as I stand at the register. I wave off the offered bag, and tie it loosely around my neck. My wide-brimmed hat is somewhat flexible and I mash it into a more distressed shape. It's not much in the way of changing my appearance, but with all the people on the street, it should be enough.

Before I leave the shop, I put my optics on. The sunlight is starting to hurt my eyes.

I leave the shop and head in the direction the Mercedes had been going. I find it, parked, two blocks away from Mere's car. There's only one guy in it. "One and one," I say.

Phoebe acknowledges. "Time to go," she says.

I put her on hold and dial the other number in my phone. I let it ring a few times, and then end the call. Mere should have felt her phone vibrating. I cross the street and head back toward Mere's car and Pedro's scooter.

The strike team wants Phoebe and me, and they know Mere will lead them to us. They'll follow her, and as soon as it is clear that she and Pedro are going to get into a car, there is going to be a scramble. If the second Mercedes isn't already prowling the edge of the market, a frantic call will be made to get it on the street. Though I suspect it's already in play.

As I turn the corner toward the market, I spot Mere and Pedro walking up the street. I cross over to the other side—the side where Pedro's scooter is parked—and slow my pace accordingly. Let them get to the car first. I keep my eyes on the crowded market, looking for some sign of people moving with purpose.

I spot one guy shoving his way through the crowd, his attention fixed on Mere and Pedro. "One following," I tell Phoebe. I think I see a shadow behind this guy and realize I'm probably telling her something she already knows.

"Two returning to one," Phoebe tells me. The other two of this trio have already split off and are hustling back to the car.

I'm tempted to let Phoebe take the remaining, but when I see him start talking into a cell phone, I realize what he's doing. He's going to identify the car that Mere is driving, and the first car is going to follow her. He'll be picked up by the second car, and then they'll double-team the tail.

That makes it easy.

▼▼

I call Mere when the second Mercedes has picked up the spotter. "They're coming," I tell her. "Follow the route."

"Okay," she replies. She says something to Pedro about her laptop, and I assume she's asking him to show her the route. Hopefully, those two can sort out a system for calling out directions, though I suspect Mere can remember the route. We planned it to be simple and straight: leave La Serena and get on the Pan-American Highway.

Phoebe's arms are wrapped around my waist and her chin is pressed against my back. The tiny engine of the scooter whines beneath me. It's not happy about the weight, but it's keeping up. We won't be able to keep up once the cars reach the highway, but we shouldn't need to.

The planned route takes us out of the heavily residential area and into a stretch of light industrial before we reach the highway. The road widens, developing four lanes, and Mere takes her time. She drives just under the speed limit enough to frustrate the guys in the Mercedes following her. One of the two cars gets into the left hand lane.

Half a kilometer up ahead, there's a light and a cross street that runs into a stretch of long warehousing.

"Miss this light," I tell Mere. "Pretend you're going to turn right."

Mere plays it well. She starts to slow down earlier and even though the light is green, she comes to a complete stop at the intersection. The second Mercedes can't figure out what she's doing, and squirts on through the intersection as the light turns yellow. I can imagine the commentary coming from the men in the car. The second Mercedes is three cars back from Mere, and he's pulled close to the center line so that the driver can try to figure out what the hell Mere is doing.

Both lanes fill up as traffic queues for the light.

I open the throttle on the scooter and swerve out to straddle the center line. Phoebe lets go of my waist, and I feel her weight shift as she leans back. I let go of the throttle as we come up on the line of cars, and the high pitched whine of the scooter's engine drops with an exhausted sigh. I squeeze the brakes lightly with one hand as I reach my other hand into my poncho.

As we line up with the Mercedes, I squeeze the brake all the way. The pistol in Phoebe's hand starts popping. The driver's side window shatters, and I reach into my poncho for a grenade. Letting go of the handlebars of the scooter for a second, I yank the pin and lob the live grenade through the shattered window. I return my hands to the handlebar, twist the throttle, and the scooter shoots forward.

We nearly get clipped by a blue van as we streak through the intersection. Behind us, the grenade goes off, blowing out the remaining windows of the Mercedes. A second later, there is another explosion as the gas tank goes up. I eke out as much speed as I can get from the scooter. Phoebe lays her left forearm across my shoulder and I hunch forward, clearing her light of sight. She presses up against me, and out of the corner of my eye, I see the gun in her right hand.

Up ahead, the brake lights on the first Mercedes flare. Someone has spotted the explosion behind us.

We're farther away than I would take the shot, but Phoebe opens up. Her first two shots go through the back window of the Mercedes. The third one leaves a hole in the back; the fourth shot hits the left rear tire. The car jerks to the left, turning toward us, and Phoebe empties the rest of the magazine into the driver's side.

The car wobbles and then veers quickly to the right, shooting off into the narrow ditch that runs along the side of the road. As I come up on the wrecked car, slowing the scooter to a stop, Phoebe hops off. She's got another gun in her left hand, and she stands at the edge of the road, precision shooting into the Mercedes. When the slide on her pistol locks back, she steps away from the edge of the ditch. She nods, letting me know that she's finished.

I hold the scooter steady between my legs as I reach into my poncho for more grenades. I throw one under the Mercedes, and after I kick the scooter down into the ditch, I lob the second one after it. Both grenades go off noisily as Mere pulls up with a screech of tires. Pedro's frightened face is transfixed in the passenger side window.

Phoebe opens the back passenger door and enters first. I follow, and Mere stomps on the accelerator pedal as soon as I'm in the car.

I put on my seat belt as Mere drives north, heading for the Pan-American Highway.

Phoebe's hair is wild about her head, still moving even though there is no wind in the car. "Secutores," she says.

I nod in agreement. The strike teams were human mercenaries.

"I like biting back," she says with a grin.

Her hate has become something else.

THIRTY-FIVE

We drive north, heading toward the Atacama Desert, one of the driest places on the planet. It's not on Mere's list as Arcadian-friendly, which is precisely why we head for it. The altercation with Secutores outside of La Serena will focus attention on the rustic city—both from the mercenaries and from Hyacinth. With any luck, they'll stumble over each other for a day or two.

Mere wants to know what our plan is with Pedro, who sits very quietly in the front passenger seat, trying his best to not be conspicuous. He didn't see what happened to his scooter, but I suspect he knows. And he's street-smart enough to know that even if I hadn't wrecked it, he was going to have to ditch it anyway. It was an anomaly that witnesses to our assault are going to remember.

They won't remember much else, but they'll remember the scooter. Our pursuers will be excited to have a clue, but it's worthless knowledge.

"He's useful," I tell Mere. "We should keep him."

"He could get killed," she replies.

"We'll get two bulletproof vests," I offer.

"It's different," she argues. "I made my choice. He didn't."

"Does it really matter now? If we drop him off somewhere, he's on his own in a strange town with no money. What's the first thing he's going to do? Call someone back in La Serena. He's just going to return there, where people know about him and his scooter—especially when he doesn't have it anymore. Someone will tell Secutores or Hyacinth. They'll find him. They'll make him talk. But what does he know? Nothing very useful. At which point, he'll have no value and they'll discard him."

"What if we give him some money?" Mere asks. "Tell him not to go back to La Serena?"

"Where is he going to go? Does he look like a kid who could just pick up and go to another city and start over? What sort of life do you think he's going to fall into?"

"This isn't fair."

Phoebe laughs quietly.

I lean forward. "No, it's not, but he's useful. He's a local kid. He can go many places without attracting attention. We lessen our risk of being spotted by having him be our errand boy. He's smart and he's cautious. He has a better chance with us."

Mere's hands tighten on the steering wheel. She glances at Pedro, who has become aware that we've been talking about him. The boy twists around in his seat and stares at me. "Are you going to kill me too?" he asks in Spanish.

He's wiry, but he still has a round face, full of young innocence that probably serves him well. His brown eyes are inquisitive and intelligent, and up close, I can tell that he's as concerned about his haircut as he is his scooter.

"You're in no danger from us," Phoebe replies in the same language.

I nod. "We're going to need your help, Pedro. You understand the risk, don't you?"

"Yes," the boy says. "Señor, are you going to kill me later?" His voice is flat and calm, but he swallows a couple of times and his eyelids flutter. He's putting on a brave face. Helping the nice American lady who had been staying in the villa hadn't turned out the way he had hoped.

"I'm Silas," I say, and then I nod to my left. "That's Phoebe, and like she says, you're in no danger from us. Other people, though, are going to want to talk to you. They won't be very nice. We can protect you from them. You help us, and we'll take care of you. Okay?"

He looks at Phoebe and me, and then at Mere, who has a more honest expression on her face than either Phoebe or I. "Okay," Pedro says. "New scooter," he adds in English, speaking for Mere's benefit. "Italian. Aprilia."

Phoebe laughs again. "Done," she says.

I nod to Pedro and sit back in my seat. The boy nods too, and turns back around. Mere is looking at me in the rearview mirror, her eyebrows raised.

"The boy knows how to negotiate," I tell her. "Why wouldn't we want him along?"

ⱽⱽ

The presence of Secutores in La Serena suggests two things: one, that they're working through the same suppositions as Mere and looking for Arcadian-friendly areas where we might have gone to ground; and two, our theory that they're still working on grabbing an Arcadian is sound. On a purely business level, keeping after Phoebe and me if they have access to Hyacinth, doesn't make sense. They're losing too many men trying to track us down. It's possible that Hyacinth and Secutores are working together and Secutores is cleaning up loose ends, but the fact that we haven't called Arcadia should also tell Hyacinth that they're in no immediate danger from us calling the cavalry. We're still on our own, but like I told Belfast, the enemy of my enemy might be a friend. The trick is figuring out which enemy is the right one to befriend. Or not. I know Phoebe wants to play them off each other, and I'm not convinced that isn't Escobar's plan with us and Secutores.

If I was under the gun to figure out a counteragent to the weed killer, I'd be buying time by getting my enemies to fight among themselves too. Us biting back against Secutores may give us a bit of breathing room from Hyacinth as well.

None of this solves the bigger problem of Arcadia and the poison within the Grove. And the question of how much Callis knows. I can't help but think he is the one who put me on to the idea of going to Rapa Nui.

After a few hours of driving, we stop and let Pedro and Mere eat. Phoebe and I stay in the car, talking about what we're doing next. Well, mostly I talk and Phoebe listens. There's a lot of brain dumping to do from the overnight session I did with Mere's computer.

Mere has the highly structured mind of a good reporter, and all of her research over the last week had been gathered into a tidy stack of well-labeled folders. I read journal abstracts, stockholder notices, corporate SEC filings, news articles, forum discussions, and more than a few conspiracy theory blog posts. There was no dearth of data to sift through, and it was a long night of reading and thinking. But when I finally read Mere's assessment, a short list of bullet points, I thought she was on the right track.

"She's methodical and tenacious," Phoebe says after I've given my assessment of Mere's thinking. "Every night, she'd talk the whole time she was making dinner. She wasn't telling me what she had learned so much as summarizing it all. Out loud. It wasn't necessary for me to be in the room, but I stayed and listened. She's a good asset. A good strategist. I see why you saved her."

I stare out the window. "The Grove thinks I had an ulterior reason."

"Because you had fallen for a mortal?" Phoebe snorts. "It happens more often than you know, Silas. But that has little to do with anything. You're trying too hard to see a conspiracy when the basic issue is that they're idiots. They've been idiots for a long time. We could have done something. We should have. But they were too frightened."

"It's changed too fast," I say. "We had no idea how quickly they were going to devour the world."

"You had no idea because you weren't paying attention. Because you were letting them gut your memories. And they did it so poorly. What could be gained by letting you remember that you've been purged?"

"So that we would think it was our choice," I say. "It was our own decisions to let go of the past, to relieve ourselves of the burden of who we were."

"Why?"

"I don't know, Phoebe," I tell her. "I've been doing it for a long time."

She laughs. "And does it make you feel any better to know how long you've been lied to? How long you've been lying to yourself?"

"No," I say. "Of course it doesn't." I grimace. "How much of what I feel and what I remember has been selectively placed in my head?"

"All of it," Phoebe says matter-of-factly.

"Who is Silas then?" I wonder. "I can't be the same man I was when I became an Arcadian."

Phoebe shakes her head. "Who Silas was doesn't matter," she says. "You *are* Silas. Who Silas will be tomorrow or the next day or the day after that is up to you."

"Is that why you never went back?" I ask.

"Partly," Phoebe says after a moment of silence. She doesn't add anything more, and I figure that's all I'm going to get.

"Was it difficult?" I ask. "Fighting the urge to return to Mother?"

"I was an orphan once before," Phoebe says, "I knew how to survive."

Maybe that was the difference. I had been part of a family. Part of a military unit. I had craved the company of others. Needed it, in fact. Becoming an Arcadian had been an easy choice for me, in the end. I hadn't given much thought to the ramifications of my decision. I was a soldier; I was supposed to follow orders. I was supposed to be part of a group.

Had Mother taken advantage of my weaknesses?

Of course she had. If I looked back on my history from Escobar's point of view, I was a dumb grunt. Manipulated over and over again by my superiors. Told what I needed to know for any given mission. Patted on the head when I returned, bloody and triumphant. *Good dog. Here's a cookie. Now go rest for a few decades.* I wagged my tail, overjoyed to be part of a family, happy to please Mother.

"It's just another survival mechanism," I murmur.

"What is?"

"Following orders. Being *happy to please*," I say.

Phoebe shrugs, a twitch of her shoulders in which I'm starting to see a variety of nuances. *Isn't that the reason we do anything?* is what I read in her reaction.

"Change happens over time. Changes happen because a system reacts to stimuli. Those species that can react quickly survive. The rest die. That's the order of the world—has been for thousands of years—and we've been at the top of that pyramid for a long time. But we're afraid now. We're looking over our shoulders, wondering what it is that is coming up behind us. The fundamental problem we face is change—how are we supposed to change when we were at the top of the food chain?"

"We get knocked off," Phoebe says. "We relearn what it is to fear."

"Is that what Escobar wants? To make Arcadia remember fear?"

"Why would he bother? He's done with Arcadia; he's working on his own evolutionary path. He doesn't want us crowding him."

"Right. He's growing his own flesh, his own tissue. Evolution takes a long time, especially when your body is already nearly perfect. So, he's taking a shortcut. He's crafting his own."

Phoebe makes a face. "Genetic modification," she says. "Splicing. Grafting."

"Frankenstein," I reply.

"Chimera," she fires back.

An involuntary shiver runs up my spine. *Chimera.* She's right. Body of a lion, head of a goat, tail of snake. The commingling of disparate species into one monstrous creation that could not exist without interference from the Gods.

A chimera would not be something that Mother would birth; it was a monster that man would build.

I recall the tree farm on Rapa Nui. There had been citrons in the grove, and I hadn't looked at them closely. Were they simply citrons or had they been Bizzaria—the chimera of the Florentine citron and the sour orange?

Had I walked past them without realizing what they were?

V V

Mere and Pedro return to the car, and Phoebe switches to the front seat to drive. We're going to drive through the afternoon and night, trying to put as much of the Atacama behind us. There's no reason to stay overlong in the desert. Pedro, his belly full of lunch, settles down in the front passenger seat and falls asleep.

I tell Mere about chimerae and the Bizzaria, the plant chimera that mixes the citron and the sour orange. By this time, I'm nearly certain the citrus trees I had seen on Rapa Nui were Bizzaria.

This strikes a chord in Mere, and she digs out her laptop and searches through her research files. Getting a hit in her data, she shows me a picture. It's a publicity still of Escobar Montoya. "Forty years ago," Mere says, "taken during a junket at a farming initiative sponsored by Montoya Industries, the construction firm of his that made their mark in the '30s." She points at the banner in the background. It's got the name of the farm and a logo. Laid over a stylized sunburst is a green sprig with a single fruit that has been rendered as a circle within a circle. "What's that look like?" she says, indicating the fruit.

"They're not concentric," I note.

"If you were to consider that image as a symbolic representation, how would you classify it?"

"A circle within another circle?"

"Or a whole that contains the whole of another thing. In other words, something made from distinct objects."

"A chimera," I nod. "Where was this taken?"

"Somewhere up north," she says, turning the laptop around and starting to type. "I'll need to find some Wi-Fi to check further. I don't seem to have that information saved locally."

"Well," I note, looking out at the sun-blasted landscape. "We're heading in the right direction, at least."

THIRTY-SIX

About a half-hour before nightfall, the western sky awash with red and orange clouds, we roll into a tiny town with a single restaurant advertising Wi-Fi access. While Phoebe and Pedro take care of gassing up the car, Mere and I head into the restaurant for a quick meal and some Internet access.

An artichoke ravioli catches my eye on the menu, and since Mere is more interested in the Wi-Fi password than food, I order her the house empanadas. The dark-eyed waitress nods knowingly as she takes out menus. She's seen too many North American couples more fascinated with checking in with their social networks than with paying attention to the local cuisine, and Mere is living up to that stereotype.

"Do you know the history of the Bizzaria?" Mere asks as she starts pulling up a variety of search results. "First found in a garden outside of Florence in the seventeenth century. People thought it was an accidental mutation."

Florence.

Mere notices my expression. "What?"

"Nothing," I say.

Her eyebrows pull together and her fingers fly across the keyboard. I watch her scan her computer screen, waiting to see some reaction in her eyes. It doesn't take long. She stops looking, fingers sliding across the track pad, and then she looks over the top of the laptop at me. And then back at the picture on her screen.

"Was it an accident?" she asks.

"Was what?"

"The Bizzaria?"

I shrug. "I wasn't there. I couldn't say."

"You've been to Florence, though, haven't you?"

"I don't know, Mere. What makes you think I've been to Florence?"

She laughs, covering her mouth as soon as she starts, subsiding into a fit of giggles. "It's almost like an Interpol wanted poster, isn't it?" she says when she has regained her composure.

"The statue of David?" I ask.

She nods, trying very hard not to start giggling again.

"I had never thought of it that way," I confess.

She scrolls down on the picture. "Is it… a completely accurate likeness?" she asks with a smile.

"It was cold that morning," I tell her. "It was cold every morning that I posed, in fact."

"Clearly," she says, the giggles starting again. With some regret, she turns her attention to her other search results.

A minute later, all of the humor drains out of her face. She spins the laptop around so that I can see what she's found. The first image is the stylized sun from the farm logo, though subtly different. "Inti," Mere says, "Incan deity. God of the sun."

I nod and go to the next tab as directed. It's a picture of a man dressed in religious garb. He's holding a stick with a sun figure mounted to the top of it. "Who's this?" I ask. The picture is drawn in a style that is several hundred years old.

"Manco Cápac," Mere says. "The founder of the Incan empire."

"Looks like someone we know," I say.

The artist has done a good rendition of Escobar Montoya, and it's not hard to see that same likeness in the sculptures in the ground-floor gallery in the Montoya building in Santiago.

"I guess he's been running the family business longer than we thought," Mere says as she spins the laptop back toward her.

"It's not as cool as a statue," I point out.

"True," she admits, "but he did get to run a whole kingdom. Up in Peru. Cusco."

"Want to bet that's where the farms are located?"

"Sucker bet," she says. She taps on the laptop keys, and then reads what the screen tells her. "Yeah, totally a sucker bet." She chews on her lower lip. "What are we going to do about Pedro? We can't cross the border with him."

"What makes you think you and I are any less illegal?"

"Oh," she says. "Our passports. What are we going to do?"

"What we always do, which is to offer lots of money for someone to look the other way. And if that doesn't work, we'll go overland."

"Neither sounds like much fun."

"Only if we get caught."

"Like I said…"

I lean forward. "We're pretty good at not getting caught."

She leans forward too, a light dancing in her eyes. "There are a lot of things you're pretty good at, aren't there?"

"Posing for a neurotic sculptor with an eidetic memory isn't all that hard," I point out.

"Too bad," she says, a smile curling her lips. "I would have liked to see *that* sculpture."

It takes me a second to realize what she's talking about, and I'm spared further embarrassment by the arrival of our waitress with our food. Mere fusses with her silverware. Her cheeks are pink, and her pulse taps at the skin of her throat. As she starts eating, her smile keeps creeping back onto her lips between bites. When she glances over at me, her heart rate jacks up.

Phoebe wanders in a little while later and approaches our table. "We're ready," she says, glancing back and forth between Mere and me.

"We'll be a few minutes yet," I say.

Mere continues to eat with exaggerated care, knowing that I'm watching her intently. Phoebe watches for a bit too, and then shakes her head and wanders off. I distantly hear her ask the waitress about ordering food to go.

Mere's heart rate has stopped spiking, but the flush has spread down her neck. I'm sure it goes further. I've been wondering how far.

▾▾

Phoebe continues to drive. Shortly after the sun vanishes and the sky goes dark, Mere leans over and rests her head on my shoulder. I wait until her breathing becomes slow and regular before I start a conversation with Phoebe.

"We're going to Peru," I tell her. "Cusco. Escobar's old company, Montoya Industries, has farms there."

"How far?" Phoebe asks.

"Mere said it was a couple thousand kilometers. How long will that take us?"

"Maybe two days," Phoebe says after glancing at the speedometer. "What about the border?"

I ask a very different question in return. "How did you get your arsenal in Santiago?"

Phoebe stares at me in the rearview mirror, that cold indifference. She doesn't even offer me one of her enigmatic shrugs.

"It's been bugging me since I woke up, more so after you showed me what was in the trunk. We weren't that far behind you. That sort of armament would take some time to procure, especially if you didn't have any local contacts. I would have had to call someone in Arcadia to find out who to talk to, and even then, without making a fuss, it would have taken me a day or two to close the deal. Either you have better local connections or you've been talking to Arcadia?"

"I called Callis when I got back to Australia," she says.

"When was this?"

"About four days after we left the *Cetacean Liberty*."

I ran through the timeline in my head. That put her in Adelaide nearly two weeks before me.

"Was it your idea or Callis's to stay dark?"

"He didn't like it."

That didn't really answer my question.

"So the two of you let things fall where they would," I say. "You let me become bait."

"This isn't about you, Silas," she says.

I growl at her. Mere shifts on my shoulder, her dream disturbed by my tension, and I relax, waiting for her to settle down.

"There's a war coming, and the Grove is in denial," Phoebe continues. "The humans want this planet. They think they can tame it. They think they *own* it. Their scientists claim to understand how nature works. They're modifying seeds, creating abominations that produce impressive short-term yields, but no one has given any thought to what their creations are going to do to the ecosystem. The planet has been a self-sufficient system for millions of years. It knows how to self-correct, to adjust itself to keep aberrations in check. The human lifespan is too short to encompass a long-term view. They don't understand the consequences of their frenzied consumption."

"And Arcadia is going to show them?"

Phoebe shakes her head. "Arcadia is going to fall," she says. "Enough humans suspect that it exists. It's a threat. The first thing they're going to do is wipe us out. That's what the test out on the Southern Ocean was about. That's humanity's new weapon. It is anathema to us. With it, they won't fear us—and fear is the only superior weapon we have against them."

"Is that what Hyacinth is doing? Building a defense against the weed killer? Are they going to share it with Arcadia?"

"I doubt it."

"Is that your mission then? To get the technology for Arcadia?"

"Why would I?"

I stop myself from blurting out a blanket response to her question. Indeed, why would she? What has Arcadia done for her? What does she need of Arcadia? Mother brought her back, gave her another life, but she's rejected that life, hasn't she? She's never let Mother touch her again. She's an orphan, a self-proclaimed exile from the only family that would have her.

"What do you want?" I ask. "Why are you even helping me?"

"I am a steward," she says, "but I don't belong to Mother and I don't answer to the Grove. Humanity turned its back on me, and Arcadia wouldn't let me die. The only family I've ever known is what I felt in the humus. I became part of the ecosystem. I was a child, Silas; I knew so little of the world. Then, all of it was suddenly thrust upon me. It was poured into me and I could not stop it. I couldn't stop it from binding to my very being. They take this from you. They numb you to who you truly are."

"Who does?"

"The Grove."

"How?"

"Mother is a chimera, Silas. She may seem like a tree, but we are her flowering roots. The Grove prunes the tree; they decide how the roots grow—what they know, who they are, what they remember. The members of the Grove don't even know they are doing this. The decision isn't a conscious one for them. The Grove is the group's mind—that's who you think of as Mother. We're all a part of Mother, Silas, and the more we all think the same thing—the more we suffer from the same fear—the more that becomes part of what Mother tells us to believe."

"If that's true, then how do you know this? If we're completely programmed by our own group subconscious, how can we know anything other than what we're told?"

"We're rhizomes. Escobar is right. We don't need to return to Arcadian soil. It helps—the soil there is very, very good—but we can survive anywhere. And the more you listen to the humus, the more you are aware of what truly matters."

"And you know?"

"I've had three hundred and sixty-five years—uninterrupted years—to figure it out," she says. "I know."

"Who we are," I say quietly, "and what we could become."

Now she gives me the shrug.

"Why me?" I ask. "Why not Nigel?"

"I didn't trust Nigel. Or Talus."

"And you trust me?"

"I trust your guilt."

I chuckle at that.

She looks at me in the rearview mirror. "We don't have two days," she says.

"What do you suggest we do?" I ask. "Hijack an airplane and fly?"

She shakes her head. "Why? We could just rent one?"

Chartering a jet. Mere had done something like that at Hanga Roa. I had been surprised at how easy it had been to pick up the phone and make arrangements for a private jet. I dig my phone out of my pocket and check if it has enough signal. "Where are we?" I ask Phoebe.

She tells me the name of the last town we passed through, and I hit the buttons that connect me to the phone's information line. "What are we going to do when we get to Cusco?" I ask while I'm waiting for someone to answer.

Phoebe smiles at me in the rearview mirror. "We're going to make some adjustments," she says. "Isn't that what stewards do?"

THIRTY-SEVEN

Mere wakes up as the plane begins its descent into the airport outside of Cusco. She is sitting in the window seat next to me, and her body tightens. Her hands claw at the armrests and she whips her head around, trying to reconcile what she sees.

"It's okay," I say. I put my hand on her arm.

She stares at me, the muscles of her neck tight. Her eyes don't stop moving. Even though she is frightened, she's trying to figure out what happened, trying to assess what sort of situation she's in.

"We're going to be in Cusco in about twenty minutes," I tell her.

"How?" she manages.

"Plane," I tell her. "We chartered one."

"How?" she says again.

"Lots of cash," I smile. "And the right sort of influence."

She presses her body against her seat. "Evidently." She lifts her head and looks over the seat backs. The plane seats about ten, and Mere and I are the only passengers on the right-hand side of the plane. Across the aisle and two rows up, Phoebe is the only one on the left side of the plane.

"Where's Pedro?" Mere asks.

"We left him behind," I tell her. As she starts to reply, I hold up a hand and cut her off. "He's well taken care of. More so than he would have been had he come with us."

"Did you kill him?"

"No. Why would I? He's been helpful."

Mere rubs her hands across her face. "Earlier, you said we couldn't let him out of our sight, and now...?

"An opportunity presented itself," I say.

"What sort of opportunity?"

"It was just as easy to charter two planes as it was to charter one, and we told the pilot to take Pedro somewhere."

"Where?"

"We didn't ask."

She turns on her side and rests her head against the seat cushion. "You have an infuriating tendency for understatement."

"Would you rather I have woken you up, screaming 'Oh my god! We've got a secret plan! You're going to love it!'?"

"I'm not sure I would have loved it."

"Which is why I let you sleep. If you were going to be disappointed, I'm not sure you would have been able to get some rest."

"That's thoughtful of you."

The plane tilts to the right, the sound of the engines increasing as we come around for our landing.

"Is he going to be okay?" Mere asks.

"Pedro? Yeah, he'll be okay. I'm sure he went somewhere were he could buy a new scooter. One he could pay for with cash. He's getting a new scooter, remember?"

"Why are we flying instead of driving? What about our passports."

"Don't worry about it," I say. "Phoebe knows how to—well, it's a long story."

"Is it?" Her mouth quirks. "When you say something is a long story, that's usually code for 'I did something stupid and I don't want to talk about it.'"

"Why do you say that?"

"You didn't want to talk about Easter Island, and it turned out that you had wrecked Escobar's garden."

"That's one example."

"Is this one different?"

I look toward the front of the plane. Phoebe has her seat tilted back, unconcerned about our approach to the Cusco airport. There isn't a flight attendant to tell her to return her seat to its upright position. "It's a long story," I reiterate to Mere.

"Okay," she says, not pushing. "What about saving me from Kirkov?" she asks. "Was that a mistake too?"

I shake my head. "No." A laugh bubbles out of my chest. "No, far from it. In fact, it may be the only decision I've made in the last few years that has truly been mine."

Mere makes a noise in her throat, and my attention is pulled back to her. A little smile haunts the edge of her lips. "Thank you," she says quietly.

I reach over and brush back a lock of her hair that is hanging over her cheek. She closes her eyes and sighs gently again. Her lips part and I want to run my thumb along her lower lip. My hand moves closer, and then she closes her mouth as she swallows. I take that opportunity to blink and force my hand to move away.

▼▼

We had ended up at an airport outside of Copiacó; we drove to a private hanger where a Gulfstream 100 waited for us. I carried Mere into the plane, while Phoebe and a large amount of cash made the necessary arrangements. The three cases from the trunk had gone into the luggage hold, and the young woman from the charter company had driven off in our car with Pedro still sleeping in the front seat. Most of our remaining cash had gone with them too.

A similar routine happens at Cusco. The plane lands, taxies to a private hanger, where a car is waiting for us. We see no one on the ground, and the pilot of the charter never leaves the cockpit. Phoebe and Mere get in the car while I retrieve the three cases. They go in the trunk; I climb into the back seat; and we drive out of the airport through a gate that, oddly, is open and unmanned.

Arcadian-style invisibility. Money makes the world go round. I have to admit that I missed the ease with which we had moved about the world. The last few weeks have been a hard reminder of how removed we had become from humanity. Our own choice, but given Phoebe's diatribe last night, I'm wondering how much input I truly had on that decision.

Given the opportunity to submit my own opinion, I also wonder if I would have chosen the same path for Arcadia and its citizens.

A half-hour later, while most tourists are still sleeping in, we're checked in to a pair of suites in a hotel along El Sol, the main boulevard that runs through Cusco. The sun hasn't burned off all the morning fog yet. Cusco's elevation is over three thousand meters; at this elevation, the air quality is usually much cleaner—the pollutants and toxins tend to sink to sea level—but I still need to be cautious. I haven't abandoned myself to the sun as much as Phoebe has.

While Phoebe strips and cleans the guns, I go next door to Mere's suite where she's sitting on the couch, legs curled under her, intent on her laptop screen. She's already on the hotel's Wi-Fi, researching the legacy of Montoya Industry's involvement in local matters.

I make myself useful and order room service. Fruit, a pot of coffee, yogurt, granola, honey.

"There's an Incan spa down the street," Mere offers. "They do ancient Incan cleansing rituals."

"Maybe on our next visit," I say as I hang up the phone.

"They have an oxygen lounge…"

"Oh, well, that's different. Do they have mud baths too?"

She grabs a throw pillow from the couch and throws it at me. I catch it and spend a few moments staring at the pattern woven into the cotton fabric. It reminds me of the facade of Montoya's building in Santiago. Dimly, I can recall the walls of the well room at the Arcadian spa on Rapa Nui.

It's the same pattern.

Are our minds actually wiped, I wonder, or do we just not remember everything? Phoebe said it was the Grove who inspired Mother. Arcadia—collectively—participated in the idea of Mother. Had we programmed ourselves into thinking she existed as a defense mechanism? As a way to explain why we did the things we did to ourselves? If Mother was responsible, then we weren't. We were simply agents of her desire. Worker ants, responding to the commands of a distant queen. An unconscious hive mind, working intuitively to protect itself. Was that worth saving? Or was my concern about Arcadia simply the ingrained survival mechanism of an ant whose only thought was to serve the queen and the nest?

"Hey."

I shake myself from my reverie and look up. "Hmm?"

"What do you know about terrace farming?" she asks.

"The Incans were very good at it," I say.

"I could go so far as to say 'exceptional,'" Mere says. "There's a bunch of sites in this region that are still in use."

"Escobar's?"

"Undoubtedly. Okay, so think of this region as being shaped like a pot. If you look at it from the side, the Urubamba River is the handle and top edge of the pot. The Andes would be, ah, the lid." She holds her hands to illustrate her point. "Along the river are these series of forts that used to protect the valley. Ollantaytambo"—she holds one hand flat to indicate the pot's arm and lid and walks down it with her other hand—"Urubamba, Calca, and Pisac." Her hands move down the line. Then she cups her hand under her other one. "Down here is Cusco."

"The bottom of the pot."

"Right. Where everything goes. Down to the bottom." She taps the underside of her wrist. "Now, back here is a place called Maras—it's known for its salt fields. Slightly uphill from it is a ruin called Moray, which is this ancient Incan installation with some serious concentric terraces. Apparently, they're deep enough that the climate changes dramatically from the top to the bottom."

"Handy if you're experimenting in different crops," I interject.

"You think?" she says. "A couple of years ago, there was a record rainfall. The sort that tends to wipe out existing settlements or, in this case, serious ancient Incan ruins. Ah, but we can't have our national heritage ruined, can we? No, that just won't do. Guess who steps in and funds the reconstruction work at Moray?"

"Hyacinth."

"Hyacinth Worldwide, in fact. Which almost doesn't happen when someone makes some noise about the fact that Hyacinth Worldwide is mainly a hospitality and services company, but then there's a big donation to the city of Cusco and plans to open not one but three hotels within the city limits."

"Hyacinth hotels?"

"Absolutely."

"So it's double duty. Hyacinth Worldwide gets into the cultural heritage business and makes it easier for tourists to visit. Everybody wins."

"And with everyone paying attention to the construction in town, which is way more exciting, no one notices what's going on at a crusty old cultural restoration site. It's the same thing they must have done on Easter Island. Move in on the land. Build a hotel and boost the local economy, and then when things are ready, lease the real prize to a different arm of the company."

"Is Escobar building something at Moray?"

"Who knows? The area's all closed off."

"So we can't take a tour bus?"

"Only if you want to hijack it."

"You think that might be a little obvious?"

"Well, it's sort of been your *modus operandi* so far. Why change now?"

"Probably a good time to change it up then. Keep them guessing."

"I'm all for that."

"Should we go now?"

"How about after we eat whatever it is that you ordered from room service?"

I concede that point. "I'll go tell Phoebe."

Mere laughs. "I doubt it'll take her more than a few seconds to pack up her guns." She pats the couch next to her. "Sit down for a minute. I won't bite." She bites her lower lip as soon as she says the words and drops her gaze to her laptop screen.

I might, I think. *Why not say it?* I wonder, and so I do.

She blushes, and shakes her head slightly, a smile fighting to spread itself across her moving lips. She doesn't say anything out loud, but I can read her lips plainly enough. *I'll bite you back.*

I sit down on the couch next to her, close enough that our shoulders brush. As she continues to fuss with the windows on her computer, I turn and lower my face toward her neck. Her hair is in the way, and I carefully lift it up with a few fingers. She shivers and sits up, her back straightening. She lifts her head, tilting it to the left. I smell her exposed neck, my mouth hovering less than a centimeter from her bare flesh. I exhale slowly through my nose, and she quivers beneath me. She grips the laptop with both hands. "Do it," she whispers.

I press my lips against her skin, carefully keeping my teeth away. My mouth stays closed, but I can still taste her. The ripeness of her flesh, the honeysuckle sweetness of her blood so tantalizingly close beneath her skin. The warm heat of her excitement. The sound of her heart, pounding in her chest.

"No," I say as I break the contact of the kiss.

I stand up and walk to the door of the suite. I don't leave. I simply keep my back to her as I wait for room service to arrive.

I hear her close her laptop and set it aside. She gets up and walks up behind me. My hands are shaking and I clasp them together to keep them still. She wraps her arms around me, pressing her head against my back. "It's okay," she says.

I unclasp my hands and raise them to cover hers. She's shivering as much as I am, and we must look silly. Standing there, staring at the suite door. I don't care. I feel...

Remember your priorities.

... safe.

THIRTY-EIGHT

An hour later, as we're waiting in the lobby for Phoebe to bring the rental car around, I excuse myself from standing with Mere. Carrying the weapons case that Phoebe put me in charge of, I wander off toward the front windows of the hotel where I can get the best cell reception. I pull out my phone, dialing Callis's direct line.

He answers on the first ring.

"Hello, Callis," I say. "Nice of you to pick up this time."

"Silas," he says after a moment's hesitation.

"You seem surprised to hear from me."

"It's, ah, a different country code from where you called me before."

"I've been traveling. It was your idea, remember?"

He's quiet for a minute. "Did you go to the island?"

"I did. What do you think I found?"

"Probably not what you expected," he says.

"No," I reply. "Did you know why Mother sent me there before? Who I was supposed to kill?"

He clears his throat. "You weren't supposed to kill anyone," he says. "That's not what the Grove wanted."

Somehow I'm not surprised to hear that response. "Come on, Callis," I laugh at him. "When have I ever not done what Mother explicitly asked me to do? When have I ever gone off the mission parameters?"

He doesn't bother to answer because anything he says isn't going to help him.

"Do you know what Escobar Montoya is doing?" I ask.

"Saving Arcadia, even if Arcadia doesn't want to acknowledge it is in danger."

227

"Are you sure?" I ask. When he doesn't answer, I ask a different question. "Did you know Talus survived?"

"Talus?" His voice isn't as confident as it was a moment ago. "What are you talking about?"

"Talus never checked in with you after the incident on the boat?"

"No," he says. "I haven't heard from him."

"Who did call you?"

"Just you and… and Phoebe."

I nod, glancing out the window at the valets swarming the cars in the roundabout. "Was he supposed to check in?"

"Yes, and when he didn't—when none of you did right away—I knew something had gone wrong."

"Oh, something had definitely gone wrong," I laugh. "Why didn't you answer when I called the other day?"

"I didn't know it was you calling."

"Bullshit, Callis. It could have been any one of us. You didn't have any insight into what was going on. You're sitting by the phone now, dying to know what's happening. You've seen the news. You know that the top floor of Montoya's building is gone. You know things have gone off the rails. You're blind and you're sitting there, wondering just how fucked things have gotten."

He's quiet for a long time. "Okay, Silas. Things have gotten out of control. I may have erred in not giving you the intelligence you needed earlier. I'm sorry, old friend."

"Apology accepted," I reply.

He coughs lightly after a moment. "And…?"

I spot Phoebe in a red sedan, pulling up in front of the hotel. "And Talus is dead. Phoebe shot him in the head. Probably a cleaner death than he deserved. I killed Escobar's grandson. And he has absolutely no intention of saving Arcadia. Oh, and do you remember that weed killer I mentioned when I was still in Australia? It's owned by a human corporation, and it's been engineered specifically for our physiology. That, *old friend*, is my report. Tell the Grove if you want to or not. It doesn't matter to me. I'm not going to answer to them any more."

I drop the phone on the ground and shatter it with my heel.

v v

The car is a full-sized sedan and Phoebe waves Mere toward the driver's seat. She slips into the back on the passenger's side and I climb in behind

Mere, putting the case on the hump between the back seats. The other two cases must be in the trunk since I don't see them. The car comes with an in-dash GPS and Mere starts punching buttons in an effort to figure out how to reset the language to English.

Phoebe sits, her hands in her lap, waiting patiently, and I'm about to turn and tell her what I just said to Callis when our car is struck from behind.

Mere's airbag deploys, slamming her against her seat, and since the handbrake is still set, the car grinds across the pavement. Phoebe and I bounce off the front seats, and I'm nearly brained by the aluminum case as it bounces around the back seat. Whatever has struck us has a big engine and it growls noisily as the driver of the other vehicle tries to force our car into one of the columns that ring the roundabout in the front of the hotel.

A burst of gunfire shatters the window on Phoebe's side. Several rounds bounce off the case in my arms, and I feel the burn of a bullet as it streaks across the outer edge of my left shoulder. A black cylinder flies into the back of the car—too big and too slow-moving for a bullet.

Flashbang grenade.

I'm already in motion before I consciously identify what it is. My hand finds the door latch, yanks it, and I tumble out onto the sidewalk.

The flashbang goes off, and in the wake of its noise and light, I hear someone screaming but it may be nothing more than my sense of hearing being completely fucked by the flashbang.

There's a man standing next to me, wearing boots and gray pants that are tucked into the tops of the boots. Standard military-style dress. I roll toward him, swinging the case into his knees. He falls, coming down to my level, and I spot the HK MP7 in his hands. I hit him in the face with the case, and take his gun.

More men are coming, pouring out of the back of the armored vehicle that rear-ended us. It's a security truck, the sort used by bank couriers. Secutores, yet again. In an upgraded transport this time. I point my freshly acquired gun and pull the trigger as rapidly as I can, knowing these guys don't default to full auto. Two men go down, and the rest scatter.

I bolt for a nearby pillar as the mercs still upright return fire from cover. The high-pitched noise in my head is no longer a scream; it's a tea kettle whistle echoing down a long metal tube. The scream of a mortar shell falling from its apogee. The distant crump of shells exploding along a trench line. The front, on so many nights during World War I.

Crouching behind my pillar, ignoring both the sudden influx of forgotten memories and the minute vibrations in the pillar that tells me it is being hit by gunfire, I open the aluminum case.

I have both grenades and a handgun. I blink, and I see Phoebe sitting beside me in the car, hands in her lap.

She gave me *this* case when we came to the elevator. Both grenades and a CZ 75—along with a few spare magazines.

I blink again and yank a grenade free of the foam. Yank the pip, release the spoon, and roll it toward the armored security truck behind our sedan. It bounces a few times, and then explodes near the armored truck. It won't do much to the heavy vehicle, but it'll make them cautious. I have two more grenades, and so I throw another one, trying to put it past the truck to flush out the guys hiding back there. I cram the remaining contents of the case into various pockets as the second grenade goes off.

A Mercedes G-class is coming from the other direction of the roundabout. The faces peering out the windows aren't frightened. More mercs, arriving in more standard Secutores-style transport. I empty the magazine of the gun I stole, killing both men in the front seat, and the Mercedes jerks to the right and slams into a nearby pillar. I drop the empty MP7, switch to the CZ 75, and put two rounds through the back passenger side window, hopefully getting one more of the mercenaries.

More Mercedes are arriving, disgorging armed men. Belfast must be bringing everyone on the payroll. I'm outnumbered and outgunned. But they're not coming in for shock and awe. They're coming in for containment. They're moving efficiently to cut me off, firing to keep me pinned down. They want to secure the sedan.

They want prisoners.

I gauge my options. I could run to my right, back toward the front doors of the hotel, and I might even make it, but that would put me inside the hotel. I'd just be containing myself, making their job easy. I jerk to my left, drawing fire from some of the approaching men, but I don't stop. I make it to the next pillar, and then keep going. I'm running faster than they expect, and in the time it takes them to recalibrate their aim, I've already reached the edge of the building. There's a narrow brick fence that separates the manicured hedges of the hotel entrance from the surrounding parking lot, and I leap over it easily.

I lurch to a stop and crab-walk back to the wall, moving toward the street that runs past the hotel. After a few meters, I press up against the wall and peek over. It takes a few seconds for someone to spot me and start firing, but in those few seconds, I get a pretty good idea of the situation.

There's more than a half-dozen Mercedes in the roundabout now, and Phoebe and Mere are being loaded into separate vehicles. The armored car has been abandoned, and the only reason would be because my grenade had actually done some structural damage or wrecked a tire.

As I creep along the wall, four of the Mercedes peel away from the hotel and accelerate up the street. There's no sense in sticking around the hotel any more, not when they've got Phoebe and Mere. I abandon any pretense of playing hide-and-seek and run after the cars. I can keep up with them for a few blocks, but once they get out of the city center, I'm going to fall behind.

As I reach the street, a helicopter roars overhead, coming in over my left shoulder. It's a Dauphin variant—sleek, distinctive fantail rotor assembly—and there are no markings on it. The helicopter dips below the buildings on either side of the street and roars up the road. The doors on both sides are open, and as it overtakes the convoy of Mercedes, people start dropping out. Leaping out of the moving helicopter onto moving vehicles like they were hopping from stone to stone on a river crossing.

Escobar's Arcadians.

THIRTY-NINE

The trailing Mercedes goes off the road first, turning sharply and plowing through a storefront on the left side of the road. As I run past, I don't spot the Arcadian who had been on the roof. He must have been launched inside the store as the vehicle came to a sudden halt, or he's part of the jumble of masonry piled atop the wrecked car.

The penultimate Mercedes waggles back and forth, and manages to dislodge the Arcadian clinging to it. The car corrects its course and speeds after the remaining pair. The Arcadian who was thrown off is recovering from his unsightly dismount as I reach him. I put two bullets in the back of his masked head before he can find his assault rifle on the strap around his torso. I strip the rifle from him, as well as the spare magazines, and then shoot him twice in the chest to make sure he stays down.

An explosion draws my attention back to the road. Up ahead, there's an open space—a promenade or plaza of some sort—and in the middle there is a round turret-like building. Atop it is a tall statue of an Incan man with a long robe and a tall staff. Pachacutec—the Incan ruler who built an empire. Somewhere near the turret, something has blown up. I can't tell if it is one of the remaining Mercedes or another car.

I'm certainly not going to find out by standing in the middle of the street with my mouth open. I sprint toward the promenade, trying not to listen to the part of my brain that is panicked about what I'm going to find in the burning wreckage.

The road from the hotel spills out into a wide boulevard that combines with several other roads into a promenade that flows around a quartered field of overly green grass. The tower rises from the center of the field, and it is several stories tall. Tiny windows along the surface suggest that it is hollow—a tourist destination, wherein they can climb up to the same height as the towering figure and get a view of the city from his perspective.

Traffic has come to a standstill, a confusion of wrecked and stopped vehicles. I can see the burning car now and it's a sedan of some kind; it's not one of the remaining Mercedes. Gunfire and screams and the occasional bleat of a horn are the cacophony that my damaged hearing is starting to parse again. Along with the *whup-whup* sound of the helicopter. It's on the far side of the tower, hovering over the boulevard.

I make my way through the traffic jam, dodging angry and shocked people who are milling about. Most of the sensible ones have already fled; those remaining are still trying to figure out what happened or are too incensed by the stupidity of their minor fender bender to take stock of the bigger picture. I feel like a steel ball in a Japanese parlor game, bouncing from pin to pin as I try to make my way to the bottom of the pachinko board.

I spot one of the Mercedes. The doors are open, and there's blood along the passenger side door, but no sign of the mercenaries.

Another explosion rocks the street, and for a few moments, there is consensus among the crowds: move away from the fire and smoke. I fight my way through the crowd, like a salmon struggling to leap upstream. Gunfire rattles in the aftermath of the blast, and I reorient myself toward the fighting.

Another Mercedes is off to my left, stuck in a morass of smaller vehicles; The mercenaries are dug in around it, sniping at the Arcadians who are circling at a safe distance. The lead Mercedes has been driven into the grass near the tower, and all of its doors are hanging open. There's a cluster of people jockeying around the base of the tower, trying to funnel through the single door.

I glance at the hovering helicopter.

Are they going to try for a pick-up from the top of the tower?

One of the Arcadians gets a little too bold, and a pair of mercenaries catch him in a crossfire. He does an ugly dance, his body jerking from the rounds, and almost immediately, he starts shrieking and clawing at his own flesh.

Weed killer rounds.

Escobar hasn't figured out a counteragent yet. This fight isn't as one-sided as it looks.

A pair of Arcadians spot me as I weave through the traffic jam, and I gauge whether I have the time to deal with them. One opens fire with his assault rifle, and the windows of a nearby sedan star up as the bullets sing around me. I duck behind the next car and return fire, aiming more for likely gas tanks in the nearby cars than either of the two Arcadians. A black Lexus goes up, spewing smoke and fire in a screen between the Arcadians and me, making it easy for me to drop all pretense and sprint for the tower.

The helicopter is rising, getting into position for its approach.

I stop at the first Mercedes. Secutores mercenaries are sprawled on the ground near the front of the vehicle, dead from blunt force trauma and broken necks. I'm carrying one of the Arcadian assault rifles—a commando version of the SIG SG 550—and I trade it for a Secutores MP7. I grab extra magazines from the dead mercs, noting the green stripe along the side of the magazine. Specialized rounds. Just what I need for Arcadian hunting.

I hear one of them coming across the grass, and before I can get my newly acquired gun lined up, the Arcadian slams into me. We collide with the Mercedes, and after avoiding his headbutt, I drop the stubby stock of my weapon down on his forearm as he tries to stab me with a long knife. I'm only partially successful in blocking his attack as I feel the knife slide off a rib. It's a flesh wound. It'll bleed a lot but it won't slow me down too much.

He whips his arm out from beneath the butt of my rifle and drives the knife at my throat. He's inside my reach and I've still got one hand on the MP7. I grab with my left hand, trying to get my arm up, but his knife catches me at the base of my neck, just inside my collarbone. I get a grip on his jacket and yank him forward, my teeth sinking into his throat. He twists the knife, trying to open me up all the way to the base of my skull.

I bite down, and his blood fills my mouth.

Most Arcadians have never been bitten. They don't understand what it feels like. There's more to drinking blood than the simple physiological and nutritional effects; there's an undeniable psychological response as well—both from the drinker and the one being drunk from. The shock is a moment of primal dominance. Your life could end in the next few moments or it could go on forever, but that decision is no longer yours. For most humans, the shock is fleeting. For all their bluster and efforts to forestall decay, there will come a moment when they are no longer in control. Some are fierce and fight it strenuously, but most—after a second of surprise—sink into a fugue of resigned acceptance.

The Arcadian keeps sawing at my neck, thinking he has time. Not aware that I own him.

His blood is thick, like fresh sap from a maple tree, and it has a surprisingly acrid chemical taste, but it flows just as readily as human blood. And its effect on me is the same. I let go of his jacket and grab his right wrist, grinding the bones as I squeeze. He finally realizes something is wrong and lets go of his knife, but I'm already bending him back. I twist, throwing him against the side of the car. He tries to beat at my head with his left arm, but I shake my head furiously, letting my teeth savage his throat. There's blood everywhere and my face is hot and sticky with it as I gnaw deeper. He gurgles, spitting blood, and his efforts to push me away are feeble, like the flapping hand of a newborn child.

I drain him until his heartbeat starts to flutter. Pulling away from his ravaged throat, I yank the knife out of my neck. The pain makes me howl, and I'm shaking with adrenaline as I plunge the knife into his chest. He stares at me glassy-eyed, his last breath bubbling out through the ruin of his throat.

I stagger away from the car, pressing my hand over the wound in my neck. *Close*, I will my flesh. It would be ironic to pass out from blood loss now, wouldn't it? I press harder, my fingers slick. I don't need Mother or the warm darkness of the humus. I can do this myself. *I can protect myself.*

The flow tapers off, and when I move my hand away, there's no sudden spurt of fresh blood. The skin around my collarbone itches fiercely, and I channel a burning desire to scratch into running instead.

The helicopter is moving toward the tower. Trailing beneath it is a long cable with a heavy hook assembly.

I still have to get that door open at the base of the tower, and then climb the stairs inside. I have no idea how many Arcadians are waiting for me. It'll take too long.

The tower is made from rough bricks. Not rough enough that a sane climber would attempt to ascend the face of the tower. But there are enough windows that someone who was more physically capable than the average rock climber might be able to make the climb.

I sling the MP7 around to my back, getting it out of the way. As the helicopter moves into position over the tower, I make a running leap. My hands frantically grab at the bricks, trying to find enough purchase to keep me from tumbling back to the ground.

The first window is only a few meters higher. If I can get a good grip, I can launch myself to the sill. My left hand catches on a nub of rock; my feet scrabble against the brick.

I'm not falling. Not yet.

FORTY

The helicopter hovers above the statue of Pachacutec, a steel cable dangling from its winch assembly. The noise and downdraft from its rotors turn the top of the tower into the yowling center of a localized storm. The statue stands on a raised platform, and it's high enough to obscure me as I lever myself onto the roof. The noise covers any clumsy noises I make.

There is a viewing area on the roof, but most of the space is dominated by the statue which fills up most of the back portion of the roof. On the other side of Pachacutec are three Arcadians: two are busy with the cable and a bound prisoner; the third is paying more attention to the stairs that descend from the roof. The cable is attached to a harness one of the two is wearing, and as I watch, he wraps his arms around the bound prisoner as both of them are lifted off the roof. He kicks off from the chest of the statue to make sure he doesn't get tangled in Pachacutec's outstretched hand.

His cargo is wrapped in an industrious web of restraints and her head is covered with a black hood. I can see enough of her clothing to recognize that it is Phoebe.

I hesitate. *Where's Mere?* As the pair go up, my stomach sinks.

The other car.

Things have been moving so quickly the last few minutes, I haven't had a chance to think about what's been going on, but it all starts to sink in. They aren't after Mere. They're snatching Phoebe.

She told me and I hadn't been listening. *It's not about you.*

Escobar wants Phoebe, for some of the same reasons he must have kept tissue samples from Nigel. But she's pure, a first generation child of Arcadia, untainted by reburial. They want her flesh to feed their chimera.

Talus wanted Nigel and me off the boat so he could take Phoebe. But that failed when Phoebe went overboard as well. Both sides floundered until Phoebe checked in with Callis. But he couldn't convince her to come in. She prefers the high ground, the sniper's position. She prefers to know a situation is safe before acting. She wouldn't expose herself, not after being betrayed on the boat by other Arcadians. She might trust Callis enough to call him, but not enough to reveal herself until after she had a chance to perform her own recognizance. By that time, I had made contact with Callis too. Knowing that she would watch me. Knowing that he could push me in the direction he wanted. Knowing that Phoebe would follow...

The second Arcadian shouts at the one watching the stairs, who turns his head. Unfortunately, as he does, his field of vision encompasses me. He brings his rifle up, and I dart to my left, putting as much of Pachacutec's legs as possible between him and me. Bullets ricochet off the bronze statue, and as I come around the statue's left side, I return fire, sending the Arcadian ducking down the recessed stairs.

The other Arcadian has nowhere to hide and so he charges me. I pull the trigger on the MP7 and nothing happens. The magazine is empty. I forgot to check how full it was before I started climbing. He's on me before I can eject the magazine and put in another. He shoves my gun aside with one hand, grabbing me with the other. As if we were going to grapple, Greco-Roman style.

With very little effort, I throw him. He bounces once, slides a meter or so, and then discovers he's out of roof. He has a surprised—and somewhat hurt—look in his eyes as he scrabbles at the edge of the roof, as if I have somehow cheated. And then he is gone.

I've just been wrestling longer than he has. Quite a bit longer.

The third guy is still hiding in the stairwell, and there's no easy way to approach him without giving him a clear shot, and so I dig in my pocket for my last grenade. Pull the pin, toss it over like I'm throwing a bean bag at a lawn party, and shake my head at the foolishness of hiding in a hole.

I drop the empty magazine from my MP7, and slap another one in.

The grenade goes off, and I'm sure the noise and flame are signal to the helicopter crew that something is amiss on the rooftop. There's no sign of Phoebe and the Arcadian who went up with her—they must be on board already—and the cable is still hanging down beneath the helicopter. On its way for the other two, who are no longer in need of it. For a second, we're caught in that moment of transition: Brains processing signals. Decisions being made.

I leap for the statue, scrabbling like a monkey up its bronze chest. I hoist myself up onto its outstretched arm, and as the sound of the helicopter's engine changes and its nose starts to dip, I leap off the statue. The helicopter pulls away from the tower, but it takes a second for that change to travel all the way down the cable. The clasp at the end of the line hangs in the air over Pachacutec. I stretch out my arm, not unlike the statue beneath me, my fingers straining for the clasp.

As I wrap my hand around the metal loop, it is yanked forward, pulling hard against my fingers. My arm follows, my shoulder complaining from the sudden tug. I fumble with the strap of my rifle, trying to get the weapon under control as I sail through the air beneath the helicopter. It's only going to be a few seconds before someone notices me, dangling down below. We streak across the promenade, roaring over the traffic jam, and I hear the distant noise of gunfire below. Something bites my right leg, down on the calf, and blood begins to flow.

Twisting on the end of the cable, I point the rifle up at the helicopter fantail and try to wreck the assembly with several bursts from the MP7. The cable bounces, dropping me a meter or so, and I shift my aim toward the main portion of the helicopter. Several more bursts from the gun and I'm out of ammo again, but at least the cable has stopped dropping. For the moment.

I hit the button that drops out the empty magazine and try to figure how I'm going to get the last magazine out of my back right pocket and into the gun without letting go of the cable, and I decide that isn't going to happen.

The helicopter turns to the north, climbing to a height that will allow it to clear the hills that ring Cusco. Discarding the empty gun, I start climbing the cable. It's slick, meant to be wound quickly and efficiently around a drum, but I've climbed worse. It's precarious work, but there's also no reason to dwell on what I'm doing. Hand over hand, as quickly as I can.

As I get close to the helicopter's landing struts, the cable starts unspooling again. It starts slow, but picks up speed. In another second or two, it'll be unspooling faster than I can climb. My muscles aching, I move faster, my hands burning as they grip and release the cable. My first attempt at grabbing the long strut misses, my bloody hand slipping from the rounded strut. Another meter of cable plays out and I have to make up lost ground before I can try again. I climb higher, and on my second try, I get my arm wrapped around the strut. I disengage myself from the cable and get my other arm around the landing gear too.

Still not out of the woods yet.

I get my legs around the strut, and hanging upside down, I wrestle with the pistol still in my pocket. One of the spare magazines goes tumbling away as I pull the gun out. A masked face peers out of the helicopter to check on the cable, and I pull the trigger twice. The face disappears, replaced by a foot jutting out from the cabin of the helicopter. The foot doesn't move, suggesting that I hit my target. As long as it stays there, I have a chance.

I put the gun in my mouth, biting down on the back of the slide. I need both hands to pull myself onto the strut. I swing up as the helicopter pitches to the right, and I clutch at the strut, fighting to stay on. When it pitches in the other direction—a clumsy attempt to shake me off—I use that change in aspect to my advantage. Both hands on the bar, shoving my butt up, and arcing my back. I pitch forward, sliding across the strut, and I push off, throwing my hands up now, reaching for the second strut—the one that runs along the underside of the helicopter's cabin.

I haul myself up, getting one arm on the inside of the helicopter cabin. The rest is easy, even with the back and forth motion of the helicopter. I get my knees up and, caught in an awkward leaning forward position, I freeze.

Sitting in one of the seats, as calmly as if this ride is nothing more than a tourist trip around the Sacred Valley, is Alberto Montoya.

But I killed him.

He's holding a bulky gun that has two holes in the front of its barrel. It's a Taser, and he smiles briefly at my confusion as he fires both darts.

The current lights up my nervous system, and I collapse on the floor of the cabin. Phoebe is lying nearby, the sack still over her head. She's oblivious to what's going on, and a second later, I am too.

BOOK SIX

PHAËTON

FORTY-ONE

"They're pretty, aren't they?" Alberto's voice penetrates my stupor. A Taser is just as effective against an Arcadian as it is a human, but since it isn't deadly, it gets overlooked. Though, as a temporary restraining measure, nothing works quite like a massive jolt of electrical current through a nervous system. My vision is still fucked up—I'm only seeing shades of gray with the barest hint of any color at all—and my legs continue to twitch beyond my control. But I can hear again, and I have control of my motion functions. Unfortunately, while I was insensate, Alberto bound my hands behind my back.

He's talking about something outside the helicopter. We've left Cusco behind, and spread out below us is a panorama of brown hills with scattered stands of trees and rocks. Incan ruins, presumably, judging from the regularity of some of the rock formations. What Alberto is wanting me to see is a cascade of white rectangles on a hillside, like a frozen waterfall. The rectangles are reflecting the sunlight, which only washes out my field of vision more when I look at them.

"Salt farms," he shouts at me, making himself heard over the noise of the helicopter's rotors. "They've been tending them for generations." He leans toward the cockpit of the helicopter, shouting instructions to the pilot, who nods and brings the helicopter down.

I'm trying to find scars or patches of new skin on him—any indicator that he's been healed—but he looks just like he did the first time I saw him at the penthouse. It's as if the parking lot beheading never happened.

Alberto grabs me and drags me toward the open door, giving me an opportunity to look more closely at the salt farms. Each plot is a rectangular area that is allowed to fill with water. The layout of the farms suggests that the whole network is a trickle-down system. A stream at the top of the hill supplies the fresh water which spills down and fills each basin. Through a network of gates and channels, the farmers direct the water. Once a basin is filled, the water is directed elsewhere so that the trapped water can evaporate, leaving behind harvestable salt.

I have a bad feeling about what's supposed to happen next.

"You hurt my family," he shouts at me, spittle flecking my face. He hauls me even closer to the edge. "I want to torture you for a very long time—for as many years as it has been since you killed her—but there is no time for that. Instead, your death will simply be very painful."

As the helicopter crosses over the lower terminus of the salt farms, he tries to shove me out of the helicopter. I don't go like he expects.

He didn't bind my legs, and I've got one foot hooked around the hoist assembly for the cable winch. He turns to pull my leg free, and in doing so, steps between my spread legs. I whip my legs together, catching him across the thighs. As I twist to my left, he falls against the seat behind him, his lower back slamming against the edge of the seat. He roars in anger, trying to extricate himself from my scissored legs, and as he lunges, hands reaching for my face, I pull my legs up and in.

The helicopter wiggles, the pilot compensating for the sudden shift of weight in the back, and all that combined momentum is enough to slide me over the edge. Gravity helps, and as Alberto gets his hands on my face, we both tumble out of the helicopter.

We bounce off the helicopter strut—rather, it's my shoulder that does most of the hard work—and we kick free of each other as soon as we can. The helicopter was fairly low as it came over the salt fields—the cliffs on Rapa Nui were higher—and it's not the fall that worries me, it's the landing.

It's impossible to gauge the depth of any of the basins, and so I try to position my body in a way to minimize the trauma of impact. In case that makes a difference.

I hit water—very briny water—and it's like being squeezed in a vise. Salt is dangerous; it dehydrates tissue and, over time, it can be fatal. Salt water—like the ocean—is a slower death. You don't dehydrate right away, but your tissue soaks up the water, absorbing the salt which becomes a poisonous residue that breaks you down cell by cell. It's a slow, painful death. The concentration of salt in this water is much, much higher, which means death is going to come quicker, but it's going to be extraordinarily painful.

Alberto is right about that part.

My skin reacts instantly, shriveling and cracking. I'm becoming both a prune and a desiccated seed pod. The only good news is that the water is denser than regular water, which means I sink less. I still hit the bottom of the basin, but the impact is a distant source of pain compared to the burning pressure of my body collapsing in on itself.

I float, letting my buoyancy aid me as I curl into a ball, slipping my hands under my butt. The next part is a little harder when I don't have something to brace myself against, but I manage to get my hands past my feet. I kick off from the bottom of the basin and shoot to the surface, breaching noisily. The sun beats down on the salt farms, making the air turgid and warm. I feel like I've jumped out of an acid bath into an incinerator. I bob toward the edge of the basin, trying not to breathe. Trying not to scream. Bobbing seems to take an eternity, a cork bouncing up and down on a lake of fire. Will I burn up before I reach the shore?

The only good news is that the plastic ties slip off my wrists with ease by the time I reach the edge of the basin, with only a little bit of my skin as well. There is no blood. There's just bubbling lines of white foam.

How did Phoebe survive *swimming* back from the *Cetacean Liberty*? As soon as I ask myself the question, I realize the answer. It lies in the enigma of her shrugs. Why *wouldn't* she have survived?

I've never been in this much pain—never has so much of my body hurt—but I'm still conscious. I'm still *me*. There are ways to kill us, but for the most part, we are immortal. Mother takes care of us. That's our secret, and our flaw. We think we need Mother, and so when we are confronted with pain—real, life-threatening pain—we run back to Mother. And when we can't get back to Mother, well, then we die. Like any other creature on this planet.

And that's our flaw. That's what Escobar has figured out. That's what Phoebe knows. We think we need Mother. We think that she can fix anything. She's our God, our deity that takes care of us, feeds us, and protects us. She is our faith, and as long as she is there, we think we can do anything. But what happens when she is gone? When there is no one to rescue us? Is that when we give up, when we default to the primal fear that lives inside all living creatures? We are alone, and the world does not care about us. We are insignificant, motes of dust in an infinite sky.

Phoebe sees the world differently. She needs nothing. She needs nobody. She *is*. Zen purity.

I clench my fist, noticing that the foaming spot has stopped bubbling. I don't need Mother's permission to die. Nor do I need her permission to keep on living. Those choices remain with me.

My philosophical breakthrough is interrupted by Alberto, who leaps over the wall from an upslope basin. He looks like a preternatural nonagenarian with sharp teeth and nails. Way too spry for his appearance. All I can do is brace myself.

He slams into me, a snarling bag of bones, and my feet slip on the crystallized bank of the salt basin. One of his hands rakes my face, tearing my skin, and the other claws at my clothing, trying to get my neck exposed. I get my hand under his chin and force his head back, exposing his neck too.

It's primal combat, animals vying for dominance. Equally matched, the fight will be decided by which of us has the stronger will. Who can take more pain, more physical punishment? Who will be more relentless? Alberto is clean and strong. He fights with that confidence— that knowledge that he is the better physical specimen. Even though I'm invigorated by the blood from the Arcadian I killed in the plaza, I'm still weak, traumatized by the salt and sun.

Be quick about it, then.

I've got his head back, and instead of trying to bite him, I grab his throat with my left hand instead. His skin is fragile, like mine, and tearing it is like ripping a snake's discarded skin. He doesn't bleed; he foams—both from his mouth and from the ragged gash in his throat. And while he's still recovering from the attack, I punch him in the side of the head, putting as much strength as I can in the blow. Bones in my hand shift unnaturally.

He staggers out of our embrace, clutching at his head which is no longer as perfectly shaped as it was. Foam is bubbling around his hand.

My knuckles are covered with foam.

Alberto comes at me again, and I sweep his strike aside, popping him in the face with my left hand, breaking his nose. He retreats a couple of steps, bumping up against the wall separating the basins, and I stay where I am. Keeping my distance.

Alberto leans against the wall, breathing heavily and noisily. His wounds continue to foam, white bubbles dripping down his face. He exhales heavily, and foam spatters from his lips.

I continue to wait for him, even though every cell in my body is screaming at me to run. To get to ground and dig as deep as I can. I stand my ground and wait. Which of us is going to break first?

"Is this hurt worse than when I took your head off?" I ask, goading him.

He shows me his teeth, his hands closing into fists, and I think he's going to charge me again, but then he spins on his heel and darts for the wall behind him. I'm taken aback that he's going to try to run, and before I can respond, he goes over the wall into the basin on the next level.

I dance along the ridges of the basin to the wall and look over. The upper basin isn't nearly as full—mid-thigh—and Alberto is splashing through to the far side. Leaping to the top of the wall, which isn't much wider than the width of my foot, I race around the perimeter of the basin. In a purely mathematical world, I'd be taking the longer—and slower—route, but conditions being what they are, I make up ground staying out of the salt water.

Alberto gets to the next wall, and opts to stay out of the water too. He hoists himself up onto the wall and starts running along the rim of the next basin. I change my course, running parallel to him on my own track toward the top of the salt farm cascade.

I can see where this is going, and I'm not interested in a foot race to the top of the hill, and as I'm running after Alberto, I start looking for something I can throw. At a nexus of four basins, I find a jumble of stones. Selecting a suitably heavy rock, I gauge Alberto's speed and route, and then throw my rock.

The missile hits him in the hip, knocking him off-balance, and he falls into a basin. When he surfaces, I'm ready with another rock—a third in my other hand. He stands in the basin, the water up to his waist, and stares at me, his forehead steaming and squirming with foam.

"Did your grandfather ever tell you what happened to Jacinta?" I ask. "How she died?"

Deliberately, he wipes the white foam off his face. His entire body is quivering from the salt water bath he's taking, but when he looks at me, all I see in his expression is how much he wants to kill me.

"I dumped her body in the ocean," I tell him. "That's why she never came back."

He leaps out of the basin, trailing salt water, and I throw my rock. His body contorts and he falls into the basin next to me with a splash. My skin burns and twitches where the salt water hits it, but I don't move.

He bobs up slowly, floating on his back. His head is even more deformed, and the foam spurting out of his skull starts to cover the surface of the basin with a web of sticky bubbles. He stares at me, still alive. Still wanting to kill me.

"I'm sorry, for what that may be worth," I say as I transfer my last rock to my right hand. My fingers are stiffening up, and it takes me a little while to get a good grip on the rock.

Alberto isn't going anywhere.

"If there is life after this one," I say, "at least you'll be with her."

He blinks.

My aim is good, and his head snaps back from the impact of my rock. He slips underwater—bobs up once, his face squirming as if it was covered with albino worms—and then he goes under again. This time he doesn't come up.

FORTY-TWO

The sun beats down on the open deck of the warship. Most of the men are huddled beneath makeshift shelters strung along the starboard rail. The less able are below deck, squatting in ankle-deep water. An eerie emptiness flowed in the wake of the storm which had blown us west from Troy, and our ship was trapped in the endless calm. We have not felt a breath of wind for many days.

"Do you ever regret not staying and fighting?" Aeneas and I are sitting in the rear of the boat, keeping an eye on the unmoving tiller.

"In which battle?" I ask.

He makes a noise in his chest that might have been the start of a chuckle. He fumbles for his water skin, takes a tiny sip, and then offers it to me. I am not thirsty, but I take it nonetheless and pretend to drink. We have to conserve what little water we have.

Our boat is leaking, and too many of the men have fallen prey to sun sickness. Our vessel is a warship, not a transport, and it was never meant to be the home for the number of men it currently carries. Though, in a few more weeks, our company might number so few that we won't have enough strong men to work the oars.

"The Achaeans were inside the gate," I say as I hand the skin back. "Priam's spirit broke when Hector died. What would our deaths have accomplished? Killing a few hundred more Achaeans?"

"What else is there for fighting men such as ourselves?" Aeneas asks.

This is not the first time he has asked this question, and I have tried to discern the answer that he seeks, but I fear my responses have never been suitable enough.

I hesitate before answering this time, glancing over at Aeneas. His skin is much darker after weeks at sea—as is mine—and our bodies are thin and wiry. We have stopped wearing our armor. It fits poorly now, and carrying the extra weight on board the boat is a foolish proposition. Very few of the men have shown any aptitude for swimming.

"I don't know," I say, unable to muster the enthusiasm to craft different rhetoric.

"Nor do I," he admits. "We have always turned to the gods for our answers, haven't we? When do we plant the crops this year? Let's ask the gods. Is tomorrow an auspicious day to smite our enemies? Why, yes, the gods think so. Shall I marry this buxom wench? The gods appreciate the offering her dowry will afford."

"The gods always appreciate a *bountiful* marriage," I point out.

"But we have no temple out here," he says, waving a hand at the sky.

I remain silent, already anticipating where this conversation is going.

"Before the men grow too weak to row, we should ask for a sign," he says.

"And how would we find this sign?" I ask. "We have no goats or pigs to offer as a sacrifice."

"We have no hope either," he says, looking at me.

"If I do this, we stray from the path we have known. We will no longer be the men we were."

He laughs, a sick wheeze hiccuping out of his chest. "We are strangers already."

"Who are we then?" I press him, seeking some sign that he was not gripped by the madness that came from too much sun.

"That is the question I want you to ask of the gods, my friend. Who are we destined to be?"

He offers me his knife and, on unsteady legs, I clamber down into the damp hold. The men, instinctively sensing I am on an errand none wish to witness, make way for me. Many of them flee for the upper deck even though they are too weak to withstand the sun's heat for long. In the darkest corner of the hold, I find the few men who have tried to crawl as far away from the others in preparation of dying. Only one of them is conscious enough to be aware of my approach.

"What is your name?" I ask.

"Tymmaeus, my lord," the sick man responds. His shoulder is festering with a foul blackness. I remember him. He had taken an arrow in the shoulder as we were boarding the boat. We had tried to get the tip out, but hadn't been successful. His wound hadn't closed, turning red and then black as rot set in. Tymmaeus tries to sit up, but he hasn't enough strength to do much more than breathe shallowly. His body is hot with fever, and his skin is slick with sweat. He was a young man when he came aboard the boat, but he looks much older now.

I show him Aeneas's knife, and he squints at the blade.

"It is a warrior's death," I tell him.

Licking his lips, he nods and tries to arrange his body to make my task easier.

"Close your eyes, brave Tymmaeus," I instruct him. "You do not need to see this death coming."

"I already—"

I don't let him finish, sliding the knife into his heart so that he dies as quickly as possible. I withdraw the knife and slit his belly.

His guts burn my hands, and I root through his viscera until I cannot withstand the pain any longer.

Aeneas has ordered the men to the oars, and when I emerge, red-handed, from the darkness of the under deck, he shouts to me. "Which direction?" He is standing beside the tiller, leaning toward me, eager to hear my augury. Eager to know that the gods have not abandoned him.

I raise my hands, puffy and swollen. Red with Tymmaeus's blood. The sun beats down, its rays inflaming my hands. I don't know how I can feel anything through the pain, but I do. It is the gentlest of caresses, the light touch of a zephyr's kiss.

"That way," I say, letting the wind stroke the back of my burning hands.

ⱽⱽ

At the top of the cascade of salt farms is a row of white-walled huts, nestled against the base of another hill that rises much more steeply. There are people wandering back and forth along the upper edge of the farms. They've been watching since I started my rambling run along the brick-lined edges of the basins. When I reach the last few rows, the watchers scatter. It is one thing to spot a monster; it is another thing entirely to meet it face-to-face. The only thing moving along the rim when I arrive is a tiny wind, blowing dust along the walls of the huts. A zephyr.

I've been thinking while I clambered up the hill, letting my brain get lost in my history as a distraction from the waves of pain coursing through my body. My skin is still raw and the weight of my clothing is a fierce torment, but my strength has not been sapped by the sun as I had expected. I have been burned by the sun numerous times during the twentieth century—a growing concern brought about by the vicissitudes of the modern world—but this time, I can live with the pain. I do not entirely know the source of my willpower; perhaps it is a reaction to seeing Phoebe survive sunlight or a facet of my conversations with Escobar or even strength drawn from my memory of the last augury I did for Aeneas.

I have lost my fear of the sun.

And with it, so too has my fear of abandonment vanished. I have turned my back on Arcadia, even as Arcadia has exiled me. I have nowhere to go. No home that I can return to. But my exile is not a yoke about my shoulders. The salt and the sun have stripped away all that dead weight.

The huts are tiny little domiciles, transitory living quarters for the farmers as they tend to their basins. I find little in the few that I break into. Most have tiny refrigerators that aren't very well stocked. What fruit I find I eat without reservation, replenishing my depleted cells. I can feel my body relax, no longer crippled by the desiccating salt of the basins. I'm a long way from being whole, but I'm strong enough to keep fighting.

Tucked between two of the huts, I find a worn bicycle. It is covered in dust and might have been green once upon a time. Wire baskets have been welded between the handlebars and on either side of the back wheel. The nut holding the seat in place is stiff, but I manage to get it started so that I can raise the seat. It has a metal bell, and I flick the ringer with my thumb as I ride toward the dirt road that runs past the edge of the farms and heads further uphill.

Ding! Ding!

Moray, the farming site where the Incans experimented with seeds, is only a few kilometers away. That's where the helicopter was going. Hyacinth Worldwide is building something there, and I suspect it is Escobar's great secret. The place where he is building the chimerae.

Ding! Ding!

The ringing of the bell is both a tribute to the dead and a warning to Escobar.

I'm not done yet.

FORTY-THREE

A long a flat stretch of road that runs along a ridge, I stop and look back toward Cusco. There's a haze of dirt stretching back toward the city, and sunlight glints off the metal bodies of a line of cars. There's too much dust to be sure, but it looks like a couple of Mercedes G-class wagons.

Secutores won the fight at the plaza. That doesn't bode well for Arcadia. When was the last time we lost a fight with humans?

Ahead of the caravan, weaving wildly around the sharp turns of the switchback up the side of the ridge, is a dark blue sedan. I watch it approach. I can't outrun it on my bike, and I'm more than a little curious as to who is leading this charge. The sedan roars over the top of the ridge, catching a little air, and slews dangerously close to me before it comes to a stop. The passenger side window comes down and I look in.

"We really don't have time for you to stand there and gawk at me," Mere says.

"It's just good to see you," I say, and I mean it. Her face and neck are streaked with dirt and blood, and there's a gleam in her eye that speaks of too much adrenaline in the last hour, but it's definitely Mere, vibrant and alive. On the passenger seat is a handgun, a model I've seen Secutores carry. I leave the bike by the side of the road—ringing the bell one last time—and climb into the car.

"What's with the bell?" she asks as I move the gun out of the way and settle into the seat.

"When was the last time you rode a bike with a bell?" I ask.

"Fair point." She drops the car back into drive and puts her foot down on the accelerator. She watches the road while I examine her more closely. Some of the blood is coming from a gash in her neck, and there's a couple of bruises forming under her right eye. Her knuckles are scraped, and there's another gash along the outside of her right forearm.

"What's the other guy look like?" I ask.

She glances over at me. "I was going to ask you the same thing."

"I killed Alberto Montoya."

"What? I thought you said you killed him in Santiago?"

"I did. I took his head off, Mere. That should have done it. But he was on the helicopter, almost as if he was waiting for me. And he looked, well, he looked perfect. As if nothing had happened to him."

"How is that possible?"

"As far as I know, it isn't. Tissue decay starts as soon as you separate the head from the body. You can't grow—" I stop. I was going to say that you couldn't grow them back together, but I suddenly wonder if that's worth the effort. What do I know of Mother's process. We go into the ground and we come out again, but who is to say that what goes in is the same that comes out again? What if Escobar's efforts to grow his own Arcadians is exactly what Mother does? She grows an exact copy of each of us.

"What?" Mere asks.

"We thought that Escobar was growing his own, right? What if that is exactly what he did? What if he's grown more than one grandson?"

"Clones?"

"Every piece of fruit from a tree is a clone, Mere. As is every flower. Nature's been doing it for centuries."

"How long does that take?"

I think of strawberry plants, shooting out runners that double and even triple the size of a harvest every year. "Not as long as you think," I say.

"Here's something else that has been bothering me," Mere says. "How old do you think Escobar is?"

"Several centuries," I say, thinking of the Incan sculpture in the lobby of the Montoya building.

"How is Alberto his grandson? Either Alberto is as old as Escobar, or he's been making babies."

I think of the familial resemblance between the two men and I shake my head. "Neither," I say, recalling something Escobar said. "Both."

"It can't be both," Mere says.

"I saw it right away and said as much to him, but he laughed it off, but I was right. Alberto is a younger version of him."

"Jesus Christ," Mere whispers.

"Yeah," I say, my hands tightening around the butt of the gun. "Where did you get this?" I ask, shaking off the enormity of what Escobar is doing.

"Our mutual friend," she says.

I pop out the magazine and press down on the top round. "It's been fired a few times," I note.

"Yep," she says grimly. The car bounces across a series of potholes, and I wait until it settles down again before I put the magazine back in the gun. "Did you get him?"

She shakes her head, her eyes straying to the rearview mirror. I twist in my seat and look out through the back window. "Did you wing him, at least?"

"Definitely." She grins.

I set the safety and put the gun, barrel down, in one of the cup holders in the center console. "I guess we don't need to have a talk about how to use a handgun, do we?"

"No," she says, "I got that covered." The grin comes back. "Much to Belfast's surprise."

"Escobar has Phoebe," I tell her. "That's who his team was after. That's who they've been after all along."

"So it really wasn't about you?"

I shake my head, smiling a little even when I see that she's giving me a hard time. "Escobar wanted tissue samples from Nigel to create a counteragent, right? He wants Phoebe for the same reason. You saw how she managed to survive exposure to sunlight and sea water. If he can figure out how to replicate the genetic coding and modify it to be resistant to the weed killer, his Arcadians will be immune."

"And it's going down at Moray," she says.

I nod. "Or it's a big hole in the ground that Escobar has filled with enough high explosives to atomize you, me, and all of the bad guys following us."

"Well, let's hope I'm right and you're not," she says as the car crests another hill and we see the white shape of Tyvek-wrapped scaffolding rising out of stony landscape.

ᴠ ᴠ

Moray is a series of concentric rings and while I had thought it would naturally lie in one of the many tiny valleys between the hills, the site is actually out in the middle of a plain. There's a high fence around the site, topped with razor wire. The fence has been lined with opaque weather-guard, keeping prying eyes out, and inside the fence, there are several frames of buildings under construction, and they're the white shapes that rise up like shrink-wrapped dinosaur skeletons. Behind the main structures, there's a landing pad for a helicopter and the Dauphin-class chopper that I was on briefly is sitting on the pad.

"Here we are," Mere announces, easing up on the accelerator pedal. The car bumps along the road, slowing down as we approach the fence. Mere runs a hand through her hair, pushing it back from her face. There are stress lines around her eyes and across her forehead, and I can hear the accelerated beat of her heart. She's holding it together amazingly well, considering the situation. "Why did you save me?" she asks quietly. "That night in the warehouse."

"Because I wanted to," I reply.

"It wasn't an order that you were following?"

"No," I say. "I did it under my own volition."

"That's out of character for you," she says, her fingers fumbling with the scar at the base of her throat.

"I don't regret doing it."

She looks at me. "Thank you."

"You're welcome," I say, my throat tight.

Her teeth gnaw at her lower lip. "Promise me that you'll kiss me again," she says. "When this is over."

"You kissed me," I remind her.

She throws me a shy smile. "All right, I'm going to kiss you again when this is all over."

"I'd like that."

"Good," she says. She stares intently at me, as if she is memorizing my face. "I'd like to laugh about what we've done."

"Me too," I agree.

V V

We don't bother being clever or coy. Mere drives up as close as possible to the installation, and we walk the rest of the way to the metal door set in the fence. Over the door, there's a security camera mounted atop the fence. Someone knows we're coming, and as we reach the door, we distinctly hear the locks cycle.

I go first, and as the door shuts behind Mere, the locks reengage. We're standing in a temporary tunnel, made from white plastic wrap stretched over a wire frame, and there's only one direction to go. "Kind of like a cattle chute leading to the slaughterhouse," Mere opines. I don't disagree with her. That is the one drawback about walking in cold to a hostile installation. You get the overwhelming sense that this approach is a *bad* idea.

Still, it is much easier than any number of assaults I've done over the last three millennia and, considering the way we went to the penthouse in Santiago, I suspect Escobar likes letting his prey wander in without any trouble. I can't decide if this is a terminally stupid way of doing things or an expression of supreme confidence.

When you get right down to it, he's gotten everything he wanted. He certainly seems to be the one in control.

Well, minus a grandson or two.

The tunnel ends, and we step out onto the edge of the first ring of the Moray installation. The original Incan site is a series of concentric circles, terraces upon which these farmers could plant a variety of crops. These rings dominate the area inside the fences. Off to our left are two of the construction frameworks, and one looks like it is a half-finished laboratory. Not dissimilar to the one built on Rapa Nui. As we approach the edge of the first ring, more of the lower rings are revealed, each one about ten meters below the previous one. Each terrace reveals a progressively more bizarre landscape.

The second terrace, just below where we stand, is filled with healthy citrus-bearing trees. Bizzaria, I expect. An enormous grove of the rare chimera.

The next ring is home to several dozen squat wooden structures. Not large enough to be sheds, but not terribly small either. "Hives," I realize. "They're beehives."

Below, stands of miro threaten to overreach their ring. Most of them are at least ten meters high. "When did you say Hyacinth Worldwide moved in on this place? Two years ago?"

"Thereabouts," Mere says.

"Miro don't grow that fast," I point out. "Nor do Bizzaria."

"And what are those?" Mere asks, pointing at the fourth ring.

The trees look like poplars, tall and slender, with pale bark. But they're too short, and their crowns are all wrong. The tree are about five meters tall, and the last meter splits into a quintet of branches. Each branch extends a few meters out from the trunk, bending back toward the ground, and each has a single bulbous pod growing from the end. The pods are different sizes, the largest appear to be thicker than the actual main trunk itself.

The fifth ring looks like an optical illusion. The tall fronds that fill every available centimeter of space on this ring look like kelp, and appear to move with the same liquid grace, but these plants are not underwater, nor is there any localized wind at that depth. In several places, the large pods from the previous layer have pulled free of the parent tree and have tumbled down onto the bed of swaying fronds. The pods, pale yellow in color on the tree, are darker within the leafy embrace of the fronds, as if they are absorbing the tint from the purple leaves.

"This is how they're made," I tell Mere. "This is where Escobar has been growing his grandsons."

Down at the very bottom, in the midst of an extensive collection of computer equipment, is a long slab on which a figure is strapped. A pair of technicians are focused on their screens, monitoring various signals and processes. A maze of cables and conduits run from beneath the slab into the workstations and into the walls of the pit.

Feed tubes.

"It's Phoebe," Mere says.

"They're going to drain her dry," I say. She's going to feed the fern layer, which will, in turn, pass along a series of nutrients and genetic triggers to whatever is growing inside those pods.

Escobar's next generation of Arcadians. They don't need Mother. They don't need Arcadian soil. They're unaffected by Secutores's weed killer.

Perfect soldiers.

FORTY-FOUR

"**W**hat do you think of my little project?"

Mere jumps at the sound of Escobar's voice, but I had heard him coming. He's wearing a light gray suit with a lavender shirt. His tie is a deep burgundy—quite close to the same color as the fronds down on the fifth ring—and the tiny detail stitched into the silk is a pair of interlocked circles. The chimerae sigil.

"We're going to stop it," Mere says, raising the pistol she got from Belfast and pointing it at Escobar.

"Stop what?" he asks as he strolls to the edge of the rings and looks down. "It's already done."

"What? What do you mean?" she asks.

"Your friend has already contributed to the project," he says. "I've drained all of her blood, and it's being passed to the seedlings as we stand here. There's nothing you can do. She's already gone."

I stare down at the still figure on the gurney. "I can take her back to Arcadia," I point out. "Mother can bring her back."

"Arcadia is closed to you. Both of you," Escobar reminds me. "They won't let you in."

I shrug. "Maybe I can get them to reconsider."

"Maybe," he muses, "but it will take some time. Time she doesn't have." He purses his lips. "You failed, Silas. You failed in every way."

"I killed your grandson a couple of times," I point out.

"I will grant you that," he admits. "And it looks like you have survived a visit to the salt baths. That's quite impressive. They've been a most effective place to dispose of certain… aborted experiments."

"'What doesn't kill you makes you stronger,'" I offer.

"Yes, that hoary aphorism of Nietzsche," Escobar sighs. "One he didn't subscribe to himself."

"Happens to be true in a couple of cases," I say. "Me and Phoebe, for example."

"Yes," he says. "She was a most perfect specimen."

"Is," I correct him.

He looks at Mere and shakes his head. "Even for one of her soldiers, he's quite single-minded, isn't he?"

"It's one of his most annoying traits," she admits. She is still pointing the pistol at him, though her arms are starting to tremble.

"Put the gun down, my dear," Escobar says.

Her only response is to tighten her grip.

"I don't mean to be so pig-headed about this," I say, looking down at the figure in the pit. "but I'm just trying to be helpful."

"Helpful? How?" He swivels his head around to look at me.

"Well, are you sure she's dead?" I lift my arm and wave.

He doesn't look away from me, which is too bad because I'm pretty sure the figure on the gurney moves in response.

I've been thinking about the gun case and the sight of Phoebe sitting calmly in the car. She knew what was coming. She knew Escobar was going to try to snatch her. Maybe she had even done something to alert both Secutores and Escobar that we were in the hotel. I don't really know, but the end result is that Phoebe got herself to Escobar's laboratory unscathed.

Escobar wanted to create a chimera, a new strain of Arcadian that was resistant to the weed killer, and Phoebe was never going to accept protection from the Grove. So what was she—a self-proclaimed steward—going to do about the weed killer? She was going to get the counteragent spliced into her own DNA.

If all Escobar had done was drain her blood, he hadn't killed her. Not yet. She was going to be incredibly thirsty and quite weak, but she wasn't dead. And whatever was growing in those pods was going to be organic enough for her to feed from. And given that it would be a mix of her own blood, the counteragent, and whatever other genetic modifications Escobar was putting into his clones, she was just going to be getting the equivalent of a highly oxygenated blood transfusion.

Brutally efficient. Just like Phoebe.

"My science is quite exact," Escobar snaps.

"I'm sure it is," I say, stepping back from the edge of the rings so that Mere doesn't wonder what I'm talking about and come to look too. "So, what's in store for us?"

"What makes you think I have any plans for you at all?" Escobar asks.

"Well, you got what you wanted." I nod toward the Incan terrace farm. "You've kicked me around a bit, rubbed my nose in things, and got my head all twisted around. What does killing me now serve?"

"Are you suggesting you might have some use?"

"I don't know what's really true about your relationship with Arcadia, but I know that at least one person there knows what you're doing. That may not have been part of your plan, but they're going to come sniffing around now that they know about the weed killer. Oh, yeah, sorry, I told them about that. They're going to be quite worked up about the humans having a weapon that can actually kill us."

"You're going to make a deal, aren't you?" Mere says. "You're going to make Arcadia bow to you. You're going to make them beg you to save them, and they'll be so panicked, they'll accept anything you offer. It's a classic scenario. Allow a threat to develop and then swoop in with a perfectly reasonable solution. God, you'd think people would have figured it out after the US government used it on its own citizens after 9/11."

Escobar raises his shoulders slightly as if the idea is interesting but not enough to fully capture his attention. "What do I need of Arcadia? I have been without them for more than two hundred years. Why would I want them to embrace me again?"

"Because you need their help," I say.

He laughs. "Their help? The combined umbrella of what my family controls makes more—in pure profit—every year than the entire accumulated wealth that every Arcadian has squirreled away. I could hire every single private military contractor on this planet—today—without making a dent in my cash reserves."

"You should," I point out. "At the very least to keep them from being hired by the other guys."

"Which *other guys*?"

"The ones you're worried about," I say. "The ones who developed the weed killer in the first place and gave it to Secutores. I mean, Secutores did wipe out that team you sent to retrieve Phoebe. If it wasn't for the helicopter extraction, you wouldn't have gotten Phoebe."

"It's a temporary advantage," he scoffs. "Soon to be rendered useless against me and mine."

"That might be true," I admit, "but that's not their only research project, is it?"

His cheek twitches.

Mere spots his nervous flinch too. "They got nervous, didn't they? When they used the weed killer, but didn't capture an Arcadian. Suddenly their secret was out. They've been under everyone's radar for some time, haven't they? You don't develop a weapon like that overnight. That's why you tortured Nigel and taped it. You wanted to show them that you were still willing to play along. That was why you let Silas and me come to the restaurant. You were going to turn Silas over. Fulfill your part of the deal. Meanwhile, they had no idea that the one you really wanted was Phoebe." Mere's figured it out too. "But we kept getting away from you, and Secutores kept getting closer. And now you've moved against them. They know you're not going to play nice. You need friends. You need to get that counteragent in place and you need to show Arcadia that it works."

Escobar snarls at her, and Mere responds by snapping her arm up, pointing the pistol at his forehead. "Don't," she says quite clearly, "I'm really on edge right now. I might not be the best of shots, but you're going to be pretty hard to miss standing right there. And I'm willing to bet you haven't received the genetic therapy yet."

"You need someone to help you smooth things over with Arcadia," I say, pulling his attention away from Mere, "That was supposed to be Talus, but Phoebe went and splattered his brains all over your penthouse floor. Which leaves me as the only Arcadian who knows enough about what is going on to help you. I'm Mother's *favorite*, remember. You need me to convince the Grove." I nod at Mere. "And you need her to keep me in line."

"Excuse me?" Mere sputters.

Escobar composes himself and offers Mere a pleasant smile. "I will need assurances that he will do his job properly," he says. "Otherwise, he could simply sell me out to the Grove. They would be taking a risk, but Silas has been a member of Arcadia for a very long time. Many will feel his words resonate within them."

"So you're just going to leave me with him?" Mere's hand drifts, moving the pistol in my direction. "What's to stop him from killing me the moment you walk out of here?"

"Not much," I admit.

"Oh, that's *fantastic* to hear," Mere snorts.

"Think of it as *detente*," Escobar says.

"Which is just a fancy French way of saying, 'Relax, this won't hurt a bit when I slip this knife in your back,'" Mere says.

"It does always hurt more than you think it will," I say gravely.

"Silas!" Mere stares at me, her eyes big and round.

We're interrupted by a shout from the lab building behind us. Escobar looks; I don't. I grab Mere's hand, reestablishing where her gun should be pointed, and mash my finger against hers and the trigger. The gun goes off, but Escobar has already moved, ducking and slamming his palm against the base of her fist. The gun barrel goes up, the round misses, and as he tries to strip the weapon from her hand, I backhand him in the face.

In the tunnel, the metal door explodes inward in a gout of flame and smoke.

Belfast and his cavalry.

It took him long enough.

FORTY-FIVE

The smoke from the RPG hit on the front door of the facility rolls out of the tunnel, obscuring Mere, Escobar, and me with the familiar stench of rocket propellant, explosives, and burnt plastic. Escobar breaks away from us, dropping off the edge of the top terrace. I don't chase him. Instead, I grab Mere's arm, and haul her toward the unfinished building on our left. If this is the lab, it's probably safe to guess that it isn't the building that serves as a barracks for any contingent of mercenaries that Escobar keeps on site. If he keeps many at all.

I suspect the cultural restoration card is quite enough to keep the locals away from Moray, especially with all the money Hyacinth Worldwide is putting into Cusco. Escobar's Arcadians are probably enough to keep the place secure, and I think he sent most of them out on the raid.

Assault rifles chatter in the tunnel, the channel magnifying the noise and making it seem like there are more guns than there are. I'm not sure what Belfast's men are shooting at as no one is near the entrance. Announcing themselves, perhaps. Making sure any Arcadians in the tunnel know they're coming.

The man who had been trying to alert Escobar is running toward us, closing at a preternatural speed. He's still wearing a flight suit from the helicopter, and I get in front of Mere to intercept him. He barrels in, and I drop and do a leg sweep. Before he can recover, I'm on him, driving his face into the dirt and putting my knee in his back.

Mere reaches us, breathing heavily, and I grab the pistol from her. I put a round in the back of the Arcadian's head and he goes limp beneath me.

I thrust the pistol back at her. "You keep it," she says.

"Take it," I reply. "I can't be two places at once."

"Where are you going?"

"Down there," I nod toward the terraces. "You're in charge of data collection. See what you can find that we can take with us."

She hesitates, and I stand up, grabbing her arm and physically putting the gun in her hand. She recoils, but I won't let her go. "There's no time, Mere. If we don't get the data, Secutores will. At the very least, we have to make sure no one gets it."

"You're going after Phoebe?"

"I'm not leaving her, and Escobar is down there. He has to be dealt with."

Her hand closes around the grip of the pistol. "Okay," she says in a quiet voice as if she is trying to convince herself.

"We're getting out of here on that helicopter. That's where you're heading."

"You know how to fly a helicopter?" she asks. "I thought you hated flying."

"It's the *falling* part that I don't like, which is why I learned how to fly those things that can keep me up in the air."

More gunfire sounds, and not all of it is coming from the entrance. Bullets kick up the dirt around us.

Men are coming out of the building shell on the other side of the terraces. I guess Escobar had more men on site than I thought, though these guys are moving slowly enough they've got to be human mercenaries.

She still hesitates and I feel like I'm missing something, but there's no time to suss it out. "Go," I insist, pushing her toward the lab. As soon as she starts running, I turn and dash to the edge of the terrace. As pairs of Secutores mercenaries come out of the tunnel, firing wildly at both me and Escobar's approaching security forces, I jump off the edge of the first ring.

ᵥᵥ

The fronds on the fifth level are agitated. Ripples move back and forth among the sea of purple strands, and the pods are nearly hidden beneath the layers of plant life that are holding them. The motion of the fronds is synchronized enough to appear driven by some sort of awareness, and I don't like the idea that the process that Escobar has built is somehow accelerating in reaction to the assault on the facility. As if the plants know they are in danger.

Would Mother react in the same way? Or are we, her children, that reactive system?

I hit the ground on the level with the citrus trees, take three steps, and jump again. As I reach the second terrace, the bees start to swarm. I see Escobar running the circuit of the third terrace, a heavy stick in his hand. He's beating on each hive as he runs past, rapping the same staccato pattern on the wood. In his wake, the bees pour out of their hives, forming sizzling clouds over each hut. They're drifting up, and I slide to a halt near the edge of the second terrace. Bee stings individually aren't fatal, but in sufficient number, they can be debilitating.

A swarm floats past the edge of the second terrace, and I remain still, trying to control my breathing. The swarm extends tendrils of bees, scouts to test whether I am a friend or foe. I close my eyes and lay a hand over my mouth and nose, just to keep the inquisitive ones from getting too curious. They buzz in my ears and land on my face, exploring me.

But they don't sting me. I must taste right. They buzz over me, moving through my hair and across my skin, and then the swarm is gone, rising more quickly now toward the surface level. The other clouds follow. Escobar's defense system is keyed to non-Arcadian flesh, which is fine with me. Anything that will help keep Secutores busy is fine with me.

Having finished rousing his bees, Escobar leaps down to the fifth level, wading through the fronds. He's trying to reach the pods. I launch myself off the second terrace. As soon as I hit the ground on the third, I run along the circuit, flashing past the empty hives, until I'm directly overhead. Escobar is trying to free the pod from the grip of the fronds, and he's tearing chunks out of the white shell in his haste. I take a running long jump, windmilling my arms as I fly through the air.

He senses me coming, and gets out of the way. I hit the pod instead, my right hand breaking through the damaged shell. Both the pod and I sink into the sea of fronds, and for a moment, the sky disappears as a dome of purple leaves closes overhead. I try to extricate myself from the pod and fronds—it's like trying to get off an inflatable toy in the middle of the pool—as something grabs my right wrist. Nails rake my forearm as I yank my arm back, and the combination of my hand and whatever is grabbing me is too big for the hole in the pod's shell. The shell, which is both slippery and hard, cracks. Fracture lines radiate from the central seam of the pod.

Whatever is inside wants out.

It also wants to eat my hand, and I make a fist with my trapped hand, protecting my fingers from the toothed mouth that is trying to take a bite out of a finger. I yank my arm back again, and the edges of the hole splinter as both my hand and the hand grabbing mine come out of the pod. The hole is large enough that I can get a better look inside, and the sight only makes me pull harder.

The thing that is inside is neither human nor Arcadian. It's *feral*, for lack of a better word.

The chimera.

It's pale and hairless, skeletally thin. Its eyes are still fused shut, and it hasn't grown lips or ears yet. But it's aware enough to know that it is hungry.

The chimera breaks through the pod with its other hand, straining to grab me. The shell crumbles beneath my legs, the monster kicking its way out down below too. It's incredibly strong; I don't want to get into a tug of war with it.

I grab the wrist that is holding mine and pull down with both arms, pressing the chimera's arm against the ragged edge of the shell. I saw back and forth, and the shell is hard enough that it doesn't splinter. It cuts, a jagged line across the albino flesh of the monster. White blood, like milk, spurts out of the wound, and the chimera shrieks.

Its tongue is deformed too, and I shudder as I look at it. Optimized for lapping up liquids.

I keep sawing as the shell starts to crumble. Only a few more slices before it breaks.

The chimera shrieks again, spitting at me like an enraged cat, and lets go. I throw myself off the pod as the monster explodes out of the shell. I'm tangled in the fronds—they stick to my exposed flesh—and I try to stumble and extricate myself at the same time, without much luck.

Fortunately, the chimera has the same problem, exacerbated by the fact that it is naked. And sexless. It is confused by the touch of the fronds— they're keeping it from moving freely, but at the same time, they're offering a rush of happy endorphins. I'm feeling the same thing where the fronds have gripped my arms. Their touch is warm and euphoric. In their embrace, I am loved. They'll take care of me. They'll feed me. Keep me warm and safe. All I have to do is lie down. Strip myself naked and let them cover me. Everything will be fine.

They're a nutrient source. Their sole purpose is to feed me through the connection between their leaves and my skin. It's a sensation not unlike the one offered by the humus when you are under ground. Held tight. Protected. Safe. Blind children suckling at Mother's tit while wrapped in her embrace. I know the feeling. I've missed it.

We all do; that's why we return. That's what she wants. That's what she tells us.

While the chimera is momentarily confused, I rip myself out of the embrace of the fronds and stumble off the edge of the terrace. I land on one of the desks in the pit, racking my body across one of the computer monitors. I roll over, groaning from having my spine stretched and my kidneys hammered. Looking at the world upside down, I spot a bloody-faced Escobar coming at me, a piece of metal in his hands.

I jerk out of the way as he slams the post into the desk, puncturing the surface. He yanks it out, slashing with it as I slide off the other side of the desk. The end of the post—a shaft torn off a piece of equipment—is sharp enough that it cuts through my shirt and draws blood. We face off on either side of the desk. He's grinning, as if he is enjoying a long awaited opportunity, and in his smile, I see the youthful glee of Alberto when he was sitting on my chest and pummeling my face.

The lower half of his face is wet with gore, as is his jacket, shirt, and tie. It can't all be from the bloody nose I gave him, and then I realize he's taken blood—probably from the technicians who had been down here monitoring the project. A nasty sort of severance package.

He feints twice, and then lashes out with his foot, kicking the desk toward me. I don't have much room to back up—the fifth terrace wall is not far behind me—and so I leap over the desk. He expects the move, and he punches me in the chest with the post as I come within range.

It hurts—having a piece of metal driven into your lung always does, but it is better than the same going through your heart. Escobar hangs on to the post, thinking he's going to hit me with it again, but I'm too close now and I get hold of his wrist, peel his hand off the weapon, and get my other hand under his elbow. I jerk one hand up and the other one out—a simple motion that moves his arm in a direction which he has little leverage against—and I feel tendons tear and bones break in his arm.

He howls and I let him go. His elbow is shattered. Everything below that point is useless.

"I can fight with one lung," I wheeze, trying not to think about the wet flow of blood running down my front. "Can you fight with one arm?"

"I don't need to fight you at all," he says.

Which is more than clue enough as to what's behind me. I dodge to the side as the chimera comes crashing down on the desk. Escobar steps back, not taking advantage of my wandering attention, and as the chimera snarls at me, I grab the end of the metal post in my chest and yank it out.

This hurts more than it did when it went in.

The chimera come at me, mouth wide. It can't see me; it's simply reacting to olfactory and auditory cues, which means its reactions are driven by the same. It's not aware enough to get out of the way as I ram my fist into its open mouth. It coughs and struggles for a second, and then I grab it by the shoulder and slam its head down on the desk. My fist goes back farther than a hand normally should, and its entire body shakes as the back of its skull comes apart.

I snap my left leg back, catching Escobar in the hip as he tries to grab me from behind. I'm not the sort to stand and stare at my handiwork. Not when there are other enemy combatants around.

He lumbers back, catching up against the slab in the center of the pit. I pull my hand out of the mouth of the dead chimera and keep my distance. He mistakes my pause for reticence. Or weakness. "Having trouble getting enough air?" he sneers.

"A little," I wheeze. "How's the elbow?"

"It'll heal," he says. "Flesh and bone always do."

"I can't let you birth any more of those monsters," I say.

"Hypocritical, don't you think?" he replies. "Given what we are."

"Maybe it is our prerogative," I point out, "given what we are." I laugh, and then fall to a fit of coughing and choking, as the pain from my leaking lung lights up my brain.

"They need to fear us," he says. "That's the only way they'll adapt. If they don't adapt, they're just cattle. If they don't want to reason, then we'll take away that privilege. They can be mindless worms. It makes no difference to me."

"But we came from them," I point out. "We were human once, you and I. All of Arcadia was human once."

"Not anymore," he says, his expression hardening. "We evolved. They didn't."

He starts to lunge at me, but is brought up short. Something is holding him to the slab. As he tries to figure out how he's caught, I grab him by the shoulder and by the knot of his tie. I push him back, bending him over the slab. He struggles in my grip, but I've got leverage on him, and I manage to push him down enough that Phoebe can grab him with her other hand.

She gets her hand in his hair and holds him down, his head back. I press my thumb against his carotid artery, and keep pressing until I have his attention.

"We're stewards," I tell him, "not mass murderers of an entire species."

I flick my thumb, my nail cutting his flesh, and as his life blood begins to pump out of his body, I release him and stand back. Phoebe—nothing more than a fiery-eyed skeletal wraith—snaps the restraints that had been holding her down, and sinks her teeth into Escobar's neck.

He doesn't cry out as she drains him. He stares at me, the light slowly fading from his eyes. I'm the last thing he's going to see, and his outrage at this finality sustains him for a very long time.

FORTY-SIX

As soon as Escobar dies, I head for the wall, scaling back out of the pit as fast as I can with a hole in my chest. The thunder of gunfire has dropped off, too much for my liking, and I'm starting to feel apprehensive about having abandoned Mere. It hits me what I missed in our last conversation, and I climb faster, a growing sense of dread that I've made the wrong decision.

At the top of the terraces, bodies are scattered—both Escobar's security force and Secutores. Escobar's men have scented strips attached to the lapels of their BDUs. They don't smell particularly pungent—gardenia with a faint hint of cypress and cedar—but it's clearly enough of an olfactory signal for the bees to distinguish between friend and foe.

I hear gunfire from the lab, the rattle of an assault rifle, and the noise is punctuated by the solitary sound of a handgun. In the wake of the last shot, all I hear is the distant buzz of bees and the faint noise of a wounded man whimpering in pain.

In the pit, Phoebe has left the slab. She's climbed up to the fifth level and is breaking open one of the nearly ripe pods. Making sure none of the chimerae survive.

I run for the lab, which is a single story building with two wings, extending laterally from a central entry. Secutores corpses lie both in and outside of the room. Some coming; some going. It looks like the door was enough of a bottleneck that they tried to turn it into a defensive position, but couldn't hold it. I scoop up a discarded assault rifle, check its ammo, and replace the magazine. Half full. Green stripe on the magazine. It'll have to do.

There's a wounded Secutores man in the corner, trying to stay conscious, and he's slipping into a fog as I approach. He can't lift his rifle in time, and I pin his hand with my boot. "Leave it," I tell him, pointing my gun at his chest. His face is puffy with bee stings, and he's leaking from a round or two that managed to slip under his vest. I lift my foot and he takes his hand off his weapon. I kick it away from him and lower mine. "You're going to die," I tell him. "Your way or mine?" I show him my teeth, and he shudders once and then slumps, his chin dipping forward.

It's been a long time since I scared a man to death. Usually it takes longer, and I'm happy it was quick. I push his head back so that I can get at his neck, and I drink enough to do something about the hole in my chest.

There are bodies and a blood trail leading into the right-hand wing. Toward the helicopter pad. I follow the trail, my gun ready. I clear each room as I go, moving as quickly as I can toward the end of the hall, where I suspect I'll find what I'm looking for. It's an old habit. Always clear the building. Never assume otherwise.

I get to the end eventually. The blood trail leads into the last room on the right. There's a temporary wooden door at the end of the hall. If my sense of the facility's layout is correct, beyond that door is the helicopter pad. I ease up to the last door and carefully push it open another few centimeters.

Nothing happens until I duck my head in to look. Gunfire rattles, followed by the spattering echo of bullets chewing through the wall next to the door. I quick-look again, drawing another fusillade. It's delayed. Whoever is shooting at me isn't at optimal efficiency. Their response time is sluggish.

I move to the other side, and push the door open with my foot. This time, there's no gunfire. The door swings open and gently bumps into the wall. I'm on that same side, protected by both the door and the wall. "How are you doing in there, Tony?" I call out.

"It's not going optimally," Belfast responds.

"I can imagine," I reply.

"It has promise, though," he says. "If you're still alive, then I made the right choice."

"What choice is that?" I ask, even though I have a pretty good idea. My stomach sinks as I wait for his response.

"Silas?" Mere's voice is weak and ragged.

"I've got your girlfriend," Belfast says. "Again. Fuck. You know this bitch shot me earlier?"

I shouldn't have left her.

I risk one more look. Belfast lets me have this one because he wants me to recognize his position of strength.

The room inside is an unfinished lab. There are lab bays, heavy installations that divide the room into several channels. At the end of the one directly in line with the door, Belfast has sequestered himself between several overturned desks, protecting both his flanks. He's resting against a crate, and there is a jumble of gear next to him.

Mere is lying on the floor in front of his makeshift fort. Her face is pale, and she's got her hands pressed against her side. There's too much blood—on her face, her hands, her clothes, on the floor around her. Too much.

I rest my head against the wall, trying to block out what I've seen. Part of me is analyzing the entire scene—calculating angles and trajectories, running through assault scenarios. None of them bode well for anyone in the room. Least of all Mere.

"Yeah, I hear she got the drop on you earlier," I call out. "I'm glad you didn't put one in her out of spite."

He coughs. "I'm a professional, Silas. Got to protect my assets. She's my ticket out of here."

"How is that going to work?" I ask, all the while trying to figure out the odds. What's his response time going to be like? Is he going to shoot her or me if I charge him? If he knows he's going to die, will he put a round in the back of her head, professionalism be damned? Or does is he clinging to the idea that I'll let him go?

"What happens to your ticket if she bleeds out?" I ask.

He laughs, and some of my questions are answered in the wet sound coming out of his lungs. "Nobody wins," he says.

"How do you figure that?" I ask. "If I walk away, I win."

Mere whimpers from the floor.

"No, you don't," Belfast rasps. "You don't know anything. Escobar is dead, I take it. So he can't tell you anything. Your bitch girlfriend dies, which doesn't help you any. And if I die, well, this whole place goes up too. You get nothing."

He's got a detonator of some kind. I don't recall seeing any explosives on the way in, but he could simply have a few bricks of C-4 on him. Maybe even a dead man's switch that closes if he dies. The whole room goes up. Given the loose structure erected around me, a fire would burn through it very quickly. He's right on that point. Nothing would be salvageable.

I sigh. "What are your terms?"

He chuckles again, trailing off with a wet cough.

There are no terms, I realize. He knows he's dying. He's just stalling me. There's a whisper of sound in the hallway, and Phoebe is there on the other side of the doorway. Her hair is pale again, and her skin is flawlessly pure. She's almost as pale as the albino chimerae. She's killed them all by draining their milky blood. She's a perfect union—both mother and child.

"Tony Belfast," she calls out. "Can you hear me?"

There's a long silence and then his voice comes out of the room. "Y— yes. I hear you."

"Do you know who I am?" she asks. Without waiting for his answer, she steps into the doorway, framing herself perfectly for him. He can't miss.

And he doesn't. Phoebe's body shakes and jerks as Belfast empties his entire magazine. Her wounds weep pink fluid—not quite blood, not quite water. There is no smoke, though, no change in Phoebe's expression that suggests she's bothered in the slightest by the weed killer component of the rounds.

I see the corner of her mouth curve into a smile as he shouts at her. I hear his gun rattle as he throws it aside, and I know he's going for his detonator. I start to move, but Phoebe's already there, leaving nothing but a ghost of motion in the doorway.

Belfast screams, but his cry is abruptly cut off.

I go to Mere instead, lifting her into my lap. "It's okay," I whisper, brushing her matted hair back from her face. She shudders in my arms, struggling to block out the gurgling wet sounds coming from behind her. She's been shot on the left side, at the top of her hip, and it looks like the bullet went through. The wound has been bleeding heavily, and she's pale and shivering. She's lost a lot of blood.

There's a way to solve that problem. I raise my wrist to my mouth.

"No," Phoebe says. She discards Belfast's body, his neck a red wreck, and she wipes her mouth clean of his blood. "If you give her blood, it'll only save her today," she says, "But she'll have to be buried if she's going to live longer. She'll have to be taken to Arcadia."

"So we'll take her."

She shakes her head. "I can't let you do that."

"She's going to die," I protest.

"Of course she is," Phoebe says, her voice surprisingly gentle. "All living creatures do. That is the cycle of life on this planet. That is the natural order of things. And who are you to break that cycle for her?"

"I've already broken it," I whisper, lowering my face to Mere's. "I saved her once already." I press my lips to hers. "And I'd do it again."

Mere stirs in my arms, her eyelids fluttering. She sighs painfully, her face tightening. "Silas…" she breathes, looking up at me.

"I'm here," I say. "I'm right here, Mere."

EPILOGUE

The dirt road is barely a road at all, and it peters out at the edge of an unruly field of untended cassava. I have to walk the motorcycle the last half-kilometer, lifting it over the meter-wide trunk of a big-leaf mahogany tree that has fallen across the break in the forest.

The shack sits on an elevated rise, looking out over an unnamed river that disappears into the wilderness of the Darién Gap. The building sags a bit, but the roof is sound and there is a short sloping overhang in the front so that the runoff from the rain doesn't pool around the building. The porch is screened with mosquito netting, and the windows on each side of the shack have wooden shutters. There's a simple lean-to in the back, a piece of corrugated metal that provides some shelter for the generator and the motorcycle.

I detach the leather saddlebags from the simple harness that holds them to the motorcycle—it's an old Kawasaki motocross bike that used to be orange and yellow—and bring them with me as I walk around to the front of the shack.

Mere is resting in a hammock that has been strung up on the porch, and she stirs as I make an effort to walk noisily across the wooden porch. The handle of a compact Mossberg shotgun sticks up from beside her. I put the saddlebags down on the small table near the hammock and undo the strap on one of them. Mere opens her eyes, starts to stretch, and winces slightly as the motion strains the staples in her side.

I take out the packaged cell phone power adapter and show it to her. "It came in." I toss it to her so that she can wrestle with the plastic packaging. I don't understand why tech manufacturers insist on heat sealing their plastic. It's like they have a sadistic desire to keep their customers from actually using their products.

"Finally," Mere says, turning the package over in her hands. I don't know how she does it, but she always manages to find the spot in the seam where the whole case can be pried open.

I unload the rest of the bag: week-old copies of *The New York Times*, *Los Angeles Times*, and *Wall Street Journal*; a couple of paperback thrillers; a six-pack of Coke de Mexico in small glass bottles; and a bottle of the local rum. The other bag has fish and fruit from the market in La Palma, as well as a block of ice in a double-lined plastic bag. I take the groceries inside and put them in the cooler.

I grab the bottle opener from the nail beside the cooler, and her bag from near the single bed, and return to the porch. Mere is out of the hammock, sitting at the table and reading the front page of the *New York Times*. I set her bag down on the table, and pop the top off one of the bottles. I put it near the paper, and she reaches up and touches my hand unconsciously.

"I'll turn the generator on," I say, letting my hand slip out from under hers.

She nods without saying anything, engrossed in the leading headline about record temperatures along the Eastern seaboard in the US, and I wander around to the back of the shack.

The generator coughs and sputters when I switch it on, and I watch it for a little while as its tiny engine whirs up to speed. It's pretty quiet, and the forest is thick enough around us that I know the sound doesn't carry too far.

Not that anyone is out here but the two of us.

The Darién Gap is a stretch of undeveloped land that extends across Central America. It is the boundary between Panama and Columbia—Central America and South America—and there are no roads that cross it. La Palma—the nearest town of any size—is more than sixty kilometers north. I take the motorcycle into town every few days, picking up newspapers and groceries.

It's a good place to heal.

Belfast's bullet ricocheted off Mere's pelvic bone, in and out, but it did a lot of damage. It's going to be several months before she's able to move without pain, and it will be years before she gets her full range of motion back.

I sleep in the ground every few nights, drawing sustenance from the rich humus of the rain forest. Every afternoon, when the sun warms a stretch of the riverbank, I lie out and let it bake my skin. It's still hard to lie still, but I'm getting better at it. My skin is almost as dark as it was when we fled Troy; it's been that long since I've had a real tan.

Phoebe is out in the forest somewhere. The few times I've run into the natives who live in the Gap and asked them about seeing ghosts in the trees, they've shaken their heads and said they've seen no such spirit. She'll come back though, when she's ready. When she's done communing with the humus.

The generator starts to purr, and I wander back to the front of the shack. Mere has plugged the cell phone adapter into the extension cord that is our sole outlet in the shack and, from her bag, she's retrieved Belfast's cell phone. It sits on the table next to her, charging, while she looks at the Style section of the *New York Times*. "Scarves are making a comeback," she says.

I make an agreeable noise as I take the short-handled shotgun out of the hammock and set it on the porch. I lie back in the hammock and rock gently from side to side.

We've settled into long comfortable silences already, like an old married couple—well past the honeymoon stage and into the long sloping twilight of our lives. It's a not uncommon relationship stage for Arcadians—we tend to not be in a rush—but there are times when I can see flickers of impatience in Mere's eyes.

It's only been a month since the destruction of the facility at Moray. No time at all…

Belfast's phone beeps, signaling that its battery has charged enough that the phone can now be used. Mere grabs at it as if it might grow wings and fly away. It has a large screen and a miniature keyboard, and I feel somewhat out of sync with the modern world as I can remember when ENIAC was first turned on. It doesn't seem like that long ago.

Mere smiles, a feral curl of her mouth, as she presses buttons. "He had a password on it," she says.

"Had?" I ask, noting the verb tense.

"Yeah, wasn't hard to guess."

I have no idea what it could have been, and I don't ask. She would tell me, but I'm learning to let her keep some secrets.

"Ah, here we go," she says. "His call log." She scrolls through the list. "'E' was Egret," she says, putting to rest one of the unsolved mysteries. She finds something interesting, pushes some buttons, and then holds the phone out to me. On the screen is a few lines of contact information.

The name field reads "Fairchild."

"Maryland area code," she says. "He called this number a lot, and Fairchild called him too. What do you want to bet this is his contact?"

Someone was paying Secutores's bill. Someone gave them the weed killer.

Escobar had given himself away when I had said that the company behind the weed killer had other projects in the pipeline. I had been guessing, but he knew what I was saying was true, which means Arcadia is still in danger.

"What do you want to do, Mere?" I ask as I put my hands behind my head.

"I want to go after them," she says.

I nod absently, staring up at the rough roof of the porch, thinking about Arcadia. Thinking about what I want to do. We've both been thinking—and talking—about what we might find on Belfast's phone, and now that we have a piece of data, it is time for us to make a choice.

Am I still an Arcadian? Do I owe Mother and the Grove some allegiance? Am I an estranged cousin but still part of the family?

Who am I?

I think of Aeneas, fighting the sea. *We are no longer who we were.*

"Silas?" Mere says my name quietly, trying to get my attention. I look at her, sitting on the narrow chair, her hands in her lap. Her red hair is loose about her shoulders, and there are lines on her face that were not there two years ago. The scar on her neck shifts as she breathes. "What do you want to do?" she asks.

Now, we are nameless scoundrels, running across the dark sea...

"I'm a steward," I say. "I have no home but the earth, and I have no family but the humus. That is who I will fight for."

She cocks her head to the side. "You have me," she says.

And I will fight for you too, Mere.

Acknowledgements

I'd like to thank Cody Tilson for the cover art. He made an artistic call that forced me to take a narrative path I might not have otherwise discovered. Erica Sage, Kristopher O'Higgins, Ross Lockhart, Jason Williams, and Matt the Intern offered useful commentary on an early draft. Thank you, all. Marty Halpern suffered through my grammatical idiosyncrasies with much aplomb (thank you, sir).

It may seem odd to acknowledge a cat, but the orange tabby who has been trying to convince me that he can fit in my lap while I type has been a constant companion during the writing of this book. Enkidu likes to sit on the pile of file boxes next to my chair and stare at me, as if to say, "Are you done yet?"

He's a tough audience.

ABOUT THE AUTHOR

Mark Teppo is a creative executive for Subutai Corporation where he manages the Foreworld franchise, which includes the three-volume epic, *The Mongoliad*. A synthesist, a trouble-shooter (and –maker), a cat herder, and an idea man, Mark indulges in speculative thinking now and again, occasionally with a Tarot deck. His favorite card is the Moon.